EL NIÑO

EL NIÑO

—

NADIA BOZAK

ANANSI

This edition published in 2014 by
House of Anansi Press Inc.
110 Spadina Avenue, Suite 801
Toronto, ON, M5V 2K4
Tel. 416-363-4343
Fax 416-363-1017
www.houseofanansi.com

Distributed in Canada by
HarperCollins Canada Ltd.
1995 Markham Road
Scarborough, ON, M1B 5M8
Toll free tel. 1-800-387-0117

House of Anansi Press is committed to protecting our natural environment. As part of our efforts, the interior of this book is printed on paper that contains 100% post-consumer recycled fibres, is acid-free, and is processed chlorine-free.

18 17 16 15 14   1 2 3 4 5

Library and Archives Canada Cataloguing in Publication

Bozak, Nadia, author
El Niño / Nadia Bozak.
Issued in print and electronic formats.
ISBN 978-1-77089-325-2 (pbk.). — ISBN 978-1-77089-326-9 (html)
I. Title.

PS8603.O998E4 2014   C813'.6   C2013-907010-9
                           C2013-907011-7

Jacket design: Alysia Shewchuk
Text design and typesetting: Alysia Shewchuk

We acknowledge for their financial support of our publishing program the Canada Council for the Arts, the Ontario Arts Council, and the Government of Canada through the Canada Book Fund.

Printed and bound in Canada

FSC
www.fsc.org
MIX
Paper from
responsible sources
FSC® C016245

For my mom

BAEZ

Baez is going to die today. The smell is like expiring sky, or a wrung-neck rabbit left too long in the sun. And also like the smell of Old Blue when, lying there in the yellow desert, palms up and swollen, her breaths had taken longer and longer to come.

That was two springs ago.

When Baez found her, Old Blue was tramping on towards the high blue mountain, arms dangling and eyes down on her shoes. Baez barked just once. Old Blue turned, shading her eyes and squinting. *My girl, my girl*, Old Blue kept saying, as Baez came running up. Baez had licked the dust and salt from Old Blue's face and Old Blue rubbed the sore part of Baez's neck where once her collar had been buckled. Then they went on together, Baez running ahead, circling back, nipping Old Blue's ankle bones. The day got too hot and Old Blue got too slow. At a narrow wash, Old Blue fell to the ground, rolling into the shadow of a skinny old mesquite. Her eyes closed. Her chest was slow to rise. Baez smelled that Old Blue was dying. Baez started to dig a hole.

She pawed at the hard, tough desert, scattering the top crust back between her legs. The crumble of dirt rained down in a steady spray. Ants circled in, sucking her saliva drips before they dried. Pent-up heat escaped from the dug earth and the ants gave way to termites, a brown, nuttier smell. Behind her, Old Blue called *girl, girl, girl*. And then nothing for a long time.

Now that dying smell comes from inside Baez. She licks it—*ch-ch-ch*—going deep, down in the roots of her grainy coat. She rolls onto her side to get at the ribs, bald and raw, throwing out her tongue and raking it back in. She might lick herself into a puddle of teeth, of bone, of tail, of fur. But at least the smell would be gone and, at last, so would she.

She is all alone in her pen. Except there is a tree. The leaves, brittle, waterless lace, drip with greying shadow. There are no other trees on this rough, rocky hillside— some man or boy must have planted this one, chiding the desert. And yet it lives. There is a cactus too. It is thick and grey and grows on the other side of the high chain-link fencing that squares Baez in. An owl lives inside the cactus trunk. It disappeared into its hole just as the moon was falling slowly away.

Glove and Tattoo have returned from the desert too. Through their trailer's remaining window, bulb light melts into new day. Three brown boys (green hat, white hat, no hat) are tied up under the lean-to. These are the night's bounties. The waxy rope that binds them together is fastened through the heavy ring Tattoo hammered into the ground back when Baez first came here. Bunches of tiny brass bells hang from the rope. Should the bounties try to get away the clattery noise will bring Glove and Tattoo out from the trailer, walking fast, yelling faster. The angled plywood that shelters the bounties is the same material as the fourth wall of her pen. On the other side of this divider her children rumble and scratch. The tight scars along her ribs and jaws still ache and if her children broke down the plywood now, she would not be able to fight back. Glove and Tattoo would watch through the window. And then wait for the bald birds to come.

Baez licks. Baez remembers. The smell of Old Blue's cigarettes mixed with the hot amber she took from the big bottle under the sink, which itself mixed in with the sharp curdle of Old Blue's paint tubes. Then there was the yellow tinge of unwashed skin, the grey of oiled scalp. Her voice was flat, rarely raised. *Ba-ez, good girl,* she would say. Sometimes at night Old Blue would sleep for an hour or two. Then when the moon had passed across the window she would get up and pull on her jeans, go out to the kitchen and paint. Baez would curl at her salty feet. Old Blue's brush would scrape-scrape-scrape. Out in the night the brown-boy footsteps would pit-pit-pit, and if they ever came in too close Baez would bark, pulling hard, raspy eruptions up from her gut, until Old Blue went *sh-sh-sh*. Night after night it went on like that, seasons ago.

Now, here, beyond this hill, a sky-scraping concrete wall stretches up-and-up towards the night's few stars. The desert ends at that impossible block upon block of flat grey. Like the deer and rabbits that still come this far south, memory and mind stop at the wall's upward thrust. Along the base, the bed of the wide, south-bound river is empty. There are rusty cans, though, and sand-filled bottles, half-buried tarps and bent nails. And then there is that wheelbarrow, helpless, tipped on its side. The sunburned men who left those things also trampled plants and cactuses, which now struggle to right their arms and hail the sun. Opposite, in the north, a jagged range of mountains runs along the horizon. The mountains are deep blue. The highest peak, a triangle, soars up from the centre. The river flowed from those mountains and that is where the brown boys still go.

Once Old Blue went that way too. And maybe it was from looking at those mountains, sharp-toothed as they are, that the sunburned men thought to lay the razor coil along the top of the concrete. It took a swarm of paddle-foot helicopters to do it. That's fine: the brown boys burrow underneath the wall, their narrow hole obscured by scattered rocks and the soda cans Glove and Tattoo crush in their fists and toss, tumbling, to the ground. When the ball caps pop up from the hole, Baez and her children are not supposed to bark at them. Let them get a good head start. Let them believe they are free for a time.

Before, when her children were babies, still too young to hunt, it was she that Tattoo would each night muzzle and lead into the back of the desert buggy—open top, treaded wheels, its body coated in the same gold as the land. Then Glove would come. The shiny helmets they still wear blinded her. The desert night teemed with the fresh tracks of those brown boys who'd just gone running into the hot bliss of a starry night, towards the rolling blue mountains piercing the faraway sky.

Now her children have outgrown her. Now they run the bounties down. Her children's tails are hacked to stumps, their ears honed to points; coats of blue-orange mottle shimmer and muscles pop, nourished as they are on bowls and bowls of mincemeat and the rabbits and reptiles Tattoo and Glove watch them hunt. Let them go. Let her shiny, flat-eyed children run down the brown boys, the hole-in-the-wall boys, the boys that Old Blue once fed and watered and watched and maybe even lived for just as Baez had lived for her, Old Blue.

HONEY

Her ponytail still smells of chlorine. And her skin is tight, like a mask too small, while her shoulders ache with that delicious kind of tired.

"Ninety-five degrees out there," the radio crackles, "and it's only ten a.m."

The land pulling past her windows at sixty-five miles per hour is a daze of blond sand, khaki brush, a sky of china blue. She keeps forgetting that she lives in a desert. Every month or so she and Keith will pack their bathing suits—plus a cooler of beer, tortillas, and Dinorah's famous *refritos*—and drive five hours west, to the coast. Each time they crest the Entrada mountain range that separates Buzzard City from the Oro Desert, Keith will shake his head at the land sprawling out beneath them. How can a city like theirs exist in the midst of such hard, parched geography? "Just look—nothing but empty."

Some two hours back, she had low-geared down the southern side of the Entradas, the roofs of brown-and-tan suburbs sinking down behind those soaring blue mountains. One of the Entradas' many peaks dominated the rest, rising up like a sloping pyramid. Then Highway 19's bright blacktop T'd at the cracked asphalt of 55 South, where she turned west. The two lanes are narrow and there's barely a shoulder to speak of, but she's really in the Oro now, squinting through her clip-ons into the pungent gold of the dirt and sand that this desert was named for. Or is the Oro so-called on account of what men used to come here to prospect and mine? To the east, low humps of chocolate mountains glow lavender, while everywhere else puffs of creosote and fizzes of blond cholla give depth to land, land, land, land, and more dry land that stretches on into forever.

A dusty black Pinto, headlights cracked and muffler dragging, rips north. She hasn't seen one of those in years. The only vehicles going south are her Ventura and the low-riding white vans with orange chevrons and "Control Corp" peeling on the sides. She slows as one signals to pass. The two agents in front stare straight ahead. Their faded green jumpsuits meld perfectly with the cactus and brush dotting the landscape. The German shepherd panting between them can barely contain its meaty bubblegum tongue. A caged window—fifteen inches, maybe, like the RCA she and Keith watch Sunday mysteries on—dominates the rear door. She counts the silhouetted ball caps of six illegals, three per side. The agents will dump them on the other side of the border, less than ten miles from Marianne's.

The AC's maxed. Keith keeps warning her about overdoing it. Does she want to blow the rad again? But the sunlight beating in heats up the black interior: dash and wheel and all that leather. Cheese in a microwave, her black pants cling, as does her matching top—a light crust of silver stars sprinkled from shoulder to chest. When she left the condo after her morning swim—suitcase in the trunk, Keith's old briefcase bursting with the "Society and Pedagogy" term papers she's going to have no excuse but to grade in bum-fuck Matchstick County—she had thought she could get down to Marianne's by afternoon. But Matchstick isn't on the road signs yet. It didn't seem so far two years ago.

A dusty brown roadrunner skids out across the hot asphalt, dragging its slender tail like a dress train. It bounces over the bumpy fur rug that might once have been a coyote or someone's dog—and which, *zip*, disappears under the Ventura and then falls away from the rear-view mirror. Orange-flavoured Tic Tacs zing between her molars—crunched three, four at a time. She's been craving nicotine since Keith left for his conference, and even dreamed of her old silver Zippo the night before—that gorgeous, satisfying sound it made each time she flicked the lid. Why didn't she just give in and treat herself to a small pack of Pilots when she filled up with gas and thin coffee? When she gets to Matchstick she'll mooch Marianne's tobacco: one delicious smoke for every six dreary term papers she grades, or something like that.

Sign says, FUEL 5 MILES. And after that it's just her and cactus and creosote, one deep-cut mountain wash after another: *arroyos*, as Marianne calls them. And it is good to be gone from the empty condo, the windowless office at the university, and for a minute she doesn't even miss Keith. But then her mind flashes to his long jaw and greying Saturday stubble, and she wants her husband's steady shadow to be there, in the corner of her eye.

A gassy burn rises. With the AC switched off, the needle on the temperature gauge drops from the red zone to the orange. She throws back one more tumble of Tic Tacs, crunches. Billows of steam rise from the Ventura's shallow hood. Her foot falls heavy on the gas pedal, catching air over an aluminum bridge under which another wide, scrub-lined wash fans out.

"Shit, shit, shit! You piece-of-shit car."

A red pickup flashes past, going north. Then she swerves to avoid the massive grey saguaro that's toppled from ditch to road, its exposed ribs splitting through the trunk. The Ventura's steaming is worse now. And then, through engine smoke, a sign in the shape of a teardrop appears. FUEL. SNACKS. SERVICE.

The attendant's skin is violet with sun, his cheekbones sharpened into triangles. "Yo! Yo! Kill that engine!" He waves a rag.

She rolls down her window. The blistering air smacks her in the face.

"Yo! Lady! The hood!"

The lever is under the seat, between her legs. The attendant pulls his greasy T-shirt up over his mouth and turns away from the steam. Like Dinorah, who is only thirty-five but looks about fifty, the attendant is probably quite young. Dinorah's eyes had popped when Honey dug out her driver's license to prove she was forty-three.

"You are blessed to look so young, Missus," Dinorah had said, pressing the collar on one of Keith's tennis shirts. "I work too hard for that. And then there's my kids. Kill your body, don't they?"

Honey had nodded, warm with pride, but then came that angry flush she got whenever someone just figured, hey, she's a woman, so she must also be a mom or at least want to be.

Grabbing her purse, she steps into staggering heat. The attendant's eyes linger over the tightness of her exercise pants. Before standing to full height, she pulls her T-shirt down as far as it will stretch. And then she does stand, and even with her shoulders caved inward and her chin tucked up she towers over this stocky man who steps away from her—lips parted, eyes up—like they always do. And then, if her height's not mind-blowing enough, what about her glasses? Or the thick gold wedding band—*This chick's married?*

The engine's steam thins into the hot air and disappears. Her skin shrivels and bakes. Behind the attendant, now bent over the sizzling engine, a soda machine glows in the station office.

The attendant looks up with a grin. "You must be rich."

"Why?" Her purse, of smoothest leather and many buckles, dangles from the crook of her arm. It is hot to the touch.

"'Cause you're killing this real nice car, lady. You should play nicer."

She frees her glasses of the clip-ons. A quick laugh catches in her throat.

"Well, anyway," the attendant says, hitching up his jeans, "she's not getting you back to Buzzard City anytime soon."

Her glasses, held to the sun, are spotted. "I'm going down to Matchstick County."

"Not there, neither, lady. You fried this sonnabitch."

"Oh, come on," she says, applying the hem of her shirt to a lens. "Last time it just needed new radiator hoses."

"Nope."

If the attendant's eyes flick away, he is lying. But it is her eyes that drop. "Do you have a phone?"

But there is no answer at the pay phone from which her

mom, her Marianne, makes their weekly calls—every Sunday at five p.m.

"It's not safe, Honey," Keith had said the last time Honey suggested they were long overdue for a trip.

"We ought to go," she told her husband.

Leaning back in his office chair, dimpled leather creaking, Keith had lowered his bifocals. His misty eyes had once been as green as spearmint.

"Let her be, Honey," he said.

A box fan whips hot air around the small office, paper rustles and flaps. A fifty-cent cola freezes as it slides down Honey's esophagus, pooling in her empty stomach. The phone's dial is caked with black grease, and now so is her finger. The ringing on the other end sounds more hollow than from the condo. She hangs up.

Her purse is as soft as a child and the smell is clean, like fresh meat. She holds it tight, fiddling with the familiar loops and buckles, the fan blowing at her back. Outside, the attendant untwists caps in the engine, pouring in icy green coolant. Thick vines of tattoo coil up his arms. When she was still teaching high school, a kid had tattooed "Now, gods, stand up for bastards!" across his bicep, so moved was he by her *King Lear* unit. She had photographed his arm and filed it in her teaching dossier under "Student Testimonials." Her own tattoo—the Sanskrit sign for healthy or, more literally, "freedom from disease"—is etched on her outer right ankle. There's a box of bandages in her desk at school for the rare days she wears a skirt with her low heels instead of long black pants.

The engine fails to turn over. The attendant is still wiping his hands when he comes into the office. "Something's sure gone wrong in there." His T-shirt ripples in the fan's breeze.

Honey crosses her arms over her chest. "Like what?"

"My boss'll fix it, but not till Tuesday." He lights a Pilot and rests a butt cheek on the edge of the desk. *Fury* is disguised within the design on his right forearm; *Wisdom* on the left.

"Shit."

Each time she speaks, her dry face sprouts another crack. She packed her Nivea this morning, must have.

"Got a cigarette?"

She pushes up her glasses and slides a cool, white Pilot from the attendant's pack. A luxurious inhale sluices her brain. She'll phone Dinorah and Dinorah will phone someone—a nephew or a cousin's cousin—to come pick her up and bring her back for her car again. So, okay, Tuesday she'll drive down to Matchstick. Except then she'll only have a few real days with Marianne if she wants to be back in Buzzard for a quick swim before Keith flies in on Friday.

"Could take the bus."

"Huh?"

"Bus." His eyes pop. "B-u-s. You know, big metal thing drives from town to town."

She feels her face heat up.

"Should be here in an hour," he says with a crooked smile. Then he promises her the car will be ready and waiting when the bus brings her back again.

He helps lift her luggage out of the trunk. But the canned goods she's packed for Marianne, the bag of no-name dog food, and the rolls of raw canvas and jars of gesso will have to stay until the next trip. There's a form to sign, agreeing to pay for parts and labour up to an estimated value.

Anything major, the boss will hold. Worst case? Tow it back to Buzzard.

While the attendant crouches in the narrow shadow of the office's eave waiting for another customer, she stays in front of the fan until the Greyhound arrives, clouded in a storm of dust. She rolls her suitcase towards the driver, who leans against the bus and lights a cigarette. The sun reflects off the mirror of his shiny pink head.

"You go as far south as Matchstick?"

"All the way to the border, lady." He looks up-up-up at her, making change for her five-dollar ticket and reaching out for her suitcase.

"I'd rather keep it with me."

"Nope." The driver clenches his cigarette between his leather lips and, straining, opens the underbelly storage bin. "It's Control. Just a rule they got." Her purse is okay. And the briefcase—once she shows him it's only full of papers.

"Let's go," the driver calls, slamming shut the luggage hold. He throws away his cigarette and squeezes past, his hand grazing her hip. The bus pulls out onto the highway, going south.

CHÁVEZ

This being Friday, they quit the fields by four. It's town day. Maclean gives them their pay envelopes and lowers the tailgate for them to hop, two at a time, into the back of the idling pickup. They're a crew of ten. Chávez gets in last. As Maclean eases the truck down the ridged-up road Chávez hunches over, counting his dollars, weighing how broken is his back against how little he's got to spend. The kids who've been picking a while will have a few bills to send home. Some send grubby letters too, though none believe they will ever get there.

Dear Granny, Please buy some Nescafé with this money.

Dear Mom, If only you could see how many tomatoes this month I picked. I bet it's more than a million.

A few have dads back in the villages, but they're crazy or old or, like Pedro, got injured up here in the north. Pedro is Abuelita's, his granny's, kind-of boyfriend. Through his pants you can see the outline of the brace that holds his leg together and on bad days he gets around with a cane that's too short so he has to hunch over. It's from Pedro that Chávez knows how to drive a car and turn a Bic into a tattoo gun.

Along with the dads lots of moms disappeared up here too. He remembers his mom had pink high heels but Abuelita says no. Because of weak ankles his mom wore sturdy sneakers that laced right up. The high heels must have been from a dream or one of those glossy magazines sold at the market. On the cement wall above Abuelita's virgin candles and hibiscus flowers there was a square photo of a girl with the same orange-coloured eyes as his and a high puff of black hair.

"She left here with only enough for a cola," Abuelita told him.

And whenever he tried to get her to speak of the factories in Zopilote where his mom might still be working, the walls of Abuelita's cement cottage closed in around them and the air got cold.

"Where? Zopilote?" Abuelita always said. "I don't know that place."

"It's over the border, Abuelita," he sometimes pushed

her. "Pedro says it's called 'Buzzard City' in English. But he told me to call it Zopilote."

But Abuelita didn't want to know about that city that swallowed her daughter and would get him someday too.

To make room in the truck he and the other boys hug their knees tight to their chests. The drive out to the main highway is muddy with yesterday's hard rain. The musty smell of tomatoes rises thick and so do the worms. Each Friday it's the same. While Maclean does his banking and shops for cases of spaghetti sauce, the other boys rush the ice cream stand and the store selling soda and chips to spend their pay. But Chávez just walks around and pretends he lives in the town he doesn't even know the name of. The way people won't look at him—or look too hard—it's a tough game. Then a couple of the littler kids get sick on the ride back to the farm, ice cream puke spraying up milky with the mud.

Their bunkhouse is just a cramped and crummy shed. It has no heat or light bulbs. Chávez is the only one awake, even being so tired. Behind his eyes bright green hunks of field tomatoes pop from the dry, grey earth, and like the ghost of an amputated limb he can still feel the motion as he stoops and picks, twists and plucks the unripe fruit, then tosses each taut handful into that cracked garbage bucket, which the biggest boy hauls and—with a heave and a curse, *fucking shit*—pours into the waiting truck. Maclean notes each bucket in his coil book; Chávez imagines stealing it so he can add a hundred ticks after his name.

Awake and dreaming, it is all the same but at least at night he is horizontal and there is no sun to burn. He hates tomatoes even if the boy with the grey front tooth and a cross on his neck says, "No way, bee-keeping's the hell of it."

Another says, no, the very, very worse is chasing chickens. Or, no, it's cleaning crabs. "Twelve hours of that slime and stink, you jam the knife in your palm just to stay awake."

There's ten boys and five mattresses. As they sleep the boys call for things like sandwiches, moms. Some boys say Maclean and his wife, in their high, wide house across the fields, sleep alone in their very own rooms. The bed he and Abuelita slept in bowed in the middle so it might as well have been a hammock, but it didn't matter because Abuelita didn't sleep much. It was always still night when, with a groan, she pushed her body away from the mattress. And when she shook him awake a few hours later she'd have baked a blanketful of soft bread. At the market plaza behind the crumbly white church, they sold the bread along with sweet corn stew, which would be brimming in the iron pot when Abuelita coaxed him off of the mattress. Chávez would pack the stew and bread into Abuelita's cart—an old bicycle Pedro had converted, with deep sidesaddle baskets and low handlebars that Chávez pushed. If he had gasoline, Pedro drove them in his two-door with the holes in the floor so you could see the road. Though it was so nice and easy when Pedro pulled up in the dark, they never counted on it.

The village was getting navy when they set out. Cats and dogs, bellies pinned up to their pelvises, followed them, going crazy for the food smells in the cart. Abuelita stopped to breathe a lot, shooing away the dogs and cats. Reaching deep into her lungs, she would point up at the remains of the starry sky. The bright one is the North Star. And that one is called Venus. It's the brightest after the moon. She said he could go anywhere in the whole world if only he knew the stars. Heaven is the only thing that never changes, she said.

On Saturdays the boys at Maclean's will make a fire and cook up food like they would eat at home. Some have been away so long they can't remember how things should taste, so Chávez cooks for them. As he stirs the chili and cinnamon into the stew—peppers and beans and a little meat—he tells them Abuelita's food was always sold out well before noon. Other grannies sold food at the market too, like salt pork, rice pudding, spicy soup, but the old men and sick men and wounded men who practically lived in the church plaza said Abuelita's food was the best. Maybe because she charged them only enough so she could buy more flour, dried corn, sugar, or Nescafé if they were out. Behind Abuelita's little house the garden was full of peppers and onions, hibiscus blossoms bigger than his head. In the shade of the high, wide palo verde they would eat the food Abuelita had set aside that morning. Then Abuelita slept: crumpled in the wooden chair, her thick grey toes to the sky, a mug of Nescafé tilted on a rock.

That's when Chávez would pack the milking bucket with a half-full bottle of spirits, Abuelita's thickest darning needle wrapped in tissue, and a clutch of ballpoint pens— blue and black and a couple of reds—then walk back to the church plaza. The market would mostly be over by then, the food-sellers, like Abuelita, gone home to nap. Some of the village men might still be there selling rugs, cigarettes, or plastic toys from their carts or car trunks. And there were always kids around. Ball-capped and sandalled, scabby knees and big teeth just growing in, they'd be sharing sodas and scrounging butts. Chávez charged ten cents for a tattoo. Always one of the kids would have saved up, and would choose from the designs in his lined notebook:

stars, skulls, and roses, jet planes too. For ten cents more he'd customize, mostly names of lost moms, gone dads. On the over-turned bucket with tongue between his teeth, he'd poke the darning needle into and out of and into and out of harassed bloodying flesh. He did wrists and necks, but that was extra too. He'd pause to clean the wound with a spirit-soaked rag and if a kid got faint, he made him sip from the bottle. Once a girl said she wanted a lightning bolt on her knee. But he said no. Abuelita wouldn't like it if he marked a girl that way. She said, fuck you, Chávez, she'd do it her-self. And she did do it, along with the knees of some other girls. He still did okay. He washed ink and blood from his fingers before Abuelita awoke and when she did she never asked where he got the money for the lemon-lime sodas he brought home every day.

And then Chávez is back in the bunkhouse again. The boy sleeping beside him has moved, struggling against the tight twist of his blanket. Roberto, this boy, sits up, looks around, not understanding the room or the shadows. When Chávez whispers, "Hey, it's okay," Roberto lies down again, his wet eyes catching in the moonlight.

Roberto says he was dreaming of home. "My mom was hanging the washing." The line went on for a million miles, squeaking all the way to the border. But it must just have been the swing set outside their window. "Right?" Roberto says his mom told him in the north there'd be grapes and peaches, "All you can eat. You seen them, Chávez? Or is it all just fucking tomatoes?"

Chávez hasn't heard about any all-you-can-eat fruit. But what about the lakes? He's heard about those, and rivers, clean ones, without rainbows of factory poison, cow shit, or dead chickens from upstream—or dead boys like he and Juan had seen in Río Loco's north-south flow and wondered how the fuck you'd drown in knee-deep water. While all he and Roberto know are the Loco's drained banks, Chávez imagines that there's a glassy paradise lake further up in the north where all the moms and dads are living, just waiting for them boys to get there. In the north there really is enough water that people can go swimming. Indoors in pools too. A white woman told him so.

And of all those moms and dads Roberto wants to know why none of them ever write home. "Huh, Chávez?"

"There's a great big hole somewhere where the letters are buried. Control takes the money out first—not that dumb—and then the fuckers buy whiskey and dog food with it."

Roberto yawns. His cousin got to an apple farm—that's really north. "They preached to them, though, made you pray before they paid."

"Fucking white jerks."

"And there's Africans."

"Blacks?"

"They come from a desert, too. They get flown over in special planes because they pick so damn fast." Roberto says watch out. "Farmers'll take an African over you."

Chávez would like to see an African. And he's never tasted a real apple. He wishes he knew where he was. Outside the old swing set creaks in the breeze. Night, now, is charcoal. Finally, Chávez dreams. He has seen this one before. The old-lady-*vieja* in the shitty blue car. Her face looks like his feels: tight from being so scared. Then, just as he lifts up the handle of the passenger door her long skinny arm with the popping veins and the blond down reaches over. It's like she's wind-milling through water, taking a broad, powerful stroke, scooping a lungful of breath. Her hand, the left, has a gold ring and is so big it could palm his whole head, and he remembers that when she held onto him it felt safe for a minute, like things would be all right. So why does she push down the door's button, locking him out? He rattles the handle. His screaming swells and swells until what comes from his mouth is a full-on siren.

He wakes then. Maclean's truck horn is blaring. And then all around him the boys jump up and untangle themselves from their sheets and grab their runners and ball caps, and after spooning porridge at the picnic table beneath the clothesline hung with Maclean's stained shirts, they climb into the waiting pickup and are in the fields while it's still dark.

BAEZ

She was born in a pen behind a gas station. There were pumps, a phone booth, a flat-roofed store. If she pulled herself up the fencing with her front paws she could see inside the store's back window. Food and jugged water were stacked to higher than the crooked doorjamb. The man who raised her was covered in brown speckles, especially his face and hands, the back of his neck. If he stayed too long in the sun the speckles leaked right into each other, like water drops into dry earth. Speckled Man had two little sons, less speckled but with the same bright orange hair and, after a time, the same shifting eyes.

When she lived with Speckled Man she shared her pen with brothers and sisters, cousins. She was left alone with her babies, when she had some, until Speckled Man came with gloves on and took them away. Like here at Glove and Tattoo's, she'd had an overhanging tree. Without it she might have boiled and cooked up along with the earth. But at night it cooled. She could breathe, smell. And at night, she could finally see: long, lean rabbits bounded past; woolly spiders tiptoed rock to rock; snakes crunched by. Coyotes came too, golden in the moon, their yowls vaulting.

What she remembers most about the gas station are the brown men. They came out with the stars. They were dusty, in ball caps. Water jugs in hand, humped with packs, the brown men ran up from the highway ditches, skidded through the gravel of the station lot and cut back into the desert, towards the jagged blue mountains in the north. They sweated a ripe white adrenaline, not unlike the smell of rabbits chased or of the orange-haired sons when Speckled Man caught them firing his gun.

When the brown men came Baez did what she was supposed to: she found her feet and bared her teeth, her eyes straining to track their low, quick figures. If they paused, winded, she caught their dry whispers, which sounded like breeze compared to the choppy stuff Speckled Man and his sons spoke, called, shouted. Sometimes mixed in with the brown men were brown boys as young as those belonging to Speckled Man and some so sun-quenched they glistened purple beneath the moon and their eyes were round like the bottoms of tin cans. The few women who appeared straggled behind, feet swelling in strappy shoes, the punch of their blood brightening the air. Then, after a time, there were no more brown men. But brown boys still came, in twos and threes or, if in a pack, a big one would lead. What was sure were the ball caps on their heads, the crunchy plastic of their bags, the water-jug slosh, and the *ka-chung-ka-chung* of their rabbity hearts.

She remembers that brown men and then just brown boys came to the station in the daytime too, but then they'd be crowded in the backs of bleached pickups driven by overalled farmers. One of her long-gone children— black of face or yellow of body—would ride in the back watching the men or boys who smelled of earth, of gasoline, the deep, oily sweat of no sleep. They sat there while the farmer bought drinks and bright bars of candy and the bigger of the orange-haired sons filled the truck, though he hardly reached the pump. And then the truck would go wobbling down the road, the men in the back clutching a candy bar and a can of drink. And not long after that another pickup would drive up, also filled with brown men, brown boys. They came and went and came and went, and all around them the desert went on living and dying and living again. Baez licks her smell. She wants to die and dissolve into the earth and just stay there, mixing up with time and dirt, nothing left. How close to death now, how very soon.

HONEY

The Greyhound leaves her and her luggage in the gravel lot of the McGarrigle gas station. Hot wind bites her cheeks while, despite her glasses, dust burns her eyes. Two boys— thirteen and fifteen, maybe—loll at the pumps, passing a Fanta. Soft orange hair peeks out from their caps, which protect their freckled faces from becoming more so. Their pointed boots are dusty, jeans webbed at the knee, and T-shirts finger-painted with car grease.

The phone booth beside the station leans like a tree in a strong wind and the animals are caged in chain-link behind the squat, flat-roofed store. The animals don't just bark when she steps forward, they roar. Marianne calls them "ancients," rather than what they are: coydogs, a half-Control dog, half-coyote breed. The coyote part of their souls is dominant, Marianne had told her between shots of whiskey. Living close to such animals had helped her reconnect with the natural order of the land, freeing the primordial part of her soul.

"Come again?" Honey had said, trying to keep her face straight.

"What I mean, Honey," Marianne whispered in her gruff, smoky tone, "is that we are all animals inside. Only we like to forget." She pointed her cigarette at the animal splayed in the corner of her trailer's kitchen, biting fleas from her belly. "This one's even more special, though," she said. She was sure it was on account of McGarrigle kicking the poor creature in the head "just for digging holes. Poor girl." Marianne paused, looking up. When she spoke it was like she was reading the words from the ceiling. "It's ever since then, Baez has been watching people. Sometimes it's like her eyes are a human's and she knows what I'm thinking before I even do. We've got our own language, hers and mine."

Honey swallowed, reaching for Marianne's bottle. In her corner, Baez yawned wide and blinked, amber eyes glistening, ears pricked up, seeming to take it all in.

In two years these McGarrigle brothers have become both taller and harder, their animals more in number. And that freckly McGarrigle dad is gone off to seal up the border with all the other local men whose ranches and farms have turned salty and whose irrigation ditches dried with the river.

"Dumb saps," Marianne said. "Wouldn't know exploitation if it came and bit them in the ass."

The teenager Honey had sat beside on the Greyhound was going down to work on the wall too. His dad was already there, he said, clicking the bald steel toes of his construction boots.

"Nothing else to do down here. It's that or move your farm north of Buzzard City." That's where all the illegals go, he said. "Those men took our jobs in the south counties, now the north ones. Their goddamn kids following them up there too." He had leaned over to watch the bus driver unloading the bags and boxes from the luggage hold for the Control agents and their dogs to inspect. "Illegals hide there, underneath, going back and forth," he told her. "I seen it once." He stood, hands on hips, to get a better view. "Only now if you turn 'em in Control gives you—guess how much."

Heat had buzzed through the open door, flashers clicked.

"Fifty whole bucks," the teen sprayed.

But he'd get more money than that joining his dad at his camp along the Río Loco—he drawled the name *law-co*. San Wren was what he called the city across the Río Loco on the other side of the border. He explained that if she really wanted to sound local she'd call the illegal boys *pollitos*, the Spanish word for "chicks." "Not like girls," he laughed but "little baby chickens. They keep squeezing through any fence or boundary we try to put up." He shook his head: part disgust, part amazement. "They're real small, those boys, quick. You know Spanish?"

"A bit." She had slid her hand into her purse so the teen would stop staring at her wedding ring.

The teen said, well, his dad didn't want him to learn it. "But I catch words anyhow. I like the way they sound." He took a deep breath and emitted a high, rolling "r," breaking static.

It won't be long before these orange-haired sons leave their sunken store and corroded pumps and go down to join their dad. As Honey tugs her suitcase through the gravel, the McGarrigle boys duck inside. The handrail is gone from the stoop and the mesh door is patched with fishing line. Her pupils pull in and out of focus until a counter and cash register materialize, behind which the boys keep watch. Shelves and drink coolers are mostly empty, newspaper racks bare.

"Can I have some water?"

The boys are unmoving.

"I thought offering water was just a given down here."

The small boy returns from the back room with a Styrofoam cup half full. The gritty contents taste of a pool, yet the drink lifts the fuzz from her brain. The brothers watch her with tight, drawstring lips.

"You two are Luke and Jer McGarrigle."

They blink. Big and small. Large and petite. Bone-rack thin and just plain delicate, twinned by desert dirt and a hard father's harder rearing.

"I was calling and calling here, for two whole days."

Luke lays his hands on the counter. "Our dad said not to answer that phone. Not ever."

She holds out her cup but the boys shake their heads. Jer, the little one, points behind her. A few cans, a Coke, a Fanta, a pair of 7-Ups, are all that's left in the drinks cooler. She takes some time deciding—inhaling the blast of cold air—settling on the last Fanta. It is gone in two long swallows.

"How do I get to my mom's?" she asks.

"Ta whose?"

She feels the downward pull of that frown she gives her students. "Marianne Moore. She's there up the road."

"No, she's not." says Jer. "She's not there."

Luke, the big one, has harder eyes than his brother. "She even left the door wide open." They themselves pulled it locked.

A forest of prickles rises on the back of her neck. "But she phoned me, just last week."

The boys look at their boots.

"Not our fault!" Jer shouts. His brother hits him, thud: heel of palm to temple. The boy's cap falls to the floor.

"Fault?" She steps back, knocking into her suitcase. "What was?" Her body breaks out in a different kind of sweat.

"The dog bite," Luke says, slow and quiet. He tells her to ask Johnny-for-Jesus. "He came here to get astringent but we was out of it." Jer's chin is patched in red fuzz and his skinny arms are muscled. She stares until he speaks. "Big Indian guy. Super kind of —"

"Churchy," says Luke. Or that's what their dad calls him.

Jer steps in front of his brother. "Dropping water almost got him banned from his own reservation. Know that? Most of them Indians're on our side too."

She waves the boys towards the door and pulls out her wallet. "Let's go. I'll pay the gas."

Jer nods at the window. Their dad took the truck when he left—a year ago now.

Fingerprints and heat cloud the lenses of her eyeglasses. "But my mom would have called us if she was hurt. My husband's an emergency doctor. Don't you know that?"

Jer shifts his pale eyes. "Where's he then? Sent you down here alone on that bus?"

Out on the road something like a short-tailed rat skids after a gecko. And there are no cars, not a single one since the bus left. She fumbles for her change purse. She needs quarters if she's going to use the phone outside. "So where's her dog?"

The brothers say she is best to just turn around and go back home. "This ain't no place for a lady," Luke says. "'Specially one that spits the image of her mom like you do. Folks'll get confused."

She digs out enough for a flaccid Clusters bar, the red-foil wrapper faded to orange, and two more drinks — Coke and 7 Up — and then wheels her suitcase outside, the briefcase slipping from the top. The mesh door slams and sun smacks her in the face. The phone booth is a slow, burning torture. She calls home, but can only stand the heat long enough to let it ring ten times before she slams down the blistering receiver and takes a break. There's no answer at Dinorah's either. Without looking back, she wheels her suitcase down the road. The barking of McGarrigle's animals fades out behind her.

CHÁVEZ

He's followed the farms too far north and east now. How come he's got so lost up here when he came to know the desert so well? He tries asking after Zopilote using the name

Buzzard City, but none of these pickers have ever been there; nor do they know where it is in relation to Maclean's farm. Only that there's a bus once a day that'll get you there. It's harder in the city, they say. Need English there. Need friends.

The worn business card that holds his place in his Charlie Brown comic says *Saint Moses Hospital, Buzzard City*. Probably Saint Moses is a really high tower of white cement with a cross on top. It'll be one of a clutch of towers — most of them glass — around which taxis will whistle up and down and back and forth just like on a highway. And beneath his feet the ground will shake with the thunder of subways and in the air the smell of hot dogs and fries and grassy baseball parks. He's read this *It's a Big World, Charlie Brown* comic enough times he's memorized all the English. On the cover poor old Charlie is wearing a too-big ball cap and his even bigger mitt is dragging on the pitcher's mound. And Chávez has read the information on the business card a million more times than that. A phone number is printed in the bottom corner along with the silhouette of this Saint Moses in profile with a corded beard and long, parted-in-the-middle hair. The cardboard is soft with the oil of his fingertips, so he holds it by the edges. It smells bleachy, like the *vieja*'s skin, so that is how Zopilote smells to him too.

San Wren is the only city he knows so far. It's right on the Río Loco. Before they started building the wall you could look across the bend and see Matchstick County on the other side, so that's why everyone crossed the border from there. And that's why he got off in San Wren when he came up from Abuelita's. The smell of charcoal and cars and whatever factory had made the Río Loco that weird orange slapped him right in the face and he wanted back to Abuelita's mattress, the spice of chilis, hibiscus sweeter than any fruit, the pop of Pedro's muffler when he rumbled up in the morning dark. He watched how people worked the soda machine then bought one for himself. Maybe it was four in the afternoon. Across from the station and through the *zip-zip* of traffic was a dull pink church with no windows, just a blank metal door. On the steps four boys were hunched over a card game. Their jeans were too big and their ball caps were worn backwards. They ate fish from tinfoil bundles, easing bones from their teeth.

He guzzled the soda and, turning his cap around too, crossed the road. The one boy who looked up had light eyes — made more so by his avocado-coloured cap. The corkscrew curls squashed underneath were thick and coarse. Staring at that hair wasn't enough, you had to touch it. Chávez showed them his coins and said to deal him in. The boy in the green cap nodded and passed him a bottle of watery brown liquid. It burned his throat, but he didn't let it show. This boy said his name was Juan. They were playing for cigarettes and also some candy that Juan said he'd brought back from a gas station on the other side of the border. Chávez won the first hand. The cigarette went behind his ear but he ate the candy—a long molasses stick, plump and sweet. No one else wanted a bite. When asked, he said his name. Chávez? Juan said there were already at least two great men with that name. He should choose something else.

No. He was Chávez, now and always.

Juan said, "Okay, Chavito, well, where you coming from?"

"You know Mendez? Left field for the Suns? Well, his village is on the other side of the valley from mine." He said he intended to cross the border and go for Zopilote.

Juan laughed. "Yeah, you and everyone else, shithead."

Chávez felt his neck get red. He took his roll of tattoo money from his pocket and said he needed to hire a *coyote* to get him across.

Juan flicked the roll and said it wasn't enough. "Chavito," he said. "You think it's a game? *Coyotes* don't come a dime a dozen, at least not the good ones who don't rip off little village *pollos* like you."

Pedro had told him the boys paying the *coyotes* were called *pollos*: chickens. Any young or sissy ones are *pollitos*. Pedro also said the smugglers were called *coyotes* because they were out to trick you. Once when Pedro was crossing, long ago before he wrecked his foot, a *coyote* had pulled a knife on him and the rest of the *pollos* he was with. They were scared and gave the *coyote* all their money and he even took the sturdy boots right off one man's feet then left them in the desert to die.

"Each *coyote* for himself," Pedro said. "Be ready, my boy."

"Yeah, I know it's no game," Chávez said. "But I don't have more money than this."

Juan took off his hat, letting his curls spring out all over. He was wearing a collared shirt with short sleeves and a thick horizontal stripe that now makes Chávez think of Charlie Brown. It was even a bit daisy-coloured, too, especially under the arms.

"What else you got?"

Chávez lifted his T-shirt. Juan's eyes widened at the skeleton key tattooed along his midriff.

"So?" Juan said.

"So I did it myself and I'll do you."

One boy put down his cards, licked his finger, and rubbed hard at the tattoo. "It's for real," said the boy.

Chávez lowered his shirt and Juan flexed his right forearm. The skin was smooth, the colour of coconut husk, with light purple veins running through.

"Juanita," he said. "For my mom."

· Chávez said okay. While he drew a design in his notebook, Juan and his friends went back to the card game and the tinfoil of fish. Juan said he liked the design. He said, "You give me a tat just like that and I take you across the border."

Juan drank deeply. Chávez unwrapped the darning needle, poured some alcohol on the tip.

In Maclean's bunkhouse the darkness thins from cast iron to the cold grey of mourning ashes. It is always this way, these long nights after endless days.

Chávez lies there beside Roberto, thinking about Juan until he's going to cry and someone'll hear. How come the bad stuff comes out at night, all the ghosts he has? Or he imagines he is back on the road and the blue car is coming. He feels the fire in his lungs as he runs towards it—and then the gunshots ring out. Something about the driver's face had looked all wrong. But that was okay because she was leaning over to open the door for him. Her left arm coming up, her face turned away.

"Where are you, *vieja*?" he says, over and over, whispering himself to sleep. "Where am I, too?"

BAEZ

As Baez clawed deeper at the hole, the earth cooled. Then it got slinky with worms and twisted roots. Baez's nails turned up a stubby plastic tube she knew came from fire-cracker guns. Then there was another tube, and another. Old Blue's fingers closed tight around each tube Baez dropped into the palm of the good hand—the hand that was not bit.

She remembers that Speckled Man and his orange-haired sons always darkened their station shack before the night was full. And her sisters-brothers-babies-cousins would go to sleep too, in a heap, breathing as one: up-and-down-up-and-down, together. But ever since Speckled Man's sharp toe landed with a crunch behind her ear, she'd come to know so much, too much, and so she never did sleep. She listened to the night, its crackle, sniffing the air. Before she saw their shadows she smelled the brown men, brown boys. She knew if one was bleeding or sick, and how recently he'd peed. She knew which of them had eaten fish from a can or maybe those wiener stubs like Speckled Man scooped from a cloudy jar and flung into the cage just to see her sisters-brothers-babies-cousins bloody themselves over a bite of salty sponge.

Then on a bug-bright night—*pit-pat-pit-pat*—three brown boys came up from the tarry road, toe-tipping slow. *Pit-pat. Pit-pat.* Loud, and louder, close. Two brown boys stayed back but the third one approached. He was dried out. His eyes—steady on the heap of her and her sisters-brothers-babies-cousins—were raw and sick. She smelled the brown boy's adrenal sweat flowering orange. He had new pee on his hands and salt on his jeans. The ball cap on his head was tangy with spent energy and also it smelled like the smoke of Speckled Man's barbequed dinners—salty burnt mince he crumbled in her bowl.

The boy's white tongue licked his white lips. He stuck a skinny bone of arm into her pen and then, fingers wriggling,

gripped the lip of her bowl of buggy water. Slowly, sloshing, he pulled it in close. His fingers wriggled in her dish.
And he opened his mouth so as to receive those wet fingers,
the pearled drops, just clinging. And then it was that a line
inside her got crossed. A fiery blaze opened in her, a great
yawn, and her heart reared like a rattle-tailed snake and her
jaws went wide, wider, widest: snap. The brown boy's hand
was muscled meat. Then the crush of bone. The brown boy's
eyes squished up. And then his mouth melted, crying, crying, pulling on the hand locked now in her jaw.

Her sisters-brothers-babies-cousins began to bark and
yap, louder even than when clamouring over one of Speckled
Man's stubs of wiener. When she felt the brown boy's fingers rip and tear she released him, warmth running down
her throat. Unplugged, the brown boy ran, hand jammed
into his belly. And Speckled Man with gun and sons came
running from the station shack. One-two-three firecrackers
exploded: one for each of the brown boys gone now into the
desert night, one dripping blood and all of them crying.

Good girl, old girl. Speckled Man gave her and her sisters-
brothers-babies-cousins new water and he dug his fingers
into that sharp biting place behind her ear. *Did good. Good
girl.* Speckled Man's shack went dark again. Air settled
back. Her sisters-brothers-babies-cousins again breathed as
one, together, and then the blood that had drip-dropped-
drip-dropped across the station's gravel dried up into a trail
of scab.

And it all went back to as it was. Again and again the
pen and the shade and water dish and shack-gas-truck-honk
and her days spent waiting for night when the brown boys
went running past. In time the water in her bowl grew

orange and rank. The field across the road turned white. The overalled farmers drove up with empty trucks and then they stopped coming at all. Speckled Man and his orange-haired sons did a lot of sitting in the shade. It went that way until the sons were taller than the pumps and she had two more litters with the biggest of her cousins. Old Blue came then. Speckled Man pointed to the holes she'd started to dig. Old Blue creaked to her knees, soothing the sore spot behind Baez's ear, the biting that was always there. Then she buckled on a thick leather collar and took Baez away to the trailer where there were no sisters-brothers-babies-cousins. And instead of a fenced-in pen and toe kicks she got a word, said again and again in Old Blue's flat clip of voice, again and again until the word was hers — *Baez*.

HONEY

Fallen chain-link droops along the road, beyond which boarded-up house trailers, like the stumps of felled trees, indicate where once life had been. Stump after stump. The irrigation ditches are so parched the very concrete crumbles, and where purple lettuce once burst in perfect rows the soil is chalky. The grocery bags that dance in the wind are not from any stores that she knows.

She turns right at the crossroads, down Route 59, where the ten-armed saguaro cactus Marianne had called Old Faithful has gone even greyer.

"Mom? Hey! Marianne?"

Marianne bought the acreage for next to nothing when the soil went white and the farmers migrated further north. A dusty aluminum trailer lurks at the far end, behind dry scrub and bare mesquite trees. The shed Keith patched is still standing, beyond which a faint path leads out to a shallow wash where leafless ironwood trees twist up, going for the sun. Along the western horizon, the soft silhouette of a low mountain range gives off a purple glow. "My mountains," Marianne calls them, capturing the textures in brown, gold, tangerine—even margarine—depending on the cut of the light. But really they are the Zari Mountains, named for the Indians who still live somewhere close and so must belong to those who share their name. Marianne said all this land is rightfully Indian.

"Mom?"

Marianne's been driving the same dull-blue two-door Tribal for what must be twenty years. Its saggy belly skims the gravel patch that is the driveway, windows pale with dust. She rubs a circle in the glass with her sleeve. The car is packed with cardboard boxes, garbage bags, and loose junk—dinner plates, lampshades, a clock radio. But the doors are locked and the handles hot. Insects pock the windshield, and on the passenger side of the glass a long, violent crack: a rock launched, a bat smashed.

There's a water pump behind the trailer. Heaving on its crooked arm, she slurps from a cupped hand then washes her face and, lifting her ponytail, her burning neck. Any minute Marianne will come striding out, smiling: *Honey, what the hell are you doing here?* But the plywood door stays shut.

It is all high-pitched stillness. The front yard is pitted with dozens of wide, shallow holes Baez must have dug. But the post by the front stoop that Marianne had chained her to is gone. The rough hole left behind suggests it was wrenched with great strain from the ground. As Honey stands and turns, she finds herself within a loose ring of rodent carcasses, dry bones, patches of fur, lumps of blackened scat which circles the trailer.

"Who needs a gun with Baez around?" Marianne had said after bringing the animal home from McGarrigle's. "Or deadbolts either."

The key with the red nail polish opens the door. A pent-up blast of heat, old sweat, and dirty fur strikes her in the face. Daylight juts through the kitchen's sealed windows, falling jagged on the floor. The wool blanket in the corner is covered in short, bristled shedding. Chewed rubber balls and some grizzled strips of rawhide litter the linoleum. With urgency and ecstasy Honey kicks away her sweaty Nikes then rolls off her socks, leaving them to dry on the stoop. She eases her puffy feet into the grey flip-flops by the door.

"Baez?" Her voice is strange, muffled, like she's got cotton in her mouth. "You in here, girl?" The words roam through the hollow interior. "Mom? How about you?"

CHÁVEZ

He forgets the name of this new town as soon as it's said. He's glad the *vieja*'s not around to hear these mistakes. When he gets to Zopilote, his English will be a million times better than that shitty baby Spanish she babbled in. At the end she was talking English mostly anyway. What if he had understood her? If she thinks of him at all, she will think he's dead. He should be dead. He is defying her and life and God by still breathing.

He breathes. He buys a pair of blue Nikes at a thrift store, good as new, then hitches a ride with a pair of brothers in

wide hats and finger-printed glasses. He tries to tell them he
is lost and wants to go towards Buzzard City.

"Please," he says.

When they hear Buzzard they shake their heads and
point down at the floor, meaning south. They let him out at
a small-time pepper farm called Fiesta, where he agrees to
the farmer's offer of a bed and cash in hand every Saturday.
No overtime. Sunday's a half day. There are bikes to ride to
town if he's got the energy. The farmer has no hair. Squiggly
veins run from forehead to crown. His eyes open too wide.
He gives Chávez a rubber bucket and a long knife for cutting
stems. The gloves are huge and smell like puke. Out in the
field a group of fifteen or so boys are crouched under a shade
tent. They share their sandwiches of meat and bright mustard and soft white bread, cold milk from canteens. They eat
fast so they can sleep for ten or so minutes. A couple of boys
from a place further south than his village sit up with him,
smoking. They say the pepper harvest could last months.
None of them know Zopilote. Only that it is too big, too hard.

"We're sons of farmers. That place would eat us alive."

But if Chávez picks a few hundred pounds of peppers,
he'll have enough in a week to buy a bus ticket and keep
moving — south. He knows that much now. Farms, like the
water, are more and more in the north part of the earth and
if he wants to find the *vieja* he's got to resist the pull of quick
money and travel back down. But with what? The farmer
pays only twenty-five cents per bucket so you have to be real
smart with the way you move your body and no matter what,
don't start to think. That'll slow you, kill you if you let it. If
you don't get ten buckets in a day, you get the farmer's boot.
In less than an hour his hands ache from grasping peppers

just right and pulling the knife across the thick stem. He's ten times slower than any other picker.

They sleep in an old barn with no windows and a curtain for a door. The mattresses are hard-packed, but at least they each get their own. These pepper pickers have dug a pit out back. Like in the desert, even if it's warm, you need a fire sometimes to stop from being scared. Evening, they sit around just smoking. He is one of the oldest because fewer boys are coming up now. They talk about the wall cutting across the Río Loco. The part between Matchstick County and San Wren is done now. They say it is as thick as a truck and high as the sky.

"You seen it?" Chávez says.

A couple say, yeah, it's a fucker of a thing but there's a tunnel you can take to get under.

"The wall's nothing. It's Ocho and his dogs that scare me," says a boy in a cap with a horseshoe logo. "You ever see him?" This boy's face is tanned dark, hands padded with callouses.

"A traitor," says one boy called Manny.

He's littler than Chávez. Over some kind of canned supper—they make their own food here at Fiesta, lining up for their turn at the hot plate—he'd told Chávez that when he came here he'd layered on all kinds of thrift-store clothes so he looked bigger and the farmers would hire him.

"Yeah, it's bullshit," says Chávez. "Ocho's for himself."

He licks a finger, rubs his Nike swooshes, stained now with squished peppers and dirt, and listens to Horseshoe Hat talk about Ocho. There are a few boys among them who crossed the border along the eastern coast and don't know about Ocho. Horseshoe Hat calls him a bounty hunter.

He says, "Ocho was a *coyote* one time. But then he sold out to Control. Now he's making a business of capturing any other boys he finds crossing to Zopilote. It doesn't matter if he gets *pollos* or *coyotes*, he turns them over to Control."

"How much he get for doing that?" Manny asks.

"Bounty's called at fifty bucks a boy," Chávez says into the fire. "Then Control drives them back to the border. Sometimes, for repeats, they put the kid in a detention centre somewhere hidden and you never hear from him again."

Manny says he knows stories of that place too.

"It's a lie," Horseshoe Hat announces. "Don't you know? Never listen to anyone with them orange eyes like this one." He points his finger right at Chávez. "They'll take you for a ride and then cut your throat." Horseshoe Hat holds his hands close to the fire, calloused palms smoking. Hey, have they heard about how Ocho got his hand bit off by a coydog? "That's why he's called 'Eight.' He's only got eight fingers. It was that coydog-bitch of El Esqueleto's that bit him."

"You're talking shit," Chávez says to him. He doesn't look up from his shoes. "What do you all know about El Esqueleto?"

But for the hiss and pop of kindling, there is silence. Then some boys shuffle, shift. They groan, stretching their cramped legs and bent backs. Someone passes a bottle of Tylenol. "Don't take more than four at a time, man."

"I know all there is about El Esqueleto," Horseshoe Hat says finally to Chávez. "She was creepy and tall and left food in the trees."

Says Manny: "What you mean 'she'? I thought it was an old man."

A boy in an Exxon cap goes, "Well, whatever the fuck she was, that animal of hers was nasty."

Manny leans in now: "Why did she keep that fucking dog? To bite us?"

Chávez says: "Can't you see? She was alone in the world except for it."

"So tell us—was she really truly crazy?"

"No, man," Chávez says. "If you ever felt a love like she had for that dog, you wouldn't say it's crazy." Now he's the one that's crazy, he sees it in their eyes. Chávez shakes his head. "Only thing she loved more than the dog was the desert." He sucks on his tobacco.

"Well," says Horseshoe Hat, "that old bitch loved the desert only because she never had to cross it."

"Yeah," they all go. "Fuck her. What's she know?"

Someone says: "She just left water out, like we were dogs or something."

"That water saved me," says the one in the Exxon cap. "Maybe without her I would have died."

Horseshoe Hat spits in the fire. "I never took from that old bitch. I'm no dog."

Chávez says, "You sure, man? 'Cause you sure talk as dumb as one."

While the other boys laugh and make howling sounds, Chávez watches the dying embers spark. In the distance the farmhouse lights blot out. Six hours now till morning.

"And she did cross the desert, you assholes," he tells them, getting to his feet. "I saw her out there dying."

Sometimes he wishes he had died out there. Because this is not alive. He's just a body working hard. He's a belly to fill, a back to ache, a bowel to move in a hidden place. He is eyes blinking in the dark of some nowhere farm and he is a brain that needs to sleep but can't sleep like the boys and boys and boys all around him. He gets up and walks back to the barn. The walls are so split he can see the moon coming through from the other side. He closes his eyes. He sees the *vieja*. He wants to forget her. But he wants his money more.

BAEZ

Old Blue's water bottle was half full. In the shade of the skinny mesquite Baez had sat before Old Blue and, head tilted back, received the warm liquid as it slid down her throat. She licked Old Blue's lips, the salt, the blood, the dirt. Old Blue's eyes kept crossing in the middle but then her sunburned face opened into a smile. From above came a razor hiss. A muscled bird with a tiny bald head had landed. Old Blue looked up. Then, very suddenly, her face melted. She looked over at the hole, scritch-scratched in the sand. *Good girl, Baez,* she said.

Across the yard, Baez sees the brown boys blink at her. And from the other side of the plywood wall, her children emit their first morning yowls. Tattoo emerges from the sooty trailer. He wears only white shorts. The food bag is loud, water sloshes. Then it is her turn. She is still. With a toe Tattoo slides the water dish towards her. Then he returns with a shovel and a pail to scrape up her shit of which there is almost none. She lifts her head, pushes herself towards him using her hind legs. His eyes on her are hard. The hair above his lip has thickened, as have the tattoos on his arms, or is it the arms themselves that are thicker? His shoulders are broad now. He is growing big like her babies did. He locks the gate behind him. When she dies will they bury her? Or will they throw her to the birds and bugs, like they did her daughter born blind, her black-and-tan son when his back leg broke?

She remembers Old Blue's trailer, hidden in brush and mesquite tree. By the front stoop under which Baez liked to sleep, there was a thick metal post. Old Blue chained her to this most of the time. While she could not reach the road, the trailer being tucked away and back like an animal shying, the chain was long enough she could go as far as the stand of ironwood trees down the wash behind the shed. She would follow Old Blue down there and wait while Old Blue hoisted food into the tough ironwood branches and left water jugs at the base. The brown boys crossed her land like they had crossed the gravel lot of Speckled Man's. Old Blue fed and watered them, while Speckled Man drove them off. She did like Old Blue wanted and let the brown boys come. So long as they stayed back under those ironwood trees, Baez stayed quiet.

Mornings, before full sun, Old Blue would pull on her round hat and take Baez walking. When they were away from the road, Old Blue unclipped Baez's leash. In spring the land erupted with bright pollen and was thick with buzzing, bugs and bugs and breeze. And there were rabbits, big ones and baby ones, unblinking lizards, foxes, rats—life to which Old Blue was mostly blind. But still Old Blue smiled and hummed, her bones creaking.

Old Blue had a favourite crop of rocks where she would sit with paper and pencil and put down what she saw. Baez chased birds and hunted lizards, spying snakes and being spied in turn. And just as there were thorns and spikes to tear her nose as she followed the tumbling, rumbling smells, there were always footprints too: small ones, pitter-patter ones. These were the tracks of the same ball-capped brown boys that crossed Old Blue's land—always heading towards the north. She followed them until Old Blue called her back. Once, though, she took a set of tracks beyond Old Blue's *Ba-ez!* The smell she followed was ripe and purple: it was the smell she licks from herself now, the smell that brings the bald birds in. The tracks bottomed out where the smell burst up as a blue-black cloud. The boy's body was a torn-up swell. Bones poked out of skin that was no longer brown and the ground was stained with leaked fats. Near was a bright spot of ball cap; yonder the sack he'd carried on his back.

Old Blue shook when she saw the body. She went yellow, fell right down like the whole ground had suddenly shifted: *crack* went her elbow against a rock. On her knees, she held her hands to the sky and then she hugged Baez's neck. She cried all the way back to the trailer where she filled her cup again and again with hot amber from the big bottle under the sink. Then she fell asleep at the table, hands hanging at her sides. Old Blue did not get up to fill Baez's food bowl. She did not get up when the man with the long black braid drove up in his stickered-up truck. He, Black Braid, came right in. *Hey, Marianne.* Baez stayed in her corner, rumbled low. Black Braid wore a wood cross around his neck. He had a bag with hot cooked food. He fed Baez from the bag. Then he shook Old Blue awake, fed and watered her too. His hands were slow and strong. When Black Braid put Old Blue to bed he pulled the shoes from her feet and tucked the covers under her shoulders and chin.

Black Braid came back the next day with a shovel. He whistled to Baez. She took him into the desert, to the dead boy. He hid the body with a blanket and with two fingers touched his forehead, chest, shoulders, side to side. He whispered a bit, looked up at the sky. The blade of his shovel scraped as he dug down into the hard-packed ground. When the hole was to his thighs, he drank a jug of water. Then he lifted the bundled body and placed it in the hole. He put the dirt back, packing it into a mound. The death smell was gone. Black Braid had some small stones in his pocket. He arranged them on the mound into a cross, like the wood one he wore, then he said some more soft words, crouching down. He whistled for Baez. They left the dead boy where no animals or birds would get him. There was safety inside the earth.

When Tattoo goes back into the trailer, there comes the far-off beating of wings. A hulk of bird touches down on the top of the trailer, among the up-turned panels that drink the energy from the sun and feed it to Glove and Tattoo's radio. The bird's bald head is small, its body muscled; feathers black and brown. Is it the same bird as Old Blue's? Its rotten meaty smell is the same. The bird bounces from foot to foot. Then in three slow, hard wing-beats it exchanges the trailer for the uppermost reaches of Baez's tree. Its white-skinned feet cling to a sturdy branch. The bird leans over and through a sharp, hooked beak hisses for Baez to hurry up.

HONEY

The dark trailer smells of old fur. She could be in a dusty flora and fauna museum at one of the national parks. Marianne's been packing. Plastic bags stuffed with clothes burst their twist-ties, and a clumsy stack of shoeboxes leans near the door. The dinner plate Marianne uses for an ashtray is heaped with crushed Phantoms. The O'Brien's bottle on the kitchen table is going on empty, the amber contents just meeting the bottom of the silver label; the rose teacup beside is syrupy with what must be years without a real washing. Last time, Marianne was giving things a quick rinse whenever the county turned on the water: seven until ten in the morning, five in the afternoon until eight at night. The bandage box by Marianne's creaky kitchen scissors is empty; whiskey and blood stain the clumps of tissue strewn among crusty bean bowls and sliced bread gone to powder. She twists the sticky lid from the whiskey bottle and sips, sloshing the burn around in her cheeks like it's Listerine.

"Mom?" Her call floats in the static. She sips again.

Each of the paintings that crowds the trailer tells a story of the desert, a vision of what Marianne calls "upmost transcendence." Watercolours—which Keith always says are inherently ironic in such a thirsty place—are tacked to the chipboard walls; stretched canvases are stacked, leaning against legs of chairs and tables. Sketches, curled into loose tubes, tumble from the countertops and roll onto the floor. A crimson dollop squeezed on a piece of glass has hardened to a knob and unwashed brushes have dried into arrow tips. Like the painting of Baez in their living room—a present for their two-year anniversary—each image is signed with a simple *MM* in the corner: a pair of flying birds and also the initials of Marianne Moore. Mother, Mom.

She remembers the flicker of laughter in Keith's voice when they first saw Marianne's trailer rising at the end of the road. "Your mother's going to live here?" He had slowed the car right down, shuddering as gravel pinged the Ventura's paint job.

Marianne had stood waving on the stoop. She'd cropped her snowy hair, as close as she could get to the root. Some kind of muscled bitch, long of snout and mottled as a bruised banana, crouched at her feet, woofing, pulling against the strong old hand gripping her collar. When the animal hushed, Honey had mounted the stoop, heart tightening at all the new wrinkles around the bright beads of her mom's eyes. She said nothing about Marianne's shorn scalp—how pink, how like a baby—just wrapped the familiar body in her arms. And she was wrapped in turn, relaxing into Marianne's same sweet odour of sweat and Phantoms. Then the animal's nose nudged between them. Honey let go of Marianne's hard shoulders. She knew it was wrong to call this animal a dog when it was so obviously one of those half-coyotes. But she'd always hated the sound of "coydog."

"Who's this?" Honey said, holding out her open hand.

"She's Baez." Marianne smiled down at the animal, its eyes of buttered orange, the skulking tail, red leather collar loose at the neck. It half-grinned, half-growled back. Keith slammed the car door and came striding up, a suitcase in each hand.

Rrrupp. The animal barked, rushing. Keith had dropped the bags then, assuming a passive crouch.

"She won't bite, Quiche," called Marianne, her Dutch accent flat. Then: "Baez!" The animal stopped and looked back.

"Offer your hand," Marianne said. Keith opened his fist. Finally the animal wagged its tail and let him touch her grizzled head.

Marianne's calloused hands were black with paint. She shoved them deep into her jeans pockets and leaned back into rubber beach clogs.

"Mom." Honey found Marianne's puckered elbow and gave it a squeeze. "Can we come in?"

Supper was a can of stew and a sleeve of biscuits. Honey and Keith should have packed more food. But they'd brought beer, which they sipped while Marianne poured whiskey into her teacup.

"Cheers." Marianne said. "Me and Baez are so happy you came."

Night swept in quickly, as if hitting a switch. The air outside grew chill, but in the trailer the day's trapped heat held thick. Honey and Keith squeezed into the single bed in the small back bedroom. Coyotes called from far off. Or were they near?

"They intend to trick you," Marianne had said. "The way they throw their voices you just can't say where they are." She told them coyotes were survivors. "When we nuke each other there'll be just coyotes left. Oh, and rats."

Marianne let the animal sleep inside. Its toenails clicked on the linoleum as it paced the length of the trailer's narrow passage, its relentless panting surprisingly loud and deep.

"She's outside the door now," Honey whispered. "It's not really a dog, Keith, is it?"

Keith's fingers found the edge of her cotton nightdress then rode the curve of her thigh.

"Quiche," she said, laughing at the nickname Marianne's accent had given him. "Don't. It's creepy when that Baez is listening."

Her husband's fingers had given a final flutter then pulled away, taking her hand instead. The in and the out of the animal's breath kept time with the gradual passing of the night.

Now Honey licks chocolate goop and nutty bits oozing from the wrapper of her Clusters bar. But for a sour smell and open can of beans, the refrigerator is empty. The chocolate bar, what's left of it, goes inside, along with the Coke. She sits on the stoop with her luggage. The Tribal stands dark and still and—keyless. Beyond it, the sun sinks into the on-and-on of textured scrub. The sugar of creosote hangs in the air. Nights never cool off as they once did.

Johnny-for-Jesus, is that the name those shitty McGarrigles said? "They're the most noble people," Marianne had said of the Zari Indians with whom she traded her paintings—getting prickly pear jam and fry bread in return. Oh, and braids of desert grass, a leather pouch stamped with the outline of coyote she sent for Keith to hook to his belt, along with the brittle rattle of the thus-named snake. With a dishrag Keith had plucked the bumpy rattle from the cotton-lined gift box and tossed the lot down the garbage chute.

"That's goddamn weird," he had said, scrubbing his hands in the sink.

From behind she had rested her chin in the well between his shoulder blades. "Poor old Mom, my Marianne."

Tomorrow she'll find the car keys and drive to the reservation. Marianne and Baez will both be there, recovering at some makeshift clinic. At first she thinks the silver-white glow in the southeast is from that dumpy Spanish-speaking factory town, San something, on the other side of where the Río Loco bends. But the light is too concentrated, too pulsing with energy to be from that impoverished place. The silver-white is from floodlights: the construction of the border wall is in overtime. Men are earning money under that light; men who might once have had farms or worked mines here in the southern counties, but who now dig a thousand miles of ten-foot-deep east-west trench, which they then stack with great blocks of concrete, reinforced with bars of thick tempered steel. From root to tip, the border wall will measure half a mile high and thirty feet thick. The only body getting through will be whatever is left of the dirty old shrivelled-up Río Loco. Marianne had asked her to clip any stories from the *Buzzard Standard* on the progress of the wall. Out of concern for the value of her land, Keith had guessed. "Which'll now be about zilch, if it wasn't already worthless before." And so Honey had tucked a few newspaper articles in among the packs of Phantom cigarettes, Vaseline for Marianne's cracked hands, and tubes of paint—hemoglobin, burnt sienna, lemony citron—that she shipped from the Greyhound station in Buzzard City to Matchstick once each month.

Apart from that floodlight and the milk of the half-moon, the stars have no competition. She whispers to those stars, to the night, to anything that might be listening, and squeezes her eyes until bright balls of colour come.

She thinks, then says: "Let Marianne put that fucking Baez out of its misery." Let this all end.

The long passage leading to the bedrooms is hung with sunsets and dawns, spring bloom, fading nights with coyotes howling at the moon. The saggy mattress in Marianne's empty room has been stripped. Honey slides open the window above the bed. Sour fur and animal breath eases out.

The pattern on the sheets in the back bedroom has been washed beyond recognition. Above the bed Marianne has stuck up a poster of a waterfall that says "follow your bliss" in cursive loops, to which she has added "ters" in bold black.

"Follow your blisters." Honey speaks the words slowly.

Through the window, shadows move against the mountained horizon — animals or else those migrant boys passing through. *Pollitos.* She's never asked Dinorah how she came to Buzzard but Keith said it's best not to assume. She could very well have documents. Many of them do.

There is no spare car key in the kitchen drawers or cupboards, nor in the coin jar in the pantry, and neither is a set hanging from the nails by the door. Marianne's knives are all packed up somewhere too. Honey locks the windows, the door, and even switches off the air conditioner so she can hear the night out there. She lies on the bed in the back room. Her glasses weigh heavy on her face. She sweats. The sweat dries. When her belly rumbles she sips O'Brien's. Outside the chain rattles on the water pump. Then comes the creak of the handle. She runs into the kitchen and grabs Marianne's scissors from the table then shuts herself in the back room.

She's never wished for a gun before now. Counting her breaths slows her heart. When she was a girl and Marianne went to night classes she would bury herself in the back of Marianne's closet, so sure was she that every creak in the wall or voice in the hall was a murderer. The time she fell asleep among the boots and extra bedding, she woke to Marianne yelling and swearing for her to come the hell out. But she stayed where she was and after a few minutes she heard fear and grief in Marianne's voice. When she did emerge, smiling, Marianne cancelled her 911 call and slapped her, open-handed, across the face.

"One, two, three," she whispers.

A coyote wails, from near and far, behind and beside the trailer, the high *you-you-you* meant just for her. *Where are you-you-you?* The animals circle in, only to recede again. Ventriloquists, like Marianne had said. Maybe there's a pack of them; or just one, outside her window.

"*¡Mira, pinche!*" a kid's voice shouts.

Footsteps rush past right outside the window.

Then, in English: "Hey!" And something garbled, something urgent.

"Go away, you little *pollitos*," she whispers, angry that kids have her so scared. There's a crack, an exploding pop that can only be gunshot. She's never heard one so close. Her body jolts out of the bed. She crouches near the door.

After another shot, sharp, fissured dog-barking breaks out, then fades. The storm passes. She stretches out on the bed, on her side, holding tight to her knees. She cries until she slips into a place that is murky and filled with shadows that are and are not Keith.

CHÁVEZ

Once he vowed to forget Juan, but that was before he knew it was going to be so hard here. He needs some bit of comfort,

a warm flame to lean into. It was one whole year ago—
more now—that he crossed the desert for the last time.
He thought he would get to Zopilote and find the *vieja* fast.
But he had no money when he got to the Roma motel so he
jumped in a truck with a farmer who called out he had a big
crop of dates coming in. They'd already pulled onto the highway when he saw her watching him from the balcony. He'd
struggled to jump out, but the other boys held him there in
the speeding truck. That was the first ghost of her he'd see.
The first of many dreams.

He went north from the date farm because he'd heard
of a place with mushrooms ready and decent food. In a few
months Zopilote sort of trickled away. That scared him.
Picking crops for sunburned men is no kind of life. Now he
doesn't even know how he'd find himself on a map. It's like
he and the pickers are on some castaway island. But learning English is like getting a boat or at least knowing how to
swim. He'll be better than the *vieja* that way. He never wants
to sound like she did, so when he's not sleeping he whispers
the lines of all those Charlie Browns so no one else can hear.
Or else, if he's really stuck for sleeping, he'll think of Juan.

He blocks out the bad parts, concentrating on the good.
His favourite bit is when he dressed Juan's tattooed forearm
on the church steps that first time they'd met. The blood
seeping through the toilet paper looked like a sun setting
into dirty white sand. In those five hours of needlework
Chávez had felt something slipping and sliding inside him.
It was just out of nowhere. Like, he'd tattooed how many kids
before? Smelled their armpits and breaths, felt the weight
of their bodies as they'd leaned into him. The feeling of
Juan had no name, just a sort of inner buzz, a good kind

of nervous that came on especially strong when that crazy curly hair tickled Chávez's face. Juan smelled like food— fish and bread and spice—and the underarms of his T-shirt were getting more and more grey from wet. When the card players trickled away in search of soda and cigarettes, Juan talked about his mom.

"Maybe my mom worked at the same factory as yours." Juan's mom had been right there in San Wren, sewing stripes on shoes, when the money stopped coming in the mail.

What about Chávez's mom? "Don't know. But she was going for Zopilote. I think she got there, too—though Abuelita says no."

Then Juan got faint and put his hand on Chávez's shoulder. It was a hot, good feeling. That made him a bit scared. Juan drank from the plastic bottle and then Chávez drank, but the nerves only came stronger.

That first night, he had waited in the church like Juan said to. The plaster walls were cool and the candles warm. Who lit them? He waited to find out. It was quiet as a cave. For many moments he was the only boy left in the world. Then he fell asleep on a hard bench. Juan came back with water jugs, bags of rough, mealy bread, cans of salty stuff, and a flashlight for each of them. The pair of old runners he brought for Chávez were too big, but he couldn't go in sandals so he put them on. Out in the street, there was only a dim light. Three boys with Indian faces and all of them smaller, even, than Chávez, stepped out from the shadows beside the church steps.

Juan said that after they crossed the desert, they would walk some miles down a highway to a motel called Roma. And that was it: Roma was the end of *el desierto* and the beginning of a new life. If they wanted jobs in the city and they had the balls, they could walk the thirty miles all the way to Zopilote. Or they could wait in the parking lot for the farmers who, in the mornings, come looking for fresh hands. Who knows where they'd end up working, Juan said. There were jobs all over, especially further north. And this being the start of spring harvest, pretty soon the boys would be making enough to buy new pairs of Nikes or Adidas — "Whatever's your brand, kids. You can have it."

As Juan made these promises he looked up at the sky and swept his arms overhead. But, one kid said, were they really safe once they got to motel Roma? Could they still get caught and sent back? Juan shook his head: if you lie low and do the work that no one else wants to, you don't have to worry about Control. "Just never complain, no matter what. North people never see us if we're happy ghosts. No sad ghosts or pissed-off ghosts or drunk ghosts, okay?"

He would be a happy ghost. He couldn't believe it was happening so fast. The Loco was low and dirty with a winter's worth of garbage, fish not just dead but opaque and flaking like they'd been cooked. The smell burned their eyes. Juan said the faraway smoulder of floodlight was the Control Corp building their wall. He said in the day you could hear the sound of drills and jackhammers, reversing trucks, even generator hum. But there was time still before they finished. The dumb fucks kept running out of money and there weren't enough men to do the work. When Chávez said, "Shit, why not just hire us to do it?" Juan laughed. It was black where his molars should have been. The water came to their knees. They carried their shoes, trudged hard against the river's quick current, then ran up the eastern bank.

Juan had walked tall and quick and though he said he'd been this route before, they stumbled too close to a ranch house. "Fuck, man," Juan shouted. Windows flashed and animals shot towards them through the dark. Chávez tore after Juan, who'd cut ahead, not looking back. But then there was a scream, high like a girl's. The smallest Indian kid had wiped out. He was on his belly, weighed down under his pack. The other two pulled him up but then the ranch dog pounced, got the kid's pant cuff in its jaws. It writhed and growled and finally they got away. The boy's skinny calf was ripped open and bleeding. Chávez stared: how was it that human beings were just made of meat?

"I can walk, I can," the boy cried.

"Shut up," Juan hissed. He tore a strip from his T-shirt and, on one knee, staunched the wound. "Up on my back." Juan knelt low. The boy climbed up, thin arms looped around Juan's neck.

They should have been going northeast, but in an hour they were back at the ranch house. The same windows glowed in the distance.

"Fuck!" Juan spat, throwing the boy, who hit the ground with a thud. Juan was turning around, spinning in the dark, craning his gaze up at the sky.

"Shit-head *coyote*," a boy said. "Don't even know where we're going."

Chávez stood apart and looked up. Soon he'd found Venus, the Big Dipper, and the big bright one that hovers over the north.

"That's the way we got to be going." He pointed them towards the right of the ranch, not the left.

Juan had stared him down. "How the fuck you know?"

Chávez said he just did. He walked on. In a few minutes he felt the others running up behind him.

After a dead-end road that a sign called *prohibido*, they were really in the desert. It got even bigger out there. An end-of-the-world kind of empty. Juan said that was why everyone called it *Las tierras vacías*. Chávez scouted daytime hideouts — in arroyos, caves and crevices, in ironwood shade — where they hunkered down. Then, at dusk, he led them through *bajada* flats. The soft dirt fanned out wide and open, the horizon disappearing into the dark. Then these high silhouetted outcrops jumped up from nowhere, snakes and spiders hiding in the cracks of the dark, jaggedy rock. Juan had punched his shoulder. "You're a real *coyote*," he said. "We can make money at this shit, you and me."

They were three nights in the desert before they crossed through the jagged Entrada mountains. They all had bloody hands to go with their dry, bleeding noses when they got to the other side. A highway blinked bright — a necklace of rich-lady gems. They crossed the flatland towards it and walked the highway single-file, the wind of passing traffic blowing them back. The neon cactus Juan pointed to had a bright golden star on top. "Roma." No more *el desierto*.

"Happy ghosts," Juan said. "Just remember."

Pickups, mucked and dented, flagged and gun-racked, encircled the motel's café. Calves at an udder. The café's windows, blazing warm orange, brimmed with the rise and fall of shadows, keeping time to twangy radio. The smell of yeasty beer and toasted tobacco leaked into the night, its air pulsing with a low, brooding energy. Somehow, the rest of the motel seemed to be sleeping. Juan said for them to keep down and out of sight.

"Men inside hate us even more when they're drunk, you know?"

It was five hours until dawn and until the farmers, who never failed to come. They hovered in the parking lot shadows, eating and drinking from the vending machine. Juan had all kinds of change. There was a muddy swimming pool where they washed their swollen feet and clothes, ripped to shreds now and blanched with dust. At the touch of that water, being across the border felt real. The boy with the torn-up leg cried into his hands.

Juan was brushing his curls with a comb wetted in the pool. He whistled Chávez over.

"Come back to San Wren with me. Let's work together." Juan lit a tobacco stub. "Look, no one died. The water we had was almost enough."

Chávez felt his face, his brow, wrinkling. "Really? Be a *coyote*?" Could he ever tell Abuelita or Pedro that?

"We're helping them, you know. Better us to bring them here than some diddler or robber. Right?"

Chávez kept watching the Indian kids. They had less money than he did and after paying Juan they would have none.

"No," Chávez said. Juan's eyes burned into the side of his face. "I can't."

Juan walked away, leaving Chávez with the weight of his mistake. He watched the moon floating across the still pool. Then Chávez got up and told the Indian kids to sit tight until morning. They'd get jobs and be okay.

Juan was neither right nor left down the highway. So he went left, from whence they'd come, his too-big shoes kicking up gravel. In a few minutes Juan ran up from a ditch and slapped him on the back.

"Knew you'd come," Juan smiled, falling into step.

BAEZ

The sun has budged again. She flicks at the biting spot behind her ear, shifts to her side, releasing the heat gathering
along her belly. In the shadow of the great grey wall, a deer
noses through the riverbed. It chews bramble, stumbles over
cans, smells for life in the block-upon-block, then turns back
north towards the mountains.

Across from her, the brown boys stare. When she first
came here, the boy in too-big shoes got free. His gunshots
still pock the trailer, and one window stays sealed with wood.
After that, Tattoo built the lean-to for shading the bounties
and Glove came up with the rope and alarm bells. That boy
was not quite like the other bounties — who just stay put and
wait; who, like her, are thankful for a bit of shade and something to drink.

Now, behind the lean-to, Tattoo does his jump-rope. The
bounties tense at the slap-slap-slap. Then Tattoo mule-kicks
the leather sack suspended from a low arm of the cactus.
He does so until his body is wet and his chest swells up like
that of the bald-headed bird above her, which he now stands
regarding: hands on hips, chest heaving. His tattooed arms
and neck are taut with underfed muscle.

When Tattoo goes back to his kicking, Baez falls onto her
hind legs and begins to scratch at the ground. Like the yard
at Old Blue's and at Speckled Man's before, the floor of this
pen was riddled with holes. One night, she almost dug her
way out. Were it not for Tattoo's stick walloping her along
the spine, she might have been free. If she were to dig a

hole now, it would take her into a different kind of freedom. She remembers how, when she'd dug Old Blue's hole deep enough, she let herself rest inside it, her flank absorbing the soil's cool. Bits of bleached white vertebrae had shone through. And there were roots, tough twists of that which had lived and died there long ago. Under the mesquite tree, Old Blue had stretched out too, feet splayed. If too much time passed between Old Blue's blinks, Baez would bark high and sharp until Old Blue would wake, her face more leathern than before.

Now, she hears one of her children, a female, cry for water. She has three females. When she dies, might the largest inherit her pen? Unlike Speckled Man, Glove and Tattoo have not mated her. She brought these children here in her belly, unborn. Coyotes heading towards the northern mountains smell the coyote part of her; the males among them come close. They sit beneath the moon and call for her to come away from the grey wall and the dry river. There is food where they are going, water, there is a sweeter sun. She tells them she is too tired. Just let her die here in the shade, she says. Her dreams of Old Blue are enough.

HONEY

Birds wake her. Their *cheep-cheep-cheep* is not unlike her five-fifteen alarm clock, so for about thirty seconds she can pretend that she's at home and Keith's strong body and reasonable words are right there beside her. After she hits the pool she'll come home to the hot sit-down breakfast Keith insists they make time for seven days a week. Tight in a ball she pinches her bladder, dozes as the room greys.

She has to find those car keys. She has to find Johnny-for-Jesus. Really? An Indian bible thumper?

Outside the air is fiery. She doesn't remember her mom's animal being so into digging. She counts a dozen holes, the deepest one where the post had been. How and why would Marianne yank that thing out of the ground? The Tribal stands sturdy, unchanged. But the shit-and-carcass ring around the trailer has been trampled and kicked from last night's running. And her Nikes are gone from the stoop.

"Fucking little ass-wipes," she whispers, blinking into the deep orange of the morning. A distant outcrop of smooth, tumbled rock is almost bloody it is so red. Behind any one of a million creosote bushes or endless cactuses, the thieving boy who stole her runners could be crouching.

Her rose-capped toes blink bright against the dirty grey of Marianne's flip-flops. Her mom'll scoff at her going around like that. "Those flimsy things are for the beach, Honey. There's snakes out in the desert. And," she'll say, "you never know when you might need to run."

"Baez?" she calls, chilling at her hollow echo. But the "MOM!" she yells is even worse.

Down the path behind the trailer, the tool shed stands open. A brown bag of Purina is ripped apart, pellets scattered across the path.

"Baez? You out here, girl?"

A flash of movement rushes through the lacy mesquite lining the path, leaves skimming her bare arm. A shadow breaches the corner of her eye, but she fights to stay focused on the ironwood trees spaced out along the shallow wash. And then there is all the scattered litter: a plastic bag, crushed water bottles, silvery candy wrappers — Igloo, Coco-Mini, others that are foreign—as well as fish cans, licked clean. A small brown ball cap dangles from an ocotillo spike. She crouches, lays her hands upon the warm earth. Then she picks up the litter, piece by piece, places it in the plastic bag. On the way back to the trailer she washes her hands in the warm pump water. The air sucks them dry.

She fills her belly with cold Coke and the solidified Clusters bar. Though still starving she will not touch the open beans, grey as they are. In the pantry, top shelf on the right, a can of flaked chicken. And as she reaches up for it, her left hand, bracing the doorjamb, brushes a nail.

"Shit," she hisses at the scratch.

Hanging from the nail is a ring of spare keys. The big square one fits the Tribal. The engine turns over on the first try.

She pumps a jug of sandy water and stashes it in the back seat. Then she stuffs the car with her own luggage, plus the rest of Marianne's bags of clothes and some spare runners, the painting stuff: boxes filled with tubes of colour, bundles of brushes, canvases upon which Marianne painted nothing other than the Oro. "There's a desert inside all of us." Marianne said she'd read that someplace. Honey glances at the violent crack along the windshield. The scissors are still on the table in the back room. She dashes into the trailer, jamming the scissors into her purse.

Like Marianne, the Tribal is dried out and wrinkled. It's the same car she drove down to Matchstick some ten years before and together they have grown old here. Honey folds herself inside the squat driver's seat, pushed back as far as it will go. She and Marianne are way too tall for women; Keith considers them both a little too thin. But down here

Marianne became that tough kind of skinny, held together with sinew and unsnappable bone.

Instead of road maps, the glove box is packed with flip-top cans of spaghetti and an opened package of oatmeal cookies. There are two left. She crams in the stale, mealy food, chunks falling from her open mouth onto her greasy spangled shirt. The engine hums. Her thighs jiggle and the steering wheel vibrates in her hands. The trailer recedes in the rear-view mirror, a tin trap not worth the gas it would take to tug it back to Buzzard. Behind it, dry land, empty land, land with no value for anyone anymore, except maybe the Indians. Right back where this place started. That's fine. Let them have it.

CHÁVEZ

On Saturdays he takes his pay and a girl bike with a slow leak in the front wheel and rides into town. If he rides on the sidewalk he gets yelled at; if he rides on the road the trucks swerve in so close one time he had to jump off or get hit. There are three thrift stores all run by old raisins with white puffs of hair. There's no one that old where he comes from and these ladies are nothing like that tough old bitch El Esqueleto who, when he remembers her now, truly had her dog's eyes — he should have seen that straight away. Maybe she *was* her dog in some way, or the dog was her. Well, crazy things happen where there is so much thirst.

While the other boys from his pepper farm — and some from other farms, too — crowd the food stores and the pin-ball arcade, he goes from one thrift store to another, looking for *Charlie Brown*s in the book bins. *You're Not Alone, Charlie*

Brown, with little Woodstock and a broken kite on the cover, is his new favourite. It makes him happier and sadder than when he closed the door on Abuelita in the middle of a warm blue night years ago now. *You're Not Alone, Chávez Brown* is the real title.

In the store with the Noah's ark scene painted on the window, there's one old lady with pearls clinging to her really droopy earlobes and half-moon glasses on a chain around her neck — she is the nicest. She doesn't follow him around the store anymore and she saves the English books with big type and lots of pictures for him. A dime a piece. She saved a paperback dictionary too and one Saturday she gave him a brand new notebook with a coil binding.

"How much money?"

She said no, it is a gift. She makes him understand he's to write down new words inside. In the front of his dictionary there's a chart with sounds so he can pronounce each word. Does he have a pencil or a pen? Yes.

"I have much pens."

"*Many* pens."

She finds a long new pencil behind the till. A pink eraser caps the end. Take it. "Young man," she calls him.

"Use the eraser when you make a mistake." We all make mistakes, she says. Mistakes are part of life, part of learning.

He says, "Truly?"

The old lady has a million cracks around her lips into which her pink lipstick seeps — like spilled water onto desert pavement. She says he just has to ask God to forgive him. "And yourself, ask yourself too."

He gives her the pencil and notebook and tells her to please write those words at the top.

"Repeat after me, young man." Then she says very slowly: "Pl-ease for-give me."

Please forgive me, please forgive me, please forgive me: he sits on a patch of grass under a flowering tree and writes it out until the pencil is dull and he has no way to sharpen it.

The other boys don't like him with his books and dictionary and the way he's always talking English to himself. Lunch comes at ten in the morning. They pick for eight hours more about, or until the day's assigned acres are done. But if they do not finish, the farmer leads them back after supper and, in the pale flood-lit dark they finish what they started. At least it is cooler. But these nights he can barely crawl onto his mattress. His hands are turning into claws. His wrists ache from all the twisting. He cannot stand straight, even when he tries pressing his back against a wall. Some boys have humps along their shoulders from carrying sacks. Nothing can keep him awake on those late nights and he has no dreams — sleep is as deep and dark as the ocean must be.

On fire nights they gather the farmer's old newspaper and spindles of dropped oak. Chávez will sit with the other pickers for a bit because otherwise they'll say he's a snob, that he's jerking off.

"Fuck you," he says back. He calls them slaves, stupid shitheads. "If you don't learn English, they're just going to keep fucking you over." Sometimes he'll teach Manny a few words. Manny's a good kid, has some balls.

There's soda tonight. Two big bottles are passed, no cups. That kid Horseshoe Hat shares potato chips. He thinks he's in charge and is always telling them he's older. He is fifteen. But he is also fifty. His eyes glimmer within a thick nest of creases. While the others listen to Horseshoe Hat talk shit about ladies and titties and who among them has or has not been laid, he and Manny sit on the barn stoop and go through his books pointing at the pictures and practicing the sounds. Manny had a TV in his village so he has a few things to write in Chávez's notebook. *Stay tuned* is one thing, though Manny doesn't know what it means. Another is *gorgeous* which means beautiful, and people up here in the north say it all the time but he can never remember how to say the different g's. Chávez has some tobacco to share. He scavenges the wet butts the farmer's wife scatters by the clothesline, wraps them in cotton and plastic and tucks them in the back pocket of his jeans.

Though the air is chilly, he sweats. Manny asks, did Chávez really know the old lady called El Esqueleto?

"Why you want to know that? Who cares about her?"

Manny shrugs and bites his nails. He says he hears so much talk about her. Once he saw her from far away. She was in her trailer and he really did think it was an old man. "'Cause she is so tall for a lady, huh?"

He closes his dictionary. There is a distant coyote call and then the farmer's dogs — three shaggy mongrels — cry murder.

"I knew her," Chávez says. "I knew her daughter better. Her daughter was old but talked like a baby."

Manny goes: Holy shit, tell me.

"You know the *prohibido* road?"

Manny nods and laughs. Everyone makes fun of the dumb Control for thinking *prohibido* means dead end but it really doesn't. "That's the nasty old road that's closed," Manny says. "We took it into *Las tierras vacías* when we crossed through Matchstick County."

"Well there was an accident, see." Chávez skips the part about getting locked out of her car. Why should he tell Manny the *vieja* hated them boys enough she was gonna let him die? Why should he tell this kid he sees her blond arm pressing down the door's mushroom-looking button each time he dreams? "There was stuff all over the road, man. But it was her mom's. Shoes, cans of food, and rolls of paper."

"Paper for the toilet?"

"Paper with pictures on it."

He says she was dumb and wandered away from the car. "At first I thought it *was* El Esqueleto, she looked just like her, see. So I followed her. She kept weaving in and out, falling into the ditch. She barfed once. It was so fucking hot. And she had no water."

"Strong, hey, for a lady?"

"And then," he whispers. "She disappeared. Snap—gone." Manny frowns.

"But I kept going and then there was a car. Poof. It came from nowhere."

"A Buick? With no plates?"

"Yeah, That's the one. It got left behind I don't know how long ago and is probably still there. Well, anyway, she was underneath." He pauses. He says to Manny, Come on. He's got something to show him. Manny waits while Chávez ducks inside the barn. He comes back with his pack—he's had it hidden under a cracked floorboard. Manny's eyes are round.

He tells Manny that he almost shit himself when that lady came crawling out from the car. "Man, she was almost as skinny as her mom and so tall. And her hands were bigger than my face. And she has this shitty old cap on and under it there was like no hair at all, but a big bloody cut." She smelled like some chemical, maybe bleach. He tells Manny he called her *vieja*—old lady—though it was pretty rude.

"Well, she called me *niño* like I was some little baby. People up here do that a lot. They got us all wrong."

"Was she pretty—even a bit?"

Chávez shakes his head. "I'd say she was a fucking mess." He reaches into his pack. The slender silver tube he pulls out glows in the moonlight. He twists it open, showing off the brush inside. "Hers," he says. "For the eyelashes."

Manny's small earthen fingers, sticky with soda drips, turn it over. He is careful, like it has been so long since he touched anything belonging to a woman. "My mom uses this too."

He says Manny can have it.

Okay. But he has nothing to trade for it.

He doesn't want a trade. Manny's just to take it. Pretend it's his mom's. Look at it when he misses her.

Manny will. He slides it into his shirt pocket. "So where's the *vieja* now?"

He shrugs. "Don't really know. In the city—Zopilote. That's where she's from."

Is that where Chávez aims to go?

"If I can ever find it."

Chávez takes out *It's the Great Pumpkin, Charlie Brown*. He doesn't like this one as much, because it reminds him of picking. He slides the Saint Moses card from the pages before giving it to Manny. His English is getting too good for comics. He's already started to memorize the dictionary. When he knows it all, no one will be able to trick him, not even the *vieja*.

When the shadowed caps rise from the fire and cut back towards them he tells Manny to get to bed. Then he hops down from the stoop and slips into the night, just far enough away so he can sit unseen. He thinks. And he remembers. On the road away from the motel, his back kept tingling where Juan had touched him. He carries that warmth still, as a wound, a treasure, a sort of tattoo.

They had slept a few hours in a ditch near a gas station, and when it opened they'd filled up on boiled hot dogs and stuffed their packs with water and candy. Then they veered west around the Entrada Mountains this time and it went well for two days, way faster without any *pollos*. There were no tire tracks or signs of Control because, Juan said, those dudes stopped giving a fuck. This was the time before Ocho and the bounty, when the only thing that was going to stop them from crossing were crazy locals or running out of water—which they did, ten or so miles north of the border.

Staggering through a shadowy grove of tall blond grasses, they'd scouted the ground for jugs with water still in them.

"Sometimes the Jesus Indian drops them here," Juan said.

But there were only jugs filled with dirt. They went on and then Juan stopped. His lips were bleeding. Some insect had bitten his ankle a ways back and now it was swollen and hard. But there were only a few more hours until it would be morning, so they kept on.

"There's a gas station and ranches up there," Juan said, pointing.

Soon a fuzzy glow broke through along the horizon. In the grey of first light it took the shape of a narrow, tin-trap trailer. Behind it by some five hundred feet was an arroyo with a stand of ironwood.

"El Esqueleto," Juan said.

They moved in closer. Along with jugs of water, a canvas sack was tied up in the branches above. Chávez climbed onto Juan's shoulders and pulled down the cache. They scooped the beautiful, beautiful rice and beans from the covered dishes inside.

"Look." He pointed towards the trailer where, through the windows, a shadow moved.

Juan shrugged. Just a crazy old skin-and-bone lady.

"She Christian too?"

"Don't know. I guess something makes her feel sorry for us."

It was getting light so they waited there. Half-asleep, he listened to the buzz of the coming day. A slammed door shot him awake.

The old lady, all in jeans and with buzzed white hair, shuffled around the gravel patch she had for a yard. She was so skinny she was almost see-through, but tough at the same time, and taller than the streetlights in San Wren. A muscled, mutt-looking bitch trotted beside her. Its coat was mottled yellow and grey, and it had a teddy-bear face like a Control dog except its nose was thin and its body too small for its head. It glanced in their direction then continued to circle the old lady, who opened up a painting easel. Tobacco smoke wafted. She paused between strokes of her paintbrush, leaning back and sipping from a little handled cup.

Stretched out on his elbows, Chávez watched the old lady while Juan dozed. Then Juan woke — "got to piss" — and started to stand up. The animal jumped to its feet. Its ears sharpened, its long, thin snout rose to sniff. It barked, pulling against its collar and chain. Chávez froze. Juan froze.

The old lady put down her brush and cast a look around her yard. When she reached for its thick red collar, the animal snapped at her. Her hand flew back.

A bird flapped low. Its cry broke the silence. The animal settled, then the old lady. It took two hours for her to put down her brush and go inside, the animal following behind. He and Juan crept away down a path and through a field behind the trailer. When they couldn't see the trailer behind them anymore, they ran.

Chávez watches as the first light of another morning washes over the sleeping boys, tucked under covers like loaves of fresh bread. Through bubbled window glass, the youngest of the pepper fields takes on texture: a rake pulled through rough wool. And somewhere a rooster does not caw or cry but shrieks and still Chávez is thinking about Juan, all their running. They had only their breaths. And that's about all he has now, too. Like the ghost Juan told him to be, Chávez gathers up his backpack and slips into what is left of the night. He walks tall, away from Fiesta Farm, and is on the main road before dawn. He guesses he ought to turn left, south, so he does.

BAEZ

If anyone came to see Old Blue, it was about the brown boys, always. About the brown boys, Baez was always confused. How could Old Blue love them and also love Baez too?

She remembers a bearded man and a spongy woman who used to bring tough old bones for Baez and fresh meat for Old Blue. Old Blue gave the man and woman painted pictures. Sometimes they would sit out and drink from Old

Blue's brown bottle. The yard would fill with tobacco smoke and laughing. The spongy woman was especially loud, grabbing onto her big belly so it wouldn't shake so much.

One late afternoon the bearded man's truck came blasting up the road, dark clouds chuffing out the back. Old Blue put down her paintbrush and shushed for Baez to stay quiet. Now the man's face was even thicker with beard. And the spongy woman's face was bruised. Old Blue was smiling at first and then none of them were. The man and woman, Beard and Bruise, both shook; hot anger leached from their pores. They talked loud and blunt. Their fingers pointed at Old Blue and at the ironwood trees down the wash where Old Blue put out water and dangled the food that the brown boys, stacked on each others' shoulders, pulled down and, with their fingers, wolfed.

Baez had kept barking at them and approached. Under Bruise's eyes were purple circles, for the blood in the skin had broken and leaked. Her big arms were spotted too. Beard lifted up Bruise's skirt. Her pale legs were splotched with that same angry colour. When Baez barked again Old Blue turned: *Ba-ez!* Then Old Blue waved her arm through the air like she was slashing down a tree and she walked away. Beard and Bruise did not go. They kept up with their voices and kicking words. Then Baez barked and barked. When the truck was gone Old Blue went into the trailer and came out with a teacup. She was shaking like Bruise had. But after she drained the teacup of its hot amber she stopped.

Now the sun is a big, bright yellow. The sky is empty of everything but its blue. Inside Glove and Tattoo's trailer a radio plays. With music comes the hot grease of frying meat. The bald bird hissing in the tree above her is hungry too.

HONEY

Road signs talk only about speed limits, nothing about the land-of-no-men where Johnny-for-Jesus roams or anything about how far to Buzzard, either. She scoops in and out of her lane as she scouts the landscape for something living, something like her mom. A distant northern peak appears from time to time, depending on the light. Her bladder's a football now. The sun, big and bald, pumps the car full of dry, burning heat. A rash spreads across her baking thighs. The weave of the synthetic exercise material coating her body is textured and sharp, the cling fusing with her swelling skin.

She skids over to the side of the road, trips going up a narrow arroyo, and, rolling her pants down to her splotched thighs, pees behind a spread of shedding palo verde. She opens her eyes as the pain in her gut recedes. The palo verde trunks are skinny and bright green, like the name says. Back at the Tribal, hazard lights clicking, she fumbles through the gym wear in her suitcase: all of it black, tight. City clothes and stupid shoes. There's a pair of blue jeans in one of Marianne's garbage bags; also a denim shirt, long-sleeved, washed and worn to the thinness of soft paper. Honey crouches behind the Tribal. The jeans, fastened with a leather belt, hang loose, as does the button-down shirt, textured with dry paint globs and bristly animal hair, which she pulls over a pink tank top that smells of Dinorah's softening liquid. Her skin tingles against the fresh, cool cotton. The soles of the flimsy flip-flops on her feet are so wafer-thin she can feel the bumpy ground. She finds a pair of white sport socks in her suitcase and grabs the old canvas tennis shoes sticking out of Marianne's pots-and-pans box. They'd be too big if her feet were less swollen. It is suddenly so quiet here. To her right, an empty irrigation canal cuts through an overgrown ranch, marked by a stretch of high metal fencing which — spurs glinting — disappears back into the horizon and the hump of hills that marks what she thinks are the Zari Mountains but who knows.

Sky above and scrub below, the narrow asphalt road winds through a stretch of flat-topped boulders that must be mesas. She brakes at every flick of plastic or glint of can. But there's nothing of Marianne, just cactus, brush, distant groves of hairy date palms, a tractor half-sunk into parched earth. And fencing, on and on, along the road.

Then a vehicle, pulled over on the opposite side of the road, ruptures the desert's otherwise smooth horizon. She brakes some yards back, waiting for it, a no-name dune buggy in tarnished silver, to speed off. But the dune buggy is still, napping maybe.

Slowly she pulls up alongside. Two helmeted heads — shiny black bowling balls — are slumped down in the front seat of the open chassis. The tires are grossly oversized compared to the body, the heavy all-terrain treads caked with dirt and vegetation. In the back there's room for plenty of cargo, passengers, both. She and Keith have come across these machines out ripping up some of their favourite Entrada trails. Why can't those people just walk? It's so much simpler. This buggy's high rear tires pump up the back end, where an oversized tailpipe juts out from the exposed engine. Along with four extra headlamps, a heavy iron telescope is mounted to the crossbar at the top.

"Hey," she calls out her window. *"¡Hola!"*

The driver's helmet turns. Then a three-fingered leather glove flips up the opaque visor. Two dark eyes, flat deep pits, look out.

He speaks some kind of Spanish then thumps the chest of his passenger, who shoots awake. The driver points at her. She can't understand his words: rapid, rollicking, muffled by the helmet that must be cooking his head.

The hand with three fingers flicks at her. "*Váyate! Deja me en paz.*" Get out of here.

She grips the wheel for support and imagines Keith watching her being so stupid. So reckless and stubborn. Just like Marianne, he would say.

"What?" she hears herself ask. "What did you say to me?"

The passenger lifts himself out of his seat, crawls into the back. His jeans are dusted with the Oro, as are his once-black Adidas. He is a young teen. So too is the driver, slim of shoulder, narrow of chest.

Honey calls to the passenger now. Her Spanish is clunky and garbled and she knows sounds idiotic: "You see old woman, a yellow dog?"

The extra fingers of the driver's glove have been cut away and the holes stitched shut. He lowers his visor while the passenger flips his up.

"An Indian?" Honey prods them. "Johnny-for-Jesus?"

Behind the driver, the other teen leans into the telescope. He swivels around, taking in the panorama of the desert, coming to rest on the Tribal. His voice is younger than that of the driver.

"*Vieja, vete a la mierda,*" he says. Old lady, fuck off.

She is stunned and, for the first time in her life, knows the sudden cold clutch of terror.

The teen does something so the telescope clicks. The barrel of a gun comes sliding out, its deep, dark hole pointing at her forehead.

"*Váyate*," the driver says again, slowly so that she does not miss a drop.

She feels the ridges of the gas pedal as she floors it, screeching away. Behind her the dune buggy spins out, U-turning in the road. The passenger hunches over the gun mount while the driver slumps in his seat. In a flash, she understands the expression "riding shotgun." The buggy's zip is crisp. Inside, helmets bob. Ahead, the road bends. Hills, new round ones, rise up, glowing orange.

Then the dune buggy is gone. She guns the Tribal nonetheless, the gas tank of Marianne's old nag now half-empty. The steering wheel vibrates in her hands. The dashboard shakes as she accelerates, paintings and junk clattering.

There's a turnoff ahead.

UNPATROLLED TERRITORY UNDER ALIEN THREAT: USE AT OWN RISK. The Spanish just says *PROHIBIDO*.

She jerks the Tribal off the main road, skirting the sign. Beneath windswept sand, the paving is wrecked with holes and yawning splits. Slowly she eases the car along the bumpity-bumps. After a mile the road turns to gravel. She skids. The main road is completely wiped away from the rear-view mirror. As the Tribal idles, rocking Honey like she's in a cradle, gasoline fumes spirit into the air. She is relieved to be alone. And then, again, she sinks into that bottomless well of terror.

A distant buzz materializes into a cloud of dust moving in from the east. Sparks of sunlight turn to chrome. The dune buggy comes at her from over a hill, kicking up rock.

She steps on the gas. The Tribal lunges. She's going too fast and skids on top of the loose gravel. "Fuck!"

The dune buggy catches up, riding parallel. The gunner's shirt ripples in the wind. His helmet glares. His rigid body braces the weapon as it trains low, on her wheels. At the next bend, a high outcrop rises, its looming crevices extending far into the distance. This section of road would have been blasted right through that mass of rock.

There is a flash of movement. A boy springs out from a crevice. He is dark-skinned. He wears a ball cap and a backpack and clutches a plastic grocery bag. Shoes too big turn his feet to boats. Why is he waving his arms like that? Why is he running right into her path? She cranks the wheel. The Tribal swerves. Honey grinds to a stop before hitting the wall of the outcrop.

A gunshot pops behind her.

She is aware that she is ducking, covering her ears.

But they are shooting at the boy, who has by now dived back into the rock. Her brain whispers that it's okay. *They want him, not you.*

Forty feet behind her, the dune buggy idles right in the middle of that *prohibido* road, straddling what might once have been its two distinct lanes. The buggy's engine revs, halts, revs.

She lifts her head, her fingers on the keys. If she inches away slowly, they might just let her go. But then the boy is running towards her. A second splits. He is so close that his coppery eyes — big as coat buttons — lock with hers. In her side mirror the buggy barrels towards them, fishtailing in the loose gravel.

The boy's hands stretch out for the handle of the passenger

door, grasping for that metal grip.

"No!" she calls out. Her left arm wheels up. She extends her reach and, beating him to it, pops down the knob, locking him out.

When she looks up from her stroke, his face occupies the passenger window. Through a layer of dust he is still very dark and his eyes gleam like new pennies.

"*Señora!* Lady!" His small palm bangs the glass, leaving a mess of prints. "El Esqueleto, *por favor.*" Please, lady. "El Esqueleto," he cries in Spanish, "don't you remember me?"

She shuts her eyes. She shakes her head. "*Váyate.*"

The next shot catches the rock behind him, as does the one after that. The boy sinks down, and then he runs ahead, quick and low to the ground, disappearing into the textures of the outcrop.

The dune buggy keeps coming, and the teen in the back keeps firing shots. She pulls back onto the ravaged paving, gunning the engine, which begins to smoke. They think the boy got into her car. And then, when a shot catches the driver's-side tire, she feels the car lose control. Instead of driving, she's riding. The roller coaster is slow and slippery, down, down into a bottomless below. She swerves. A great boulder looms. There is no time to call out. She squeezes her eyes shut. Her tongue, when she bites it, tastes of Christmas ham. After the great echoing smash, the world is washed with silence, like an ocean wave pulling back.

CHÁVEZ

Some forty miles down from Fiesta Farm, there's a river called Ruby Rock. That's what the sign says when he brushes

away the dirt. He knows "rock" and "ruby" from his dictionary. Last night he'd slept on the river's damp banks, lulled by
the gush. His backpack is his pillow—extra jeans inside, a
T-shirt, books in English. For breakfast: canned fish, same
as for lunch and dinner. He follows a path to the main street.
There's a motel called El Cheapo some two miles up.

He has enough for a pair of eggs and a coffee but a sign
in Spanish and English tells him, NO BOYS ALLOWED IN
THE MOTEL CAFÉ. FORBIDDEN. *No se permiten a los niños.*
But there are boys sitting right there at the counter. There's a
blond boy, a freckled boy, a boy that might be a girl. He says
this to the lady in the apron in his best English. But the lady
just snaps her long nails and sloshes hot coffee. He leaves,
swearing in his best Spanish.

He buys a can of Splash from the machine in the courtyard. Sun rises over the cracked road, fields of earth beyond.
Here the soil is getting dark. Fewer and fewer white fields,
empty fields, or dried-up irrigation canals. In time some
other boys straggle out of the shadows, gather around the
soda machine. When the farmers start to come out of the
café, wiping their mouths on their curly forearms, he and
the other boys stand up.

He waits for a truck that looks decent and ends up in line
for one that says *Bob Guthrie* on the door. "Got twenty-two
full carrot beds to dig, and—ask anyone around—I won't
shirk you, boys."

Chávez swings his pack onto his back, climbs in. He is
one of fifteen boys. None of them know where Zopilote is,
just that it's far from here. Then one in a sideways cap says,
man, he's going in the wrong direction.

Chávez covers his face with his hands. He speaks to this

kid through his fingers. "You mean this Bob guy's farm is even more north?" He tries not to moan. "But I need to go south."

"Yup. North." The kid nods, smoothing out his eyebrows which, weird, have a bit of grey in them. "What you want down there in Zopilote anyway? Place's set to eat you."

"Money," Chávez says, watching the road spin out behind. "A lady there owes me a real bundle."

Nights at Guthrie's after the other boys are sleeping he writes in his coil notebook from the Noah's ark lady. He writes English words he wants to remember and also, more and more, he writes letters home to Abuelita. Thoughts get all piled up inside him after tramping them down-down-down like he's supposed to, but when he writes letters the thoughts come out fast and heavy—pens ripping right through the paper—and then he burns them in a jar with matches. He writes about the things he can't stop remembering, hoping if he gets them out of his head they'll quit making him so sick. Like when he had a cold Abuelita said to always blow the snot out rather than suck it in—how can you get well otherwise? He writes about being with the *vieja*, or how lonely it is when you can't sleep, but mostly he writes the bad bits about Juan. How once when they were crossing some ranch boys caught them and punched him and Juan in the face and then tied them to the fence and left them there until Control came.

"Those guys got fifty bucks for each of us," he writes. "And then we crossed right back over the next day."

He writes about how Juan and he took their *pollos* deep into the desert without enough water and they all almost died. He didn't realize it until after, that they were dying, but that's how bad it was. He writes to Abuelita that when he was dying he saw her swimming around like a ghost, disappearing behind a cactus, and then the Jesus Indian with the long braid and all the stickers found them. "The *pollos* barfed up the water he gave us and, Abuelita, you should have seen the hatred burning in their eyes — hatred for me and Juan. The Jesus Indian knew we were the *coyotes* and so even with all his believing he must have hated us too." He tells her about the two *pollos* he is sure *are* dead because of him, and he asks Abuelita to please forgive him though he knows she never could. "They swim around too, Abuelita, they go dashing through the rows of peppers or whatever." With fingers ink-stained and the tip of his tongue bitten, he writes how this kid named Ocho started hunting them down in one of those weird desert carts they got up here. He writes that Ocho's called that, "Eight," because two fingers got bit right off. He writes, "But I stole his desert cart, Abuelita, it even had a gun. I drove it like Pedro taught me." He writes that Juan is gone now. "Just gone." That's all he can say about it.

For a year he had been with Juan — every day. They slept side by side — making the desert or the church steps their bed — and they ate the same food, crapped at the same time in the morning, even started walking with the same right-leaning gait, or that's what someone said. He knew everything about Juan — about his life, about his heart. He knew he was funny and cared about stuff even though he had to talk tough all the time: that was just to stay on top in a shithole border town like San Wren. Kids there do whatever they have to to get over the border and make some dough, only to drift back down again, wait around, go back over. Juan wanted to *really* get ahead. He was different that way. Especially, though, Juan was different for how much he loved his mom. They'd spend days walking San Wren looking for her or waiting out front of the factories when the shifts changed. Once there were all kinds of factories there, for shoes and jeans and electrical stuff—that's how come the Loco was so orange—but now most were shut up. Maybe the factory owners had gone someplace where they had cheaper and cheaper slaves—cheaper than ladies like Juan's mom.

"Like my mom too," he wrote. "Right, Abuelita?"

Juan said his mom had long, super-curly hair like his, jeans, a sparkly ring, and a gold coin necklace that rested high on her breastbone. She was a pretty lady, Juan said. So many times poor old Juan thought he saw her in San Wren and even grabbed a few ladies by the elbow, but it was never Juanita. One lady slapped him and called him trash. Juan would get mad at his whole life and San Wren and fucking rich people everywhere and swear he'd not be a slave to anyone. He said the world was an open and a free place, if only you were smart and saw opportunity.

Chávez writes, "Juan told me he wanted a tattoo that said 'opportunity,' but in a symbol—something to make people think." But he wanted a surprise: "You choose, Chavito, but nothing weird or ugly." So Chávez thought about it and thought about it and then on an afternoon on the church steps he inked a symbol of opportunity into Juan's left forearm. The whole time Juan was looking at some village girls across the street who'd just come in on the bus. "Man, they better watch out," he kept saying. "They're just too sweet for this fucking place." Juan said he couldn't remember the last time he saw a girl like those ones and he wouldn't shut up about them. When the tattoo was done, Chávez dressed the wound and Juan was patient and in a few days it was time to take off the dressing.

"A fucking keyhole?"

Chávez nodded.

"Man, you're a big dummy, I didn't say I wanted that."

"But you said to surprise you."

"Okay, yeah," Juan said sucking back on a soda. Juan's cheeks were getting red. His mouth was orange from the drink. "But this is fucking sissy." He made Chávez promise to design a cover-up tattoo. "Otherwise kids'll think it's some fag thing we got. Like I'm matching your key or some shit, fuck!"

Chávez was jittery inside. He wanted to turn things back. "You just gotta get used to it."

"To being a fag?"

He said Juan was being stupid. "Who cares what kids think?"

Juan stared at him for a long time.

After that Juan kept hinting it was getting too dangerous to keep up the crossings. "Let these shitty little *pollos* get over on their own. I need another line of work," he said. Stories came of more and more kids dying in *Las tierras vacías*. Which was what Control wanted, funnelling them into the worst, most dangerous parts where they were welcome to go and try to cross because they were just going to die.

And while the bounty had been in place for a while, now some real-time mercenaries were moving in — ones that knew the desert. One of them was Ocho. Juan said he knew Ocho a little — he'd worked on farms up north and then, to make more money, he worked as a *coyote* out of San Wren. Though Chávez had seen Ocho's vehicle tracks on their crossings, Ocho was still just a story. Juan's eyes sort of got glassy and far-away when he was talking about Ocho, so Chávez started to hate Ocho and to hate Juan a bit, too.

Juan wore long-sleeved shirts now, hiding his tattoos like he was someone else. Their last night in San Wren he had on the checkered one with the missing cuff buttons, the tear on the right shoulder a perfect "L." Chávez showed Juan his ideas for a cover-up of the keyhole he hated so much but Juan grabbed the marker and scribbled them all out. Then Juan pushed him. Chávez fell, cracking his elbow on the sidewalk. Juan called him a freak, a spray of spit raining down.

Later they walked along the Río Loco and saw in the twilight and the not-too-distant west the swashing of lights. And over the river's rush and San Wren's outlying traffic, he heard the motor-hum of backhoes and pump-irons, generators firing up all those floodlights. The wall was closing in. It was really going to plug up the border's ratholes, burn out its nests of boys, forcing them to find a way out of the south by some other channel, route, or maze, of which little boys with not enough to eat can always find many. Juan said again that it was coming time to quit while they were ahead.

"And in a way, Abuelita, we almost did."

BAEZ

Old Blue started staying up by the window the whole night, just waiting for the brown boys. The trailer would get blue with cigarette smoke. The clock on the wall would be ticking. Baez would bark, just once, when she heard the pitter-patter of footsteps. *Shhhh!* Old Blue would wait, give the boys time to eat and drink. Then, when they were gone, she'd grab some water jugs from the tub and whatever food she had left on the stove and Old Blue would whistle— *Come on Ba-ez, good girl*—and by the swish of a flashlight they'd take the path to the ironwood trees where the old water jugs would be empty and food would be gone, just like the brown boys too.

Once some boys were still under the trees. Old Blue's body had hardened. Baez was already unleashed. Old Blue pulled at Baez's collar, shushing. Sharp fear leaked from Old Blue and the brown boys both. The boys were young, weak. Their wet eyes blinked. Old Blue made her voice low, held out her hand as she'd done once to a cornered rabbit, and then she found her knees and crawled into the shadows, cooing in her choppy language. And then she cooed the singsong language that the brown boys knew.

Baez kept back. Old Blue held out the pot with her dinner in it, dinner that Baez, too, had eaten, but from a bowl on the floor while Old Blue stood by the sink. And slowly, the biggest of the brown boys reached out his hand—scratched and cut—until his fingers connected with the silvery dinner pot. Baez felt the line rise inside her and upon its crossing she opened up into that fiery pit that was always bright and blazing. How could she let him take food from Old Blue while Old Blue was herself made only of bone now? Baez leapt and sank her teeth into the squish of his arm, pressing until her jaw locked.

Old Blue screamed, pounding her. Baez felt her body cave as Old Blue's fists punched ribs, neck, eyes. Then her jaw clicked open and the brown boy—his eyes pinched— took back his arm, punctured and slippery with blood. The dinner pot fell. And all the brown boys went running, and she chased them far into the desert, as far and fast as she could get until the line was redrawn and the fire inside went out. And then she turned back.

The golden squares of Old Blue's windows floated in the dark. The perfume of her trees sweetened the night, as did the sugar of the boy's spilled blood which lingered, wilting, in the air. Baez crept in towards the trailer. Old Blue had stacked new water jugs beneath the ironwoods but there was no sack of food in the branches. Baez crawled under the stoop and was asleep when Old Blue came out calling. *Ba-ez! Ba-ez! Ba-ez! Here, girl!* So Baez broke out, away from the shadows. Old Blue fell to her knees. *My girl,* Old Blue said— sang—her arms around Baez's neck, soothing the sore place behind her ear, the tumbled-up signals it sent.

Now Baez lifts her head and calls through the heat to her children—a low, gravelly yowl. Glove and Tattoo come to the window. But her children are silent. They do not understand her. It was only Old Blue who did.

HONEY

Her left eye is smashed. Or, no, it's just the lens of her glasses, the frames of which are still clinging to her face. Sun leaks through the shattered windshield. Warmth drips down her face. A fierce tightness pulls at the back of her head, yanking her ponytail. Her right arm is twisted back, the elbow going in the wrong direction.

Footsteps circle the Tribal. There is a cough. An angry laugh. Someone spits.

"*¡Hola!*" Then what must be a name.

The young voices are roughening into those of men. The

words they use are simple at first. It is Honey's kind of Spanish: good enough to custom-order her tamales at Tony's and to remind Dinorah how Keith likes to find his dress shirts hanging.

Match strike. Tobacco whiff. "Where's that shitty little *coyote*?"

They kick the bumper, jolting the car. "*¡Hola!*"

Through the broken glass of the passenger window a hand reaches in and up. The nails are raw-bitten and the smoking fingers stained pumpkin. The hand unlocks the door and yanks when it doesn't open. The top of the upside-down door scrapes the dirt. The next yank is harder. A tumble of bags and boxes spill out. The pressure on her body eases, but the pain in her ponytail gets worse.

"*¿Hay alguien?*" Is she in there?

She lets herself be dead. Monica, their friend from the emergency room, tells of women getting guns up the crotch. When the assailant or, hey, the boyfriend, finally pulls the trigger, the bullet takes out the top of their skulls.

Through the gap in the clutter, a head pokes in: dark hair in spirals and soft stubble sprouting on a round chin.

"*Oye. You there?*" They just want to talk business. Can't they make a deal with him?

The one with the glove says to hurry up. The one with the curls falls forward, into the car — kicked in the ass. Cigarette smoke wafts in with him.

Checkered sleeves cover his roving arms. He paws through the rubble and junk, tossing pots and paints and magazines. Then he stops sharp, pulls back.

"Nothing in here, Ocho. Just the old white lady."

"*¿El Esqueleto?*"

Yes. The Skeleton. But she's dead. "*Está muerta.*"

Ocho says he wants to see her. Ocho. *Eight*—that is his name.

The car sinks as Ocho leans inside. He clears his throat. A hot wet gob lands on her neck.

"*Perra.*" Bitch.

The spit smells like adenoid. It is thick jelly.

Ocho pulls back. "The kid's worth way more than fifty bucks. Fuck!"

Someone kicks the car. Then something smashes through the back window and the dune buggy's engine turns over and they go.

She wipes the gob from her cheek. Her face is all there, nothing crushed. Her right arm pulses, hot and swollen. If she leans her head more to the right, there is less pain in her scalp.

Dry white light and drier air enters through the open passenger door. In her purse, wrenched from between the seats, she feels Marianne's kitchen scissors. One handed, left-handed, she reaches behind and cuts her ponytail free from the headrest mechanism around which it has formed an impossible knot. Then, right arm pulled into her chest, she moves, swatting away a tumble of terry cloth towels, balled socks, paperbacks, torn canvas. Finding the seat-belt's heavy buckle, she clicks it free and falls out onto hot gravel.

It is bright and boiling. Any sweat that breaches the surface of her skin is sucked away. If her arm was broken it would be unbearable. Like the time she fell off her bike and broke her collarbone. "A lucky break," she always called it: the doctor who set it turned out to be Keith. She pulls one of Marianne's T-shirts from the spillage and wrestles it, one-handed, over her head; her face pokes through the head-hole like she's a Muslim woman or a nun. Footprints circle the wheezing, belly-up Tribal. Its shot wheel is flabby. Along the gravel shoulder, the dune buggy tracks skid wide and sloppy, disappearing over a low, cactused rise in the direction of south — at least she thinks it is south.

A stretch of bluish mountain ripples in the heat. But the Zaris are still in the west. There's a box of Tic Tacs in her purse, a can of Coke from the rest-stop where she had a taco breakfast, an empty pack of matches, loose tobacco, smears of chocolate. Makeup and mirror. Marianne's kitchen scissors, her wallet with not much left in it, a fistful of keys. No clip-on lenses. She squints.

Keith's briefcase has been flung, open, into the road; sixty term papers lie scattered far and wide. She cannot imagine being the person who would care enough to collect them. The cracked water jug in the back seat has soaked bags of clothes and bedding and boxes packed with canvases. Her right elbow dazzles with pain as she barely manages to wring the dregs from a soggy lime-green T-shirt— *Buzzard City Air Show*—into her open mouth. She hears Keith say, "Rate the pain, Honey, on a scale of one to ten." A nine. Or, no, maybe an *ocho*. Then she twists the cloth into a rope and, with her good hand, the left, and her teeth, she knots the ends, slides the loop over across her chest, and lays her wounded arm into what is now a sling.

The driver's-side mirror hangs from a tangle of wires. Her face is washed in dark blood, as is the denim shirt, splatters mixing with dried paint. She pulls back her T-shirt veil, cringing at the gash that stretches from forehead to mid-crown. Then, again with one hand, she snips the bloody hair away from the wound, evening out what is left from the hacked-off ponytail. She walks towards the main road, keeping the sun and the Zari Mountains to the right.

In the ditch, where she vomits up a mouthful of burning taco, she finds a ball cap half-buried in the hot sand. The canvas is the same dirty green as the flesh of an overripe avocado. Some child has drawn a sun on the front in thick black marker. With her left hand she adjusts it from a small setting to the largest then fits it onto her head. She keeps going — and going, for two hundred footsteps. She'd better count. She'd better keep track of her position. The gravel turns to rough pavement. Okay, that's good. She must be going in the right direction. Except all of it spins out and tumbles together: nothing looks the same and none of it changes, either.

She turns to see how far she's gone. Someone is following her. Even at a mile away, she knows it is the boy with those big penny eyes. The dune buggy didn't get him. Not yet. She watches him come. And then — maybe she blinked too long — he disappears. He was never there.

Her scalp crawls beneath the grimy cap. But if she takes it off, the sun will cook her head. Monica speaks of staph infections neglected so long the bacteria enters the bloodstream, infecting the brain.

"You'd think we're in the Third World, I swear," Monica will say, sipping her wine and reaching for a cracker. "Or the Dark Ages. Whatever happened to basic hygiene?"

When the Coke can boils up and starts fizzing, she guzzles it, tosses it away.

A Buick straddles the shoulder ahead. The wide oblong

tail lights are broken, and both the trunk hood and bumper are dented. There is a gap where the license plate should be and the tires are too narrow for the body, which, were it not glazed in dust, would be turquoise. Fine sand blanks out the windows and side mirrors while, as in a kindergarten painting, fingerprints have been pulled across the dusted trunk, swirling around the silver slot where the owner's key might still fit. Shards of tail light mix with gravel across which she crawls, pulling herself into the patch of cool black shadow beneath the car's low belly.

Did she sleep? Pass out? Is that what Keith would call the warm wash of gloom that just happened?

Footsteps wilt as they come up the road, sinking into the hot highway like fingers into ice cream. And there is a hollow rattling, rocks clatter against tin — a can, a cup. Now they or he or it is circling the car, cutting into the bright hem of sunlight that seals her in. The kitchen scissors are dull with years of Marianne snipping string, opening envelopes, depriving newspapers of their best photos.

And then it is quiet. She waits. Her shoulders fall back into the ground. She pulls herself and her injured arm out from under the car, draws the scissors. The sky is streaked with cloud and jet-stream and though the sun is that much lower, the sheer muscle of it still blinds. She shuffles, one kneecap then another, along the Buick's thrown shadow — and freezes.

"*Hola, Esqueleto*," the boy whispers, pushing back his cap. "Really, you thought you could hide?"

CHÁVEZ

Chávez writes to Abuelita about how on his last night in San Wren he sat on the church steps waiting for Juan to get beer and cigarettes. The fried eggs and black bread they had eaten sat like a stone in the passage to his belly.

"But the hot food reminded me of you, Abuelita," he writes, "of your creased forehead and cracked hands, the crackle of your radio that never came in right. Of mornings in the market — do the dogs still follow you like they did?"

The big dish of clock above the bus station said it was gone eleven. Up and down the street in front of the church, diesel-powered buses chugged, competing with clanky bikes, sun-washed cars, low-riding pickups. Fumes and cooped-up energy blotted out the stars. When the midnight bus pulled in Juan was still not back.

Chávez and Juan, but mostly Juan, knew the kids who hung around the dried-up fountain in the plaza. They'd been in San Wren for a while, waiting like Juan for what they called "opportunity." Under grey-blue street light they passed cigarettes and murky bottles. Chávez eased in and out, asking for Juan. Some boys were *coyotes*. Some were lone wolves, saving up to make the trip on their own. Others still were in the business of selling you all the stuff you needed to take into the desert: canned fish, bottled water, sweat socks, pocket combs, rosary beads. Some sold knapsacks or shoes. None had seen Juan.

A boy in a palm-tree T-shirt, Gilberto, said: "Seen Ocho, though."

"Shit," the other boys swore. "That fuckhead's gonna screw things up for all of us."

"Now he has a gun, you mean."

"A fucker of a thing, courtesy of Control. Bet a maniac like him would use it, too."

Gilberto ignored them. "Hey, Chavito, seriously, Ocho had a message for you and Juan." Chávez had to pay a cigarette to hear it. "Stay out of the desert. It's his run now."

Chávez shrugged. "So? I never even seen the guy." Inside he felt sick. He bought a drink from one of the boys hawking sodas to anyone who walked by. The fountain hadn't even trickled since Chávez had been in San Wren. It was really just a big empty bowl glazed in green rust.

"Don't Juan have a gun?"

Chávez shook his head. "No way."

"You better go from here, Chavito," the boys in the plaza all said. "Tell Juan Ocho gets most of his bounties along the *prohibido* road."

Then they spoke like he wasn't there: "Ocho'll recruit Chavito, I bet. That kid knows the desert the best. Shit, that's the reason Juan hooked up with him. Right?"

A boy who was bigger than the rest by a foot and with the start of a moustache jumped over and thumped Chávez in the temple. "Imagine, kid, you could make some real dough, working for Ocho. Plus you get to drive that funny car."

"Dune buggy," someone called out in English.

"No, man, it's *dude buddy*."

"Really?"

Laughing rushed through his ears—at him, with him. All around him were high, smiling cheeks and rows of glistening teeth.

Chávez swatted the moustache boy away. "That's bullshit. More to life than money."

They all laughed. "No there ain't, Chavito. Money *is* life. You die without it. Same as water."

"I believe it now," he writes to Abuelita from where he is, lost somewhere in the north. "Anyway, it's less hot up here at least."

The further north he goes the more water there is for the fields, so the fields are getting bigger and so too the vegetables in them—but they taste like the chemicals the farmers spray on their crops. Or, rather, the chemicals men like Pedro and boys like Chávez spray on the fields. And the further north he goes the more farms there are with these massive spaceship-looking machines. With a machine like that, a farmer can cut a crew of twelve down to just two: one guy to drive it and another to ride up on the back, making sure the carrots or corn or whatever is coming down the chute. He saw one such machine way in the back of a mammoth cornfield. But it must cost a million bucks to buy one and most men around here don't have that kind of dough so there's still work for regular human boys like him. Because of that machine, even he, a slave, can afford to buy a bag of potato chips. And because of that machine a farmer without one can't hardly compete unless he pays his slaves just dirt, which is about what Chávez earns even picking so fast and steady he wants to die at the end of the day. But he eats chips anyway—a big bag a week bought in town—because they taste so good.

"They'd be too salty for you, though," he writes to Abuelita.

The soy field where he works now is soft with yesterday's rain. His Nikes sink in, leaving deep prints. The rows are green and frothy with leaves browning at the tips. The plants grow to the hip, burst with fruit beneath. After he fills his bucket with pods he's going to curl up for a quick ten minutes before the farmer comes. There's a permanent hunch between his shoulders now. Each time he bends over it gets bigger, like a camel hump almost; too bad his isn't full of water. He threw down his gloves some rows ago, his hands being calloused into their own kind of leather. Somewhere off, one of those fancy combines hums. He heard that a boy fell under that same one last week, before Chávez arrived here. They say he had slipped on some wet ground. The driver—a man from Chávez's side of the border—was so tired after going eighteen hours he didn't see the kid go down. Now the kid's got only his right foot, the other shredded off. The farmer put him on a Greyhound for the border and hired a replacement off the next one that came in.

Birds call back and forth; their high-pitched xylophone is answered by something like a crow. The bucket is almost full. Once he fell asleep picking—did a face-dive right into some pepper plants.

"Hey!" Two boys from a village near his wade towards him through the rows. He stands and squints. Nights and mealtimes Reyes and Díaz curse this place, the muscle aches and the shitty pay just for starters, and they say that come end of season they'll be going back home. They say, it's not so bad being poor.

"Think," they say. "All we are here is slaves."

Like he doesn't already know that. But he is always surprised by the boys that whistle while they work and take pride in what they do. Others make it a race or a contest to pick the most—that's how they're getting through.

Chávez can't make his mind bend that way. And he hates the land here, too. Beneath the flat humid sky there's nothing to look at but dirt roads, fields, or mud. Pickups patrol the highway, keeping watch for the pickers—boys and men— who might be out walking, bike-riding, hitching to another farm town, north or south, depending on the season. The trucks slow as they pass. Soda-sucking teenagers, freckled and zitted, throw cigarette butts and swear words out muddy windows. He can understand what the words mean now but wishes he couldn't. At least the soy bean farmer feeds them well. His wife, the mother of his three pink kids, stirs ground pork in with the ribbon noodles they get for most suppers. And Sundays the whole family even sits with them to eat the exact same food. Before eating, though, the farmer makes them all take off their hats and bend their heads while he says a long, breathless grace that no one understands.

Reyes and Díaz wear matching ball caps for the Zopilote Suns. They bought them almost-new at the thrift store in town. Compared to the sun logos he drew—so long ago, it seems—on Juan's cap and on his own, the store-bought design is clear and bright and the stiff caps perch like crowns on Reyes and Díaz's curly heads.

"What you want?" Chávez winces into the sunlight. "Time is money, you know."

They have grape on their breath. They throw him a cube of Hubba-Bubba. His cracked fingers fumble with the wax paper. They say they know who he is—Chavito the San Wren *coyote*. "You got them eyes."

"So?" He tries not to let them see him stiffen.

Well, so, he ought to know the border wall is closing in. Fewer boys will be coming up now. "Chavito, you'll see."

The gum coats his tongue with a taste that is not grape so much as just big, bright purple. Jars of such glop are set out on the picnic tables in the morning—they're supposed to spread it on slices of white bread and top it off with a layer of salty brown paste that someone says is called PB. The grape stuff is J. He has these sandwiches for breakfast and lunch, even dinner if the noodles are not enough.

He licks his sweet lips. "Can't you see I got to finish this bucket?"

They tell him boys in San Wren were saying that Chávez had sold them out and teamed up with Ocho.

"Not me," he says.

So who, they want to know. Does Chávez know who Ocho's sidekick is? What kind of asshole would sell out to Control like that?

Chávez crouches down, feeling for bean pods under the leaves. He doesn't have an answer for them. He says he can think about that until the end of time and he'll never know why boys betray boys.

"Some are just rotten inside. Some don't think what they're doing is wrong." He says, "They're just playing their part in the game. So what? If not them, maybe it would be you."

They just stand there watching him, waiting to say what it really is they came to bug him for. "Zopilote," they say. "Take us there too."

He stops, dragging his hand through the lush plants at his knees.

"Teach us your English and help us get away from these asshole farmers." They say they will pay him. Isn't he a *coyote*?

"Go away," he says. "I don't want your money." Then he calls them shitheads. "I'm not a *coyote* anymore." And not just anyone can go to Zopilote—only the strongest get there and if they have to ask for help then they're not up for it so fuck off home to be poor.

Reyes and Díaz walk away. Their caps bob in the distance.

He turns up his collar against the sun. The combine encroaches with a buzz, offsetting his belly, rumbling already and it's not even lunch. He'll have to wait an hour, or he'll never get through until suppertime. Suddenly he just has to lie down. Knees to nose, he curls in the shade of his rows. Behind his eyes he sees Abuelita sleeping, naked toes sticking up in the grass, and he feels Juan's hand flat on his shoulder blade. He wants Juan still. Wants him more and more. And he hates him too, like God must hate Chávez for wanting Juan in the first place and not being like the other boys. There is a great, dark hole that lives in him. It lies, half-sleeping, waiting to smother him with sadness and never let him go.

Before he picks up his bucket again he looks out at all the ball caps moving through the fields—all colours and sizes, different patches and pins on each—and he wishes to get far, far away from them and everything they share.

BAEZ

Wings, heavy and turgid, beat the thickening air. Her tree shakes, its shade shudders; a second bald bird has touched down. If their heads were any smaller, they would not have heads at all. Then they could not hiss like they do. With her good arm Old Blue had thrown fistfuls of dug earth at the birds above, sputtering as the dirt rained back down on her. Old Blue had shouted, torn her clothes, pulled at the white fluff that was her hair. With a squawk, the birds lifted themselves and flapped off for the hills. Old Blue was quiet then. She fell down again. The birds returned.

Somewhere off, Baez hears an engine buzz. One of the bounties whimpers. He wants water. They all want water: brown boys, her children, the animals nosing in the dry riverbed below. The water they get is yellow and lines her bowl with sand. It is worse than the water that came from Old Blue's pump. Old Blue would go without water—no drinking, no washing—so she could leave jugs under the ironwoods, or save it for Black Braid to take.

Black Braid was a brown man, but not quite the same brown as the brown boys or the brown men who came before them. Black Braid's brown skin was taut, tight. He smelled of the silver-foil food bundles he brought Old Blue: spicy meat wrapped in bread, of which Baez always got half. After Black Braid loaded Old Blue's water jugs in his stickered up truck or the desert buggy, also crazy with stickers, Old Blue got in the front. They bobbed off.

Baez stayed chained to her post. She watched long-eared rabbits criss-cross the yonder gold of land and waited for the sun to move across the sky; right when its rays penetrated the ironwoods in the wash behind the trailer, Black Braid and Old Blue would come up the road, yesterday's empty water jugs rattling in the back. There might be another heavy bottle of amber, food in cans. And Baez got a brown bag with pellets that were the same colour and flavour as the bag itself.

Old Blue did just about everything standing. She'd only sit down to have a fast sleep; arms folded, chin to chest. So all day, while she waited for the boys—they came at dusk—she stood in the yard and painted, dripping colour, cigarette ash, amber down her clothes or into the dirt.

She was painting when the blue truck came up the road. Baez screamed, ran, pulled so hard at the chain the collar choked her and the post slipped just a little, affording her one more inch.

Baez! Old Blue shushed. Old Blue's heartbeats were coming fast, travelling down through her arms and out the tips of the fingers gripping hard at Baez's collar.

The man left the truck parked by the road. The animal inside was Baez's cousin — an old brindled male. Hot breath clouded the windows and its screams rocked the cab but, unlike Baez, it did not show its teeth. The man came close. He was sunburned. He had yellow hair and yellow eyes to go with his yellow hat. Yellow Man. He shouted for Old Blue to hold off her animal. Old Blue knelt. *Shush, Baez, good girl.* So Baez stopped screaming. Yellow Man stopped hollering. He came towards Old Blue — one boot, two. He pointed at the ironwoods where some water jugs were visible. Old Blue shook her head and folded her arms, leaned back in her shoes. She was a whole step taller than him. Yellow Man spat, then pointed again at the trees. Old Blue shook her head and pointed at the blue truck in the road. Yellow Man flicked his hair, came close enough he could look up into Old Blue's eyes. Baez showed Yellow Man her teeth. Then he yelled. His arm slashed the air. When Old Blue called out *Baez!*, Baez charged. Yellow Man walked backwards and then he ran, his slippery boots skidding. Inside the truck, the animal who was her cousin threw itself at the windows and doors, yowls projecting forth as if escaping from a deep, dark hole. Just as Yellow Man reached the road, her long teeth found the cuff of his jeans. Then came a long ripping sound. Yellow Man dove, wriggling away. In its fury, his animal set off the truck horn: once, twice it blasted. Baez jumped back from the road. With a strip of pant leg in her mouth, she watched the truck drive away.

Dusk fell. Old Blue moved inside. And just as light was failing—bats deking low—the blue truck came back. It parked up the road, headlights off. Old Blue was talking to herself, walking all over the darkened trailer, looking out the windows. Baez barked when the pitter-patter of brown-boy footsteps came up past the trailer. And then from the road there came a crack, like thunder. It burned her ears and it sent Old Blue to the floor, clutching her heart. There was another crack, another. The pitter-patter footsteps turned to quick, frightened running and disappeared. Then the truck chugged off. Outside, in the ironwood tree, the food bundle swung heavy. The full jugs of water knocked over.

Next dusk, the blue truck parked up on the road and stayed. Later, six fire-cracker shots exploded in the sky: two for each group of brown boys that came through that night. Most ran on before they got to the ironwoods, bypassing water and food, which Old Blue found, untouched, in the morning.

Old Blue went back to painting in the yard. But she faced the other way now. Now she could see the road.

HONEY

He is maybe twelve. His jeans are chalky, sneakers big, and his T-shirt might have once been white but now is the same beige as the land. The tips of his ears are tucked under his dusty blue cap, whose shadow does nothing to mute the glow of his eyes. The Sprite can that glints in his small hand rattles, to warn snakes away. A *serpiente de cascabel* was on the road back there.

"Huge," he whistles, extending his arms. "And it keeps spirits away too." He gives the can a slow shake.

"Spirits?"

"Sure, Esqueleto," says the boy. "Spirits, ghosts, witches, skeletons—just like you."

The boy's Spanish is fast, riddled with slang and crested with sharp intonations. It is hard to understand him. The water from his jug is hot. He stands above her, dribbling a stream into her open mouth. Her throat, when the liquid hits, tightens at first and then, like a vacuum, sucks up the moisture. Her brain brightens. Fuzz lifts. She lowers her scissors. This boy is going to help her. She's going to get home and tell the police Marianne has wandered off.

He has two two-litre water jugs, a vinyl backpack; tins of Heinz spaghetti and jalapeño sardines in a grocery bag. He recaps the water, taking none for himself.

"Take me main road?" she asks in slow, sparse Spanish, aware of the mistakes as she says them.

The boy frowns. "You want Zopilote?"

Dinorah calls Buzzard by its Spanish name too. The sun catches the blades of the scissors. She holds them out, demands to know who stole her Nikes.

He shrugs and reaches around the scissors, going for her ball cap. She ducks. The boy laughs. "You know—your hat is for the Zopilote Suns."

"What?"

"You know, baseball?" His fingers—nails chewed to

black squares, knuckles red with open scrapes—smooth the plastic jugs, saggy with sun. She catches the handle of the one closest; water sloshes as the boy pulls it away.

He says, well, the Sun is his favourite team. Mendez—left fielder—has family in a village not too far from his. "Look." The boy leans in, tapping the front of his cap, where a jagged sun is drawn in the same thick black marker as the one on the green cap she found. He tells her he drew the logos himself.

His eyes narrow. "Who gave you that hat, Esqueleto? Or maybe it's something you stole?"

"Someone drop," she says, startled at how little Spanish she actually has. "Much, much garbage here."

The boy squats, digging at the gravel with a plastic take-out spoon. A beer tab and a shard of green glass are among the discards he flicks towards her feet.

He says, low, "I can just leave you here."

The inside of her purse still smells of rose lotion, peppermint gum, the swimming pool.

"And you would die then," he says, his penny eyes following her fingers as they trace the contours of her handbag.

"But, me, am already dead," she says. "*¿Si, niño?* A spirit, *un esqueleto*, you said."

He pushes back his cap and lunges for the one she wears, fingers snapping the brim. His hand, when she catches it, is hot and rough.

"Mine," she says pinching him until he gasps. "I need. Or die."

They sit close, following the Buick's shadow as it moves with the sun. When the boy's spoon snaps, he tosses it away. They watch the horizon waver in the heat.

"Hey," the boy says, "you eat snakes?"

She scrunches up into the upturned collar of Marianne's shirt.

"Me neither," he says. "But I know how. We could get one good with your —." He snips the air, fingers dancing.

"Scissors." She whispers the English word. Her head gets heavy and falls forward. The slow burn sinking into her body pulls her awake. The Buick's shadow has shifted, and the boy with it, leaving her to cure in the desert's full sun. She moves into the boy's old spot.

"So what now, Esqueleto?" he says, looking up at her with those orange eyes. The boy slows his Spanish. "I gave you water in the *Las tierras vacías* and then you locked me out of your *pinche* car?" His voice fades in and out: a distant radio, a half-dream.

"Marianne," she says. "A woman and dog, you see? I need find."

Birds wheel in the above, and the heat buzzes like an idling motor. The sun finally cracks its shell, descending into its own rich bleed. Her head thuds back against hot metal.

The boy hovers over her until she crumples up again. His shoes are tied so tight the sides overlap in the middle.

"You need to go from here. There are bad boys out hunting. They will hunt you too."

He bends close. The sandpaper of his lips brushes her ear and the neck of his T-shirt gapes open. His little-boy chest is caged in — four, five, six flat rib bones.

He opens a jug of water and she opens her mouth. He pours in a long sandy dribble. Then he leans his head back and swigs, throat bobbing.

Her fingers are swelling, on her good left hand as much

as her injured right. When the boy is not looking, she twists off her wedding ring and zips it into a pocket inside her purse. The skin is purple-pale where for five years the simple band of gold had never once been removed.

"You go, *niño*. Leave me now. Johnny-for-Jesus come, take me to my mom."

She flattens out against the ground and rolls under the Buick. The ground is not quite cooking, and what there is of air is thin. She hugs tight to the familiar skin of her purse.

The boy, rattle shaking, sneakers scuffing, circles the car. Then he stops. His grocery sack rustles and backpack zips shut. And then, when his footsteps finally go, she falls into an undertow of thick dreams. When she wakes again, into grey light, her hat and purse are gone.

CHÁVEZ

Chávez closes his eyes against the carried sound of the combine and the calls of pickers as they compete with each other over how fast they can fill a bucket.

"I beat all you assholes!"

"No way, check it out, this kid's only doing them three-quarters."

He thinks about what happened that night. After waiting in the plaza, he went back to the church: Juan was still not there. All that about going for beer and cigarettes was bullshit: Juan would be clear across the Loco by now, gunning straight for Zopilote to make it big 'cause he'd never in a million years work on a farm. Or that's what he said. Across from the church the bus station was dark and on the street the traffic had thinned to a trickle — mostly drunk old men weaving around in their trucks with soft tires. He gazed up. Paint was peeling off the church's high cross and the metal doors were dented like maybe someone had kicked them in. The moon showed almost full but there were no stars. Instead, the city night had a low charcoal ceiling.

His body was heavy as he climbed the steps. He'd slept in there before, but usually just naps. The old women in their head scarves would bless him if any came in. Sometimes he'd wake up with some coins by his head—maybe a bus token, a bible, a piece of fruit. The door's handle was warm and the hinges creaked as it opened. He tasted the church's cool on his tongue—like snow must be—and then down on the street tires screeched. The smell of rubber hit his nose—black and hot-peeled. He was frozen. Why couldn't he move?

Soft soles touched down on the steps behind him: two, four, six, all the way to the top. His heart got so small and so tight it might have, for a minute, stopped beating.

"Chávez?"

Ocho was in black jeans and Adidas, his face sprouting hair. On his right hand he wore a smooth leather glove. He looked regular—or his face did—tanned dark and with blackish eyes. He could have been a village kid like any of the others.

"Come on," said Ocho in a normal voice, a kid voice. Ocho just wanted to talk. He gestured to the souped-up silver buggy parked on the street.

Chávez climbed into the passenger seat, so low it was like sitting right on the ground. But the huge rear tires jacked up the back, where the engine was, open so you could look right in. The back seat was big as a bus but there was only a tripod and it was missing whatever should have been hooked up to it. Butts jammed the ashtray full and the dash was coated with stickers all in English —music groups he had no idea about but badly wanted to. He tried to memorize the names but couldn't get his mind to make the sounds.

"You like rap, Chávez?"

He shrugged.

Ocho pressed a button on the tape deck. The low, bassy beats that came seeping out were layered with deepening teen-boy voices, voices birthed of their own beats; they half-talked some kind of drip-drop, tick-tock poetry that did and did not rhyme. Mixed in and mixed up, the words cut out, only to bust up again, rhyme by rhyme—he didn't under-stand what the voices were saying but he knew the meaning. That music was about rising high and up, about rhyming and dancing as a way of not getting stepped on, of not step-ping on others, too. One day he would find out where that music came from and wherever that was he'd find home. He was that. Rap.

"Yeah, you like that," Ocho said, bobbing his head. "How's it you couldn't, kid?"

Ocho's T-shirt was red, his hat was wide-brimmed like what an old man might wear, but it looked good on him. The gold chain around his neck was thick. He gave Chávez a Coke and a Delight bar. He wanted Chávez to come and work with him. He had a plan: clean up the desert like Control wanted and then when those fuckers were sitting back all relaxed and getting fat, he and Chávez would start moving kids through professionally—"I mean using vehicles." Ocho said soon it would not just be boys coming through.

"Girls too?"

Ocho shrugged. "A fucking tidal wave." It only made sense. "You think all those sisters back home are going to stick around after our grannies die? What the fuck?"

But then there'll be no one left. What happens to a country when it's empty?

Ocho turned down the music a click. "Not empty, Chávez, just moved. Don't you see, the desert's ours now— no one else in there but Indians and crazies. Imagine if we outnumbered them rich white people up north? We just need a leader and then we're taking over." Ocho leaned back in his seat, head keeping up with the pulse of the beats. "Maybe that leader's going to be a girl. Maybe she's dreaming of making the crossing right now. Maybe," Ocho said, "we'll be there to help her do it."

"For a price," said Chávez.

Ocho winked. Everything has a price.

"So why me?"

An old man in a bright white shirt slowly crossed the street. He stopped at a pay phone, checked the coin return, disappeared down an alley. Ocho's music picked up tempo. *One-two, one-two*, a voice not-quite sang in medium-cool. Chávez knew English numbers all the way to ten. Then there was something like a stuck record needle scratching at a groove, back and forth, back and forth.

Ocho smiled. "Because you're the best. Isn't that what they say around here? Isn't that what Juan says?"

"You talked to Juan?"

Ocho nodded.

"And?"

Ocho reached into the back seat for a Coke. Cracking it open, he leaned back and took a sip.

"I'll tell you what I told him. Either you work with me or I want you the fuck out of my desert. I'm taking down all you shitty *coyotes*, right. Then you and me and Juan will run the place. Control doesn't matter, kid. I got them eating out of my hand."

He pulled off his glove. The spot where his first two fingers had been was sealed in scar, shiny red and bubbled.

While Ocho wriggled his fingers back into the glove, Chávez traced a sticker on the dashboard. It showed the silhouette of a man caught in the crosshairs of a gun. The man was in a hat and had his arms folded over his chest so his elbows jutted out: that gun couldn't silence him. He wasn't scared at all. In Zopilote Chávez would buy a radio and tapes like Ocho's. The Delight bar was getting soft in his hand.

"And what did Juan say?"

"He said no fucking way."

So that's what Chávez said too.

"Whatever," said Ocho, turning the keys in the ignition. "But if I see you out there again, I'll be forced to shoot you."

Chávez stepped out of the desert buggy. With music thumping—he already forgot what kind Ocho said it was— Ocho drove away.

BAEZ

The desert buggy returns heavy with water and food, cans of fuel. Glove disappears inside the trailer, plastic bags hanging from his wrists. Tattoo fills her bowl. When she does not come, he coos. She cannot move. He stands and kicks the water towards her, then the food dish, releasing a cloud of flies. The whistle from his lips is shrill. The stone he throws pings off her raw rib, landing with a sharp thud. She lifts her head enough to growl. Then lets it drop, lolling, on the hot ground.

Her children bark and yowl. They throw their bodies against the barrier. It waffles, waves, threatens to crash. Glove, from somewhere, shouts. Then Tattoo shouts. Then the bounties call, cry, followed by the bald birds, hissing. The noise swirls around her, twisting with the heat, with the flies, with her Old Blue dreams.

When the yard is again silent, the gate of her pen rattles open. Though Tattoo holds him back Glove crouches over her. He smells of meat and blue smoke and he smells like Tattoo. The leather of his glove is soft on her head, almost cool. And his bare hand is strong beneath her jaw. When he coos, she opens her mouth. A rubber nipple finds its way between her dry lips. Water trickles down her throat. She swallows. Before Tattoo and Glove leave the pen they clap their hands at the bald birds whose heavy wings lift them away, leaving her to sleep.

She lies back down. She remembers the brown boy in big shoes. He had come from the direction of the north, going against the flow of all the other boys. He stood on a ridge above her and Old Blue then shimmied down, ledge to ledge, tripping over his feet. He came close. She barked at him, driving him back up a sharp peak. There he squatted, watching. Old Blue woke. She called out to this boy, lifted her good hand at him, waved him to come, and — *Baez!* — hushed her when again she barked. The boy in the big shoes slid down to a lower ledge. His eyes were orange. His hat was blue. He crouched, set down a plastic bottle with dirty glue instead of a label. Then he threw a roll of paper — the bathroom kind. It unravelled as it soared through the air, landing in the partially dug hole. He threw words at Old Blue too. Old Blue nodded. *Okay, okay, okay.* Baez brought Old Blue the paper roll. Old Blue took her arm out of the sling and gathered up the spilled lengths. Then—the boy coaching her—she tossed it up into the branches. The boy clapped his hands, smiling. Old Blue caught the roll when it fell, then tossed it, up and up until the tree dripped streams of glaring white paper, stark against the blue above and yellow below, the rocky rises in between.

When the boy was gone—south into the desert from where she and Old Blue had come—Baez retrieved the bottle he left, dropped it into the sink of Old Blue's lap. Old Blue's good hand held the bottle and Baez got her teeth on the cap and bit it loose. As Old Blue drank, Baez licked the dribbles from her master's saggy throat. When it was her turn to drink, she titled back her head and allowed Old Blue to pour the liquid between her lips. The paper ribbons waved, twisting. Old Blue smiled and leaned back. Then the water came gushing back up through Old Blue's mouth. Baez licked that up too, hot and acid, then—*scritch-scratch*—she went back to her dig.

Now Baez finds her feet. The water in her bowl is thick and still, almost a jelly. And, of the food Tattoo left her, there's less than the day before. Each day fewer pellets, less mushy meat, or it's just bread soaked in sweet soda. Before, there were many boys to catch. Sometimes two white vans would come to collect them from Glove and Tattoo. The white vans had orange dashed on the sides and the men that got out were dressed the same: black boots, black glasses, pants and shirts that matched the thick, thorned cactus that grows here, everywhere. And they were tall and old like cactus too.

These Cactus Men gave Glove and Tattoo paper money then drove the bounties back over to the other side, a dozen or so of them stacked like logs in the back.

But the wall turned the flow of brown boys into a trickle, dried them up like the riverbed. Or else the brown boys have all made it through. The other side of the wall will be empty of them just as it must be empty of brown men. Gone up north, where there is water—and what else? Green fields? Somewhere there will be a silver lake around which brown men and brown boys live with some animals, some fires. The lake will be there in the rippled brown mountains, yonder where the sun begins, where their hunters—Tattoo and Glove and the Cactus Men—let them live. Unseen, unheard, they live.

HONEY

The early sky is streaked rose. Beneath it the *prohibido* road looks less ugly. That she has been lost out here for an entire night rises inside her with a cold nausea.

"*¡Niño!*"

She steps around the car, squinting into the distance. The boy has left her an Evian bottle of hot dirty water. His prints disappear off the road, into the distant hills beyond. A crumple of tissue caught on a fuzzy cholla cactus waves like a ghost. Inside the paper, her lump of chewing gum still smells of peppermint. It goes in the pocket of Marianne's jeans. She drinks the water, her teeth straining the grit, and walks down the road in the direction she thinks is south, back to the main road and the Zari reservation. She pictures herself walking into the café—"Whoa, am I an idiot," she'll say, ordering a bucket of icy Coke. She forgets why she's even here, so consuming is the humiliation of losing control of life, of everything. When she comes to another unfamiliar crossroads, she keeps straight.

She remembers feeling lost in the vast spread of this landscape even when she and Keith were just walking straight up to McGarrigle Station. It was the same time of year but not nearly this hot. Marianne's animal was scooting in and out alongside. She had put her hand on Keith's bony shoulder and then, when she dropped it, he scooped it up, and they went on hand in hand. ·

"I'm dying of thirst," she had said.

"We're going too fast," Keith replied, as they turned onto the main road. "We ought to pace ourselves in this place."

So they did, taking in the golden ground and azure sky, soft mountains in the distance.

"God, it can be beautiful here," she said. "Even this scrubby south."

Keith said the farms were white with salts from too much growth and irrigation. Then he whistled and the animal came trotting out from some low distant brush. "Well, Marianne was right, she's not a bad dog."

Honey was telling Keith about the poor thing getting kicked in the head, "Must have some brain damage, you think?" But then the gas station rose, shimmering, up the road. A sign promised Coke.

McGarrigle, dressed in denims, freckled face scorched to ketchup, pumped gas into a Cadillac with a fake silver tire decorating the trunk. His sons, knobby strawberry blondes, sat cross-legged on the stoop, lips blue from the ice pops they sucked on. With a bucket of water, they ran over to

Marianne's animal, smothering her with hugs in the shade of the phone booth.

McGarrigle nodded at Keith and pushed up his hat. He called his boys to tend to the customers. "Marianne's kin," he said.

Inside the store, the brothers watched her and Keith pick cans from the shelves, a pack of wieners from the freezer case, cold sodas, one of which Keith opened before paying. He passed it to Honey, who took a long drink. The boys narrowed their eyes, and the big one shook his head.

"It's stealing," he said. "You gotta pay for it first."

"It's just we're so thirsty," Keith said reaching for his wallet. "Nothing more than that."

"How old are you, kids?" she asked, bending over the brothers.

The youngest said six; the older, eight.

"You want a dog?" they said to Keith.

He smiled. "A dog?" No, they couldn't take a dog. He and Honey lived in a busy city, in a bubble high up in the sky. "Where would it play?"

The boys said, "There's no outside?"

"No. And that's not fair to an animal to live like that."

Keith stacked their purchases into the plastic bags the older one finally surrendered.

"They're good. Our dogs." He nodded at the window. Marianne's animal was laid out on her side in the shadow of the phone booth. "Like that one."

"Okay, show us," Keith said, his voice soft and warm.

Her hand found the base of his wet spine. "We've got a long walk back."

"It's okay, Hon. Just a quick look."

The wieners in Keith's plastic bag began to drip, a dark spot forming on the ground near his runner, the Velcro straps curling. Inside the pen the big brother milled about, clapping hands and barking orders at the animals that rushed the fencing. The chain link bowed. Some jumped, aiming for the barbed-wire edging. And away from the others, in its own cage, a male coyote lay in the shade. Its eyes flickered. Keith poked Honey and nodded towards it.

"Know what that is?" he whispered.

"Your mom's was the oldest." McGarrigle had come up behind them. "Marianne taking care of her?"

"She always wanted a dog. I think she was a little lonely out here. And I was always worried."

"A woman alone needs protection," he said. "You know that the Oro isn't safe."

"How's that?" Keith frowned.

McGarrigle laughed through his nose. "Goddamn migrants hiding in the ditches, coming in the dark. They steal anything they can get, leave their shit everywhere — excuse my French — steal the few farm jobs left around."

"Right," Keith said neutrally.

"Your mom's animal got one by the hand. Kid was trying to steal her water. You imagine?"

"We saw it, didn't we, Dad?" said the boy at McGarrigle's knee. "Bit three fingers clean off."

"Two, son." McGarrigle smoothed the boy's orange hair. "A rancher just up from Marianne got robbed not six months ago. His wife beaten up."

"Mom didn't say."

McGarrigle shook his red head and took a cigarette from his jeans pockets. "Until they seal that border, I told

Marianne, she'd better get a gun."

Keith shifted the plastic grocery bag, dripping wiener water on his foot. "Let's go," he said to Honey.

"Keep Marianne's one tied now," McGarrigle said, looking from Baez to Keith. "She'll go running back to the desert."

"That's where she came from, isn't it?" Keith nodded at the coyote in the cage.

"In part, sir, you're right."

They walked away from the pens, Keith looking back at his trail of dripping meat. "What a creep," he whispered.

And because Honey didn't think that those few wieners would be enough for four, what with Baez counted in and Marianne looking so underfed, they decided to stop for meat at the ranch Marianne had recommended. The garden was overgrown with nopal paddles, tough ones, well-spined, and the flat-roofed concrete house was dark with late-day shadow. They had already followed the signs around to the back porch when Honey realized this must have been the place that was attacked.

"Everything okay?" Keith asked the bearded rancher who answered their knock; his chunky wife, in flowered cotton, moved in the back. The man just handed off a brown-paper package soaked in beef juice in exchange for Keith's twenty bucks.

Keith and Honey looked at each other, both swallowing deep, and stepped down off the porch. Then the screen door squeaked open behind them. The rancher's wife, her face burned a deep cherry, stood on the stoop. "So that Marianne still giving cheese to rats?"

"Excuse me?" Keith smiled.

The woman growled. "Whose side is she on?"

The rancher then pulled his wife inside by the arm. It took a minute before the echo of the slammed door faded.

When finally they got down Marianne's side road they all, Keith and Honey and the animal, ran towards the tall blue figure when it appeared, waving, on the stoop.

Here, now, Honey can't look behind her down the *prohibido* road anymore. She'll just think she's going the wrong way and she feels crazy enough already. She steps over the bones of something that might once have been a pig, smooth and white as Ivory soap, the pelvis watching her with its holes like eyes. The road curves to the west around a jutting hill. The adobe chapel on top is as white as angel cake. It is a steep climb up through brush and scrub, sharp prickles. Something scurries over her toes and bites her. It stings like a doctor's needle.

The shrine is shed-sized, white and sunken as a marshmallow, topped with a Christian cross. Inside, blistered plaster is going to powder. The air is warm and stale. The dirt floor is piled with rocks and cans—fish, lunch ham, beer, soda—and pooled with light from the cracked roof above.

She crawls into a corner, pushing away litter, and pokes the lump of gum into her mouth, sucking, chewing on the tissue. Spots of sun move like bubbles across the dirt. The flutter in her heart slows. There is less fear. No hunger in her belly, no dryness in her throat.

She smells Marianne's rich tobacco and hears the slow rumble as, somewhere near, her mom clears her throat. Yes, her mom, her Marianne, is still alive. She wouldn't just wander off. Not even after her beloved Baez. She opens her eyes again and the light is deeper. She must have slept. When she looks down at her dusty blue costume and tennis shoes she believes that she really is Marianne, but how can that be because then where is Honey and who is even thinking this and—

In the sharp angular shadows, an arm's length away, the boy crouches with her purse. His head rests on his knees. He watches out the low doorway. A deep red *S* is scratched from left elbow to wrist. Outside, birds call: sharp and high. After a minute the boy opens her purse, rummaging inside.

"Give!" Her voice cracks the childish Spanish.

The boy jumps up. Litter flies.

She coughs. "You a robber. You a bad *niño*. Bad boy." She finds her elbows. She struggles to lift herself up.

He stands above her with the water jug. When she tips back her head, he pours in a slow stream. Then the boy drinks.

"Alone?" she asks. If she shifts a little to the left she can see out the door.

The boy says there is no one else. He squats, examining Marianne's scissors. "You need new glasses."

"Need my mom."

The boy puts the scissors back.

"You know her, yes?"

"*Sí.*"

"Where?" she whispers. "How far?"

He crouches near, his face close. "She's near here. In *Las tierras vacías.*"

Honey repeats the name putting together a possible meaning. Empty lands? Wasteland?

"*El desierto.*" Now he waves his arm, cutting the air near her head. "Nobody's supposed to go in there," he says slowly. "Not even Control. If you go there and you die, it's your own fault. You know what I mean, *vieja*?"

She nods. In English she says: "No-man's-land." When she repeats *el desierto* the boy studies her mouth as it stumbles up and down the syllables like a series of steep hills.

He takes off his cap and runs his fingers through his thick, unwashed hair. "I thought you were her. You know? I thought *you* were El Esqueleto." He makes a sound that might be laughter.

He is poor and desperate, proud to wear what she assumes must be his big brother's shoes.

She says, "I pay you money, all you want. Much, much money."

The boy shakes his head. He steps around the shrine, looking out the windows, tripping over stones and cans. "Just like El Esqueleto, you don't know the rules here. How come she thought she could beat this place? And now you, too?"

An unopened can of spaghetti is on the altar. He pulls back the lid and with a plastic spoon shovels orange mush into his mouth. He points at her with the spoon. "They think you are El Esqueleto."

Her good hand braces the wall. Again she tries to wriggle up. "Who thinks?"

The boy watches her. "You even have your arm in a sling." He squints. "You sure you're not her?" Then he considers something. "No, hers was on the left and yours is the right."

The morning is bright now and the shrine is turning hot. There is not enough air for two. She is almost on her feet when she grows faint. She falls. Her elbow smacks against the floor.

He kicks some gravel at her.

"*Niño*—my mom, help find her." She stares up at him. She can hear her heart. She is trying not to hate him. She is trying to remember he is just a boy. Not that long ago, he would have been a baby, toothless, hairless, lovable.

"Pay me."

She nods.

"I want five thousand dollars. Can you give me that?"

Like a soccer ball he kicks the spaghetti can elegantly through the door. Then he reaches behind his back, lifting up his T-shirt. He shows her his spine. It is scarred with black ovals, the most prominent at the base. From a backpack, he says. From helping others cross over. But he is done with that now. Now he is ready to start the life he has always dreamed of.

"Five thousand? That's plain extortion," she says, in English.

He unzips his backpack and takes out a red leather dog collar. But now the leather has been chewed apart. In a flash she sees Marianne and then the gaping hole in front of the trailer where that animal's stake had been yanked.

"You know whose?"

She nods. "Baez."

He shakes the collar at her. The loop and buckle clatter. "The dog is with her."

Her eyes follow the collar back into his bag. "Okay. Five thousand."

"And if you rat me out or try to get help —"

She shakes her head. "I won't."

"I leave you, if you try that. And if I leave you, you will die. And so will El Esqueleto who you say is your mom. She'll live another few days, if that. Then the dog eats her."

"But she live —"

He says he thinks so, but they have to move as fast as this desert lets them. As he speaks, he tries not to smile, drunk as he is on the thought of all that money. "And we go my way. Do what I say. Otherwise, Ocho will catch us."

She nods. She says she is sorry. "So fast. They shooting me."

The boy looks hard at her then goes back to her purse. "I saw your driver's license, *vieja*. Visa, MasterCard. How much money in the bank?"

"Enough. Much. I pay for you *coyote*."

He passes her the plastic spoon. "Spaghetti or sardines?"

The spaghetti's salt will restore her electrolytes. But the expiry date stamped on the side says five years ago. She gives him back the can. "So you the *coyote*. And me?"

The boy shrugs, snatching the spaghetti. "You are the *pollo*. That's what we call them. Especially a big one like you."

"A chicken," she says. "No—*gallina*?"

"No, *gallina* is just the bird. *Pollo* is after, when it's killed and cooked."

"*Arroz con pollo*," Honey remembers out loud. Dinorah has made that several times, leaving it in the fridge covered in tin foil. Heat and serve when she and Keith get home.

He fishes through his knapsack, drawing out a piece of thick, cottony paper. He unfolds it: the ruins of a sunset, twined *MM*s in the corner. "El Esqueleto gave us water," he says. "She tried to help us."

The paper is soft. It smells like Marianne. She lifts her face to the sky-lit ceiling, eyes closed against the shafting sun. Were they not whispering it might echo in here and with each echo, a new crack in the wall and a crumble from the plaster.

"Yes," Honey whispers in English, "because she knows how life is not very kind."

CHÁVEZ

When, at lunchtime, the soy farmer's red-plaid back has disappeared down between his rows—he likes to surprise them with random inspections—Chávez reaches into the open window of the farmer's pickup and scoops a couple of road maps from the seat. The pickers around smile and look away.

Later, alone with a flashlight, he finds the town he's near—Capricorn Creek—and he finds Zopilote, only of course it goes by Buzzard City on the map, which he can never get used to. His face burns with sick when he sees just how lost he is—a whole territory north and east from Zopilote. He can't sleep for that and then his mind spirals into thinking about what Reyes and Díaz said about Ocho. The last time he crossed the desert with Juan, two knob-kneed *pollos* followed behind them: another pair of round-faced Indians from the mountains, south of the south, where their people farmed rocky slopes, raising goats for milk and bees for honey. Once, pink-skinned, white-haired northerners travelled down to look at those Indians and buy their brightly dyed cloth embroidered with birds and flowers and listen to their ancient stories, nodding like they could understand. But, the *pollos* said, guerillas running guns and drugs up the Río Loco were driving them out of the mountains. Now the northerners keep away along with everyone else. They have found some other mountain to go to with their money and their short pants, their big black cameras resting on hard, swollen bellies.

These *pollos* had Indian names too hard to remember so Juan called the younger one Mario and the older one Diego.

"After my uncles," Juan said.

Mario wore big sloppy rubber sandals, muddy with farming, muddier, even, than Diego's leather lace-ups.

Before even handing out water jugs and plastic bags — the candy inside already starting to melt — Juan had tucked the brothers' soggy money into the pocket of his jeans. Then they'd sloshed across the Loco, their throats tightening at the river's thick stench. Coming ashore, they cut west, following the curve of the river's dry banks, away from the drone and glow of the construction site not five miles to the east by then.

When they were into the salt crusts of former ranchland near El Esqueleto's trailer, Diego, the older boy, slowed right down. They waited for him to catch up.

"Fuck, Chavito," Juan spat, "why's he hobbling like that?"

Mario said it was nothing. Diego caught up. They all kept on. Then Diego's limping shadow got to the size of Chávez's thumb.

Juan shouted at Mario, "We're gonna have to leave that faggy brother of yours behind."

Mario looked at the ground. His bangs were cut straight across his forehead and his high cheekbones glistened. His T-shirt showed a cartoon fish riding a bicycle and lots of English words and Chávez remembers staring at it, impatient for the day he'd be able to read that language. Probably now he could.

He remembers that when Diego staggered up, his water jug empty and plastic bag dragging, his face was red and about to burst. He finally said his feet were killing him. He had grown out of his boots last year. Juan made him take them off. Diego cried while he did it. In the glow of the moon, they saw that wet sacks of blister covered the boy's heels and his toenails were jammed with blood. When Juan told them to, they all ripped material from the extra T-shirts in their packs. After wrapping Diego's swollen feet, Juan told Mario to take off his sandals. Mario did and then Juan used his pocket knife to slash the backs off and tops open. Then he tied what were really just rubber soles around Diego's bulging feet. Mario put on his brother's bloodied boots. There was lots of room in them, he said, stuffing the toes with balled-up socks.

They went on, past the gas station, onto the highway then cutting northeast towards El Esqueleto's place, which humped up on the dark horizon. Juan led them down the trampled path to the treed wash behind the old woman's trailer. Her windows were gold and from them leaked radio voices and the smell of burned cooking. Her animal started barking so loud it seemed its very jaws might split. Something was different this time. The buzz of energy in the air was new. Then a pair of gunshots rang out from the direction of the road. They ran without getting any water or food.

They were okay for another night. Then out in the *bajadas* these blinding white headlights came. The lights flashed, on-off, on-off. There was the zip of an engine too, but distant yet. Then the headlights went out for good. He and Juan knew it was Ocho but neither of them said it.

"Who's that? What's he want?" Diego whispered.

"Shut the fuck up," was all Juan could say.

They walked until the sun made them stop and they lay in the shade of mesquite trees, moving with the shadows and hiding when they heard even the creak of the breeze. The cotton wrappings on Diego's feet turned red and brought in flies. The next night they reached the big old house trailer with ragged tinsel and bleached Christmas pictures and the mountain of desert trash behind. Juan said the man was like a devil Santa Claus with all the crappy decorations and the way he drove around in his blue pickup with the back full of garbage instead of presents in a sleigh. He would diddle you and then sell you to the Control. That's why he lives in *Las tierras vacías*, Juan said.

"Preys on us, see?"

That kept the *pollos* puckered up and quiet. Inside the Christmas trailer a radio or something was loud, like a crowd of people were laughing; it echoed through the desert night. And the dog tied up in its pen was too old to smell them much or hear them when, in the white glow of the trailer's bug light, they drank the part-jug of water that Christmas guy had in the back of his truck. He always had something they could drink. They even drank from the dog's dish if they were dying.

The night after, the serrated edge of the Entrada Mountains rose up. Beyond, the big pointy one in the middle was visible. The sky was going from blue to purple to black.

"There's a valley and then a dirt road and we get to the final pass," Chávez told the brothers. "From there you can see the highway lights."

Juan kept looking behind him. Or maybe that is just how Chávez remembers it now, reading more into it each time he thinks about it, over and over. How come bad memories don't ever wear out but good ones fade so fast? Their climb was slow. After the first miles of rising grade the ground turned rocky. Diego fell, his face melting as he swallowed pain and whimpers. They dropped their water jugs as they were emptied. Then Juan made them stop.

"But it's there," Chávez said. "The highway's down on the other side. Just let's get through this pass."

Juan said no. "We got to rest. You yourself said every hour we take a break. Look, that kid's feet are killing him."

"What about Ocho?" Chávez asked. The name choked in his throat so he kind of squealed it.

"Ah, we lost that guy." Juan grinned. "You worry too much, Chavito."

"Ten minutes," he remembers saying to Juan. "Then we move."

They had huddled on a sandy flat, tangled with sweet sagebrush and barrels of stubby cactus. Above them, the mountains blotted out the sky. Below, flat rolling hills spilled out. Moon and stars picked up the nubbly texture of the endless scrub.

Diego and Mario stayed close together, passing last mouthfuls of water and soft secret words.

"These two were a bad idea," Juan said, flipping his cap backwards. "I'm sick of these *pollos*. Basically they're all fucking stupid." He stood and spoke down at them. "We're far behind now, because of you."

Diego and Mario watched as Juan pushed up the sleeves of the checkered shirt he wore now. The tattoos on his arms were thick and dark.

Suddenly he pointed behind the brothers and shouted, "Look, *serpientes*! Fucking rattlers!"

Diego and Mario jumped up, stumbling away from their spot. Their faces were pale, eyes red.

Juan laughed. "Hey, Chavito, see them squirm, dude?"

Chávez looked away. "Not funny."

When the brothers sat down again Juan said to him, "You make sure they don't run. I just got to piss."

He remembers how the brothers were cross-legged and how when they looked at him they were just praying to death that Chávez would be good and honest, not like the other *coyote* whose piss just then was hitting hard against the dry earth.

When did he hear that rumble? Had Juan stopped pissing?

"Listen," he had whispered to Diego, holding the eyes of the older brother.

The motor came grinding its way up the climb. Chávez got to his feet.

"Grab your packs," he yelled.

He found his own and then saw Juan's pack was already gone. Had Juan taken it for his piss? He still can't remember when he thinks back — over and over — that part of the night is gone. Then the motor got close and the whir of it was furious. Gasoline exhaust poisoned the air.

"Juan!" he hollered. "Juan!"

Beaming headlights came sweeping in, bathing the Indian brothers in whitewash, their fear naked. Like them, Chávez stayed frozen, as if dissolving in the very rocks of the mountains that hemmed them in.

There came a gunshot — a bright, quick pop.

"Run!" he screamed — really screamed, at the top of his voice, summoning all the fear and anger that he found now raged inside him. "Run, motherfuckers!"

At that, the three of them had scattered. He remembers flailing arms, tripping feet, eyes peeled back: away, away from that light, away from the engine, away from the thumping music cranked on Ocho's stereo. He took one look back. The dune buggy's body faced him full on. The vehicle was bearing down on him. Through the headlights he saw two round, slick helmets—like spacemen, soldiers, jet pilots. One helmet was driving: Ocho. The other helmet belonged to the gunner, standing over Ocho in the back.

He heard his name. "Chavito!"

But Chávez just stood there, squinting against the pain of the blinding light. Where were the gunner's eyes in all that shine and white? If he could find those eyes he would be able to move: to run, to drop dead, something. But there were no eyes, and no way into the gunner's heart, brain, soul.

The next shot whistled above his head. There was a sharp, needling pierce deep in his ears. His body jerked. He turned and ran back into the dark, craggy hills, climbing and falling, skinning his palms, ripping his jeans. The high mountains lurked above and beyond. It was only when he could not run anymore and he fell down in a mess of exhaustion that he remembered the *pollo* brothers.

He squeezes his eyes shut. He hates this memory worse than any other. With all the breaths of all the pickers clouding up around him, the walls close in and then the whole world closes with it. He tiptoes out for a smoke and then decides, fuck it, it's time to go again.

Before the sun comes up, he quits the soy farm, the crisp smell of which he's not even used to yet. His backpack is weighed down with hoarded food—bruised apples, a sleeve of cookies, two cola cans. He walks the seven miles it takes to cross into the next county—going in the right direction this time, according to his map.

BAEZ

The bounties sleep, drool darkening their shirts. The one with no hat is light around the eyes, like he has lost his mask. Their backpacks broil in the desert buggy. They smell sweet, with flesh, with fruit.

When those squat shadows rose behind Old Blue's trailer, the humps of back came first, then the billed caps. Because of Yellow Man and his gun, Old Blue started waiting on the stoop as the brown boys tiptoed in from the path they'd cut across her back field. Old Blue would call to them in their language and then, with Yellow Man's firecrackers going overhead and Baez barking, Old Blue would shield them with her long thin body, run them back to the ironwoods and, standing over them, hurry them to eat and drink. She wrapped their feet with strips of white cotton, wiped blood from their scratches, packed their bags with candy and the foil bundles that Black Braid brought and that Old Blue herself needed to eat—her jeans were so loose now that she tripped on the dragging cuffs. And after the brown boys had gone on and the smoke of Yellow Man's firecrackers had dried up, Old Blue would march up to Yellow Man's blue truck and knock on the window. Through the lowered glass, Old Blue passed Yellow Man water and food as well as words, high-pitched ones that pierced the night air. Baez always got that same food in the morning, scraped from the road where Yellow Man dumped it.

Then the blue truck stayed away for one night, two nights, three. When it came again it was bright afternoon. Baez was chained up, asleep in the shade of the stoop. Old Blue had gone with Black Braid, her easel propped up against the shed. The truck didn't stop at the road this time but kept coming down the lane towards the trailer. It travelled fast, sliding in the gravel. The ground beneath her belly shook from the rumble. Yellow Man got out of the truck. She exploded, charging, pulling back her lips, her teeth shaking from the root. There was in the world only the shuddering blur of Yellow Man, against which she seethed and writhed, the insides of her tearing apart. Yellow Man slammed his truck door. He carried two things. The rock in his left hand he threw at Old Blue's car. It hit the front window with a thud, followed by a long, bony crack. And in the right hand, he carried a stick—silver spike impaled crossways through the tip. Yellow Man wound up and came at her. Baez jumped away as the stick caught her in the shoulder. The hollow smack reeled through her body and the spike pierced deep. As Yellow Man pulled, tearing muscle, ripping flesh, Baez flew back. She skidded, gravel scraping her flank. Then she twisted up and sprang forth again. But Yellow Man was in his truck, racing away.

The rock had dented the ground where it landed by the car. A piece of paper, covered in words, was tied around it with string. When they came back Black Braid and Old Blue read the words out loud together and when Old Blue started to yell, Black Braid put his arm around her and pulled her in. *Baez!* Old Blue spun away from Black Braid. *Baez!* With hands shielding her eyes Old Blue followed the chain to where Baez was hiding beneath the shady stoop. Baez crawled out to meet Old Blue, trailing blood and bugs.

Now the sun inches towards its summit. Tattoo and Glove are in the trailer. They will be sleeping. The panels on the rooftop swallow up the sun's throbbing light. Despite the

shade of the lean-to the skin of the bounties gets browner —
the knees of the boy in the green cap are almost black. In
the riverbed below, a snake with diamonds on its back twists
among rocks and cans, until it is seemingly sucked down
into a hole where, once, fish might have slept. It was not that
long ago.

HONEY

They go by night. It is cooler by at least ten degrees, maybe
more. The boy says El Esqueleto was alive when he saw her
two days ago. He gave her water before moving on himself.
She was way past the Christmas trailer —

"Where?"

"The Christmas trailer." Some kind of garbage man in a
blue truck, he tells her. Or so she understands. "It's almost
at Zopilote, you'll see. For a crazy old *vieja* like her, that was
really far." He says maybe she had enough water to get there.
For her and the crazy dog.

She swallows her million questions. It is better just to
walk.

Tip, tap. Walking sticks the boy has made from the
spines of dead cactus are taller than he is. One for each of
them. *Tap, tip.* After a mile down the rough *prohibido* they
cut west, into the desert.

"That's it," the boy says.

Now they are officially in what he calls the "empty land,"
the *vacía* land — from here to the Zopilote highway. They
step away from the gravel shoulder and paving, into the
dusty flat beyond. After they go a pace, he stops and snaps
off a mesquite branch, the leaves fanning wide. He walks

back to the road then turns around. Crouching low, twisting left to right, he works backwards, brushing away their tracks.

Centipedes as long as her middle finger scuttle across the sand, shrill night birds curse in the above. Razor cholla and ocotillo spikes catch their pant cuffs, a scrape or scratch with each blind step. In spring these plants are graced with delicate flowers—sea blue, bubblegum, canary—or so Marianne paints them, with the colours Honey sends from Buzzard.

She remembers watching Keith through the window as he grilled the rancher's steaks and hot dogs over the fire pit out back. His back was rigid and he stood right over the smoke, disappearing in the dark cloud when the meat burned. She helped Marianne refry the beans but could not find the right moment to ask about the attack. After a silent supper, they sat out by the orange glow of the coals, sipping beer and coffee, Marianne smoking. Whenever Keith went to gather kindling, she snuck deep hard drags off of her mother's tobacco.

"I won't tell," Marianne smiled with a wink.

The sun set slow and then, like shutting off a switch, the sky went indigo and the coyotes cried like babies, coming in close. Light, cracking footsteps sounded, moving in on the ironwoods lining the wash. The animal perked up. Marianne pointed her finger: "Sit."

"It's just *pollitos*," Marianne said.

Keith sipped his beer. "Remind me what that means, Marianne. My Spanish isn't up to snuff." Twilight turned the lenses of his clip-ons a dense, polished onyx.

"Chicks," Marianne said. "Little chickens." Then she waved

into the dark. "Just innocents. They won't hurt us. All they want is to find their moms and dads. Those people you got working for you in Buzzard left their families behind— these kids, in other words. We have no idea."

The next dry snap was closer.

"*Jesus!*" Honey clutched her throat.

The animal lunged at the sound. And then it yowled, baring sharp teeth matte with plaque.

"Mom!" Honey jumped up, knocking over her lawn chair. She found herself in Keith's arms. They stood there dumb and useless while Marianne yanked at the animal's collar, her hardened body straining to maintain hold.

When night settled, they folded up the chairs and Keith stomped out the fire.

Later, when Keith had fallen into a raspy sleep, she found Marianne painting at her easel. She was wearing the same floor-length bathrobe Honey had bought her for Mother's Day when Honey was still teaching high school. An O'Brien's bottle stood open and she had a cigarette going.

"Mom," Honey said, "that dog's going to bite someone."

Marianne did not look away from her canvas: a towering date palm, whose lime-green fronds and ravaged bark looked flat against a muddy purple background. "Hmm?"

"Apparently she already has—one of those migrant boys or whatever you call them—that's what McGarrigle says." She took a pull on Marianne's damp Phantom, emptied the rose teacup of its whiskey. "I mean, what do you think that guy bred it for?"

"*Her.*" Marianne said, tossing down a paint-stiffened rag. "My dog is a girl, okay?" She took the cigarette back from Honey's fingers.

"You really leave water out for those boys?"

"How can I not?" said Marianne.

"McGarrigle won't like it. Doesn't he know what you're up to?"

Marianne snorted. "Sure." With a slosh she refilled the teacup, threw the whiskey back. "Around here they call me 'old hippie bitch,' among other things."

"Mom!"

"It's okay, Honey." Marianne turned back to her painting. "A bitch is just a female dog, anyway. Nothing wrong with that."

Now the desert night gets so dark Honey might have her eyes closed. The boy has a penlight. It lends them a dim shaft of grey into which he leads her. When she slows, he takes her good hand, tugs a hard lead. His skin is hot and rough, the grip strong.

"Don't let me out of your sight," he tells her.

The boy won't give back her ball cap, not understanding her argument about finders and keepers. And he's got her purse slung across his narrow chest. He promised her wedding ring was safe inside but wouldn't show her. Instead, when they left the shrine, he'd handed her a bottle partly filled with water and he carries another himself.

Though his legs are less than half as long as hers, the boy moves faster. They only have so much night and so much water. "Don't you want to get to El Esqueleto before she dies?"

After an hour's walk, a ten-minute stop. She loosens her sling. The cotton is rubbing the back of her neck raw. While her arm is no longer swelling, the pain rating still hovers at an eight. "Show me the collar."

The boy swears, digs around in his bag, and then holds it up. She still doesn't want to touch the mangy, bitten leather.

"You don't believe me still?" The boy zips the collar away and they go.

At orange dawn they stop in an empty creek bed. There is an overhang of mesquite. They huddle in shadows. A faded can of 7 Up, heavy with sand, teeters upon a rock. Why would someone carry a tennis racket out here? The cracked handle nudges an aerosol can, the label peeled. VO5? Easy-Off? Pam?

The boy points to the horizon where the rough outline of low, red hills is breaking through the passing night. "Water comes from those hills. If it ever rains, this creek will fill."

"And when is rain?" The bottles they carry are almost empty.

He finds two large clear plastic bags in his knapsack, shakes them out, and pulls them over the living branches of nearby mesquite shrub. Then he gathers the openings, tying them shut with what might be dental floss. The bags puff like balloons. He is thin, this boy, his shoulder blades jut through his T-shirt like nubs of wing. She would like to know how old he truly is. But really he is ageless. He was never a boy nor will he be. Around his eyes he already has wrinkles and the palms of his hands are thick with callous. Monica's blond, lanky Kevin would die out here. Maybe this boy would kill him, like he could easily kill her. She wills herself to think like Keith, to rationally assess this boy, to act with empathy but not sympathy, to put her own health and mental stamina before his. If she dies, he'll never get his blackmail money. He wants to find Marianne, therefore. And he wants Honey to live.

"Where's my hat, *niño*? My green hat." She tells him her face is burning.

He grips his knapsack, inching away. "It's my friend's," he says. "I made it for him."

He has a fine-toothed plastic comb. With it he pulls thorns from his ankles. Then she tries.

"*Tatuado*," he says, pointing at her tattoo.

She tells him it means "good strong body" in an ancient language.

The boy lifts his T-shirt. The tattoo of a skeleton key extends vertically from hip bone to just below the nipple. The tattoo's lines are thick and bluish, homemade.

"*Llave*," he says.

She nods her understanding. "A key."

To prove he did the tattoo himself he pulls a kit from his knapsack: Bic pens in black, red, and blue, along with sewing needles, a jackknife, Wet-Naps in packets fill a vinyl pencil case. "I did all the kids in the village. That's how I got the bus fare north." Then he did tattoos in San Wren, the border town where he lived for a whole year.

She gets him to understand he is skilled. The boy shrugs. She should see the tattoo he did for his friend. "My best tattoo for my best friend." Gently the boy touches the inside of his right forearm. "Here. His mom's name: Juanita. And a broken heart."

"Her heart?" This was one of the first Spanish words she learned: *corazón*.

"His. My best friend's."

Like him, she removes her shoes and rolls off her socks so they can dry. Her feet are spongy and swollen, the toe-nails still perfectly lacquered with rose. Thursday night she'd done them fresh, a glass of wine resting on the back of the toilet. Classes were officially over and Keith—as of seventeen hundred hours—was officially in the air. She ate Dinorah's deep-fried chicken rolls—ignoring the calorie count—while watching the news, then smoked two Pilots on the balcony: crisp wine, crisp toes, crisp stars. It was going to be a good spring, even if Keith was going to be away for most of it.

There is a screech behind them. A pair of hairy, horned pigs scuttle down the creek bed.

"¡Mira! ¡Jabalíes!"

As the boy jumps up to look, her purse tumbles to the ground. She snatches it back, buries her face in its soft leather, sucking in the scent of mint, powder, the reassuring chlorine of mornings in the pool. Her ring is in the pocket like the boy had said.

She gives the boy a pair of Tic Tacs, another for herself. The candies are stark and clean against their fingers. "Like candy, niño? Sweet teeth?"

He shrugs. He points.

A snake—black and diamonded—coils in the eaves of an ironwood's sculpted stump, unaware of the bow-headed hawk above, etching a circle in the bold blue sky.

Or is it a buzzard?

"Zopilote?" she says, of the bird in the sky.

The boy nods. There are many out here.

As day passes the plastic bags fill with condensation. He carefully removes them from the shrubs, drains them into a water jug. His trick has yielded a good two cups of water.

"Smart boy," she says, after she has tipped back and swallowed her half of the warm liquid.

He almost smiles. "I take care of you, remember."

They lay languid, in the hot sink of sand. Ants crawl in the crooks of her fingers. She is too tired to fight them.

"In a month it will be so hot birds fall dead from the sky," the boy says.

He opens a can of spaghetti, hands her the spoon and says to eat half. It tastes of tin and something tangy and though she gags on a soft chunk of noodle, she forces herself to swallow.

"You found. In mom's car." She passes the can back, shaking her head. When he doesn't understand her Spanish, she tries just yelling it louder. Finally he nods. He found lots of stuff in that car wreck. With all the boys crossing by there, soon there will be nothing left.

When the sun has fallen, they go. She rolls up her pant legs. Her calves are torn and scratched. She drags the saguaro stick behind her. Her water bottle is empty.

"More water, boy?" She asks him ten times, twenty.

"Be quiet." Then, "Shut up." Then, "There's water just ahead."

They come to an abandoned mining well by greying light. From the hole beneath the splintered wooden cover she never would have seen, the boy can reach only half a jug. She takes her turn at the warm liquid then goes on after the boy, whose breathing begins to labour.

Night descends. Great rocky mesas loom, sailing like black liners across an ocean that is now so big it is gone.

They stop. There are a couple dozen Tic Tacs left. She gives them each one.

"People look for me," she says. "Johnny-for-Jesus. Or Control."

Not Control, the boy says, surprised. "Control doesn't come in the *Las tierras vacías*." They think we'll all die crossing here. But if we don't and get up north, people give us jobs. You don't know that, *vieja?*" He adjusts his jeans and starts to walk again.

She scrambles behind, tripping over brush and rock. Her purse is heavy. She throws away her makeup mirror, a bottle of hand lotion, notebook, hairbrush. But not her keys or her wallet.

He has stopped to watch her with steady staring eyes. To this boy she is little more than the lucky winner of some undeclared lottery. In a flash she understands that because her life is comfortable and productive it is somehow worth more than his. But she did not ask for this to be so. Getting him to see that her and Keith's privilege is not their fault is an abyss as vast as this desert.

Finally he looks away and calls for her to hurry. Then the boy darts off through dark. She finds him bent low, his fingers grazing a set of tire tracks. They are fresh.

"Ocho and the partner?"

He nods. He says he and Honey will follow the tracks a ways.

They pass a grove of skeletal cactus, burst ribs fanning out, arms twisted at the elbow. Then on a rise appears a shack that the boy says is full of snakes. There is a dump of litter nearby. Candy wrappers glint in the moon, some bent metal.

She falls asleep walking, lands hard on her knees.

"Get up." The boy wrenches her good arm. "*Ándale.*"

She can't move. She curls on the hot ground.

He crouches close and whispers: "Stay here a minute, *vieja.* I'll follow the tracks on my own. Okay?"

His footsteps fade away into the dark desert.

She tries calling out, but her tongue cannot find English or Spanish. There is nothing to do but be still. There is nowhere to look but into the face of the sky. A lozenge, a mint, a moon, with softness in the centre, it bobs in the above. She is tethered to that moon. There is an invisible twine. She will last only as long as it does, until dawn, going where it takes her. Or maybe it is just that she, like a gunshot cowboy, is slowly dying.

When she wakes the dark shadow of an animal is moving in close. It breathes loud. Its back is in silver, or else it is just moonlight that makes it so. A hackled body of pure muscle, not even bones inside.

"Baez?"

The animal is close enough she sees its eyes are truly made of amber, ancient bugs trapped inside. It brings the smell of urine and heat and ripped-open garbage.

Don't put your hands or feet where she can't see them, Marianne says from deep inside her. *Honey, are you listening?*

The pink tongue flicks between tight-pulled lips, keeping time with the air that sings, up-down, through the wet holes of its slender nose. Shoulder blades shift as it slinks in. The animal screams—or else she does—then the boy is there.

CHÁVEZ

Cool wind dries his wet brow. He's some days west now but still feels so far from Zopilote because the trees are fat and dripping shiny leaves. The highway's just a back road really, lined in brush and low oak and bursting with the delicate lavender flowers the farmers call weeds. He walks until half

the cookies and both colas are gone — two in the afternoon —
then sleeps for an hour under a swath of brush, backpack for
pillow and hands tucked between his knees. He dreams of
birds and wakes up hungry for eggs, wishing he'd saved the
second cola. He goes on along the ditch. Up ahead is a sign
shaped like a valentine, hand-painted. BERRIES. He follows
the arrow down a tree-lined avenue, canopied in a rustle of
green leaves. The trunks, thick as his waist, loom high. The
farmhouse is sided in what looks like orange safety plastic.
Behind it, acres and acres of green fields stretch into the
horizon. A tractor, unseen, grinds away. He watches the
fields for signs of pickers. Flies buzz to get at the moisture
in his eyes.

The farmer comes out from behind the house. He says
his name is Peacock. His face is red, and the white hair on
his head and arms and growing up the neck of his shirt
glows like light around a candle. Above a set of crystal-blue
eyes, the white eyebrows are thick and fuzzy as tomato
caterpillars.

"Our berries are organic," Peacock says. His flat accent
is different from the other farmers. Maybe he is from else-
where. "Means we use no poison. You understand?"

Chávez nods. "Yes, I do understand, sir. Very clearly."

Peacock widens his eyes at Chávez's English. "Three
bucks per ten pounds and all you can eat at mealtimes. No
smoking or shitting in the fields."

"Okay." Chávez follows the farmer back to a series of
wood-panelled outbuildings, the first of which is where he'll
be sleeping. The inside is crammed with bunks, three high.
He opens his mouth to ask how far it is to Zopilote but then
he freezes.

The boots. Those boots. At the foot of a lower berth are the boots. Though they've been cleaned up and polished enough to wear to church, he sees the ghost of blood stains and remembers how the boy's swollen feet had popped with blisters. And he hears how Juan had laughed.

"Rest'll be back from the field soon," Peacock says. "They can bring you to supper."

He takes the bed roll and lump of pillow from Peacock's blond hands, and when the door shuts behind him he sits on the bunk nearest the one with the boots. The mattress beneath him is thin enough the bed slats jut into his thighs, while the bedding in his arms smells of the dry sun.

He smothers his face in his pillow, fighting back the rising memory of that last crossing with Juan. But his mind is stronger than that sack of sharp poking-out feathers. The flashing lights behind his squished-up eyes turn into the stars he had counted waiting for the first sign, however slight, of daybreak. How many stars had he counted? The same ten, twenty, thirty, over and over. Then his thoughts would spin out, and, losing count, he'd have to start again. "*Uno-dos-tres-cuatro* . . . *uno-dos-tres-cuatro*—*fuck. Uno-dos-tres* . . . *Uno-dos-tres-cuatro*—Juan.*"

Juan. He'd find Juan and it would be all right. Ha-ha. They'd pretend to check each others' jeans for shit stains and laugh about who was more scared of Ocho and then vow to never come back, not for any *pollos* again, forget it.

At the thought of Mario and Diego, his stomach falls. He remembers over and over how he saw Diego's chewed and bloody feet and saw Juan's bag was gone and heard the hard sound of his piss hitting the ground. Chávez had sat high on an outcrop, head between his knees, shaking. In the whole world Abuelita alone would forgive him. Or would she? There was so much forgiveness to ask for—where would he even start?

When the sun broke that morning he'd picked up his own footprints and followed them back to where Ocho had ambushed them. The foot of the mountain pass was sloped, thick with dull green agave and bottomed out into a scrabble of mesquite. If they had only climbed a little higher, Ocho's dune buggy would not have been able to reach them. But they did not climb higher because Juan made them stop.

"Just you wait," Juan had said to those brothers—he always did: promised, pledged. "The peppers up north are coming up fast. In a few months you kids'll be rich."

He found Juan's footprints. He found where Juan had pissed on a round pink boulder some ten paces away. He followed the prints, leading away from where he and the *pollos* had been sitting; and then they just stopped and went nowhere. Juan himself had taught him how to brush away his own tracks. Here, maybe, he'd done the same.

Back near where they'd sat, Ocho's tire tracks skidded through the soft dirt. Chávez drank the last inches from a dropped water bottle then followed after Mario and Diego. Their prints led east. At first they hit hard and strong, but then Diego had started limping behind, winding around like crazy, stopping and starting. He had fallen once, twice. Mario kept back-tracking to help: pulling, dragging, holding his big brother by the hand.

Their trail led deep into the mountain pass. Chávez had looked up at the steep face and hoped they had not gone too high. They must have taken turns gaining purchase on the ridges, skinning their hands and knees like he had. He had climbed with the ghosts of them, smelling their fear, pick-ing up their signs in broken brush and disturbed rocks, and when he came to a wide plateau he shouted out for them, crying loud and angry for them to come back. Scrambling up into that high country, he went fast, his heart choking, and then, at a round, jutting boulder with a long deep crack that Juan always joked reminded him of a human ass, he lost them. All signs of those brothers had been wiped away from the earth. Until the boots. Right there in front of him.

BAEZ

It was well before dusk when Yellow Man came again. Now he had Speckled Man's orange-haired sons with him. There was someone else in the truck, too. It was not Speckled Man. But it might have been Beard. Baez could never see anything clearly until dark. But she saw they had guns. And they had animals, a bulky male each. Gripping leashes and weapons, they crouched in the back of Yellow Man's truck, which was parked close, just at the top of the lane.

She took to her feet, ran to the end of her chain, barking.

Old Blue called — *Baez!* She followed Old Blue in the opposite direction, down the path to the ironwoods. Old Blue's scent was steady. Her footsteps even. She threw a length of rope into the branches. And then, when she caught the dangling end, hoisting a warm, scented food bundle high into the tree, her shirt rose up and gaped open; the cage that held her organs was rickety, deflated skin hanging.

Behind them the animals in the truck were on their feet now too, tails pointing up and stiff. Maybe it was because Baez was still bandaged that Old Blue grabbed her collar, shoved her, barking, into the trailer and locked the door. Inside, Baez pulled herself up into the kitchen sink. Dishes crashed to the floor. Through the window, she watched Old Blue pick up the stone that Yellow Man had thrown — she needed two hands — and walk, head high, towards the pickup where she plunked it into the bed. Maybe it landed on the boot of the bigger orange-haired son, for he jumped back and words came from his black gap of mouth. Old Blue held her hands out, open. The animals, pulling at their leads, took in her scent, tongues working in and out between her fingers. She caressed their heads like she did Baez's. Then Old Blue turned back towards the trailer. But she stayed in the yard, pacing around with her arms out like wings. Baez barked, scratching at the window screen.

Ba-ez!

She hushed.

Outside, Old Blue kept flapping her arms, calling out to the brown boys who would be coming in: *Pollitos, pollitos, pollitos,* she cried.

And as the sky darkened they came, they always did, popping up in the field. Darkness cut their figures in fine relief. Now Baez could see, darkness bringing clarity. But the intensity of smells and sounds still out-powered her sight.

¡Pollitos, pollitos!

Ducking low, the brown boys came running in towards the ironwoods. Behind Old Blue, the truck's headlights flashed. Baez bashed her skull into the window screen, each time feeling it loosen.

With guns and animals, the orange-haired sons hopped out of the pickup. Old Blue, her arms held out in a stiff cross, headed them off, yelling. The sons bore rope that they'd looped in the way Speckled Man had some seasons before, when Baez had dug herself out of the pen. The small son let loose with his gun, its firecrackers bursting into the sky, and then they let go of the animals who tore towards the ironwood stand, knocking Old Blue to the ground where she lay clutching her hip.

Feet scuttling in the sink, Baez had the screen loose enough to squeeze her head and shoulders out. Up the lane, Yellow Man's head darkened the cab. He blared the horn in warning as she leapt from the trailer and landed, four feet on the ground. Old Blue was on her hands and knees now. She turned, her face a blank circle of white. *Baez?*

The ironwoods creaked beneath the weight of the brown boys who were hiding in the branches. The orange-haired sons had regained the animals' leads, but still they screamed, jumping and clawing at the trunk. The sack of food swung in a wild circle, hitting the big son in the head. He smacked at it with his arm, but missed.

Baez entered into that hot rush of night. With one howl she had all their eyes—those glazed holes of the orange-haired sons, the bright yellow ones of the animals she herself had birthed in the pen behind the station, and those wide brown rounds of the boys in the tree. She jumped and lunged, tearing into fur and flesh, twisting to get at the thick muscle of neck, the veins within. Somewhere close, footsteps hit the ground; the brown boys went pounding off and away. Somewhere else, another set approached. Then a body came from behind her, a strong bone of arm closed around her neck, pulling, choking. Her teeth sunk into that bone as far as they would go. The bodyweight fell from her back, crawled into the shadows.

The animals went away with a whimper. She stood and growled, facing down the guns that the orange-haired sons pointed at her. She shuddered at the feel of the firecrackers coming. But then Old Blue was there, yelling and crying until the sons turned and, like their animals, went back to the truck.

The sweet blood in her mouth was Old Blue's. With her arm bent up and bleeding Old Blue staggered into the dark trailer. Baez crawled under the stoop, licking her raw cuts and scratches. The truck did not come back. But when she heard the pitter-patter of more brown-boy footsteps, she rushed them, barked them away from the trailer, from the ironwoods, from the land she would no longer let them cross. Let them take their pain to another place, this one had had its fill.

The night was long and it was empty. Above her, the trailer creaked. Old Blue paced, back and forth, back and forth. Doors slammed. Then came clattering and a crash. Old Blue came out with a big zippered bag. One arm was held tight to her chest. With her good hand she locked the bag in the car. Then she went back inside and paced some more. When the sky came grey, the car was full.

Now the sun is directly above. Half of her last day has passed. The shade of her tree falls in a wide, jagged circle. Flies needle her bald flesh. She shifts, flicks her tail. Beside the flies, a bounty, just one, is awake. His pants are wet in the front from where his bladder has leaked. He watches her and he cries, not bothering to lift his bound hands to wipe the drips that muddy his cheeks and chin. Instead of closed shoes, this one wears rubber sandals, his foot-wrappings loose and trailing out in streamers. The trailer door creaks open. Tattoo is shirtless, shiny. He strides towards an old brown cactus where he stops and undoes his pants. Then comes the gush of pent-up pee. Tattoo goes back inside, and soon all three bounties are asleep.

HONEY

They fall in and out of rhythm. The Zari Mountains recede behind them in the southwest. They seem to be veering east, cutting towards that lavender-and-chocolate range she remembers from the drive down. The Entradas are still not in sight.

She has to close her left eye and squint through the unbroken right lens of her glasses.

"Where is she, *niño?*"

He is lying. There is a trap ahead. At any moment he will dash away and leave her for the teens in the dune buggy who are lying in wait for the stupid trusting white woman that she is. And Marianne, is she also their hostage? She thought kidnappings only happened in the city.

"Look, *vieja.*" Birds fly above them towards a cluster of squared-off outcrops. "There is water."

They climb, pulling themselves from ledge to ledge. Winded, she stops and leans back. Morning is full-on now—a second night has passed—the sun a surging furnace of energy.

The boy grips her hand and pulls her on, deeper into the looming rock, the tightening static of the air. He drops her hand and she stumbles, tearing a hole in Marianne's jeans. She catches a flash of herself as nothing more than a bulb of brain tailed with narrow spinal cord. Like a tadpole she wriggles further into the vast dark of open life, blind to its turns and contours. Blinkered, limbless, she can only move forward.

The boy is gone. She calls out, bracing for a sudden crashing blow to the head, but then comes upon him after squeezing down a narrow crevice. He leans into a pool of water that cuts deep into the rock. He drinks from cupped palms, splashing his arms and face, cooling his bare feet. He is alone, a boy in the world, untethered to any people or place that she, at least, can imagine. She watches as he slips off his T-shirt. Like strumming a guitar, he runs his finger up and down the tattoo on his belly before rinsing his shirt and pulling it back over his head.

She crouches beside him, drinks like him. The water is warm. He calls the spring *ojo de agua*. Eye of water. There is a spa resort with that name west of Buzzard. The hospital had its last Christmas party there. The "eye" was a turquoise swimming pool that no one went into, dressed for cocktails as they all were. She tells the boy he is so smart to know these places.

"Good *coyote*."

"Wash, *vieja*," he says.

The face reflecting back in the water is gold with sand and scratched. Her glasses will not sit straight. Her feet scream with shock and relief when they hit the water. She takes off the sling, washes her calves, her arms, face, and neck.

The boy stretches in the shade of an overhang: eyes closed, knapsack for a pillow.

"My mom. How she look?"

The boy pretends not to hear.

She leans over and nudges his sneaker. "Marianne," she says, "she sad? She scared?"

The boy crosses his legs and runs his fingers along the rock. She slings her arm in the T-shirt, oily with her sweat and rubbed skin, and tries to imagine him showered and clean, sitting on her leather couch digesting a well-balanced meal. She'll have to take him into the city if she is going to pay him. She'll get Dinorah to interrogate him. What will Dinorah say to this boy? Will she chide him or hug him close? Maybe Dinorah will turn out to be a distant relation and offer to take him home. He could be rehabilitated yet. First, he would have to learn English, go to school with regular children so as not to be ghettoized like other migrants in Buzzard. He is obviously intelligent in some innate, potentially dangerous, way. The makings of a corporate mogul, or a drug lord.

"Not scared, not sad," the boy tells her in simple words. "She had the dog. She had a tree. I gave her water." But he reminds her they have to get to her fast. At least as fast as what Honey thinks of as the no-man's-land will allow.

The line on her finger from her wedding ring has already darkened. She takes it from her purse, tracing the engraving inside: her name, Keith's name, the day of their marriage five years ago.

"Who is he?" the boy asks.

"My husband? He is good man."

"A good man."

She shoves the band onto her fattened pinky, twisting it to fit. "A wonderful man. An excellent doctor. In ER." While he doesn't get the Emergency Room part she manages to tell him how they met. Her translation of "lucky break" leaves the boy with a sour expression.

"His name?"

"Keith."

"Dr. Keith." He pronounces it carefully.

"Dr. Keith pay lots for helping me and Marianne," Honey says.

The boy looks at her, big-eyed that she would think to remind him. "Of course he will pay. My life will be better then."

She tells him they are good people, willing to help him. She tells him that a woman named Dinorah—a friend, she calls her—comes from the other side of the border too. "She know what you can do." Does he want to go to school, for example?

Now his face clouds. "I don't know. Something to make money, something not picking fucking fruit. You think that's it for me, right?"

"You no English."

"I can learn, *vieja*."

She agrees. Anyone can. She tells him once Marianne didn't know how to speak English either. "When she learn, she free. Now your turn."

"My turn to be free." As the boy opens another tin of spaghetti he repeats her words even more slowly than she had. He offers her the first bite but she pushes it away, touching the hard bits of his fingernails.

"Old food," she says. "No good now."

He shrugs, laughs at something, perhaps her stupid words. He asks how she knows Spanish.

"Nowhere," is all she can think to say.

She sleeps somewhat, wakes to find the boy has somehow got hold of her purse and is going through her wallet. He looks closely at one of Keith's business cards then zips it into a pocket on his bag. Money is scattered between his bare feet.

"Boy," she whispers.

He starts, his body twitching.

"What you do?"

"Look." The plastic coating on her identity cards has started to melt. Her Visa sticks to her library card, which is now glued to her faculty ID and driver's license.

"You don't look like her now," he says, holding up the driver's license. "Maybe it won't even work now. Control would say you lie. Like any *pollo* going north to pick lettuce. You are not who you say." And you are old, he says counting out her age on his fingers.

"How much money for that?" she asks, snatching back the license.

The boy is wrong: she is still that woman in there, with her lean neck and blond swimmer's hair. Six feet tall. Corrective eyewear. On September 15, her forty-fourth birthday, she will have to make the annual trip to renew the stickers on the Ventura's plates. Marianne will be there to celebrate with her this year. Will this boy? Or will he just be a topic of conversation? Keith will steer her, guide her, help her get over—what? This. That is what Keith does: guide, advise, chairing so many damn medical committees because he is not just a good doctor but a good man. His hands, when he reset her collarbone, were so warm and soft and capable, so free of a wedding ring. The spell of comfort and well-being he cast over her was total and unquestionable and as-yet unbroken. Keith will know what to do.

The boy shrugs. He could get some money for her ID. "I could sell who you are. Who you were."

"Much, you think?"

He casts his arms wide. "I don't deal any more with *pollos*. It's dirty money, blood money. I find some other job."

"Your mom need money?"

"I have a grandma only. *Abuelita*." He says the name with a slow, curving lilt.

"Everyone has mom," she presses. "I have my Marianne. Who yours?"

The boy tells her his mother had eyes his colour and wore pink high heels. She went north to work in a factory. He thinks she made it to Buzzard City though his grandma says she only got as far as San Wren. "She sewed clothes and sent money home to me and Abuelita." And then she stopped. Like his friend's mom, Juanita. Both of their moms are gone. Many women are gone. In his country Honey would be an old woman, just as he calls her, a *vieja*.

"What name your mom give you?"

The boy ignores her and just speaks on about his friend. His eyes shine and some slight upturn plays on his lips.

And where is he, the boy's friend?

"Lost somewhere. We got separated leading some *pollos* across. Ocho came and shot at us and we all ran, scared. Ocho got the *pollos*."

"And your friend?"

The boy shakes his head. "You're wearing his hat." The thought of his friend tempers the orange sheen of his eyes. His shoulders lose their angular tension.

She says the boy will have a better life in Zopilote. "Don't worry. Please. I care for you there." She does like Keith or Marianne, trying to find his eyes, to share a smile.

Worried? He has never worried before. What is it even to

worry? He picks up the scattered coins and drops them into the zipper of her wallet. In paper, there is only one bill: a ten.

"You have a job?"

"Teacher."

The boy whistles. He taps his right temple. "Smart *vieja*." But not so smart out here. "You should not have left the car. The Jesus *indio* would have found you."

She catches her wallet when he tosses it. She rummages through its pockets. He missed the picture of Keith she had long ago tucked into the billfold. It was taken before she knew him, when he was married to his first wife, whose half of the photo has been cut away. His hair was already grey, contrasting with his dark tan and open smile.

The boy takes the photo and peers into it, holding it close to his face. "He is an old man. But he has a good face. No kids?"

"No kids. Just me and Keith. Big love, lots of love." She takes back the picture. Then says, "Who is *indio*? Johnny-for-Jesus, no?"

The boy calls him the Jesus *indio* but doesn't know his real name. "He left water for us, like El Esqueleto." But he and Marianne broke the rules by coming into the *Las tierras vacías*. "Only strong ones can come through here. *Coyotes* like me and Juan."

Juan is the name of his lost friend, the lost son of lost Juanita, the owner of the hat on her head. He tells her how everyone wants to go through the *Las tierras vacías*.

"The land of no man," she says to him in English. She asks if that's why there is a bounty.

"Only the strong boys should be in your country, *vieja*, no ill boys, or slow or weak." But didn't he himself break the rules by helping boys cross? No. He justifies this by saying he makes no guarantees to them.

When she asks if he had *pollos* die on him or if he had to leave them behind, his face drains of its bit of softness and his shoulders square up.

"Yes. I did."

"Died?" Honey whispers. "*Pollos* like me?"

He shakes his head. "No. I lost them and found them again, that's all." Then he says they're lucky he did even that, didn't have to. He takes care of himself first. He says he is perfect for her country, therefore. "Don't you think, *vieja*?"

"Yes," she says. "I think."

Her keychain is a plastic cruise ship, a souvenir from last summer with Keith.

The key to their Ventura is capped in bright red plastic. The one for the condo is marked with blue. It is nice, in the sky, she tells him. "High, thirty-three. Up."

He frowns, unbelieving. "One day I will see this, how you live."

She smiles.

"You don't believe me?" he spits.

"Yes, I believe."

When he asks if she makes pictures too she cringes. "No. My mom."

The boy would like to draw comics. Did he say already that he knows how to tattoo?

"Yes."

He wants to see Honey's ankle again. One day he will get his lines that thin. The boy's finger traces a shape in the sand. A chess pawn? No — it is a keyhole. He touches his left forearm. "This is tattooed here, on Juan." He met Juan in

San Wren. They got together taking over *pollos*. "Together we were the best."

"Look," he points at a dark spot moving across the horizon. A coyote, he says. "Or else it is that crazy dog, the dog of El Esqueleto."

No. "Baez have big, big head."

The animal stops, watches them, its ears peaked. When it is gone again the boy goes back to drawing shapes in the sand. Or he writes *Juan,* only to quickly erase it.

"You read, write? How?"

The boy throws a stone at her foot. He shouts. "I went to school, *vieja.* I tried hard and I read each day. You think we're stupid?"

"No. Just underprivileged, underdeveloped," she says in English. "Buzzard, school, need money," she says, trying Spanish again. "Many boys and girls no go school. You see?"

"I'll teach myself," he says. "I'll speak English perfectly. And you'll still speak shitty Spanish."

He goes back to his shapes, his *Juan*s in the sand.

Honey looks deep into Keith's photo, perhaps as he is looking at the one of her he carries. He might right now at this precise moment be swimming in his hotel pool, getting his blood flowing after a long day sitting, listening, shaking hands with his international counterparts, nodding at their eager English. When he phones the condo he'll assume she drove to the coast like she had lied and said she might. She closes her eyes. Water rushes against her skin as she dives into the Olympic-sized pool where she does her laps, resting only on Sunday when she bike-rides instead. Somewhere, a whistle blows. A coach barks encouragement from the deck. As her body cuts through the resistance of the water, her mind fuses with her arms, hips, bringing consciousness to her physical rhythm. Then there is the comforting fatigue that invades her shoulders as she climbs back into the Ventura, hair still damp, skin tight. Her belly weakens in anticipation of Keith's protein-rich breakfast. She hears the boy's Spanish but cannot respond. She is in the pool again, dissolving into the push and pull of her daily battle. Wriggling and blind, pressing ahead.

CHÁVEZ

Light thickens, gives to gold then falls across the floor planks, warming his back. It is quiet. He hears that on farms way in the north, pickers have to find their own places to live. They sleep outside in tents or under bridges and then walk long distances to get to the fields. He has to get out of this work. He hates it more than any other picker, he is sure. The smell of sweat and dirty sheets clouds the air, hard work and the zing of burgeoning testosterone. His stomach growls and thirst tightens his throat. Then the pickups pull in. The yard fills with chatter and clatter, the water pump creaks and creaks.

A crowd of ball-capped kids—boys and teens—spills into the bunkhouse, their shoes heavy with caked mud, knees and hands crimson. Straw clings to clothes, lips, hair. They smell bright with coconut suntan lotion and the rotten fruit caked under fingernails and in the treads of their shoes—some kind of sticky jam stew. They claim their beds, peeling dirty clothing from their humid backs, groping through gym bags and plastic sacks for something cleaner.

Most nod at him. Some smile, tell him their name, and others, too tired, simply look his way and blink. Mario comes in last. He finds his bed, unlaces his sneakers, lies down — hat on, eyes closed.

"Hey," Chávez whispers. "Mario." Mario does not respond. That's because Mario was just the name Juan had made up for him.

Chávez leans over and touches the boy's shoulder. "Hey."

Mario sits up. Through the shuffle of bodies, the rustle of tossed shirts and pants, his bleary eyes land on Chávez.

"You?" His small voice gets lost in the clamour. "Those eyes."

"Me."

They stand, step forth.

"I thought you were dead," Chávez says.

Mario's face is less round. It has been almost two years. His gaze is tight: if he looks away or blinks, Chávez might disappear. And his voice when he speaks has both deepened and lost its Indian accent.

"What are you doing here?"

Chávez takes off his hat and removes the fold of dollars from the inside band. "It's your fee back."

Mario shakes his head.

"How about Diego?" Chávez looks around the bunk-house for the brother. Though he sees the older boy in his dreams, he cannot remember his face.

Mario says, "My brother was not called Diego. You called him that."

When he asks Mario what their real names are, Mario just shakes his head. "My brother died in the hills. Not far from where you left us."

Chávez looks down at Mario's boots. "But not you. You lived." He wishes he could say he would give his life so Diego could have lived, but then he would be lying.

"God chose me. God left me alone, with no brother. I don't know why yet."

A crowd has gathered around them. One face is darker than the rest. Is this what they mean by black? Is this an African boy?

"I didn't mean to leave you," he says. "I ran scared. But I went back and you were gone."

A sharp clang resounds from across the yard. There is a flurry of movement and bedsprings. Mario fades into the jostle of the supper rush.

"Bring me mine, hey," some boy calls weakly from an upper berth.

In English someone else keeps saying he can't open his hands because of some bee stings.

"One of you untie my boots?" The African boy sits on the edge of his cot, holding out his hands which are wrapped in ice packs. "Lost a whole day's pay," he says, shaking his head.

Mario bends over on one knee, changing into the boots that were his brother's. Chávez shoves the fold of money into the pocket of Mario's shirt.

"Please forgive me," he says in English, the way he's practiced, and then, though it's more difficult, he repeats the line in Spanish. Then he walks out with the other pickers, turning back at the door. Mario is tucking the money between the bee-stung hands of the African boy.

BAEZ

She got the hole so deep the top of her head was lower than the rim of the ground. Behind her, Old Blue's legs and shirt were splattered with dirt. With closed eyes, Old Blue picked at the sand and root and rock. She opened her mouth, ate from what was in her palm.

The morning after Baez bit Old Blue, Black Braid arrived early, sounded his horn. *Marianne!* Baez came out from under the stoop. Black Braid knelt over her, his wooden cross swinging and his dark eyes narrowing as they travelled over her fresh cuts and scratches, the shoulder where the Yellow Man's stick had struck her.

Marianne!

The door to the trailer opened. Black Braid disappeared inside. Then he came out and drove away, fast. He drove back with cans of soda, food in a white bag, water with which he filled Baez's bowl. Black Braid and Old Blue spoke in the trailer above her while she hid in the shade of the stoop. When they came out, Old Blue's arm was wrapped in the grey towel that had hung by the bathroom sink. But it was not grey now. Now it was stained dark, as if all the colour that should have been in Old Blue's face had drained into that piece of fabric. They crouched over Baez. Old Blue kept her towelled arm tucked in. Old Blue and Black Braid spoke. Old Blue cried. Old Blue filled Baez's bowls and chained her to the post then pressed her face into her fur. Old Blue climbed into Black Braid's truck and then they drove up the road.

Now, an engine sounds, coming near. A not-so-white white van chugs up the path towards the trailer; the orange arrows on the side are chipped and bleached out. Behind the plywood, her children take to their feet, yowling. Their caging rattles. Jittery scent cuts the air. The Cactus Men are two. These ones are sunburned, near as tall as Old Blue, with bristled faces. Instead of eyes glassed in black, theirs are silver reflections of the desert. But the shaggy, saggy greeny-brown from head to boot is the same. Some Cactus Men came to Old Blue's once too. They walked about the trailer, the fields, wrote in their notebooks and went away. Then, like now, a brown-and-yellow dog was belted into the front seat. It is not the same dog that Speckled Man once mated her with, but it could be. And it could be her mother, too. She has that dog's blood in her just as she had that other dog's children in her womb.

Glove leads the shuffling brown boys to the white car. Tattoo carries their packs. A Cactus Man opens the back door. Their dog's barking rollicks the buzz of day, fuelling the frenzy of her children again. Amid the shaking, breaking, cracking air, the second Cactus Man locks the hands of the brown boys behind their backs with bracelets, and, hands under armpits, lifts each up into the rear. When the door slams shut, the brown boys, through the window glass, turn into sharp black silhouettes.

The Cactus Men give Glove some bills of crinkled paper then disappear into the bright dust. Glove and Tattoo count the money that once would have stacked thick. Once, there were many boys for Glove and Tattoo to catch. Soon the Cactus Men will not have to come with their dog or their money. Baez will have died by then, her children released into the desert. Then, maybe, the Cactus Men will take Glove and Tattoo back over the grey wall too.

HONEY

The soles of Marianne's tennis shoes are starting to crack. Rocks keep getting in. And the left one is rubbing her heel raw. She would kill to get her Nikes back. But it is every boy for himself here. She would have stolen them too.

The ground is scaled crust. Somewhere below there must be burps of moisture, for some things do grow: silk-haired cactus and squat twists of tree; creosote and low, silvery bushes in whose branches wrens have nests and under which rabbits hide. The holes they see dug around a mesquite are from coyotes, which, the boy says, can get deep enough to grasp roots and suck the moisture from them. And there are snakes, some alive and many dead, bellies baked. Their carcasses are strung out beside dropped water bottles and cans and diapers and rolls of toilet paper; a comic book, a dusty boot. She picks up a toilet roll and puts it in her purse. She does not pee here. The boy says to save it up. Don't sweat, either. With each drop of moisture she doesn't replace, she loses a little bit of her life.

They stop and the boy eats the last tin of spaghetti.

She says again it is bad, as in expired, but cannot make him understand.

He smacks his lips and rubs his belly — "Yummy-yum, *vieja*. Too good for you?"

He says they are almost out of water again. He says a person can live maybe two days here without it.

The pain in her arm is down to a five. She opens and closes her stiffening right fist and with this hand touches her head. The cut is closing. Beneath her palms Marianne's jeans are soft. She rubs her legs, releasing the smell of that animal.

"Tell me, again. My mom, she say what to you?"

He opens his mouth to speak, but staggers instead. He doubles over and clenches his belly, dropping the plastic bag.

The boy's face is slick with a different kind of sweat and his eyes water. He pushes her hand away from his forehead and walks on.

"The hills there," he points. Then the boy halts, crossing his legs. "Please," he groans. "Please go away." His shirt sticks and his body rolls with trembles. "Go," he says, his face is beaded. "Go, go," he hollers, gripping his gut and clenching.

"Go? Where?"

He screams something. His face is pale then it purples. She picks up his bag and water bottles and huddles in a stretch of pale grass, some yards away. She rocks on her heels. The sky lightens.

He calls to her. He waves for her to come. He is reduced in colour and size, his jeans swallowing him. Beneath the bill of his cap his eyes are blistered and his cheeks are streaked with the dry salt of tears.

"Fucking spaghetti," he whispers, his voice shakes. "I am vacío." Empty.

He takes his bag and bottles without a look and walks on towards what are now red and lavender hills.

"You need salt and water," she says. She knows this from Monica. Or was it Keith? The boy lets her put a hand on his thin shoulder. He blinks up at her. The hand that dangles limp at his side is cold and wet.

"Let me help you," she says in English. "We have to do this together."

They pull each other up a slope that grades into a ledge

obscured by scrub and tree-shell. And the mountains? Gone now, receding back and back like a forgotten dream.

At the plateau the boy drops to his knees, curls into a ball.

She ties the boy's plastic bags around any living green she sees within the scrub, forming neat balloons. Dawn has come and gone. In a few hours the boil will be on. The boy sleeps in the shade of a high, curved boulder. Figures move along the southern horizon sprawled below. They are too far away to call to.

The boy opens his eyes. His head is hot in her hand. She pours the last of the water into his mouth. He sleeps again—if he dreams, it will be of sparkling rivers and cold Coke. His lids flutter, birds beneath.

She drapes him in one of the T-shirts he has in his pack. She takes her purse and an empty water bottle. In the plastic bag, she finds the boy's penlight and Juan's hat, which she pulls on.

"I go not far," she tells the boy, shaking him.

"Once there were two little *pollos*," he says. "*Vieja*, I'm sorry they died."

"It's okay," she tells him in English, too tired to use his language. "You can only do your best, little boy, that's it."

When he is still again, she slips down into the desert basin. She can hardly breathe. Like in outer space, there is no oxygen here, it is just dry.

Up on the hill, she spots the boy's boulder, a soft, tumbled egg rocking on its wide bottom. She closes her eyes and locks it in.

North and west. She stumbles over pant-cuffs, Marianne's denim clothes stretched and torn, burned by the sun right through to the skin. Behind her the hill with the boy's oval rock has disappeared into the horizon and before her, hills stretch on, rippling out. Marianne is in this place. She will find her and she will still be alive.

To remember her way, Honey speaks what she sees, loud and full, using all her voice:

Boot prints

Snake tracks

Plastic blue razor

Jackson's sardines

Frigo mango juice can

Luna Springs water bottle

Scarecrow cactus

Stick like a bone

T-shirt rag

Hills rolling like m-shaped birds

And every five hundred steps she drops a hot metal key from the cruise-ship ring. Thud, in the sand: condo, car, desk, Xerox room, pool locker, Marianne's trailer. The keys to the Tribal are still stuck in the ignition.

Tire iron

Heart-shaped rock

Ocotillo skeleton

Behind her the dropped keys glisten, nuggets of shimmer and shine. And up ahead, there is a shallow wash. In it, a twist that is barely an ironwood tree, bottomed by a brittle patch of creosote. She huddles beneath the tree, drinking in its shade. A rumbling erupts through the hot sand. She sits up. A cloud of dust comes barrelling down — no, up — from the south. The low-riding dune buggy materializes, a gutted scream, a tarnished gleam. As it nears, the driver's helmet shimmers, then the passenger's: or rather, the gunner's.

She stays still.

Sand explodes, some ten feet off.

The second shot, taken from fifty feet, is as wide as the first.

She flattens herself. She is part of the earth.

The teens hoot and *wheeeeee*. An animal, maybe ten yards away, rushes past. Mottled orange and grey, perked elfin ears, and dropped tail. A coyote. It goes north, into the distant hills, feet barely touching the ground. Its motion is sleek against the azure sky and white sand beneath. There is a puff of dirt with each of its footfalls. It bounds forth, close to her tree, its eyes pierced with terror. Behind it, the dune buggy, sun-drunk, spins out after its target, the gunner hooting. Then, along with the coyote, it disappears into the horizon and is gone.

CHÁVEZ

Yellow jackets had hidden in the fingers of Ishmael's gloves. His right hand got stung four times, his left just once. He keeps them iced overnight, going to and from the chest freezer out in the yard where the pickers keep soda and beer. In the morning the swelling is down.

Mario picks far away at the other end of the field, while Ishmael and Chávez get rows alongside each other. Ishmael shows him how to clear the plants fast but without getting too many nubbly green fuckers — Peacock shits his pants over anything unripe. Peacock watches them so they don't eat too much and will even check to see if their tongues are red. The pickers get to eat the bad fruit: wormed, misshapen, overripe, and under-grown. Peacock's sons do the watching too—they march up and down the rows in their big brown boots and shirts with no sleeves and if their sunglasses are not on their faces they wear them on the backs of their necks.

"That is just stupid-looking," Chávez says to Ishmael.

They laugh. They speak English together because while they both go "huh?" over each other's accents, Ishmael's Spanish is worse than Chávez's English. They say how if these farmers were smart they'd plant their crops on something like a factory conveyor belt so all them pickers wouldn't have to break their backs bending over.

"Know what?" Ishmael says human beings are not supposed to plant that may strawberries or any other crop. "It's crazy!" You should have a few rows for your family, your neighbours, and that's it.

Chávez nods. He thinks about Abuelita's little garden and her market cart and how she herself told him it was time he went north. "Come back when you have enough for a house, some land. Make a life for yourself, by yourself. I am almost through with mine."

"But here," Ishmael says, "they worship one god."

"What god?"

"The god's name is profit." Ishmael stops picking and looks hard at Chávez. Bits of straw are sticking out of his dense, curly hair. How does African hair feel to the touch? Does he comb it? And will Ishmael ever get a sunburn? And if he tattooed Ishmael's skin, would the ink even show up?

Ishmael says, "You do realize we're slaves, right?"

"Slaves—sure." He wipes his face on the back of his arm. Berries suck. The plants are so low you practically have to crawl on your belly to get your hand under them. "But only for a while."

"And then what?"

"Oh, I got some money coming."

"Like your granny's going to die and leave you a million?"

"Naw. Just a debt that's owing. I'm going to Zopilote to collect."

"To where?"

He smiles. "Buzzard City."

Ishmael sizes him up, eyes narrowed. "West, isn't it? Down a bit to the south? That's where I'm gonna go."

On Saturday they take bikes into town. There are all these old-fashioned Christians: ladies and girls in bonnets and long skirts, men with beards driving horse-and-buggies. The ladies sell homemade bread as good as Abuelita's and speak a weird flattened Spanish. He and Ishmael eat on the curb and then he looks through the book bins in the thrift stores while Ishmael hunts for T-shirts with sports team logos. He had thought the pink people in towns stared at *him* — but Ishmael really gets it. Eyes pop out of people's heads — that's before they look away. And any store they go into, they get breathed on right down the back of the neck.

"They're not all bad," Ishmael says of these pink people. He wants to go to Buzzard because he figures there he won't feel so black anymore. Chávez tries not to think about Ishmael as black and after a while it works. He is his new friend who is very smart and careful the way he watches the world with his narrow brown eyes and who happens to live inside a warm purply skin.

The night air is chill. Peacock gives them firewood, only they have to split it with an axe that is dull and heavy. Some pickers have bought marshmallows to roast, but most spent their pay on cigarettes, canned peanuts, and soda. Others, older ones, have beer and whiskey but hide it because Peacock is some weird kind of Christian. "A fucking wacko."

Chávez tells them that "cock" means a penis and the pickers all laugh. Then he translates "pea." That's fucked up, they all say, screwing up their faces. What the hell? "It's like if your name was Mr. Bean-Dick. Or Lentil-Wang." Chávez smiles. He doesn't tell them his dictionary says peacock is also, technically, a bird.

One or two pickers say that if you want to get to Zopilote you need to have a bit of dough. Otherwise you sleep on the street and some pink fuckers stomp your ass.

The flames crackle, shooting sparks up towards a full-faced moon. Blossoms sweeten the air—grape hyacinths are popping—competing with the sour smell from the town's beer factory that the western breeze draws in. He sticks close to Ishmael. He keeps catching Mario watching him from across the fire but then Mario always looks away. Ishmael says he gave the money back to Mario. Without knowing what it was all about, Ishmael told Mario not to be a fuck-up and just take it. Ishmael said to him and then to Chávez, "You two are as good as even."

Someone passes whiskey. There is talk of *Las tierras vacías.* Chávez translates for Ishmael. "Empty land. Even though, really, there always seemed to be lots of life around. Birds and boys and crazy whites."

"Ten times it took me to cross," says an older picker, between sips of Bud. "Each time Control caught me. But that was before."

Another says, "Me, I got over in twelve."

A kid in a cap with a bumblebee on the front tells them

he got rounded up and almost died in the back of Ocho's buggy. "Then some kid with these scissors came and got us out." Bumblebee says that kid saved them from who-knows-what. "He got left to deal with Ocho."

"So he got a shit-kicking in other words?"

"Butt-fucked too, I bet."

"Yeah, I heard Ocho's a fag for sure."

"Or just bored. Like being in jail or something, the way he lives just him and his dogs and that other kid."

"Yeah, what's his name?"

No one knows. Just that he has lots of tattoos.

Then Chávez says, "So what's with the dogs?"

Bumblebee shrugs. "Like he used to have a gun but that got robbed off him."

The kid with the beer goes: "Control don't want no dead bounty, right, so he takes them down with the dogs."

Ishmael says it's the same as where he is from. "Some of the dogs are wolves, though, I swear, and they only go for our black asses, no one else's."

What country is he from?

No one has heard of the name.

"It's small," Ishmael says. "But it's in the Bible."

He and Ishmael walk back to the bunkhouse. By flashlight they throw all their money onto Chávez's mattress. Next Saturday they'll have enough to get as far as a chicken farm Ishmael's heard of, further west near Lucinda County.

"That's where you make the real dough," he says.

They find the town on Chávez's map.

"How much savings you think we need?" asks Ishmael.

Chávez scrounges in his bag for the book he's reading: *A Christmas Carol*. The cover's ripped off and the pages are brown. He passes Ishmael the bookmark, holding it by the edges.

"So this Dr. Keith owes you money?" Ishmael says.

Chávez says, "It's his wife. We got to find her there. I got five thousand owing."

"No way? What for?"

He takes a breath, leans in, and tells Ishmael the story — or most of it, anyway.

BAEZ

Scritch-scratch.

Finally her nails had hooked into the tough, muscled roots by which the mesquite drank. Chomping and chewing and sucking, she wrestled a hairy tangle from the earth. On her belly, she pulled herself from the hole, plopped the roots into Old Blue's lap. With nose and paw, she prodded Old Blue awake. Old Blue did not move. From her face there still came a misty whiff of air. So she butted Old Blue until the old woman fell away from the tree, crumpling into a limp pile. She barked. Old Blue's eyes opened: however tinted were the whites, the green pupils as yet pierced into focus. Old Blue's good hand found the dirty root in her lap. She kneaded its tendrils then she held it out, shaking her head. *Good girl, Baez.* So Baez ate the root, jawing until its molecules were sucked clean. And when she looked up, licking her lips, Old Blue's eyes were closed again.

After he'd taken Old Blue away, Black Braid had come back to the trailer. He was alone. He filled her bowls. When he knelt down, cooing at her from where she hid under the stoop, his face was blank, backlit by morning sun. Then he left again.

Nights alone she barked the brown boys away — one or two at a time now, few, fewer, few. And nights Yellow Man came with his truck, but just flashed his lights and did not stop. Then Black Braid did not come. Her bowls dried. Searching for any lost traces of Old Blue, she stretched her chain to the ironwoods, roamed the section of field through which the brown boys came trampling. She killed mice, lizards. She laid their bodies out in a ring. And she chased a white-tail rabbit, blasting ahead until she connected with the very tip of its tail. And then the collar choked her. As the animal criss-crossed away, she strained forth, cutting off her air until she felt the post in front of the trailer slipping. She ran and tugged, ran and tugged, struggling against the chain's reach. The fur around her neck thinned, the skin beneath burned, and when a night of that passed and day came again the post popped out of the ground. She ran then, into the desert, towards the mountains. There was nowhere else to go. Behind her, the chain dragged and the post clattered, bumpity-bump, across the gravelled terrain.

The hunger in her belly is heavy, pulling her back to her hilltop pen, to the hot ground where she lies, to the food bowl that is — still empty. Since the bald birds landed there is less bird call, snake slither, and no more rodents squeak. And since the bald birds came she drags her fallen hips into the corner to squat. Like Old Blue, she stays in the thin shadow of her even thinner tree. The sun keeps moving across the sky.

Night cools. Instead of heat, it is the dark that oppresses as does the pain in her arm, which shoots to the surface. She talks it down. She follows the tire tracks as they snake north, saving the boy's penlight for when cloud washes the moon away. She is slow, with her two left feet. Her breathing is as heavy as a dog's.

In the whole world no one knows where she is right now. Neither does she. She is in the swimming pool, her body slicing against the defiant strength of the water, sputtering at a noseful of chlorine. When she blew out the candles on her thirty-eighth birthday cake, she had promised herself she would swim a minimum of fifty laps, six mornings a week, for the rest of her life. Her first nights with Keith, she'd brought her swimsuit to his place and set her alarm for five-thirty.

"If you don't like it, that's too bad," she had said.

"And if I love it?" Keith had replied.

Half a mile on, the tire tracks converge with those of the coyote the teens had been hunting. It had run hard, maybe reaching the hills before they got it. But then the tire tracks skid, and the paw prints peter out into a final stagger. Now the coyote is a humped-up carcass, on its side some twenty feet off. An eye glows in the moon and the pink ribbon of tongue lolls in the bloody sand. There is a hole in its belly: life oozes out while ants burrow in.

The tracks continue north. After three hundred and twelve footsteps — she counts them — yellow headlights shine through the dark. Closer still, there is music, then the carry of voices. She stops when shadows rise; the pair of black silhouettes is crisp against the night.

The two teens lean against the dune buggy, passing cigarettes and drinks. They wear wide-brimmed hats instead of helmets, their bodies snugged up in tight jeans and their high-top Adidas long and sleek. Dust and smoke glow in the headlights. Their shrill, tight-lipped whistles break the air. When a lone coyote howls back, the teens laugh, whistle again.

They have a small fire going and a smell hangs in the air like they have roasted processed meat. The music turns to a low, bassy beat: the sound of the poor and the angry, of blacks and browns, white kids going along for the ride. That slice of self-awareness comes again. She knows she has little to lose—or is it that she has a lot? She cannot think beyond getting water for the boy and the need to know that Marianne is okay. There is nothing outside of those things. Her two feet step towards the light.

"¡Hola!" she calls out. She hugs her purse, her slung arm.

The teens get rigid. The taller silhouette must be the one called Ocho, the one with the glove. The shorter one—she thinks of him as Curly—is the one who reached into the Tribal and thought she was her mom. But for a difference in height, they cut the same slight shadow: wide hats, belted waists, narrow chests.

She calls to them, again, in Spanish.

The music cuts out. A can falls to the dirt, liquid soaks in. It is so quiet she hears the emptying glug.

"Who's there?" Ocho calls, his voice cracking.

"¡Hola!"

"What the fuck?" they say in English.

The teens pace in the sheer spotlight the dune buggy

casts. Then Ocho grabs Curly by the scruff of the neck. He pushes him. "Go look. See what's out there."

Curly falls into the dark, some few feet away from where she now crouches, perfectly still, in something thorny and dry. He is motionless, waiting for his eyes to adjust to the dark. She waits with him, her adrenaline surging. Then he undoes his fly and reaches inside. His piss hits the ground hard. He waves it around in a stream. He wipes his hands on his jeans, zips up. He curses, scuffing around, then yells out to Ocho: he can't see anything.

When he trips over her crouched body he falls to his knees. "*¡Pinche!*" He finds his feet and, lashing out, he kicks.

She tucks in her injured arm and rolls away from his shoe. "*Agua*," she whispers. "*Por favor.*" Finding Curly's wrist, she pulls him close. "*Shhhh.*"

His breath smells of stale beer and tobacco. She is close enough to feel his thumping heart.

"Hey, what you see?" Behind them, Ocho's voice is cracked and nervous.

"Nothing!" Curly calls back. Then he leans into her: "Esqueleto. Get the hell away from here."

His arm in her grip is taut and sinewy. "Water, *agua*," she says. Struggling with Spanish, she manages, "I begging you. Some water."

"Esqueleto, you are fucking crazy. Why do you come out here, if not to die?"

"I helped you," she whispers. "You and the *pollitos*—I gave water. I gave food, no? *Ayúdame*," she whispers. "Help me. A boy sick. A boy like you."

"Hey!" Ocho screams. A gunshot pops, wild, into the night.

Curly's hand goes right for her injured arm, crunching down on the slung-up elbow. "Who's this little *niño?*" he hisses. "The one who got in your car?"

His face is so close he could bite her cheek, her lip. She grips his hot moist shirt. She says she doesn't know, the boy has no name. She says his eyes are orange and then tries begging him again.

He pushes her off. "Get out of here. Before Ocho sees you."

When she gropes his arms he punches at her. His fist connects with her shoulder, then a thigh. His shadow falls over her. She covers her head with her hands, curls up to protect ribs and guts. She closes her eyes and waits for more.

But Curly runs from her. After calling out to Ocho, their engine revs and the dune buggy rips away.

CHÁVEZ

Ishmael shakes his head. "You were a *coyote?*"

"Please forgive me," he says, like the Noah's ark lady taught him. He looks Ishmael in the eye. He feels different after telling someone, like he has taken off a dry clay mask. He even touches his face, brand new as it is.

"And that one with the boots, it's him? Mario?"

Chávez says yes. "God must have made it happen this way, right?"

Ishmael considers this. He says Chávez is lucky and unlucky. Unlucky that the one named Diego is dead; lucky he and the other one—Mario—are alive.

"You think Mario will forgive me?"

Ishmael says yes, in time. "I believe it." But maybe he

won't forgive Juan. "What happened to him?"

He tells Ishmael that after losing the others he headed back to San Wren. He was sure Juan would be there. He tells him that after walking south a day and a half without water he picked up tire tracks that may or may not have been Ocho's. He followed them, and so ended up zig-zagging all over the desert. There was no sign of any other boys. He felt alone and very scared.

On the second day he came to a pair huddled up in an arroyo. The older boy had a welt on his cheek the size of a tomato and coloured the same. Chávez paid them ten whole dollars for a boiling hot can of Pepsi and he told them how to get north to the mountains.

"Where's your *coyote*?" he asked them.

"Ocho got him. But we ran."

He pointed at the red lump on the boy's cheekbone.

The boy stuck out his chin. "Yeah, I got a wallop, but we got away in the end."

"He alone? Ocho?"

"No." They said there were two now. But all they remembered were the shiny helmets.

"Like spacemen?"

"Yeah."

"How about two Indian kids?" He finished the Pepsi and then crushed the can under his heel. Back in the village they used to do this — one on each foot — and pretend they were wearing cowboy boots.

No Indian brothers either, they said. He made them promise that if they saw them — Mario and Diego, he called them — to say he was really sorry.

He went on. His throat baked. He moved heavy, as if

through a swamp. He was going in a circle. Water caches he and Juan knew were drained. So he drank from stagnant dregs collected in abandoned irrigation wells, thick with drowned bees—chunks of which he tried to chew, stingers catching in his teeth. Maybe it was his time to die now, for all the bullshit he'd done. Abuelita would never know what had happened to him and that was better. She could stick up a picture of him next to the one of his mom, but then he remembered she had no picture of him and no one else in the world did, either. Except for the tattoos he had done, it was like he was never there on earth. He didn't want it to be that way—he wanted to live.

He went where birds and animals led him, drinking at their mountain trickles or dipping his fingers into moisture left in cactus crooks. On and on he went, looking for Juan. In a low, scrubby valley he watched a rattler sunning itself on a flat grey stone right near one of the Jesus *indio*'s caches. He threw a rock, then another, driving the snake beneath the stone. He drank a jug on the spot and put another in his pack. He picked up some buggy tracks. The Jesus *indio*'s? Then another set. Ocho's? He took the older set, reasoning them to be Ocho's—otherwise, the jugs would have been punctured.

The tracks cut clear for a mile, running out at a wide, rugged outcropping. He climbed up, the rock warm on his hands. Chávez tells Ishmael how at the crest it was narrow and jagged. He crouched, squinting out. Far in the south something gleamed that might have been nothing or might have been the border wall if it was going to be as high as Juan kept saying. Suddenly—he thought he was dreaming—a dog barked. He ducked back, his stupid fucking big shoes tripping him up. The barking came again: sharp and high. He crawled to the edge and looked down — way down.

"I'd know El Esqueleto anywhere, man."

"Really, it was her?"

Chávez nods. "And that goddamn dog too."

Ishmael swallows. "Holy shit."

Chávez smiles.

BAEZ

When night was shrinking, she had cleared the hole of its roots. Above, the mesquite sighed and moans leaked out, draining into the porous air. Or was that Old Blue who sighed, her jaw dropped, mouth slackened? In her good hand, Old Blue clutched a small triangle of hard grey stone. She'd plucked it from the mound of earth against which she leaned. The triangle's dull edges were furrowed, for it had been chipped away from some larger piece. Old Blue had held the triangle out for Baez to sniff and lick clean, which she did. Then, with thumb and finger and shirt sleeve, Old Blue rubbed that shard until it glowed silvery with warmth. Old Blue held it to her lips then, and spoke into it. And Baez went back to digging the hole — *scritch-scratch* — adding length to the depth and width, and more earth to the mound growing up behind her.

After running away from the trailer, she had slogged through the flat, tangled desert, the chain snaking out behind her, the post clanking at each rock and soda can, catching on cactus, twisting around shrubs. Soon she was trailing uprooted plants, patches of caked rodent fur, human garbage — cloth, plastic, paper. It weighed her down, the chain, the post, all those trawled trappings, eroding the strength of her already aching body, sending rabbits and rats fleeing, snakes retreating. Brown boys, when she found them, ran from her. She ate shit, carcass, shallow root; she drank from a still puddle thick with larvae. When the sun was hottest she hid in an arroyo—chain, post, and accumulated dregs piled beside her in a heavy nest. Upon a sharp jut of rock she rubbed at the leather collar, each slip cutting further into her balding neck.

At dusk, she woke. Night was taking size and shape. The scent of an animal brought her to her feet. The silhouette of a male coyote was watching her from high on a distant hill. Its yowl pierced the sky. When, in a snap, it disappeared, she followed the arroyo up towards where it had been. Up in the hills, she picked up the coyote tracks—marked with mouldering urine, a coil of scat—and, dragging the snaking chain and the anchor, she went on towards the mountains.

Now Glove returns to the trailer. Tattoo retrieves the fiercest of her children: a bitch with a long whippet nose, short bulge of tail, eyes small and black, muscled hunter's body. He muzzles her and, holding tight to a shortened lead, walks her around the yard, up a hill, back again. Then he unfolds a chair and, with the female at his feet, sits in the trailer's shade with a thumping radio and no shirt. Black glasses blank out his eyes, a ball cap shields his shorn head. The bitch's hot black eyes are on Baez, sucking her of life like her lips had once taken her milk. When a third bald bird lands in the tree above Baez, Tattoo's bitch barks at it, straining at her muzzle, tiring herself out. Then, like Tattoo and his animal, the birds fall into sleep. The deep part of afternoon settles in.

HONEY

The last time Honey saw her, Marianne said: "Transcendence can't be taught, Honey." Then she handed Honey a rolled-up canvas, held with a brittle elastic band.

Honey had glanced back at Keith. His long body was stooped over the trunk, wrestling with one of her suitcases. When she looked back, Marianne's eyes were pinched. Dutch crackled through her rasped whisper. "It is caught. Not taught."

"And have you caught it, Mom? Transcendence?"

The animal at Marianne's knee barked, sharp, just once. "I think so, Honey," Marianne smiled. "Yes, I do."

Honey had smiled too, pulled Marianne into a sudden hug. Her mother smelled unwashed, a bit lemony. Keith had said he'd noticed it too, the smell.

"Mom, are you safe here?"

Marianne had stepped back. Then she put her dry, cracked hands on Honey's face, cupping it. It was so early in the morning and yet whiskey smudged her breath.

"Don't listen to that cranky McGarrigle. I've been through a world war, Honey, don't you forget. You learn about people in a war. And you learn not to believe what you hear on the news or read in history books. Right? You're the brilliant Ph.D. philosophy doctor."

"Actually, that 'Ph.' stands for phony," she said. "Get it?"

But Marianne went right on: "Tell me: why is it so hard to see that we are all one people, a common species?"

Honey shook her head. Her stomach gurgled against the instant coffee and freezer-burned bread served for breakfast. Or maybe it was the side of spiced beans. No eggs. Not for some weeks now. Marianne said she'd thought of getting herself a chicken.

Honey had watched as Marianne's fingers, stained periwinkle, found a Phantom in the pocket of her button-down. Old sweat and smoke and oil paint wafted, almost visibly, from the denim as she moved.

"If that McGarrigle had no other way to feed his brats he'd cross the filthy Rio Loco too, or climb that goddamn wall they're threatening to build—a goddamn wall! Put yourself in the other man's shoes." Marianne bent down and, cigarette between her lips, ran her fingers back and forth between the animal's sharp triangles of ears. "One day I'm going to walk all the way there to Zopilote. Just to see. Just to say to all these people dying to cross the Oro that at least one old lady cares. That's me." And then she promised Honey that with the animal she was not afraid. "Don't you worry about us, Hon," she said.

Honey made herself smile. "Well, I just love this painting, Mom."

"But you have to unroll it, first," Marianne laughed. "You haven't even looked."

She peered down the tube. And she told Marianne to come up to Buzzard anytime. "Open invitation, Mom. Stay as long as you want. Bring your paints."

"Who'll take care of my critter here?" Her fingers pulled furrows along the animal's back. Its tail flicked in pleasure, eyes trained on Keith, leaning against the hood of the Ventura, reading the map. "And who'll look out for the boys? Can't have them dying on me. No. I have things to take care of here, Honey. I stay put."

Keith came striding over, wiping his forehead. "Anything else?"

"Just our anniversary gift." She unrolled the canvas. Marianne's painting showed a night sky and some kind of canid animal baying at a low moon. They were quiet, taking in the painting's thick textures.

"Maybe you don't understand it," said Marianne, leaning back into her heels.

"We do, Mom," she forced herself to say. "It's just so striking."

"It's really one of a kind, Marianne," said Keith. And then he kissed her mother's cheek.

"I love that the moon is baby blue," she whispered. "And that's Baez, Mom?" She pointed at what might be a lion, a tiger, a wolf, a mix of all three.

Exhaling tobacco, Marianne said, "It's how I see her in my dreams."

"It'll go nicely in our living room. You know we can see this far south, Mom? The condo's that high up. You can't imagine the view."

"Maybe I can imagine," Marianne said, dragging her tobacco. "Maybe I don't have to go anywhere to see something. Maybe I can just think it."

While she'd pulled Marianne into one last hug, Keith tucked the painting into the trunk, slamming the lid.

"I sure as hell won't miss that dog or whatever it is," Honey sighed as they turned onto the main road.

"But in case you do, you have a picture of it."

She had laughed along with Keith.

"Poor Marianne," she said, clipping her dark lenses onto

her glasses and leaning back into the leather seat. As the car flew past the McGarrigle station she caught a flash of the coydog pens. "It's a different world down here, isn't it, Keith?"

Now she crawls one-armed through low thorned shrub. The boy's penlight picks out where the dune buggy's engine dripped and her hand grazes its residual heat. Butted cigarettes litter the ground, along with sneaker-prints and crushed Coke cans, from which she drinks down trickles of hot sweet sap. How far away is the store these came from? The embers in the fire pit still glow. The smell reminds her of the activated-charcoal tablets Keith takes when he's travelling instead of that horrible pink stuff. She finds a stick, picks a coal from the fire, and douses it with spit. Then she puts it in her purse.

In some nearby brush a torn plastic bag is badly hidden. Curly must have left it before taking off. Inside is a can of sardines, a gallon jug of water, a bag with squashed bread rolls. She drinks from the water jug. Her belly hardens and her brain clears. The homemade bread is soft and soothing in her mouth. The crust smells smoky. Whoever made it would never in a million years think of Honey as the recipient.

She holds tight to her purse and her sore arm and follows the buggy's tracks back the way she came. Night begins to lighten. After the coyote carcass, at which a wild pig—what the boy calls a *jabalí*—picks, the land takes shape.

Twist of tree
Ocotillo skeleton
Rock that is shaped like a heart
T-shirt rag
Cactus like a scarecrow

White stick of bone

Luna bottle

Juice can

Sardines in salsa—Jackson's brand

Blue razor

Then her keys, drop by drop, glimmer through the sand. They burn to the touch, so she leaves them.

Rolling hills like m-shaped birds

Snake tracks

Boot prints

The day is getting hot and there's nothing around for shelter. If she stops, she's cooked. And then there is the egg-shaped boulder on the hill. The boy is still lying in its shade, draped in a T-shirt.

He reaches up for her. Maybe he thinks she is his mom.

She gets her hands around his hard, thin body, pulls him up so the tree supports his spine. He drinks from the water jug while she unwraps the coal.

She breaks it apart, giving him half. "You eat."

He tells her she is crazy.

"Doctor Keith say eat it. Or"—she says in English—"do you want to die of dehydration?"

He takes the chunk of burnt wood into his palm, crumbles it into smaller pieces and, looking away from her, licks them up. He washes the charcoal down with a chunk of bread.

"*Niño*," she says leaning in, "Ocho's friend give water and food for you."

His red eyes open wide. His lips are black with ash. "Friend?"

She nods. "With curls. *Rizado.*"

The boy looks away. Honey waits, then touches his shoulder. "What?"

When he looks back the otherwise cool orange of his eyes has been flooded with something fiery, something like pain.

"What? What?" she says.

His shoulders cave in now and he covers his face with his hands. He is still.

She squeezes the bony shoulder. "Ocho know where is my mom? Or Ocho friend know?"

The boy shakes his head. He is doing all he can not to cry. But if he did cry, there would be no tears, just parched and empty gasps.

She helps him lie down on the rock, bundles his bag and slides it under his head for a pillow.

"I hope not," he whispers. "We have to get to her first."

CHÁVEZ

The town of Lucinda's about two hundred miles east of Zopilote and just about parallel. A sandwich shop—Lucinda Lunch—and some blinking tavern are all that's lit; even the bus station's lights are off. Out front, a white van is waiting, *Jelinek Poultry* painted on the side. He and Ishmael duck into the restroom where men come, it seems, to spray urine on the wall and spit tobacco juice on the floor. He shows Ishmael how to stuff his shirt with extra clothes. With his jacket zipped up Ishmael looks ten pounds heavier and a couple of years older. Ishmael says yeah, Chávez does too. A few teens and a couple of men are lined up at the van, but he and Ishmael hang at the back.

"Pay's two-fifty an hour. Board and bed deducted," says

the driver. "So's your boots and gloves. And goggles too."

He waves them into the side door, which another man slides open with a swoosh.

Across from him, Ishmael falls asleep, the hood of his sweatshirt pulled over his face. Chávez talks to the kid beside him, Tony, who's passing around a bag of corn chips. Tony's looking for his dad.

"Someone said he was up here rounding chickens. You?"

Chávez nods at Ishmael, whose slack arms are hugging his backpack. They are saving up to make a start in Zopilote, he says. They both have some English so that should make things easier. They figure they need about five hundred each to get fake papers—you need those in the city.

Tony says he'd like to go to Zopilote but until then working chickens will be okay. Like Chávez, he's had enough of stooping over the fields.

"That's for the little *niñitos*," he says. Those who don't know better yet. "Not like us," he says, brushing crumbs from the start of a moustache. Tony has been picking for three years. What about Chávez?

"Two."

The van slows. They leave the highway for a gravel road. Blue light rises in a halo glow and the smell of bright, acrid chicken shit hits them even before the driver opens the door.

"Okay," the man says. "Outta there. Split."

There's three hundred thousand birds among Jelinek's sixteen chicken houses. Chunky men in jeans and boots and "Jelinek" hard hats point out a block of low concrete outbuildings behind some chain-link: that's where they'll sleep. The one with the solar panels is the canteen. The job's rounding up the birds and loading them into cages, which are then stacked in trucks to ship out for processing. It's a twenty-four-seven operation.

Chávez says to a hard hat, "Where's Jelinek?"

The men laugh. "Who?"

He and Ishmael take their pillows and bed rolls, gloves and goggles and rubbers, and, along with the rest of the passengers, follow a hard hat to the barracks. Their shift starts at six in the morning. Breakfast bell's thirty minutes before that.

They call it "chasing" but you don't really have to run. The birds are so fat and top heavy they can't hardly stand never mind run around. Plus it's dark in the chicken houses — they've got no windows on purpose — so the birds lay right down like it's their naptime, making it easy to scoop them up and cram them into a cage. The smell of bird and chemical follows him into his dreams. Plus he sees over and over the image of a chicken man bulldozing a mountain of feathered carcasses into a dirt hole in a field. They're the ones that have died of disease.

Ishmael just says, "Wear your mask, Chávez, like all the time." And they promise to get out of this place fast.

There are mostly men working here. The few boys have lied about their ages like he and Ishmael have. Most come from the south like him, but there are Africans and Chinese too. The white people are sunburned because they get to work outside. They are the managers or they drive the big machines. They live in Lucinda and come to work in their own cars. The one or two Lucinda men who sign on as chasers work a single shift and never come back.

Days are dark. The chicken houses are like caves. Earplugs muffle the scream of poultry but do not drown it out.

Ishmael says, "Pretend you are a robot, man."

The real job here is blocking the chickens from their minds. Even with a mask on, disinfectant chokes his lungs and behind the goggles his eyes pool with the poison smell Jelinek's candy-pink soap can't wash out. He wades through the dark house, arms outstretched like a sleepwalker, a froth of living feathers at his feet. Before scooping the birds by the ankles, the catchers kick them towards the cages, tossing those already dead into a waiting backhoe. When he's got a load, the driver—an unlit cigarette behind his ear—drives the bodies out to the pit. Chávez sees some men cry at all this death. He sees others stomping living birds and ripping them apart with their hands. He just keeps his mask pulled up and his eyes low. Except for Ishmael, he talks to no one.

The white van brings new workers every day and every day workers leave, walking the twenty miles back to the town of Lucinda. Two really black African men come. They are as thin as saguaro cactuses and so tall they barely fit in the van. While others pass free time snacking, talking, shining shoes, these men stretch on their bunks, eyes blinking up. Ishmael speaks to them. They know very little English. They say they are like Ishmael. They came here with a special work permit, but that has long run out. It is the same with the Chinese men, who are not from China but another country no one has ever heard of. In fact, these men hate the Chinese. Because of the Chinese they had to flee and now here they are—like him and Ishmael—chicken slaves.

There are only so many beds in the barracks so when they get off their shift at seven in the evening the beds are warm with the bodies of those who are now chasing chickens in the houses. Nights carry a chill. Men gather around electric heaters. They drink powdered hot chocolate and take turns showing off their scars—missing fingers, chemical burns—telling about the really bad farmers, or talking big about how they got here: how long they went without water or how Control just about caught them and one time . . . Chávez plugs his ears to block out what he thinks of as bragging stories. These old guys don't know anything about the desert.

Like the chicken houses there are no windows in the canteen either. It's funny but they never get served chicken. There's lots of pork but Ishmael won't eat it.

"Against what I believe," he says.

"What's that?"

"That pigs are dirty swine."

Plates in hand, they join a line to wait their turn at the metal tables with the steaming hoods. Lucinda women in puffy white caps and Jelinek smocks ladle food onto their plates. The women are taller than all of them except the Africans. The men keep their eyes low.

"Those guys are not men to them," Ishmael says.

They carry their plastic trays to a corner table. Talk is made between spoonfuls of macaroni.

"Where does the colour come from?" Ishmael says of the sticky orange noodles.

"From hot lava, from orange peel, from searchlights, the flesh of yams and squash husks, like the kinds we have back home."

"No," Ishmael says, "I bet it's from a lab somewhere. Scientists make it."

"And then terrorists use it in bombs."

"We have sand that colour, or close," says Ishmael. "I am from a desert too, you know."

"With elephants, I bet," Chávez says. "And giraffes."

"No," says Ishmael, drizzling ketchup on his meal. "But there are jeeps and big guns, kidnappers and pirates, and the girls are beautiful in long bright robes."

Ishmael thinks the girls here are not beautiful. Many are fat but wear the shortest shorts right out in the streets. He can see their ass cracks when they bend over! Where are their brothers, husbands, fathers? He wants to know about the girls where Chávez is from.

He shrugs. Never noticed them.

"Wah?" Ishmael shows him the food in his mouth. His teeth are orangey-pink. "How you don't see girls?"

"I'll be better in Buzzard," he says to Ishmael. "Maybe I will see them there."

A bell signals the end of twenty minutes. He slides their trays onto the racks by the trash while Ishmael grabs packages of cookies called Bear Claws.

As they head back to the chicken houses, the smell of grease and starch gives way to bleach. Across the fields, the backhoe is dumping carcasses into the pit.

Chewing their cookies, they each pull on one of the smocks hung in rows by the main doors.

"Not much longer, Ishmael," he says. Then they'll find the one he calls *vieja*.

"Imagine, Chávez, the look on her face when she sees you." He shakes his head and laughs from his belly.

The final bell peals, loud. The manager — Vernon — is tapping on his watch saying how come them all's so late.

"Day's a wasting," he says. That is his favourite expression.

Vernon has a big, hard belly and stubby arms, and his watch cuts deep into the flesh of his chubby wrist. He's not the worst one—that's Mike. Mike jokes that Ishmael and the other Africans—Manu and Peter, who do the night shift— are natural at chicken chasing on account of being voodoo.

"Don't the Africans tear the heads off the chickens and drink the blood from the necks?"

Inside the dark cave, the smell of fear rises with the great rustle of squawking and clipped wings. A patch of tile on the ceiling has peeled back: bright sun comes shooting in. The birds are hysterical. Whether this light tells of freedom coming or the dawning of their end, its radiance is absolute, at once drawing them in and pushing them back.

Chávez tightens his mask. He and Ishmael gaze out at the sea of feathers, each to have its turn at slaughter.

"From *gallina* to *pollo*, like in Spanish," Chávez shouts over the rampaging birds. "You know, there's two words for chicken. *Gallinas* are alive. *Pollos* are slaughtered and cooked."

"Like cow to beef?"

"Sure. But, you know, we are coyotes to them chickens."

"Because we have to be, Chávez," Ishmael shouts. "That's all we can be for now."

Through the obscurity of their goggles, they look at each other before wading in, kicking away the piles of flesh and feather that collapse on the slick floor.

In five hours it will be time for supper.

BAEZ

She had followed the coyote. And that coyote followed her in turn: it was she who was being tracked. The chain and post had picked up more roots and branches, plus a shoe, a T-shirt, a broken bottle. She was slow, lugging her load like a sled. And also she stopped to rub her collar against the sharpest juts of stone, and, twisting her neck, she bit at the loosening leather, but just gnashed her shoulder instead. After a stretch of flat land, a dense outcrop rose up. She stepped up through a narrow corridor barbed with cactus; a fresh, hormonal musk clung to the looming walls of rock shimmering above. Climbing the steepening grade, she slipped on the smooth bare stretches. Stopping to rest, she bit at her collar. Then the coyote calls came: the sound lurched above like a bird dodging a breeze. With a grunt she pulled ahead, straining to gain purchase on the next climb. She did, though she slipped and slid down the other side. When she picked herself back up and pushed ahead, the collar dug deep into her windpipe. She gasped, choked. With each tug she strangled herself. Above her in the craggy rock, the post was hooked into a narrow split, the chain dangling taut. She was stuck.

The desert crackled. Moonlight ebbed and flowed as burrows of cloud swept across the sky. The corridor in which she stood was shadowed in blue, the walls disappearing into the black above. And then a yowl: it came from nowhere, everywhere, bouncing back and forth, rock to rock. She twisted, biting at the collar, gnashing the muscle in her shoulder, and then she stopped: sharp triangles of ears rose up above her. Then up popped the thin snout, taut body, dropped brush of tail. The male coyote peered down at her, lips pulled back into a low yip and howl.

Now one of those bugs is moving in on the grey cactus. It is just like the bug that had crawled up Old Blue's loose, fleshy neck: flat and shivering with hairs that are also its legs. When she saw that bug on Old Blue she had pulled herself up from the hole, crouched, and then leapt, pouncing on her master's chest. Old Blue's eyes stared up, her hand on the spot where the creature had been.

The sun darkens and begins to fall behind the trailer. Tattoo and Glove muzzle her children, two at a time, and then release them into the bowl of valley below. While Tattoo turns up the radio her children run, wrestle, twist; dust coats their bodies, turning them into ghosts. Glove has a plastic bag with a bright mush of meat inside. He tosses handfuls of it into the air, pitting the one with more coyote against the other, whose long coat and round nose bespeaks the Cactus Men. Tattoo and Glove goad the animals, tripping around, laughing. When each of her children has had its turn at the meat, Glove and Tattoo water them and, sitting by the trailer, talk: which of the animals will they take out hunting tonight?

HONEY

The boy is hidden between humps in the rock. The roll of toilet paper has disappeared. Keith would have buried those expired cans in the sand, Monica too. Instead she let her *coyote* make himself sick.

When he crawls back out, the boy's body percolates with sweat. The beads and sheen dry quickly.

"Boy, *niño*, it's not so hot. Let's move."

The boy's eyes are almost neutral, drained of strength and will.

"*Niño*, what is your name? Tell me. Hey?"

"I'm no *niño*," he whispers. "*Vieja*, don't say I'm so 'little.'"

Marianne would be cradling him. He is only a child. She shuffles closer. Getting him under one armpit than another, she drags him to the tree. His body is hot and lean. When he is propped against the trunk he eats the rest of the charcoal, along with bread and water.

He sleeps, slumped up. And when the day is done, she gathers up their things. The plastic bags have collected a few inches of condensation. A "still": now she remembers that is the name of this contraption. She pours off the liquid, drinks her share, saves the rest for the boy. She traces the tattoo on her ankle. This bit of ink remains constant. Is that why this boy tattoos his friends? When he dies, they will all remember him. Suddenly, out of nowhere, the boy reaches out and grabs her ankle. His squeeze is fierce. So is his whisper: "Where you going, *vieja*?"

"Nowhere without you." She has to pull hard to get her foot away.

"Good. You stay where I can see you always, okay?"

"*Te prometo*," Honey says.

At dusk, he gets up and pulls on his knapsack. "We get to the Christmas trailer next."

It is not far down the side of the hill. The boy trips, slow and clumsy now. She grabs his hand, tugs him along. They stop every ten or fifteen minutes. They drink the water. It is better in full glugs than sips, he says: let the brain soak it right in. The stars are not out yet, though the bats are. They swoop low through a purple sky.

"You talked to Ocho?" he says.

"No. Other one. I told you." She makes spirals with her hands.

"*Rizado*."

"Yes." She asks where Ocho comes from. Why he would hunt boys who are like him?

The boy shrugs. "He was just a *coyote* like me and Juan until they called the bounty. Like a price on our heads, see?"

She nods and repeats the word he says for bounty.

"Then," the boy goes on, "Ocho, he started to double dip, kidnapping the same *pollos* who paid him to take them across and then turning them in." After a while no one would cross with him so he just started hunting anyone in the *Las tierras vacías*. He came away with enough money to buy the dune buggy and live on this side of the border.

"Who pays Ocho bounty?"

"You do."

She shakes her head. "*¿Qué?*"

"All you in the north." He lowers his cap. "He comes cheap, no?"

They follow the penlight until it dies. Then they stop, resting in sparse brush until moon breaks free of cloud. They veer east, away from the place where she met Ocho and Rizado—Curly—crossing a flat expanse of something like gravel, each footstep yielding a tinkle like so many broken dishes. First sun beams along the horizon. Low planes drift overhead, flying towards what must be the airport in Buzzard City. It must be Buzzard City.

"She's not far now, *vieja*," the boy keeps promising her. He says she has to believe him.

She says something like, "What other choice I have?"

He thinks about that, smiles, and says: "None."

The air is heavy, the heat coming fast. Soon they will have to stop moving. She turns her sling into a bandana. With the material tied over her mouth and nose, she can breathe.

Then a tower rises up, its reflective glass looming in the distance, beyond what looks to be the spikes of northern mountains. It is her condo tower. The three antennas at the top are the only way she's ever been able to tell theirs apart from all the others. She waits for the boy to point to it or otherwise comment, but he trudges on, head down.

She points. "What is it?"

"What?" the boy snaps.

"Nothing." Just a miracle, a mirage. *Un milagro. Una ilusión.* She challenges herself to remember her Spanish words, learned in topic clusters. Shirt, shoe, hat, purse. *Una Camisa, un zapato, un sombrero, un bolso.*

Her condo tower turns out to be a high, rocky outcrop. The antennas, armless saguaros. The boy picks up a partial set of animal tracks leading right up to it. A few of the prints are perfect, undisturbed. The animal, a coyote or a dog, was dragging something behind it—a rope? The tracks end at the outcrop. The boy tells her he's been here before, in this very spot. This is where he found the dog's collar.

They have to climb up the rocks. Does she see that gleam up there? The boy pulls himself towards it. He stops to breathe. In a minute he calls for her to follow. She re-knots her sling then finds him in the mouth of a narrow corridor of a pale pink rock. The gleam belongs to a long stretch of chain. It hangs down the face of a high, tapered rock and is clogged with garbage and brush, a fishing net pulled from a filthy sea. The metal post at the top is wedged between the arms of a jagged V cut into the rock.

The red leather dog collar the boy takes from his bag fits onto the loop at the end of the chain. This time Honey takes the collar from him. The gnawed leather is rough and cracked.

"How?" She turns to the boy. "How Baez get free?"

They look up at the chain, hanging perfectly straight, pulled down by the sheer weight of the links and the wreckage.

"How? El Esqueleto's dog is from some other world."

She feels an ache for the animal and a fear—both for it and of it. She tucks the collar into her purse. "Mine."

The boy does not protest.

They pick up Baez's tracks on the other side of the outcrop. Though the boy says the tracks will lead straight to El Esqueleto they fade out at a low hill that bristles with mounds of melon-shaped cactuses. The animal is just gone.

"Now what?"

He says it does not matter. He knows where El Esqueleto is. He says she is waiting for him. She even tied *papel de baño* in the tree above her so that he would see her.

"Toilet paper?"

He is toeing a plump globe of cactus. The needles are two, maybe three inches long. When the boy tells her to empty her purse, she does. Then he gloves his hand with it, and with that hand picks up the scissors—"*tijeras*"—and jams the blades into the cactus. When he has hacked off the top he mashes the insides with a stick. Honey does as he does, sucking up the moisture, swallowing the pulp. The damp flesh is clear and has no taste. That the boy knows to do this gives her hope.

She makes up names for him: Bruno, Jaime, Diego. "Or," she says, "your name, that's Juan?" Is this boy himself the friend he lost?

"No." The single word punches the air. "Just don't call me anything. Don't even think about me at all."

There are no trees here. The land stretching before them is bare and pale. In time a human figure rises along the horizon, like someone laid out flat, with toes to the sky. *Un milagro?* A miracle? A mirror? Mirage?

"Look! Someone!"

She runs towards it: jeans, white runners, a grape-and-gold T-shirt. Then she stops sharp. The someone is a dead boy with a leather face. He has no eyes or nose and the pony-tailed hair — dusty black — is more like a wig, like the crown on a department store dummy. The water bottle in his hands is empty but for an inch of bright pee. Up ahead, the flat land dips into a deep gully. This boy had his eyes on that gully too, had also felt a surge of hope — there might be shade ahead, some source of water.

"He is fresh," the boy says. "Dead maybe a day." Any longer and there would be nothing left. The sun and animals take care of flesh really fast here.

She finds herself on her knees, scooping sand over the limbs, shrunken now beneath the clothes. "Help me!"

The boy just watches. "Save your energy, *vieja.*" He says every bit of sweat she loses has to be replaced.

"This is you, *niño,*" she says to the boy, unable to look up at him. "This is Juan."

She pushes the hot dry sand over the tough face, hands, the bottle of pee. If she goes hard she can erase the sight of him from her mind. Otherwise it will be scorched there forever.

"Come on, come on," the boy keeps at her. She'll have to dig so fucking deep to keep animals away.

Finally, he starts kicking sand over the body too and then when the dead boy has been replaced by a mound of pale sand, he lays two sticks on top, forming more of an X than a crucifix. He crosses himself. He crosses Honey, kneeling beside him. His fingertips burn.

She whispers in English to her *coyote*: get out of this place, little boy, and don't come back. To the boy in the ground she says she is sorry. "Whoever you are."

The boy pokes her shoulder. They have to go.

They find shade in the lip of the gully. Below, the basin is lined with ocotillo. The spiky limbs, still tipped in dried pink bloom, wave and curve as if under water. Swaths of white brittlebush partly shroud the hulk of an abandoned Chrysler, its trunk sprung open.

Bruno-Jaime-Diego-Juan sleeps. She listens to the crackle of the hot air, the whisper of death it carries. She wills herself to remember how many strokes it took to complete a lap in the pool, or the time when she and Keith were at the coast and she swam so long her tongue got fat with salt and how scary it was when she couldn't speak. Then there is the cool silk of her bathrobe after a warm bath; falling asleep to the sound of Keith taking a bedtime shower. And she recalls newspaper stories of hikers and campers getting lost—and found—in the desert. One of Keith's colleagues, a respiratory specialist, spent twenty hours perched on some rock face high above a famous canyon, only to be spotted by search helicopters and pulled out. At his homecoming party he was sunburned burgundy, bitten and scratched, but smiling, gracious. He said he had recited opera arias to stay calm. And, no, his life did not flash before his eyes. That only happens when you think you might die, which the respiratory doctor did not.

She sticks to laps in the pool and her Spanish. Verbs, for her, are always the worst.

Eat / *Comer*

I eat / *Yo como*

You eat / *Tú comes*

She/he eats / *Ella/él come*

They eat / *Ellas/Ellos comen*

We eat / *Nosotros comemos*

What is Marianne reciting right now? Her Dutch school-girl songs? War songs? Or maybe she is going over her Spanish too, though hers has always been strong.

"It happens when you're European," she had said once. "We, that way, are gifted."

The boy's breathing shudders.

"Okay, *niño*," she says, shaking him awake. "Bruno-Jaime-Diego-Juan, we gotta move. We gotta get to Marianne."

Then a rumble swells up through the earth, followed by the grind of an engine. It is too loud to be the dune buggy. Her face must betray the surge of hope that Johnny-for-Jesus is coming, or the Control, for the boy's eyes ratchet hers. There is suddenly a ferocity in him.

"*Vieja*," he says, pinching her injured forearm. The sudden pain takes her breath. His fingers dig deep. "You don't tell on me," he whispers, his voice like a grizzled old man's.

When she says nothing, he pinches her again.

"Okay. I no tell."

"Because then you never see your El Esqueleto. Right? Or" — he pokes the wedding ring on her pinky — "him."

"Okay, okay," she hisses, prying off his fingers. For each one a white half-moon throbs in her red skin.

The engine closes in, drowning him out. "Men are bad here, *vieja*. Remember." He taps his temple. "Remember men will kill you in a second. First they rape you. You know, rape?"

Una violación. She says the word. She knows the word.

"You are nothing to men here. You are like me, just garbage."

She nods. She places her fingers on her lips. "*Silencio.*"

CHÁVEZ

"Okay," he says, when Ishmael asks him to tell the rest of his story again. He's told it a few times, and he loves the way he holds his friend's attention hostage with his words. "Her crazy dog wouldn't let me come close so I drank some of the water from the jug before I left it for El Esqueleto. I guessed her dog would come up and get it—which it did, I saw."

They are on Ishmael's bunk, going over the map. They have drawn a red-Bic line from Lucinda County over to Buzzard City. A whole fold over—but they'll get there. They have to save enough for the bus and a bit extra for getting by until they find the woman Chávez and now Ishmael call the *vieja*.

"Vee-eh-ha," Chávez coaches his friend.

He says he didn't know if El Esqueleto understood that he wanted her to mark her tree with the toilet roll so he'd be sure to find her. He thought by the time he made it back with help—who was going to help her, he didn't know—the animal would have struck water at the bottom of its hole. Crazy fucking bitches, those two.

After he left them he had crept up to the Christmas trailer. There was no truck, no dog, the door locked. He went on, picked up Ocho's tracks on the other side of an outcrop and followed them south and west. He stopped where the tracks did: an old rancher's shed that Juan and he had passed by and once or twice had slept in. It was full of trash now. He'd slept off the hot part of the day. When he woke he saw that a bag was hanging from a rafter above him. To reach it he had to stack rocks in a teetering pile from which he leapt, barely catching the bag's corner in his fingers. He did this twice before he got hold of it and the bag ripped apart. Juice boxes, cigarettes, canned sardines, a bottle of water, and packets of salt tumbled out. Ocho was well stashed all over *el desierto*. Chávez filled up on the drink boxes, packed the water and salt, and at dark he went on, following Ocho's trail further south. He made it to the end of *Las tierras vacías* then stopped at the *prohibido* road. High walls of rock narrowed into a corridor. He crawled into a crook where he could see what was coming up the bend.

"I remember I was hoping I'd dream of a way out of there. Like maybe God would tell me what to do."

The sound of engines woke him—the sun had hardly moved. From where he was hiding he saw Ocho. His buggy was chasing a shitty blue car. He knew that car but really had to think about from where: it had always been parked in the gravel patch by El Esqueleto's trailer. He never saw it *not* parked there. Always, its windows were coated in dust, and lately, the windshield was smashed up. Now, it screeched to a stop not fifty feet off. He saw El Esqueleto's face inside: he swore it was her, all crumpled and scared. His brain did a back-flip. How was she driving her car here and now when he'd left her half-dead maybe only a day ago? Something was happening. Some bit of God's grace had sent this fucked-up old lady to pick him up and take him out of this desert and into the north. Why not?

"Sure she was crazy," he says to Ishmael, whose eyes are

wide and brow washboard rigid. "But I could've used a fuck-ing break."

"Still could," says Ishmael.

But Ocho's desert buggy was getting close. So he ran—he remembers the fire in his lungs—and then the shots rang out and as he got closer to the car something about the woman's face looked all wrong. But, there she was leaning over to open the door for him— *Help*, he called, running towards her. It was like she was going for a swim—he shows Ishmael—her left arm coming up, her face turned away. He was already thinking fuck you Ocho and double-fuck you Juan, but when he got to the car the door would not open.

"She had locked it."

"We have to find her," Ishmael says, shaking his head like he always does when Chávez tells this part of the story. "She owes you big time, man."

"I know she does." Chávez lets his head fall back. It feels so good to not be alone with the *vieja* anymore. "For two years it's all I can think about. Dreaming, dreaming. She's living it up in Buzzard and I'm killing her chickens."

"But," Ishmael says.

"What? But?"

Ishmael takes a deep breath. His nostrils stick together. "You have to try to forgive her too."

BAEZ

She remembers how the coyote had moved towards her down the rocks: like rain it had come, dropping slowly from one step down to the next. It did not lift its eyes from her. She tugged on her chain, bit at the collar, writhed. The coyote drew close. And though she lifted her tail and barked, the coyote kept its tail down, its hackles smooth and teeth concealed. The golden circles of its eyes glowed through the night, brightening as it advanced forward, shoulder blades kneading. The musk of its scent subdued her. The coyote circled, came up from behind. She braced her legs, allowing it to mount. Its body was taut. Not heavy. Just strong. It struggled to gain purchase on her hind quarters. As it thrust its seed deep inside her, its teeth bore down on her neck. She yipped and howled, strained, but she was powerless until it finished and withdrew. The coyote pulled away and was gone back up the rocks. She fell back on her haunches, then stood and shook herself, sending the coyote's scent flying like so much water. Behind her, the chain rattled and twisted where it was stuck. But the collar — that fell loose from her neck. It thudded to the ground, the leather wet and ragged where the coyote had chewed it through.

Now the sun is falling under the burden of the day's slow-churned energy. She shifts. The ground beneath her has cooled by a degree. Her side is numb where the texture of the earth has been stamped into her furless flesh. The hill and valley are as quiet and still as she; any bits of life have been consumed by the bald birds waiting above her. Inside the great grey cactus, baby birds — now orphaned — cheep-cheep, pecking at each other. The strongest of them will bite its brothers and sisters until they are gone and then itself tumble, wingless, from the nest.

The engine chuffs, just above where they hide, barely concealed by a rocky overhang. The air fills with blue-black exhaust. The valley is not far below. They could still run down there. There is room for two under that Chrysler. Beside her, the boy's eyes are blinking like crazy. He is thinking the same thing. His fists are tight, bracing himself to take off.

But they both stay rooted to that meagre hiding spot. Finally, the engine cuts out. A door clicks open then slams. The driver's boot-tips breach the ledge above. Blackened nostrils and a whiskered chin, the bill of a yellow ball cap, hands on bony hips. How long has it been since he has seen a woman? Does he sense her body close? He steps over to a gentler grade, scans the gully below, and descends the slope. His eye is on the hulk of car and twisted metal decorating the basin.

They crouch as they move in on the pickup truck: navy blue where it is not rusted out. Behind them, its driver slides down into the gully, moving towards the Chrysler. His denims are slack and cowboy boots snub-toed; a yellow-and-grey ponytail grows out the back of his cap.

She whispers, "*Silencio.*"

The boy nods. He puts a dirty finger to his cracked white lips. Then he says, "*Las llaves.* Get the keys." He keeps low and climbs up into the truck bed.

Though the window is open, the ignition is bare.

Where's the boy?

Beneath a stretch of tarp, the truck bed brims with scavengery. Pop cans, beer bottles—Coors, Pepsi, no-names—jumble with Evian, Perrier, and Agua Libre. A handsaw, rubber shoes, rags torn from jeans, T-shirt bits layered between sardine cans, disposable razors, a tire iron. And there are bones, of animals and humans; a gecko carcass dried to a husk, a brittle tube of canvas, and pieces of Marianne—her T-shirts and socks, her crockery. Her paintings. There is Keith's briefcase, student papers, Honey's toiletry kit, now empty.

Honey pulls herself into the truck bed, filling her sling with Marianne's watercolour sunsets and canvas rolls of cactus fields. "Mom, my God."

The boy watches from his side of the truck's piled-up trash. He drinks from a pop bottle and slides a *Sports Illustrated* into his knapsack.

Behind them the driver grunts as he hauls himself up from the gully. His boots scrape close. The boy grabs Honey's arm and pulls her down, the tarp blanketing them.

"*Shhh!*"

It is dark underneath, hot and rotten. She holds the boy, trying to shrink her body, his body, to get them both to disappear. His lips tickle her ear. He whispers that he knows where this man lives.

"It's the Christmas trailer. Close to El Esqueleto," he says.

"But if he finds us," she says in English.

The man coughs, kicks a tire. There is tobacco.

The boy shakes his head. He says something about trust. "*Confianza.*"

Then the tarp crinkles back. A few inches of light fall in. So does an antenna, a road sign with bullet holes, a bottle with a few inches of liquid.

The engine fires, the truck shudders as it pulls away.

"*Confianza,*" Honey says, giving her body over to the flow of the engine, the way of the boy.

She drinks from some bottles and a few empty cans, burning her mouth on hot, rank liquid. The boy's eyes blink at her. He pulls back the tarp enough that she can see the sky unfurl. The blunt white sun hangs heavy.

There will be water at the Christmas trailer. Where the driver lives.

The truck bounces. Honey rolls, crushing her sore arm. She mashes her lips to hold in the pain rating: nine-nine-nine. They stop and again the driver gets out. His boots scuff the ground, whistling recedes as he walks off.

She does not know what she has done to get here. This slow burn of punishment: eye for eye, hell for hell for Honey. Is this how God goes?

When she shifts and tries to sit up to get a look, a clue, of where in the world they could be, the boy's eyes flash. He pulls her back into the heat and rot beneath the tarp.

The man is back. A flip-flop is tossed inside. Next: a plastic bag with a cigarette lighter and a hairbrush, a soda bottle that is not quite empty. The door slams. They move.

She slides up against the side of the truck bed where there is some shade. This should be the driver's blind spot. The way is rugged, off-road all the way. They are still in the no-man's-land part of the desert. Her teeth shake and the trash spills. Marianne's pictures, canvases and paper, fly and flap. Femur, rib, jaw rattle against the metal bed. The bones chatter and sing, more alive than she is. She buries her nose in her purse: leather and chlorine.

They stop. Honk, slam, the driver's slow footsteps are joined by two more.

"Marty," says a man, voice gravelled. "Where's Andy today?"

Marty's yellow cap meets another, of denim.

"Had some shits again this morning. Purina just doesn't sit with that dog." He, Marty, calls the other man Bob. Rob? Todd.

Dry, white-patched elbows lean against the tailgate. The long fingers that grip the side of the bed are stained a rich nicotine, and several are ringed with silver and turquoise.

Says Todd, "What you got today?"

"Migrant trash." Marty pauses. "And you know those kids're getting younger." He speaks through a cough and coughs through slow, spittled speech. "Trash's gone from razors and bibles to all candy and Gatorade."

Todd says, "So what's in the boxes? S'all papers and stuff." A meaty paw reaches into the truck bed, shifting the broken-down cardboard.

Marty says there was a car wreck. "Way down, that *prohibido* road that used to lead straight to the reservation."

"Uh-huh."

"Well, this was all that was left worth taking."

"A wreck or a shootout?"

Marty considers. "Left a mess behind, that's all I know." He chuffs a cough. "Looks like it was old Marianne's anyway."

"Who?'

"Samaritan bitch. Todd, you know, pal of Johnny-for-Jesus. Down in Matchstick County. Look, it's her clothes here."

"Whoa," Todd whistles. "Sure I know her. And these're her pictures?" The paw sifts around, pulling out a roll of paper.

"Yeah," says Marty, "she was some kind of *artiste*."

"What's this one supposed to be?" Gravel voice rakes. "Hey Marty?"

"Don't know. You want it?"

"Naw." The paper is tossed back. "You try the Zaris?"

"I did," Marty says.

"They know you smashed that, uh, Marianne's car window?" A match strikes crisp. Crisper tobacco creeps into the air. "That's the talk."

"Well, yeah," Marty sniffs. "Johnny gave me grief for that. But looks like she listened."

"And her animal? Where's it at?"

"That thing should be shot too. Just as crazy as the old lady—had to fight that thing off with my goddamn stick."

"Well," Todd says after a time, "you ever find any tires, always needing those."

The door slams.

When they're bumping back along the road, she pushes away the paper and plastic and cardboard. She breathes.

"What'd he say?" the boy whispers. "Tell me."

She shakes her head, her teeth rattling. The truck lurches, and the boy falls into her shoulder. She takes his hand. He squeezes back. *Bruno-Jaime-Diego-Juan.*

Honey lifts the tarp, catching flashes of the passing horizon. The sun is starting to sink down into late afternoon. The truck stops twice: to scavenge and for Marty to urinate. She thinks the boy will leap up and they'll have to make a break for it, but he says for now they are going in the right direction. This is so much faster. So they hide under Marianne's flattened cardboard. He has found a pencil. With it he cleans the dirt from his fingernails. Then they slow for a long rough stretch, five to ten miles an hour. Barking explodes far off; they drive towards it. Then the truck stops and the engine dies. Dusk falls fast.

"Andy," Marty calls to his dog. The barking reaches a flurry. Nails scratch the truck's metal. Marty coos: "You better now, old man?"

A muscled body bounds up into the bed of the pickup. Bark turns to growl. Through coming night, a light falls from what might be a porch, catching the animal's fur: so grey it is almost green and shabby, balding. It snaps at its master's haul, nosing through the desert residue. Then the dog finally senses them: it breaks into a fit, luring Marty back from where he has retreated.

"Andy! Shut your trap."

The truck bounces as Marty lowers the tailgate and climbs up. Monica doesn't tell her about the rape cases she triages in emergency. But Keith knows the numbers. "One in three women, Honey, will be raped or beaten in her life." Each term, during her "Educating in Crisis" lecture, she relays that statistic to her students; and every time, the room falls into a hush as the young women think, *Will it be me?* But how many of her male students, the few she has, will wonder whether they will be the one who beats, who rapes? The scissors in her left hand are hot and familiar. She peeks through the cardboard that blankets her. The grizzled old dog lopes around on top of the tarp, frantic to get at the issuing smells. Marty gropes for its collar. But the dog whips its head around. Marty stumbles, loses grip. A hollow smack is followed by a whimper. The dog, now weakened, is tugged off.

Marty mutters. He clears the tailgate and the truck rises. A door—tin or aluminum—slams.

As she lifts off the tarp, light catches the boy's eyes, like brown beer bottles in the sun.

"What? You don't run inside to him, *vieja*? You don't beg him to save you from me?"

She says, "We promise. *Promesa*." Then she squeezes his shoulder until he nods back. She tells him in English that she trusts him. He says something she doesn't understand. Then they climb out of the pickup.

Marty's place is an actual RV, a house on wheels, maybe even the real Winnebago brand. The roof is loaded with antennas, satellite dishes, solar panels. Jaundiced cutouts of Santa and tin reindeers with no noses cling to the walls, and grizzled, rat-tail tinsel frames the windows and the door. Rising behind is a high dark heap that might be an outcrop did it not reek of hot corrosion and old fruit. There are no lights to indicate neighbours or any kind of infrastructure. More and more of these boondockers have been popping up since the canal was decommissioned. They prefer to retreat further into the desert instead of following the agricultural work as it heads north. Somehow they get by, their very survival a protest against the forces that have taken their farms and jobs away. Through the two yellow squares of uncurtained windows Marty moves. He goes between table and appliances, chair to cupboard, his neck and jaw flexing as he chews at something tough. His head tilts back. The inches of brown liquid in his glass go down the hatch.

Between the RV and the garbage mountain there's a high chain-link pen where Marty cordons his dog. A lean-to shed slumps inside. The boy clears the fence, landing in dog shit. "¡Pinche!" He pulls his plastic grocery bag from his pocket and disappears into the shed.

One foot after another, Honey circles the RV, running her good hand's fingertips over the dirty metal. The boy calls this land *vacía* but that's wrong. What makes it so empty are all the people here. Without anyone looking at it or trying to change it so much, life in this place would spill over, but quietly so. All on its own. Television laughs inside the RV and through the windows the smells of cooking leak—gas station nachos or close to it. And then a microwave dings. She touches the familiar texture of her purse. Marty's aluminum door is dented, from shoulders, from boots. And the metal is warm against her cheek, the knob smooth against the palm of her hand. That commercial—"Leggo my Eggo." Right? Marty laughs. His smoker's hack rumbles like the one Marianne was starting to build. She closes her eyes. She twists the doorknob, finding it locked. Hoarse barking breaks loose from within the RV. The dog claws and scratches on the other side of the cheap pressboard door. Then come the bashes and head-butts. When Marty swears, angry and slurred, the animal's alarm turns to whining. Honey crouches as she steps away into the surrounding dark. Behind her the TV cuts out.

The boy has crawled through the open window of the pickup. She holds a finger to her lips and gestures at the RV: silent, still, more guarded. "Marty," she whispers. She tries to say in Spanish that the bad man has heard them.

After a minute, the whine of the TV again opens up the heavy silence. A live studio audience breaks into a round of applause. The boy shrugs. He shows her a stick with a nail stuck crossways through the end. "See that?" He says the sticky brown on the nail is blood. He emerges with his knapsack full of bottled water. There's also half a pack of Pilots, a bag of salt peanuts, a can of beer, and a box of tissues. Look: a whole cup full of change but that's too heavy and besides

Honey is going to give him money soon enough in Buzzard, right?

They crouch by the pickup, drinking Marty's stash of water. He shows her the length of rope and canvas tarp he found in the shed. Marty's face appears at one or other of the RV's windows then disappears. His dog barks once, twice, for there are coyotes in the night. Their calls compete with those of what can only be owls. *Tecolotes.*

They eat the sardines from Ocho, Marty's peanuts.

"Juan wants a pickup more than anything." The boy looks up at the stars. "He's saving up. Then, he always said, we'll drive to the ocean. You been there?"

"Yes," she says. "I love the ocean. I love to swim."

The boy says he does not know how.

She must look shocked, because he rattles on about how would he ever learn when the Río Loco barely reaches to his knees and there's no pools where he comes from? He and Abuelita share the same water for a bath. She lets him go first.

"I teach you. You want swim?"

The boy wipes anger from his mouth. "No. I don't." Then he jumps up and goes. "I just want my money," he calls back. Or that is what Honey thinks she hears in the words gliding towards her through the thick night air.

Ahead, he hunches into his footsteps. The back of his neck is delicate. The knobs of his spine bulge in a way that is painful to see. When he was ill he had needed her. Now he moves like a machine. A machine fuelled by thoughts of reward money. Her mother could live or die because life is cheap in his world, and Marianne's old anyway and so is she. The *vieja*. The *vieja* with the bottomless purse.

The heat defies them to move. Her slung arm begins, like

a heart, to beat. Then it just throbs. She cannot remember how many days or nights they have been here. This is a test of God. If she wants to survive she will have to come to truly trust this boy who is leading her deeper into a hell — without beginning, middle, end — and extorting hard-earned money from her and Keith.

The boy points west at a low sprawling hill. The base is ridged with deep arroyos patched with ocotillo and brush.

"We're close," he says.

Beyond the hill, mountains rise clear. They could be the Entradas.

As day begins to break, he moves fast against the coming wall of heat. Or she is just struggling. Is this what it means to be half alive? You sort of cling to some knotted-up ball of will just to get through to the next toppled cactus or dry creosote bush. *One more lap, come on, one more*, a coach is calling from the pool deck. It is only for Keith and Marianne that she is still walking. What else, who else?

They settle in the shadow of a rock where the ground, she has learned, is always cooler. The arroyo is coming up — but still so far away. Vultures swim above. The sun brims.

The boy says it is too hot to go now. They have to wait until night.

"No." He keeps prolonging this fucking trip. What about Marianne?

"And I can't let you die either. Running you into the ground," he says.

"You want me to pay."

He stands. The sand he kicks sprays her in the face. "So? What else?"

"Who you anyway?" she says, standing too. "A *zopilote*, that is what." A buzzard.

She does not understand his fast, vicious Spanish. He juts out his chest. Like the men at the market when they see her coming with her ingredients list and stuffed wallet.

With her teeth and good fingers she tightens the knot holding her sling. The cotton tastes like canned soup: salty tomato or maybe vegetable beef. It is because she is so numb that the pain rating plummets down to about a five or six. Around them the land is much the same as when they began. On and on it goes: an indeterminate circle of sun and sand and sky closes in, recedes, yielding nothing but itself to break up the horizon.

"You trick me. Right, *niño*? Like any other *coyote*." She says Marty wasn't going to rape her. A lie. How stupid she was to trust the boy.

The boy wipes his hands on his jeans. Scratches criss-cross his burnished face and skinny arms. What looks like a sparse patch of hair has emerged above his upper lip. The beginnings of a moustache or is it just dirt? Filthy clothes hang from him in rags, their original colours having faded into his very skin, and his skin into the dry swallow of their surroundings.

"A trick?" he says. "Like El Esqueleto? She puts out water and then lets the dog take us down." He pauses. "We stop here. We rest here. You are stupid otherwise."

"No, I go," she says.

She walks on, towards the arroyo and the low hill beyond, the mountains beyond that.

"Marianne! Marianne!" Her voice echoes and dies. "Marianne!"

The boy thuds up from behind. *"Perra!"* Bitch. He yells for her to do what he says. He is the coyote, the boss here. Just as she turns, his head butts into her crotch and hands shove her thighs. She topples, grappling with him with her one good arm, catching his laden knapsack. He straddles her waist, squeezing to hold her down. She pushes him from her body and as he wrenches away, she winds up and, left hand open, swats him across the face. She catches his cheekbone, the butt of her palm connecting with his jaw.

She kneels on the ground, wind gone from her chest.

His hand to his cheek, the boy gathers his knapsack, plastic bags, his fallen hat. "Fuck you," he says in English. In Spanish: "I hope you die."

The flame in his eye, the tightness of his lips: he is more than a bad boy, he is a war boy. And he is no longer a boy, therefore.

He walks north and east towards the hill, mountains beyond growing more defined. "Bruno!" she calls softly, cradling the hot pain pulsing in her arm. "Jaime! Diego. Juan?"

He is too far ahead to hear.

CHÁVEZ

A muddy night in sticky June he and Ishmael wake up before the overnight crew comes back and by the half moon they walk away from Jelinek's Poultry—five hours along the narrow shoulder and that's not counting the three times they jump into ditches or bushes when flag-waving pickups come skidding to a stop. He tastes chicken shit in his mouth no matter what he eats or how much he brushes his teeth so he buys some Trident when they get to Lucinda. The sticks are soft and white. With each chew his mouth gets a little more numb. He tells Ishmael the taste reminds him of the *vieja*. She had stuff like this in her purse. Useless junk rich people waste their money on.

Ishmael folds a stick into his mouth. "But does it kill the shit taste?"

It does.

"Then how's it useless?" He says maybe that lady had some horrible taste in her mouth she wanted to get rid of too.

The man selling bus tickets speaks fast and hard and eyes them in such a way Chávez says to Ishmael, "That guy's going to tell the cops on us."

Ishmael says it'll be easier in Buzzard City. "We won't stand out so much." But they agree that if they have to run, it's each one for himself.

The bus—only one a day—comes through at three in the afternoon. It's twelve-thirty now.

Lucinda's the biggest town he's been in. There are two Chinese restaurants. The Italian one smells like home just a little. Six churches and six taverns—that's so the sin and the forgiveness balance each other out. There are no old-fashioned ladies with bonnets selling home baking but at the gas station you can get stuff that's plastic-wrapped. While Ishmael searches the drink coolers for the kind of milk he calls "normal"—Ishmael hates the chocolate kind or any brand of soda—Chávez watches as drivers (their cars and trucks idling in the lot) pump orange goo onto hot dogs plucked with tongs from a revolving wheel. The goo is the same colour as Jelinek's macaroni. One driver with sunglasses perched on his ball cap catches him staring, so Chávez turns to browse the racks and racks of chips. He buys a bag of crinkled ones and, like Ishmael, he gets a carton of milk.

There's a library in Lucinda—also the first he's seen. It's red brick with white pillars holding up the small, peaked roof. Across the street is a park edged in sweet bushes buzzing with bees. Kids run around in a patch of sand while the moms in sunglasses talk and smoke.

Theirs is a splintered bench set back from the street. They stretch out their legs. His muscles are tight and his left knee nags again. Doesn't it look bigger than the right one? Cigarette smoke and laughter drift in. All the dads of the kids there must be working someplace. Maybe they are the asshole managers at Jelinek's. Maybe they are the ones who threw cans at him while Ishmael was pissing in the ditch.

"Even the dogs are fat here," he says of a golden dog with long, silky hair. When it squats, the owner, a grey-haired man carrying a newspaper, looks away and then stoops down and gathers up a heap of turd.

"Dogs are filthy swine," Ishmael says, passing him the chips. "Look at people here worshipping them."

"I thought that was pigs that were swine."

"Them too. But in a different way. I mean, you're not going to think about eating a dog like you might think about a pig."

He crunches the chips. The salt works better to kill the chicken-shit taste than the gum did. No, he'd never eat a dog.

"They're just like people." Chávez says El Esqueleto's dog made him think dogs are smart and even have souls. "They get born normal creatures. It's us that turns them evil."

Ishmael frowns at him—he doesn't know that part of Chávez's story yet.

Of all the kids playing in the sand, one is darker than the rest. Even from far back, his eyes are bottomless black and shaped like sideways teardrops, like those of Diego and Mario and other Indians from the mountains in the south of the south. The blond woman wiping the dark kid's nose has long, sieve-thin hair; she keeps tucking wisps of it behind one ear then the other. Her jean skirt's hemmed in diamonds and her flip-flops are fancy ones, the thick soles wedged. That kid of hers was fathered by some chicken chaser—likely one that's even shorter than her but a really sharp dancer, and now he's gone and moved on to another farm and doesn't know he left a kid behind. Chávez says this to Ishmael. "Yup." The kid's going to have a hard time here. Maybe he'll get arrested and sent back to—where?

He licks his fingers and brushes crumbs from his rap T-shirt. He bought it from a chicken chaser—five bucks and a pack of cigarettes—who said he got it in Zopilote. The picture on it is the same as the sticker in Ocho's buggy: the silhouetted man standing up to the crosshairs that have him caught, but not stopped, not put down. The shirt is so big it might be a sack, and the cotton's faded to charcoal from being washed a million times. Above the picture the lettering's so cracked and peeled it says PU LIC   MY.

In his heart he still hears the beauty of the beats Ocho played him. He wonders if up here he and Ocho could ever be friends.

The blond mom straps her chicken-chaser kid into a leather harness and then, after tucking her hair, clips on a leash. That makes them laugh. Chávez says, "She's got herself a *pollito*."

"You know she'll always, always, always remember you, right? Or at least she should."

"Her?" He thinks Ishmael means the mom. The diamonds on her skirt and shoes catch in the sun—there's no diamond ring on her finger like the other moms. But Ishmael means the *vieja*.

Chávez thinks about that. "I don't want her to remember me at all," he says. "I just want my money."

BAEZ

She had run away from the rocks where the coyote mated her. Soon after she found tire tracks and in a deep gully the remains of a car. The hungrier and thirstier she became, the sharper her eyes, nerves, and the desert brightened, became more alive. For the hot part of the day she followed a wide sandy wash edged in twists of black, burned brush. Garbage fire still heated the blue swirls of air. By night she crossed over a low swath of hills. At the bottom was a rough snaking path that might once have been a road. The long white trailer at the end was sunk in the sand, its walls covered in bright pictures and the windows hung with ragged twists of silver. The mountain of tires and bones and metal was higher than the trailer and just as wide. Out front was Yellow Man's truck and the musk smell hovering in the air was that of her old brindled cousin, who was chained, sleeping, in the pen out back. She herself slept in a distant patch of brush.

When day greyed Yellow Man came out, peed while still standing in the trailer doorway, the screen open only an inch. The orange arc of liquid caught in a soft wind, filling her nose with the scent of urine. Yellow Man fed and watered his animal which then hopped in the back of the truck. They drove away. Her cousin's shit-filled pen stood open. She consumed what remained of its water and food then waited until she felt her bowels. She squatted and shat in front of Yellow Man's door. She went on.

In a sandy arroyo not far from Yellow Man's, she had picked up the smell of Old Blue. The smell came from the direction of the mountains and that is where the footprints, when she found them, were going. Old Blue had been falling, weaving, as she walked. Old Blue had stopped in the shade of a big rock. Old Blue had dropped a water bottle. Old Blue had turned and walked back towards home then changed her mind and continued on to the mountains again. Old Blue began to smell of something—age, expiration—her energy thinning and her body evaporating into the wavering heat. Then the footsteps came to a rocky rise. They rounded the bottom, looking for some kind of well-worn path that was just not there. Baez lost the footprints, but picked them up on the other side. And the smell was suddenly so close it hit her—smack—in the face.

When Baez found her Old Blue was not blue anymore. She was the same colour as the desert. Her bright, burned face was salty, so was her neck. The arm she held to her chest was wrapped in a sling of bandages. Old Blue tried to talk but her voice had become that of a man almost. Her hands were twice their size and the black of her pupils had pushed out all the colour. Old Blue touched the raw spots on Baez's neck where the leather collar had been; she clucked and cooed at that. Then she pointed at the mountains and slowly, hand to knee, found her feet. The bottoms of her pants were torn; her shoes just clung. They went on together, Old Blue bent right up. A hill was rising before them, big and pointed. The land began to climb. Old Blue shook her head and fell and only when Baez barked and tugged at her clothes with her teeth did Old Blue crawl, one arm and two knees, to the skinny mesquite where she fell down and stayed.

Then Baez started to dig.

She looks down now at her front paws, nails thickened to black bone, splayed open on the rough ground. The earth pulses underneath. She is too tired now to find the source. Tattoo and Glove are standing on the rise. Taking turns with the binoculars, they gaze out into the valley and the flatlands beyond, unfurling with low sun. Shadows are long. Then they muzzle a wiry bitch and a thickset male streaked with shiny scars. They load them, along with water and cans of drink, into the desert buggy. They drive away without filling her bowl.

HONEY

By the time she reaches the arroyo, the boy is gone up and over the hill and into the rocky horizon beyond. She has a small bottle of water left. And her wedding band is gone: either it slipped from her pinky finger during her scuffle with the boy or he stole it while she slept. She follows her footsteps back to the torn-up patch where they struggled, rakes her good hand through the dirt. She churns up sticks, stones, insects, bottle caps, but no gold band.

The land is a swath of open, no shade and no soul. *Pollo, gallina.* What's the difference again? Cow to beef, pig to pork, *gallina* to *pollo*: which is the living bird and which the cooked meat?

She walks, again, up the arroyo. The wash is cut deep. The sand is marked with tough leafless ironwood and tufts of brittle brush; rocks along the bed are tumbled smooth, while higher up they are jagged and sharp. The land starts to climb. A broad saguaro stands some twenty feet high, the trunk and branches pocked with woodpecker holes. The heat is too thick. It is like syrup. Like honey. Inside, her body is burning up. She stretches out on her side in the long sausage of the cactus shadow. Keith's picture—his smiling face both strange and familiar—is clasped in her good hand. She rates the pain in her other arm: still a five, then a four, then she can't feel it anymore. Her heart is slow, a tap left to drip. She moves when the sun does. Above her, a brown red-cheeked bird dips in and out of a hole it has drilled in the cactus; further down lives a family of mice. And there is a tarantula, the first she has ever seen, picking its way across her very footprints.

The sun is at its zenith. Somewhere in the distance a motor *zip-zip-zips*—above her or below her she cannot tell, behind or beside—but it is too quick and high-pitched to belong to a truck. Then it goes. The cactus shadow moves; she follows. This is what the boy wanted from the beginning: to lure her out here and leave her to die. Is it murder? Has she been murdered?

"Marianne?" says a voice.

A shadow, a human one, leaks into that of the cactus.

"That you, Marianne?"

A thick, brownish hand grips her good wrist. Keith's picture flutters away.

"Get up, Marianne. Come now."

She clings to the arms that lift her, staggering, to her

feet. A bottle is pressed to her sore lips. Water infuses her tongue, dribbles down her chin. Through haze and smashed glasses, there is brown skin, black hair, wood cross, a deep voice. Sunglasses perched on a long knuckle of nose. She hugs this body. It is the last body on earth. An adult body. A man's body.

The man steps back, holding out her picture of Keith. "You're not Marianne." The voice is both gentle and direct. He is wearing a long-sleeved white blouse with a standup collar, and over that an orange reflective vest. The cross on his chest hangs from a strip of leather and the brim of his safari hat is broad; his army pants are covered with all shapes and sizes of pockets.

"Johnny," she says, "Marianne is lost." They need to find her.

Johnny-for-Jesus nods. Johnny's neck is thick. "Let's go," he says.

She falls in behind him. A long black braid swings down his back.

His dune buggy is some steps away, facing west. The body is red beneath the dust, the tires wide and fat, and a naked chrome engine pokes out the back. Stickers—Jesus this and Jesus that and the outline of a fish—plaster the bumpers, while the otherwise open top is covered with reflective vinyl shades. A dirty white flag with a bright red crucifix flutters on top of an antenna and the rear is stacked with water jugs like the two he is carrying.

He stops at a tangle of creosote. "See that?" he says, kicking around with a lace-up boot. "Some boys camped here, maybe last night." He replaces empty water jugs with the fresh ones he carries.

He tosses the old jugs into the open back of the dune buggy. "Get in," he tells her.

The seats are boiling and smell of burned matches. "Where are we going?" she says.

"Do some rounds for now," he says. Then he helps do up her belt and hands her a Ziploc bag of sticky dried fruit and warm, softened nuts.

The desert inches away, the sand going from white to straw to buttermilk. Through mirrored sunglasses, Johnny-for-Jesus watches the horizon. "Holler if you see anything moving."

She guzzles water, chews gummy figs and raw peanuts from the baggie on her lap. The nuts and fruit mash up in her mouth, forming a thick sweet paste that is so familiar she might cry. She dozes, wakes when the motion stops.

Johnny-for-Jesus has made a shade tent from a thick white tarp and a collapsible aluminum arch. They sit on a canvas blanket, huddling in shadow. Her good fingers fumble with her shoelaces, but he says she better leave them on for now.

"I don't have too strong a stomach for blisters," he says. "One thing I can never get used to." His hands gently squeeze her sore arm, fingers to shoulders. She says on the pain scale it's back up to a six. "Nothing broken," he says. "But we'll get you to the nurse's station. She'll pump you full of Gatorade too." He says she looks like hell—worse than that, even, especially the broken glasses.

She drinks as much water as he gives her, a jugful at first.

Johnny-for-Jesus rips open a packet of dry dates with his teeth.

"Desert food," he says. He pops a date into his mouth then passes her the packet. "Watch for pits." Behind his sunglasses, when he lifts them, his brown eyes are rimmed in red and pinched at the corner. He squints at her. "You really fooled me into thinking you were Marianne." Laughter whistles through this nose. He leans back, pokes her knee. "Maybe it's the denim . . . Or the hairdo."

Her eyes tear from the water and sugar.

"There was a crash," she says. She describes the picture in her head: the silver dune buggy with the gun rack, the helmeted riders, the boy who lured her into this no-man's-land. "He lied and said he knew where Marianne was."

Johnny-for-Jesus nods and reaches for a date. "How do you know he's lying?"

Johnny's jaw clenches as he chews. He rubs his crucifix between his fingers and looks out at the western horizon, the high country of some distant mountain she assumes, as a Zari, he must know the name of. She realizes she's never really talked to an Indian before. But being such a Christian makes him less of one, somehow. Right? Does he call himself Johnny-for-Jesus too?

She swallows the sweet lump in her throat.

Beside her Johnny releases a long slow breath. His nostrils flare. "Any news on the animal?"

She tells him supposedly Baez was with Marianne. The boy left them about ten miles from the road to Buzzard with nothing but a litre of water and some toilet paper.

He whistles. "She got far, that tough old Marianne." He laughs. "She always threatened to do it, but how in the heck?" Now he fingers the end of his long braid. The way he's twitching, Johnny-for-Jesus must once have smoked.

"But why was the car all packed? You know about that?"

Johnny-for-Jesus nods. He tells her some locals kept coming around to bother her. "She was putting out water for these boys, just like I do, only I don't lure them onto tribal land, see. If I do, the council will kick me out." Johnny opens and closes his fists. "Council's looking at land as property, see, just like you people. But when the end comes, it's all going back to the Lord, you know?"

Honey nods.

"So I stick to this no-man part though even that's against the rules too. Otherwise you're just asking for someone to fuck with you. Marianne was finding that out the hard way. Like I did. "

She tells Johnny of being at Marianne's with Keith those two years ago. "We heard them, these *pollitos*."

"Lots of them around her place," he says. "But don't call them that. They're not animals. They're boys. The Lord's children. Just happens they're born in a part of the world that's crapped on."

"Sorry," Honey whispers. "Of course."

"Anyway," Johnny-for-Jesus says, "there were way more of these kids passing over ranches and down the main highways before word spread about what the boys call *Las tierras vacías*. And I guess her animal kept them away too. Must have scared the shit out of them if they ever got too close."

Johnny spits a date pit into his fist. A single bead of sweat trickles down his temple.

She shows him the animal's chewed-up collar and describes the chain. "It's just so loyal."

Johnny-for-Jesus nods. "That dog's well trained. Like you

can walk right up to Marianne's property line and she'll just look at you all lovey-dovey. But one step further" — Johnny claps his hands — "she'll go nuts. That happened to at least one boy. Marianne saw it. Kid got bit, went running. Marianne was sure he died out here, bleeding, but who knows how bad the bite really was."

"She told me none of this."

Johnny's not surprised. "Here she's bringing the boys in close with the water and food she leaves, but then the dog's scaring them away. I said to her she only loved the boys on her terms. She only loved them when they were on the other side of the property line, a safe distance away. That's not Christian. You got to love without condition, as does our Lord." Johnny takes off his sunglasses, holds them up, looking for smudges. "Marianne didn't like hearing that. She said I should believe in the earth mother and all that, like I was some prehistoric ancient." Johnny-for-Jesus sweeps an arm across the landscape. "But I see the Lord out there in all of it. So what?"

Johnny stretches out his left leg, gropes in a bulging pocket near his knee. "Here." A bumper sticker: IT'S THE SAMARITAN WAY. "That's what I am, Samaritan. Before being Zari or anything else, you know? Like the Lord's children are my community."

Honey says thanks and that she thinks she understands. She lays the strip of plastic across her thigh and smooths it down, like a band-aid, before tucking it into her purse. She scans the surrounding desert. "So where is she?"

Johnny-for-Jesus says he doesn't know. After Marianne's arm stabilized, he says, he drove her back to the trailer. Baez was already gone.

"Dog must have freaked out, being left alone those few days. You say she dug that post right out of the ground? Shit." Well then it was Marianne's turn to freak out. "We drove around looking for that Baez, but no luck. Car was packed because she wanted to drive up to you folks, and she would have, but Marianne wasn't going anywhere without her dog. It's funny but when I went back to the trailer a day later I knew already Marianne'd be gone after the dog. I followed her tracks as far as I could. Then they faded out. Poof." Johnny's fingers snap. "Like the Lord, seeking in the desert for forty days and nights. Maybe she saw the light."

After a long buzzing silence Honey finally says, "How could she do that to me, to Keith?"

Johnny shrugs. "You don't know Marianne. But that boy does. And I bet he can tell you where she is. What'd you say he looked like?"

She tells him: hat with a sun drawn on the front, jeans, dirty shirt, oversized runners, knapsack.

"Sounds like all the others."

"But he's got weird orange eyes and a tattoo. A key." She touches her rib.

Johnny shakes his head. "They all got tattoos now." Johnny says, "Come home with me. Leave them be. Marianne's been gone a week now. She's either in Buzzard or she's with the Lord."

She won't believe what this Jesus Indian in the orange vest and big cross is saying. "No. She's close."

"So you do believe this boy?" Johnny leans back on his hands. His soft voice does not soothe.

"Help me find him."

Johnny waits to speak.

"Drive me over the hill. That's it. I bet he's there."

He considers. "Okay. But that's as far as my gas'll go. Then we got to go back." He might even have to stop at Marty's to trade for some fuel. She takes his hand when he extends it, allows herself to be pulled to her feet. He looks up at her and laughs. "Wow. You sure you're not her?" he winks.

Johnny packs the lean-to into the back of the buggy. The cross flag, up close, is homemade: a pillow case painted thick with acrylics, maybe Marianne's. The paint's texture is rubbery and glossy beneath her fingers, the bristled strokes controlled and neat. Johnny fusses with the jugs, empty and full. Then he tosses her a box of granola bars. She fumbles a one-handed catch. Foil-wrapped bars spill across the dirt: manna from heaven, is that what they call it? Her teeth tear open the packaging. She eats one—the chewy kind with marshmallow—then another, before Johnny is even in his seat.

"The boy was there with her, Johnny," she says, chewing on a third bar. "He might be my last link to her—right?"

Johnny shrugs. "People disappear in the desert all the time."

"People?"

"Boys." He fires up the engine. The gas gauge is at a quarter. They lurch forth. In the distance a rabbit dashes. Then something—a fox maybe—goes bounding after it. "Like the signs say: enter at your own risk."

Johnny cranks the buggy's wheel to the left then reverses so they face the hill. The climb is slow and bumpy. They burble and grind; wheels crunch and water jugs slosh. When they crest the hill Johnny brakes. Below them the land opens wide and flat, just the same as the land she's come through:

sandy arroyos, brittle vegetation, saguaros—arms raised or fallen, thick of trunk or dry ribs fanning out—and glints of tin and tufts of colour that is not flower but treasure turned to trash. Ahead, the Entradas glow along the horizon. That high triangle peak stands out from the rest.

"Where's Buzzard?"

"About sixty miles that-away," he says, pointing at the Entradas. "As the crow flies."

He tells her to open the compartment above her knees. Inside are maps, leather gloves, and a pair of binoculars. "You see what you can of him," he says.

Johnny switches off the engine. She sits straight up. With one hand she focuses the binoculars. Birds mostly, darting geckos—and she zooms in on every dropped piece of trash.

"Pass 'em here." Like a searchlight, Johnny scans the landscape, coming to a sudden stop. "He happen to wear a blue hat?"

"Yes." Honey squints in the direction of Johnny's glasses. "With a sun."

In a patch of mesquite, a dark bundle, a hump of something living.

Johnny passes back the binoculars. He starts the engine. They creep down the hill, veering to the right where the grade is gentler.

"Got to get to Marty's," he calls out, nodding at the gas gauge. "Not good."

Through the cloud of dirt and dust the vehicle churns, Honey trains the lenses on the boy. The hump of him moves.

"Fuck!" she shouts at the thought of losing him.

But he waits, unmoving, choosing to hide rather than be chased down half-alive.

Even at two yards away, his neutral colours are barely visible through the branches. She unclips her seatbelt.

"Just stay." Johnny takes a jug of water and a packet of dates from the back seat and—"¡*Hola!*"—approaches the boy's hiding place. He crouches down, knees wide, his orange vest glaring against Oro's pale monochrome.

The binoculars are on Johnny's seat. She manages to zoom in on the boy, partly visible over Johnny's shoulder. He drinks, eyes closed, not missing a drop. Johnny gestures to where Honey sits in the vehicle. The boy lowers the water, shakes his head. When his shoulders shudder she thinks he is going to vomit. But his orange eyes are actually crying. Wetness muddies his face. Johnny squeezes the boy's upper arm, so in need of muscle and fat. He is as exhausted as she is, as thoroughly wrung-out. He lives in a purely physical place. But a body can only have so much adrenalin. Then what? That he has tears inside him is sort of miraculous. She has nothing like that left and she can't imagine ever having it again. The salty water that falls from his eyes is elemental: it is life itself.

Johnny helps the boy to his feet, pulls him into a kind of sportsman's embrace. They pick up the boy's bags, walk towards her. Johnny keeps a hand on the boy's back. The boy is madly chewing the dates stuffed in his mouth. He wipes his cheeks, the right one red and swollen where her hand struck. When she catches his eyes beneath the peak of his cap, he looks down.

"Okay," Johnny says, "he'll show you if you still want to go."

"You're not coming?" she asks, when Johnny says he'll see her later.

The boy's face strains, gleaning from the English that he's going to be alone with her again.

Johnny shakes his head. "I'll give you food and water and even the binoculars, but I don't have enough gas." Johnny says she has no reason not to believe the boy. "Trust him. He will take you to where he left Marianne. And then on to Buzzard where you will pay his fee. You don't have to see him ever again, he says."

In Johnny's sunglasses her red face is narrow and distorted; the green ball cap appears ballooned.

"It's hostage-taking, isn't it?" She glances at the boy. "Isn't that what he's doing?"

Johnny shrugs. "It's lots of things. But this is where I stop. I got a long way to get back."

She loops the binoculars over her neck.

A hand to her good elbow, Johnny helps her out of the vehicle.

"What's his name?" she whispers as Johnny stuffs her purse with dried fruit and granola bars.

"Won't say."

The boy, whose pack is full of food and water, thanks Johnny. He and Johnny banter a bit, even laugh, the smile transforming the small bony face into that of a child. Then the boy steps back from the dune buggy, falling in beside her.

"Lord bless," Johnny calls out as he drives into the sun, now cresting in the west.

The flag bobs, the driver's head bounces, and then the buggy nips over a hill and Johnny-for-Jesus is gone.

CHÁVEZ

The sun is too hot and the bees too many so they cross the street to the library. A fat old tree with pointy leaves shades the lawn. They sit cross-legged underneath, leaning on their packs, but there must be an anthill nearby—they get right inside their socks—and then Ishmael starts to sneeze his head off. People are coming and going from the sidewalk to the library, books under their arms.

"Let's try," Ishmael says.

So they take off their caps and push open the library's heavy glass door, stepping into wood and quiet and the smell of glue. It is a place of calm and peace—a church or a thrift store only a million times better. A few heads turn but then look away again. They take turns going to the bathroom— Ishmael figures out you need to tell the man with the tie and short sleeves at the desk that you need to go and he'll give you a giant wooden spoon with a key on the end. When it's his turn he uses his best English with about five "pleases," and in the spotless porcelain sink scrubs his hands and face even better than he did back in the bus station.

At a wide table of dark shiny wood, he and Ishmael hunch over the Buzzard City newspapers. After his body cools and his ears get used to the breeze of turning pages and the click-click of the librarian's date-stamp, he becomes aware of his smell—sweat and dirt—and the sour odour of his backpack. No one looks at them. To these nice Lucinda library people he is as see-through as a window. But then why does his dark skin feel as bright and blazing as if he's sitting there on fire? And Ishmael is so black against the flat grey walls of the library it scares him. A cop could just walk right in for them. Maybe the librarian with the half-moon glasses like the Noah's ark lady's has called them already. Would it be the regular cops in the black-and-white cruisers parked behind the Italian restaurant? Or is there Control up here too? From a million miles away he would recognize the low-slung trundle of those shitty white vans.

The two chairs at their table are the only ones empty in the whole place. A lady in a floor-sweeping sundress considers sitting in one, but—her eyes vacant—just leaves instead. He watches Ishmael, who is smiling at his paper. Then an old man plunks himself in the chair next to Ishmael. He wears a camouflage baseball cap and shirt done up to his wattle neck and a sweater and a jacket. He smells nice, like hot coffee. While the old man and Ishmael read their papers, Chávez scans the headlines for words he understands, gently flipping and folding the crinkly pages. It gets busy with kids— skinny and red-faced from all the giggles they're trying to keep inside. The tall ones are really tall but could be the same age as him and Ishmael, and their backpacks—patched with reflectors and badges and a million zippers—are for books, not fuzzy toothbrushes and cans of oily fish. One kid has a violin case. Another wears baseball cleats. Two girls with long golden legs wear thick, pink-rimmed eyeglasses. When the dark kid from the park comes in with his mom he tries to meet his bottomless eyes. Then he tries to imagine he's that kid and that woman is his mom. He hopes the kid learns to fall in love with girls like he was supposed to.

When the clock above the magazines says two-thirty he pokes Ishmael's arm.

"Hey, Ishmael," he whispers. "It's time to catch that Buzzard bus."

BAEZ

And she dug and she dug. A day passed. The bald birds came, then the boy in big shoes. He had his water and roll of paper, which Old Blue tossed up into the tree, sending the bald birds squawking. And another day passed. Old Blue's purple smell hung in the air. And she dug and she dug and it was when Old Blue's hole was finally done — wide and long and deep — that Baez felt the coyote's offspring first stir in her belly. She stilled. The feeling came again: a very remote wriggly sucking, the first sapping of her blood. If she didn't eat and drink soon, her babies would die inside her, right along with Old Blue.

Finally Old Blue's breaths came out small and white and jittery — like puffs of rabbit tail. And then, at the first sign of grey, the breaths grew calm and long — snakes. By morning there was no more rising and falling in Old Blue's chest. When the body began to stiffen, Baez crawled on top of her dead master, spread out sphinx-like, and put her head on the side of the hard, slack face.

The bald birds came swooping. Baez nudged the body — heavy in death — towards the hole. It thudded to the bottom and something gave a loud crack. The bald birds hissed, the muscled hulks of them diving to get at the carcass. One latched onto Old Blue's finger, tugging to get it off. Baez barked them away and with her hind legs she began to push the mound back into the earth from whence it had come. All the while the bald birds shrieked, flapped, spewing their ancient bilious scent. And then the hole was full up. Old Blue was safe inside. In time the birds thumped away. Baez waited, blinking against the day.

Now, as dusk falls further, the high grey wall blackens. In the valley below a single small body emerges from the brown-boy hole. The figure is humped with a sack. It runs up the dry riverbed and towards the mountains where the desert buggy drove some hours before. This figure is wry and slender, goes faster than the boys that came before, its laboured breath lifting up and away in a cloud of silver white.

HONEY

They move away from the sun, towards the jagged line of the Entradas now stabilizing in the distance. Buzzard's on the other side. The heat sucks like a vacuum, drinking the moisture from her eyes, her mouth, from deep in her nose. Her lungs fill with hot air. She drops to the ground, crouching by a mass of dried-out snaking ocotillo. The plant's branches are hollow tubes pocked with holes. She thinks of insects, of dinosaurs. Above her, the boy gazes north through Johnny's binoculars. They will wait until the sun is behind them.

"You see my ring?" she says, holding up her pinky.

The boy doesn't answer.

It is just a ring, a thing.

"He is your friend, the Jesus *indio*?"

She says no, her mother's. "He good man, I think."

The boy agrees. "He helps us though he shouldn't. He breaks the rules." The boy crouches next to her.

"So why Ocho no shoot him?"

"Because he is *indio*. Some say this is his land, the land of his people."

"That what El Esqueleto think."

"What is she thinking about now?" he asks.

His voice is firm. He really does not know what Marianne is thinking but he wants to. What does an old woman have to be thinking to wander, willingly, into the desert? To surrender herself to this land, and, possibly, die here? Will his thoughts bring him to the conclusion that Marianne has done all this, in some indirect way, for him?

She says, "She think about water or a pretty colour."

"She is thinking about you," he says.

"Or she is thinking about the war." She tells the boy her mother lived in Holland during World War Two. She saw real Nazis. She saw what humans do to each other.

The boy does not know this war. But he does know Nazis. He lays his index finger under his nose making a moustache.

"Yes. Hitler."

His orange eyes get big. How did El Esqueleto get away from the Nazis?

"On a boat, all alone. She no speak English."

"How old was she?"

"Fourteen."

He whistles. "Did she ever go back?"

"No," she says.

They go.

The swath of flat begins to climb towards the looming Entradas. What comes ahead is dense with shrub and brush. Newsprint litters the ground—Spanish and English and is that Chinese?—a toothbrush, a crusted sock, a photograph so bleached out it could be a picture of the sun itself. The boy stops. Canine footprints again graze the dry sand.

Up and up, the footprints cut a clean straight path. Then the prints peter out only to begin again, three yards up.

They walk two miles, three, four, taking turns with the binoculars.

They walk another mile.

The boy says, "You see that hill?"

"Yes."

"You see that tree in front with the white? Like ribbons?"

"White? Yes."

"That's it."

Somehow the boy goes steady. She just feels like he calls her, *old lady*, barely able to focus her eyes so total is her exhaustion. Like an astronaut returning from the moon, she has aged twenty years in just a few days. After a hundred yards he stops again and looks through the binoculars. Then he pokes her good elbow and, passing the glasses, tells her to look. Her stomach clenches when she sees the narrow arroyo. Baez is sitting, back turned, beneath a wizened mesquite draped with white streamers. A high serrated outcrop looms beyond. The animal is waiting, watching, waiting some more.

Then she sees the footprints. She crouches down, her fingers following the textured lines of the long tread with the wide toe left by Marianne's sturdy lace-ups. For years and years her mother has worn the same sensible brand. She looks up at the boy. How can her neck feel such ice? In English she tells him she is afraid. She doesn't want her mom to die, not like this.

"Why, *niño*? Why she come out here, *Las tierras vacías*?"

"You go to her," the boy says. Then he hands Honey the length of rope he stole from Marty's. He is close. She reaches out and touches his arm like Johnny-for-Jesus had. This boy has strength in him she cannot imagine. But she can feel it, so she keeps her hand on him until he tells her again to go. "It is almost over, *vieja*. Soon you will be home."

She grips the rope in her good hand. Until the dog is leashed, the boy will stay where he is and keep watch.

Marianne's remaining prints are sporadic; Baez's, which run parallel, are also irregular. She wants to scream for Marianne to come out. And she just wants to scream. The animal continues looking north, away from her. Her hand grips the rope, sweats. The loop is taut, held in such a way she can throw it over the animal's head and pull it into a leash. Back-and-forth-back-and-forth her eyes scan the arroyo for Marianne, any piece of her, then shift to the animal: its twitching tail, mottled coat, broad ears folded like the page of a book: dog-eared.

And then the ears stiffen to attention.

"Baez." She says it softly.

The animal springs to its feet, turns. Its yellow eyes watch her come in.

"Baez! *Ba-ez. Here I am, good girl.*" She allows her voice to lilt, like adults talking to babies, to old people, to kittens. Does the animal really smile back? With three quick barks she comes bounding towards her. Honey's neck disappears into her shoulders. She has to plead with her muscles to relax, to not be afraid, for that will only make things worse. When Baez is but a few paces away she can already smell what is now that familiar hormonal reek. She closes her eyes.

Paws press heavy into Honey's legs then climb, settling on her abdomen. Those plaque-coated teeth match its eyes. From the smile, or something like it, on the animals' face, she knows the barking is in glory, relief. Its neck is bald where the collar had been while its left shoulder bears a long, nasty pink scar that she does not remember from before. Baez jumps back, runs circles around her, then paws her again, licking any bit of flesh she can access: a hand, a wrist, a bare knee through Marianne's torn jeans, which she takes in with wild sniffs. These are still Marianne's clothes.

Honey is on her knees. Baez tenses, allowing Honey to, one-handed, pass the rope over her head. With teeth and fingers she knots it, turning it into a leash. She holds the animal into her, restraining it but also hugging it close.

"Where is she, girl? Where's Marianne?"

"¿Vieja?" The boy calls. He has cut in from the side and is now standing under the tree where Baez had been.

Panting with happy calm, Baez turns towards the boy. Her wiry muscles harden in Honey's arms. The vibration building beneath fur and flesh erupts into machine-gun barking. As Honey grips the rope, the animal's teeth snap to get free.

"Go!" She screams for the boy to get the hell away from that tree and he does, dashing across a narrow arroyo and up into the outcrop from which it flows.

She frees herself of the sling so both arms can hug tight to the animal's thick neck. Her face presses into its bristled spine, breaking its pull. The barking cuts out. She opens her eyes. The boy is crouching in the distance. Some new form of pain sears in her injured arm. Baez has nipped her.

"Fuck!"

The animal growls at her now, licking its lips. Then growls turn to panting. Its eyes are held to the boy in the distance.

Baez pulls Honey to the toilet-paper tree. The rope burns her palms. She stumbles.

An empty jug of water lies slumped in the shade. Footsteps and paw prints trample the ground. A few animal carcasses—rodents, a rabbit—rot in the distance, and a wide patch of disturbed earth forms a mound near where she stands. Around the tree's base someone has formed a ring of small rocks, glass shards, and old nails. Honey picks up a triangle of rock that might be an ancient arrowhead. It goes in her pocket. She shades her eyes and finds the boy.

"Come," she calls.

He concedes a few feet, twenty or thirty, before the animal is on its feet again, barking.

"Bad girl!" Honey winces as, with both hands, she double-knots the rope to the tree, leaving Baez three feet of leeway. "Look what you did," she says rolling up her shirt sleeve.

Two berries of blood ooze from the punctures on the back of her bad, right forearm. But Baez's eyes are on the mound of earth. She strains to get at it. Honey bends, running her fingers over the long, loose-packed bump. The animal barks and dashes at her, lunging against the rope, the tree bending. Pain and anger compete in that tight mongrel face, two halves of a whole writhing against a vast, swelling sorrow.

Honey understands. She is standing on Marianne's grave.

"Hey!" The boy is shouting at her. "Hey, hey, hey!"

Echoes pop all around her, particles of voice falling through the static air. She blinks at the world, the red and blue and rock, swimming as it is. The sun is burning the back of her neck. So hot the flesh might go opaque, like steak in a frying pan. How long has she been just standing, Baez staring up?

Marianne is in the oven of the earth. Baez put her there, like a bone, a dead bunny: a sack of impossible love. Honey is in the earth too, for an alive, beating part of her has leaked down from her belly and out the bottom of her shoes.

Honey takes the arrowhead from her pocket—from Marianne's pocket—and, her eyes holding the animal's, touches her lips to it , and sets it on the grave, upright.

Moments pass. Her feet continue to leak: rooting her, gutting her, both.

"Hey!" The boy is still there, he is still alive.

When Honey believes the animal understands she unties Baez, drops the rope to the ground. She holds out her fingers. Baez bows her head. There is that scar behind her ear, the size of a boot tip. Honey touches it, soothing it.

"Goodbye, girl. Take care of her."

Then she walks towards the rocks where the boy is perched. When she reaches the outcrop she turns. Baez is sitting on Marianne's grave, just like Honey said.

CHÁVEZ

Buzzard City is written on everything from his bus ticket stub to the front of the station to the flags hanging from the streetlights alongside the flower baskets: pink, blue, wedding white.

Is there a festival on?

The bird on the flags is indeed a *zopilote,* its wings drawn back, talons sharp, going in for the strike.

"What does a hospital look like?" But Ishmael has never seen one either. They crane their necks. None of the buildings here have crosses on top like he'd thought, or a bearded saint like the one in the corner of the *vieja*'s business card. Of the glass — sheets and walls and towers of it — none is the kind you can see through. It is more like mirrors — tinted pink, gold, silver, green, purple, blue — and it's stacked so high as to block the moon.

There's no one to ask about Moses Hospital — everyone's in their cars — and, it's weird, but nothing is open and it's only ten o'clock at night. The glass cube that is the bus station is still visible down the block. There were some black policemen — one was even a lady with her hair looped up in shiny braids — walking around there. The police went really slow in their big shoes, with one hand on a gun the other on a stick, so they left. Now they share a square of light cast down from a Pepsi sign throbbing above a café too full of pink men to go into, though the smell of cooked food weakens him. Ishmael has the business card. He stares at it, trying to find some new information in the faded lettering.

"When you seen her last?" he asks Chávez again.

Chávez shifts his backpack, glancing up and down the block. "Don't know. Two years ago now, I guess."

"Don't worry," Ishmael says. "We're going to find her. You got through the desert, through the picking. This city's nothing."

"Yup, okay," he says. Were it not for Ishmael he'd still be picking berries and dreaming about this place. He can't believe how wide the roads are, how the pavement isn't all broken up with holes — and where are all the bicycles, the open plazas, the drunks who stagger through them? Some army of grannies must get paid to keep the sidewalks scrubbed and swept.

Ishmael says if they walk around they will find life.

Maybe they will find the hospital without having to ask. "We can't just stand here, right?"

The men in the Pepsi restaurant are all alone. They sit with fallen shoulders and face out like they are students in a class; the blank night reflected in the window glass must be their teacher. A lady behind a counter at the back does the cooking. She is dark-skinned, her black hair piled up under a net, and when she waddles out from behind the counter, he sees she is wearing bright pink rubbers. Chávez thinks if there is a God that lady will be his mom. In one hand she's got a giant glass of soda and in the other a plate heaped with food — red-yellow-brown — which she sets down along with a bill in front of the man closest to the window. The man gets his hands around some kind of sandwich and opens his mouth so wide he might crack his jaw; biting down, juice and bits of onion come shooting out the end.

Ishmael tugs his sleeve. A police car passes on the other side of the street. "It's twice now," he says.

They go north, away from the bus station, leaving the zone of the big glass towers. The streets get narrow and dark. They stick close to the walls, following shadows and going single file, Ishmael in front. The cars that pass have music pumping and the buses are all lit up blue; the heads inside are all dark-skinned, even that of the driver. It is otherwise quiet. Then a green car stops. It's so low to the ground it almost has no wheels.

The music cuts out and the man inside, just a mouth and a hat and a hand on the wheel, leans out the window: "Hey, need a ride?"

Chávez stops. He reaches for the card. This guy might know about hospitals.

Ishmael shouts "No!" then runs up the street between two brick buildings. Chávez almost doesn't find him. "You crazy?" Ishmael hisses. "You know what that guy wants?"

No.

Ishmael says he is pretty stupid. "He wants to fuck your ass."

"My ass?"

Ishmael says, hard and angry, "People here'll eat you alive, man." He says, "I thought you were smart."

They go on. Lights are on above the shut stores and from the windows come voices and TVs and smells of home cooking. He feels all the time like someone's following, and he starts at every damn cat or rat or fluttering bit of garbage. Though there's no one to see them, they obey the traffic lights.

Ishmael says of the walk signals, "Look, even the flashing men are white!"—and Chávez thinks the red hands telling them to stop are an Indian's hand—"'Cause they say Indians are red but really they are brownish."

"So maybe it's an Indian wearing a rubber glove?"

Chávez says, "Maybe." He agrees that if the flashing man was brown or black no one would see him. He'd be an invisible man, like them. No one would pay attention and people might get hit by a car.

"What people?" Ishmael says. "There's no one."

After ten more blocks—the street goes on straight and forever—they pass beneath a train bridge and come up in a place even darker and instead of stores there's just metal screens that stretch on and on like a wall or a fence. Then there's a window someone forgot to bar. It's filled with boots—rubber boots, silver-toed construction boots, boots for any kind of cowboy—and beside it a shadowed doorway. He sits there. Then Ishmael slides down beside him. He feels sick. Hungry sick. There's no food left so they each get a piece of Trident.

And he is tired, even though he slept the entire way on the bus. But he gets so he could sleep forever sometimes and it occurs to him that if things ever got bad, he could kill himself. How? He has no weapons—just his hands and his own ideas. So it would have to be jumping, like in front of a fast-moving car. But, really, he doesn't want to die. Okay, so does he want to live?

If they stay far enough back in the doorway no one can see them. He leans on his pack, draws in his knees, and closes his eyes against thirst and hunger, the shooting pain in his knee where another chicken chaser banged it so hard with a shovel. The cars in this part of Buzzard drive slow. One or two go swerving around, drunk. A muscled bulldog trots right down the middle of the street, its nails clicking, and then a few minutes later two guys in white sneakers come by, also right in the street, whistling and yelling a name he can't make out though he understands their "Come home!" They have sweatshirts on with hoods pulled up and maybe it's because the hands dangling at their sides are dark-skinned that Ishmael says "Hey" and steps out onto the street. The guys don't seem surprised. They are glad to see Ishmael. They just want to know where their dog went. Ishmael points up the road where the bulldog disappeared and then shows them the Saint Moses card. Where is this place? One guy pulls back his hood. His face is about as dark as Chávez's and his hair is cut very short. Were his face leaner, he could be a picker.

Ishmael comes back with a lit cigarette and he says the hospital is near the bus station, but on the other side. They share the cigarette, and go back. Just like in the desert, it's better to move at night. He thinks, is that why God made them so dark? Like they are meant to keep to shadows? But then he tells his brain to fuck right off and follows Ishmael on.

There's a puffy brown man lying in the gutter on the other side of the bridge. He's not dead but drunk. His shirt is wet with alcohol and sweat and something sticky is smeared on his pants. Chávez gets the guy's feet and Ishmael takes him under the arms and they sort of slide him onto the sidewalk. There's a squashed pack of cigarettes in his shirt pocket and the leather wallet in his pants pocket is full of bills. In the wallet there's also a rubber ring in a clear plastic wrapper that might be some kind of bandage.

"Trojan," he pronounces, remembering the English "j" is hard, not like the "hoh-tah" of Spanish.

"I'm no thief," says Ishmael, when Chávez slides a few bills from the wallet.

"But this guy has so much."

"Doesn't matter. In the eyes of God that's a sin." Ishmael's eyes are steady and strong.

"But we saved him from maybe getting driven on."

So Ishmael straddles the guy, grabs his collar, and shakes him going, "Hey, hey, wake up."

Finally the hoods of the guy's eyes crack open. Ishmael says, "Hey, hey, can we have some money?"

The guy snorts, "What the fuck, what the fuck" and then says, "Yes."

Chávez peels off two wrinkled twenties and then jams the wallet into the guy's front pocket.

"That's okay with God?" he says to Ishmael.

Ishmael thinks so.

The Pepsi restaurant is still open. They agree that Ishmael should go in alone because he looks older and his English is good. "Just act really normal." They go over the menu board through the window and practice the order: "Two Cokes, two hamburgers, two French fries."

Chávez pictures two single fries in a big carton. He asks Ishmael, "Shouldn't you make a plural of a plural? "'Fries-es'?"

No. "Just 'fries.'"

Only a few of the men look up when Ishmael goes in. The lady behind the counter frowns when she turns around and sees him but she gets used to him fast. Ishmael looks so dark inside the place with this fake lighting and the whitish walls and checkered floor. He stands ruler-straight, hat off, hair puffed up into an Afro. One of the chasers at Jelinek's had some clippers and for two bucks gave cuts. He gave Chávez a real shearing last week, but when Ishmael held out his money the chaser just looked at Ishmael's hair and shook his head no.

There's a kind of concrete park with a water fountain; they lean against a planter of bitter-smelling pink flowers and eat from the greasy bag. The food is some of the best he has ever tasted. It even takes away the ache in his knee. Then they wash their feet in the pool; the bottom sparkles with coins.

"Better?" says Ishmael.

He nods and says he is grateful to that drunk.

The sky is muddy. The water in the fountain flows and spits. He knows he should be astounded by that water but it is just as he expected from Buzzard City: that free water, plus the coins in the pool, could keep him alive in this city for his whole life, maybe — if he was careful, if he lived only at night. He will have to learn how to navigate this place where the stars don't mean much.

He wakes to the sound of an engine's steady rumble and grind. There's a little car coming towards them right on the sidewalk. Along with wheels it has whirling scrubber brushes and a tube at the front that the driver uses to suck up cigarette butts. He elbows Ishmael. Though the windows of the little car are dusty, they can see the driver's orange headphones, blue coveralls, and dark skin. Instead of hiding they just stay where they are. The driver jolts a bit when he catches them in his eyes but goes around like they are not there.

"Let's follow him," Ishmael says. "Let's make that man see us."

There are more cars on the street now — the sky is that dark blue before dawn comes spilling. They get their backpacks on and walk behind the street sweeper, then Ishmael goes running up ahead of the vehicle, circling the guy while Chávez stands right in his way with his hands out like the flashing Indian hands. The driver stops. His yells are muffled. He backs up and goes the other way, faster. He follows — Ishmael is out of sight — then stops to watch some kids skateboarding. Railings, steps, and flower planters are their obstacle course. They push hard with their feet as they, by magic almost, clear a planter or slide along a railing like it's a wave. The scrape of their wheels followed by the hollow thud as they hit the pavement is smooth and soothing. One kid skates over and says, man, does he have a cigarette? Chávez turns and runs.

The street sweeper and Ishmael are on the next block, in front of a pink glass tower with a concrete plaza and massive bronze discs like a giant's loose pennies. He remembers what Ishmael said about the god here being named profit. The street sweeper works along the tower's glass doors—the regular kind of see-through glass. Inside there are potted cactuses and spongy couches and a guard—a white guy way too old for a job—who is hunched over a huge desk. He's reading on the sly. Behind him, taking up the whole wall, is a giant painting of a desert—crinkled orange mountains, lemon-coloured sand, cloudless sky of beaming blue. He squints in case the writing at the bottom says MM, but can't make it out.

"Hey, outta the way, shithead!"

Ishmael has backed the street sweeper into a corner where there's a row of waist-high ashtrays made of giant pebbles. Who thinks up this stuff? Did some men somewhere agree to make ashtrays look that way and for the couches to be slabs of sponge? He finds no meaning in it except do-not-touch. Finally the street sweeper yanks off his earphones and cuts the engine.

"Look, kid, I gotta quota to cover tonight," he says. His accent is kind of sing-song. "And I got another job to go to after this one. Quit fucking with me."

Ishmael holds out his palms as he steps closer to the man, who's making a wide-eyed grimace.

"What is wrong with you, kid?"

"Hospital," Chávez calls, running up. "Moses, Moses."

The sweeper's face clouds then softens. Out on the street a bus swooshes past—the first in hours.

"Show him," Chávez says to Ishmael, who fishes the business card from his pocket.

The sweeper looks around. His nostrils flare as he grabs the card from Ishmael. Just glancing down he says, "Oh, yeah, Saint Moses is close." Then he scans them, up and down, back and forth. There is some grey in his hair-like-Ishmael's. "You sick?"

Chávez nods but Ishmael says "no" and tells the street sweeper the truth about how Chávez led the wife of that doctor across the Oro Desert and he's come to collect his *coyote* fee. He's been picking crops for two whole years to get here. The doctor will know who they are. "Or at least he'll know Chávez."

"The Oro Desert, huh?" The street sweeper says he heard there was some nasty shit going on down there. "Like an apocalypse happened. Or is happening."

"*Un apocalipsis* —?"

"Yeah. End of the world, man. Like in the Bible."

Clappity footsteps sound behind them. "Hey, what's going on?" The guard has a cigarette between his lips, one hand on a long black stick.

Ishmael squeezes Chávez on the elbow. "*Let's go.*"

The street sweeper turns over the engine of his little car. "Hey, no problem, man," he shouts to the guard. "They're with me."

The sweeper's hand is strong on his shoulder. "Come on." His voice is low, meant only for them.

Ishmael gets to ride right inside the car while Chávez balances on the side, his hands gripping the door handle, squinting against the rising dust. They chug along, passing the skateboarders, the water fountain, the Pepsi restaurant. The sweeper lets Ishmael hold the wheel and though Chávez can't see their faces, he knows they, like him, are smiling.

The city is waking up now, the sky cracking orange. Men in black leggings and silver Nikes go running past. One waves at him. The sweeper lets them out across the street from a high building of pink, speckled brick and rows of squat, glossy windows. MOSES, it says on the front, the metal letters all spaced out. There's a roundabout driveway and in the middle a concrete man in a big shirt or else it's a dress. A deep groove parts his long hair in the middle and the cord of his beard goes down to his belly. From across all those empty car lanes, Moses' ping-pong-ball eyes look straight into Chávez. But their peeled look is blank, saying nothing about what he and Ishmael should do now that they've finally arrived here.

BAEZ

Old Blue came back from the dead. She dreams of that, of that first real whiff of Old Blue's tobacco and paint tubes and oiled skin and salt feet that came tickling up her nose. Baez turned. Old Blue was dragging herself up from the southern horizon. Lightness swooshed through Baez's body, bright and also very loud, like an airplane overhead. There was no pain. It was all rushing light. She barked and ran towards her.

But it was Golden. She was dressed in Old Blue's clothes. And it was the wrong arm from Old Blue's that was hurt. As she ran towards her Golden's smell grew strong. It was the smell from before. When Golden and Grey drove up to Old Blue's they had a chemical smell, blank, like the flat glasses Grey and Golden wore over their eyes. When Old Blue was outside or just not looking, Grey's long thin fingers would trace the muscled spine that divided Golden's high, arched back. Puffs of cloudy yellow scent would discharge between them. And though Golden could have no children — Baez smelled that right away — her female smell was strong, seasoned, and hung in the air long after Old Blue came back in.

When Baez reached her, Golden's voice was high and her body hard. Baez licked and nosed at the clothes she wore, each time releasing a bit more of Old Blue from the soft fibres. Golden had the big-shoe boy with her. He waited back on some high rocks. Golden carried rope. She was aching as she moved. Baez let her loop the rope over her neck. The feeling of its constraint brought safety, soundness, a certain interior melt. Then the big-shoe boy moved in. Baez did what she was supposed to. She barked, she bit against Golden's body when Golden held her back. When she tried to run the rope cut into her neck. She was roped to Old Blue's tree.

Golden stood for so long. She started to smell like pain itself — a throbbing orange and slow, leaky blue. Then the boy shouted and woke her up. Golden knelt and talked to Old Blue through the earth. She marked Old Blue's mound with the triangle of stone. Then Golden undid the rope from Baez's neck and left her alone to guard Old Blue. She watched them go — Golden, who cut the same tall silhouette as Old Blue, and the small boy loping a step ahead of her. Big and small, they went as one. Then they became dots, swallowed into the rocks. Above, the sun arced across the sky. In the bright of the desert Baez was and was not alone.

HONEY

There is a path on the other side of the rock, as well as a stampede of small footprints that lead up to it, cutting in and out of the sand.

The boy says don't worry about the footprints. He says, "We'll get to the highway tonight."

Ahead, the Entradas are taking on texture. The path twists through the hills towards them. The small, little-boy footprints reappear from time to time. Some are no bigger than her hand and look fresh. A gang of eight, ten, maybe a dozen boys came through here. The biggest feet took to the front: *coyote* to the *pollos*. They were cautious, but for a time they imagined themselves unseen, and so went on quick and easy, gunning for the mountains ahead. Almost there, almost there, the leader among them must have said, just like her own *coyote* has promised.

The boy loves the binoculars. The strap cuts into the back of his neck as they fall heavy down his chest. He stops, scans the horizon, then nods it's okay to go.

They snake in and out of the hills, winding up, staggering down, and when they come to high bald humps of rock, he clasps her hand tight, pulling her up. They stop to rest after a jagged pass, for there is not enough light to climb, and wake to find lowlands—*tierro baja*—stretched below, after which more hills rise.

"Where are the Entradas?" she asks. The mountains seem to have disappeared.

He laughs. "We are in them."

He passes her a granola bar and the binoculars. He points to her arm. Why no more sling? She rolls up her right cuff. The poke-holes left by Baez's incisors grace the surface of her hard, red flesh.

"Hurt not bad," she tells him. But her neck and shoulder are stiff from the pull of the sling, now tied around her knee where her jeans are ripped.

"I'm sorry your mom died," he says very suddenly, without looking at her. "But she will be happy in this place."

"A happy ghost." She tells the boy in English she thinks that is what Marianne wanted. "To save you and protect you. What's wrong with that?"

The boy shakes his head. He does not understand. Can she find the tire tracks in the land below? She zooms in on the spot where he points. A vehicle has torn up the sand, spinning circles, cutting deep ruts. Within the pattern of the tires, the pack of footsteps they have been following erupts, casting off in all possible directions: a dozen boys scattered into the foothills.

They climb again, stopping on a hot plateau. Below this hill is a low basin of valley, filled with brush and a dry creek bed. Through the binoculars, the boy spots a narrow road leading back into the hills: some kind of dirt pass, down which wagons and horses might once have travelled.

"It is our road." The boy says they will pick it up and take it another hour, just to the other side of the valley.

The upper rim of the valley is cactused, nooked and crannied. As they move down, toeing what is solid, hand-holding over the steeper rocks, the road becomes increasingly visible, hidden back among a stretch of ocotillo, bramble, jumbles of roots. A vulture skims the air. The white sun blinks in and out.

Ahead, the boy has stopped. He turns. One finger is to his lip, the other points at a shimmer of chrome.

The dusty silver dune buggy is camouflaged in overgrowth. The search lamps on top poke out, like gophers from their holes. Ocho is laid out under a shady mesquite, soda bottles littering the ground. The other one, Curly, is slumped a few feet away; a wide-brimmed hat covers his face. In the dune buggy's rear, four boys are roped, their mouths blanked out with silver tape.

Morning hums. The boy crouches. With a stick he pokes at some ants moving through the sand. A gecko darts behind a cactus, the boy jumps, startled. He removes his knapsack and the binoculars, piles them on the ground.

"You stay, *vieja*." He says if he does not come back she's to follow that road to the highway.

He takes off his hat, wipes his face, then puts it on backwards. It changes him. He is older now, his chin narrower, upper lip definitely rimmed with soft hair. Quickly, before she can restrain him, he turns and creeps through the brush towards the dune buggy.

She watches Ocho through the binoculars: he ripples beneath his tree; Curly remains still. How long before the heat forces them awake? Ocho's hands are folded over his chest, the gloved one on top. Curly, meanwhile, wears his partly buttoned sleeves rolled to the elbow. Some kind of tattoo disappears into the folds of his crossed arms. Both are crusted in dust, as are the bounties in the back of the dune buggy, lying face up, eyes to sun. They are slowly broiling. The smallest might be eight, the oldest fourteen. All are in ball caps, sneakers or flimsy rubber sandals, cotton T-shirts, dusty jeans. Their bags, piled on the ground, have been slashed open: sweatshirts, comics, rosaries, cigarettes, empty bottles, canned fish, handmade maps spill out.

Then the boy pops up. Crouched over, back flat, he moves in on the buggy. He pulls Marianne's scissors from his pocket. They catch the sun. One bounty sees him, then they all do. They surge, begin to wriggle. He shushes them. The boy uses the scissors to break open the ropes on their wrists. The knots are tight. The boy's face is screwed up.

The day is getting hot. Ocho and Curly shift.

Except for the smallest, with a green hat that says *Twins*, the boys in the buggy are free now. They rip the tape from their mouths then gather around as the boy—her boy—wrenches with the scissors, working through the tough fibre of the little one's ropes. Then this one is free too.

The boy whispers directions, his lips moving like crazy and the freed boys nodding in turn. Then he points in the direction of the hidden dirt road. They gather their knapsacks, grappling for disgorged contents. With face-splitting grins they pat the boy, her boy, on the back, rub his arms, offer him what they have—a tin of fish, a small can of juice. But then something catches her eye. Ocho is not only up on his feet, he is crawling through the brush towards the buggy.

Her mouth goes dry. Then her mind blanks: swept clean, numbed out. She is aware of life and time slowing down, of herself being both detached from what she sees and also intimately connected to it. The action she takes does not come as a choice. It is just a series of exertions, movements, sounds that flow outward from within.

She pops up from her hiding spot and starts screaming her head off: "Go! Run!"

In their clamber to get away, the freed bounties knock the boy to the ground. If any of them see this, none turn back. Then they are gone. When he falls the scissors pop out of his hand. Quickly he comes to his knees and is pulling himself up, but Ocho has already got him head-locked. A piece of the rope the boy has just cut from the bounties now binds his own hands, in front, so they cover his crotch.

She crouches back in the underbrush. Fire-cracker Spanish carries through the valley. The voices are hard, not in depth but in anger. How many minutes pass? Enough that the heat of the day comes on full. Enough that her mind casts back to Marianne on her stoop, Marianne leaning over the stove, Marianne contemplating a canvas, Marianne expiring against that dying tree, toilet paper fluttering. Was Baez even with her then? Or did she find her already dead and then dig her mother's grave? Honey's chest convulses with something that in a different place would be a tidal wave of sadness, a final heave before collapsing into grief.

"*Hola*," a voice whispers. It is right behind her. "Esqueleto. Don't you move."

Curly's hand is tight on her bad elbow. The binoculars and knapsack dangle from the crook of his arm, as does her purse. Bruno-Jaime-Diego-Juan is by the buggy. With downcast eyes, he is smoking a cigarette and sipping a can of Coke. His face, though sunburned and swollen and scratched, is pale. He is not just shaken, he is stunned.

Curly tosses the boy's pack into the back seat as well as the binoculars, which land with a thunk. He gives Ocho her purse.

She thinks her hands will be tied. But instead she also gets a Coke. It instantly glazes her brain. A dense, cottony confusion lifts. They tell her to sit on the ground. She is too tall, they say. They need stairs to see her face. Ocho laughs.

Curly laughs. The boy's eyes do not look up from where a horde of ants skirmish over a spongy chunk of something bready. The chunk is carried aloft, as a trophy.

Like Ocho, his friend is dressed in dusty black Adidas and snug jeans, but while Ocho wears a tight red T-shirt, Curly is in a farm-boy's checkered long-sleeve, worn open. His chest is bare beneath. Both wear wide-brimmed hats which cast rich, inky shadow where their eyes and noses would be.

Despite his glove, Ocho is deft as he unzips her purse. The bumper sticker flutters to the ground. Ocho laughs through his nose.

"Ah, you met the Jesus Indian."

He calls for Curly, who peels off the backing from the sticker and smooths IT'S THE SAMARITAN WAY onto their pocked and gritty bumper. Ocho, meanwhile, is flicking through the cards in her wallet. He sounds out the information on her ID, glances at Keith's photograph, then jams everything back and throws her purse to the ground.

He asks where all her money is.

She shakes her head. Something inside her has unravelled. She cannot speak. Her words are all gone. Her tongue a nub.

Ocho steps close to her. "Esqueleto," he says, "I want something from you." His voice is slow. He holds up his gloved hand, pushes back his hat. His eyes flash: brown with black flecks. His pores ooze cigarettes. She guesses he is fifteen. He stands above her. With his bare left hand, he gently removes the dirty green cap from her head.

"Come get it," he calls to Curly, dangling the cap from his left pointer-finger like a hook.

His friend scuffs the ground with the toe of his Adidas. He is a few feet behind the boy.

"Hey!"

Curly looks over.

"Don't you want this thing anymore?" Ocho calls, his eyes not leaving her face. Curly steps up and snaps the cap from Ocho. He looks at it. "There's a million caps. So what?"

"Is it not yours?" Ocho says.

"It *was* mine," the curly teen answers, dropping it to the ground where it lands, deflated.

Ocho turns back to Honey. "Say something, *vieja*."

"Take me to road." Her Spanish cackles. "I give money there."

"Huh?" Ocho does not understand her shaking voice, her thick accent—both. He walks a circle around her. He says, "We thought you were El Esqueleto, but Chávez here says you are just her daughter. Chávez says your mom is dead." Ocho says he is sorry for that. Now they are all orphans—all four.

She is still. The Coke can, though empty, is heavy in her good hand. *Chávez*. Her eyes flick over to the boy in the backwards ball cap. The ants have broken the bread chunk into two pieces, one large and one small, and are splitting now into two groups.

Her head is scorching. Everything goes white for a second.

Ocho leans in. He holds his glove under her nose. He peels it back, revealing a rough lump of glossy red scar from which three digits stick out: thumb, pinky, and ring finger. "You know what did this?"

Her eyes remain glued to the mangled hand: a salad fork,

a garden tool, a permanent gesture to "rock on." She says she doesn't know.

Really?

She says again she doesn't know.

"Well," Ocho drawls, "Chávez says he knows where the dog is, the dog that did this." He looks back at the boy. "Right, Chávez?"

The boy squishes his Coke can beneath his heel. The tin crinkles. "*Sí*."

"Well, he's gonna show us where. But only, he says, if you say it's okay."

The boy named Chávez wipes his face, smearing grime. His eyes stick to the ants, the itchy chaos of their battle.

"And he says something else. Know what?"

She shakes her head.

"Says you got some kind of deal he's gotta honour so we got to drive you up to the road first."

Chávez's body gives up a belch. He is smaller and thinner now, his T-shirt must have stretched.

"And then?" she says to Ocho.

"Huh?"

She tries it again. "After the road?"

Ocho laughs. "Then you go for a cold beer, *vieja*. And you go thank God He blessed you with such a fine *coyote*. I'm gonna say the same prayer. 'Cause now *Las tierras vacías* is ours. We three got it all now. Our free-trade zone." He turns, calls out, "Right, guys?"

Chávez has righted his cap, the bill's shadow blanks out his eyes. His lips stiffen into a yes.

The curly teen calls out that yes Ocho is right. Smiling, he digs around in the back of the dune buggy. Finding a white T-shirt he strips away his button-down. For a moment he stands bare-chested in the sun. Then he takes off his hat. A mass of curls springs from his head. He squints up into light. His skin is the colour of coconut shell; his torso, though thin, is well muscled. He is a beautiful, beautiful boy. And when he lifts his arms to pull the shirt over his head, she sees he is Juan. The homemade tattoos on his inner forearms are just as Chávez described. The right arm shows Juanita and a broken heart; the left is a simple silhou-etted keyhole, the match to the *llave* on Chávez's stomach. And then the shirt is over Juan's head and the button-down again covers his tattooed arms. She understands the nature of Chávez's love for this Juan and she is sorry for the boy and very afraid for him if anyone finds out.

"So?" Ocho is saying to her. "You understand, *vieja*?"

She doesn't understand. She is only watching Chávez. He is a scared lonely kid just surviving. He needs so much. She has so much. There is so much between them.

Ocho speaks to her again in slow baby-talk Spanish. "There is nothing you can do for him," he says of Chávez. "He is a *coyote* through and through. He can't run away from that. So don't even try to help him." He waves his lumpy hand in front of her eyes. "See? Like any other *coyote* he bites the hand that feeds."

"Listen to Ocho." The boy's voice is flat and hard. "Tell him okay and we'll take you to the road."

"Chávez —?"

The boy's eyes finally meet hers. Ocho does not see their exchange and neither does Juan. And nor do they see it when Chávez flashes Keith's Saint Moses business card at her. She remembers him taking it from her wallet. He rubs his fingers together—the sign of money—and then as quick as he produced it, the rectangle of cardboard with her husband's name and contact information disappears into his jeans pocket.

"You fight hard, Chávez," she says in English. "Johnny-for-Jesus will help you. I will call him from Buzzard and he'll find you and you can go with him and he'll bring you to me and we'll get you new shoes and clothes and after you have a long bath you can watch TV while eating supper and we have an extra room in the condo and Keith always said he wanted a son and now you've done so much for me and with Mom dying I think it is all meant to be and maybe her soul's in you now, the last person to see her alive, that's you —"

"¡Basta!" Ocho shouts.

Then the boy says, finally, "Quiet, vieja. No one understands you but you, okay?"

Honey looks at Ocho and Juan. Then back at Chávez. These boys are tiny and fleeting against the might of the land that spills out, uninterrupted; forever, it seems to go. There is land. There is sky. There is so little left of her. Each boy for himself: that is the rule of this no-man place.

"Okay," she whispers. "Let's go."

CHÁVEZ

Chávez loves Ishmael very much as a friend. He could never feel that love for him like he once had for Juan. He has shoved that kind of love down now. That love is in the desert. He left it there that last night. Though he has told Ishmael the story about how he quit being a *coyote*, he always says that after they drove the *vieja* to the Zopilote road, they stopped for the night and he managed to escape: nice and simple. What really happened is something he will not tell Ishmael about. He dreams it sometimes, his mind betraying his vow to never think about it again.

The dreams always start with the music on the dune buggy's stereo cutting out—the same swishing, dishing one-two-one-two rap as before. It is dark: the half-moon-and-a-bit covered in cloud. And then comes the feeling of climbing what must have been a pretty high hill and the sudden push-pull of when Ocho finally stopped driving. All the jiggling had made him sick. Twice he swallowed mouthfuls of hot vomit.

Beside him, the Esqueleto's bitch had smelled of rot and death. What name did the *vieja* call it? Baez. Its eyes were dull and its coat patched with bald spots, especially around the neck. They were both bound to the gun rack—he by the hands, she by the neck. Was that sadness in its yellow eyes? While Juan untied the dog and led it away, Ocho took care of the ropes around Chávez's wrists, going slow with the knots because of his missing fingers. Ocho's breathing was shallow. Somewhere, footsteps sloshed in gravel. He didn't know where he was. The dark sky was made ghostly by a hazy blue light so he guessed they were close to the border wall.

In that blue light he saw a small trailer with sloped sides and lots of panels and antennas sticking up off the top. He felt sick thinking Juan lived in there with Ocho. He would crush and crush and crush whatever was in him that had made him once feel love for Juan. If ever it reared up, he would cut it down. He swore to that. So how can he tell this stuff to Ishmael, who is his best and only friend? Ishmael, who Chávez loves so much? It's a good kind of love, he knows it.

When he stepped out of the vehicle, Ocho retied his wrists and they followed Juan into the cage where he was settling the bitch beneath a tree. While the bitch got a tall plastic bucket of water in her corner of the pen, he got a two-litre jug. The door rattled closed and then the keys jangled. He drank all but an inch from the jug, soaking his shirt, and fell asleep in the corner. Keys and the rattling of the cage woke him, but he kept his eyes shut until whoever it was had left again. He was on his back, bound hands at his crotch. The dog's jaws were working away as it devoured its bowl of food. With wrists tied he spooned the dish of cold spaghetti Juan or Ocho had left, then he drank the rest of his water.

The dog was laid out on her side, the flat top of her head facing him. She must not have had a voice left then, she'd barked herself sick when Ocho and Juan drove up and found her still guarding El Esqueleto's grave. It took hours of goading her with food and water—and a fierce kick when she bit Ocho's glove—but finally she let them leash her. For some reason, the dog wanted to live, to be contained by them. What did it want with life? he wondered. What did he?

When the dog woke, she flipped over to face him. The darkness in her eyes was lesser, replaced by being sad. He wrenched at the ropes and then scanned the pen for anything sharp. There was a jagged rock in among a pile in the bitch's corner. He crawled close and she jolted, got to her feet. They froze. The dog's growl was weak. He told her what he was going to do. He just needed that piece of rock. He said he knew she was sad her old lady was dead. He was sad too. He was alone too. The dog lay down again.

With his legs open like a butterfly he clutched the rock between the soles of his sneakers. Then he held the rope to the sharpest edge and sawed away, one fibre at a time. The rock slipped about every second or third try, stabbing into the butts of his wrists. Soon the ground and his crotch were wet with sweat from his forehead—what didn't fall stung his eyes and wetted his cracked lips. The night sky was lightening, the unlit trailer taking shape. He looked up. The dog was watching him, tail flicking and ears twitching. The rope was thick and tough and the rock kept slipping. As the sky turned grey, his heart raced and his movements grew clumsy. Then he felt a coolness. The dog's shadow fell over him. It lowered its head. Its nose was warm and wet against his wrists. He willed his body to relax, to lose all fear. He drew his hands into fists and held his wrists apart as far as the rope would stretch. The dog slobbered as it chewed, its hot breath smelling of meat. He watched the bald spots tensing on its neck—the wounds from where it too had been set free. There was one behind the ear too: a round of pink flesh. As the fibres snapped he pulled his wrists wide—and wider—until the rope finally gave and his hands separated, a frayed bracelet on each.

He climbed the tree to its top, shimmied out on the highest branch, and got hold of the fence. The chain-link buckled at his weight. Hands like stars, he clung tight, jamming his wide toes into the links. The dog's eyes grew round beneath him. He pulled himself over the fence's spiked edge and shimmied down the other side, soft-landing in the gravel.

His backpack was still in the dune buggy. He filled it with all the cigarettes and candies he could scrounge and, finding no keys for the ignition, he sat down in the passenger seat. The sky became light. Above him the gun barrel was pointing up towards where the moon had been. Carefully he stood alongside it and ran his fingers over the components, the black metal smooth to the touch. He didn't know if there were any bullets or if, when he pulled back on the trigger, the thing would really fire. Was there an on-off switch? He put his pack on and lowered the barrel, aiming the gun at the trailer.

There was a great open silence after that first shot. His body buzzed with reverberation and he thought maybe he had burned his trigger finger. And also he had sort of slipped, fired wide, the bullet blasting off the top corner of the trailer. The dog had bounced up to her feet — her figure clouded in the corner of his eye — but the dog, like the morning itself, did not make a sound. His next shot was aimed at the trailer's door but the right-side window shattered instead. He remembers the ringing in his ears — the great wa-wa-wa — and thinking very clearly that nothing would be the same for him because with each shot he was cutting out some of the cancer growing inside. Juan was a cancer. His mom was a cancer. The desert was a cancer. He had to make himself well, not sick.

"What the fuck, Chavito?" It was Ocho. His high, angry voice escaped through the smashed window, just then catching the glow of the coming sun.

He didn't know what the fuck. "The keys," he shouted after a minute. "Bring me the keys for this thing or I kill both you fuckers."

Too much time passed so he fired again. The bullet went wide, pinging off a panel on the roof. "You both got to bring them," he shouted in a voice he did not recognize. "I want to see both of you." Then he added, "Hands up."

One of them shouted okay. The trailer door swung open. Neither Ocho nor Juan had a shirt on, no shoes either, just black jeans. The buggy's keys dangled from the pinky of Ocho's gloved hand. Chávez clung to the gun, his finger on the trigger. As they stepped towards him he saw how they looked so much alike—their bodies wiry and strong, hair above their lips the same thickness and colour as that which sprouted just above the waistbands of their jeans, thinning out as it climbed as a vine up their bellies. They both held their arms like a cactus—squared at opposite angles. Juan's tattoos showed bold. Chávez promised himself he would never do another tattoo. Kids and the *vieja* too think the feeling or person they're getting written on them will go on but nothing can last forever. Like you could never know what was coming, how in a week or a day something might make you a whole new person. He didn't want anyone to look at their skin and remember him, he who embedded that deep, dark reminder of time past into their living bodies.

When Juan and Ocho were four feet away, he lowered the gun so it was aimed at their heads. He told them to stop.

Ocho said, "Now what?"

Juan suddenly started yelling at him—"You crazy, crazy shithead"—and he stepped in towards him. The bullet whizzed close to Juan. He grabbed his left shoulder with his right hand as he fell to his knees. But when he pulled back his hand there was no wound. Juan's eyes were round and wide when he looked at Chávez—like a baby feeling pain for the first time.

"I don't care about your life, Juan," he said. "You fucked me over. You know you killed two little kids?"

Juan stared, scared to blink.

"You know?" Chávez shouted. "They're gone, dead in the hills because of you."

Juan shook his head. He didn't know.

"It's on you both now," he said. And then when he told him to, Ocho tossed the keys into the front seat of the buggy.

"Okay?" Ocho yelled.

His eyes kept hard on Ocho and Juan—back and forth between them. "Now go back."

Ocho obeyed, stepping backwards. Birds called, unseen.

When Ocho and Juan were on either side of the trailer door Chávez dove down for the keys, scooped them up, and jammed the biggest of them in the ignition. The engine turned over. He got both hands on the wheel and pulled the gearshift into reverse, just like crippled-up Pedro had taught him. He floored the gas pedal and, with a screech, swung the dune buggy around. Without looking back he left that place—down the hill, along the low riverbed, towards the Entrada Mountains in the north. On a high ridge in the foothills, the buggy ran out of gas. That was fine. He had himself, mind, heart, feet, and that was enough. One more time. This was it. He would cross the mountains just once more, and knowing that it would soon be over filled him with the energy of having a full meal, a week of good sleeps. He kept his eyes on the mountains as he went forward. And the whole time he climbed, pulling himself from rock to rock, he kept his promise to himself and never once turned back to see how far he'd come.

BAEZ

After Golden went away Baez still held the smell of her clothes and of Old Blue therefore. But the smell disappeared into heat. It did not take long. She was waiting to die then and she is waiting to die now. And then, like now, the sound of a desert buggy carried in from somewhere far off. A boy who was Glove and a boy who was Tattoo came skidding up. They had the boy in too-big shoes with them now, slumped up, hands tied and hat down. That low bass music was playing in the parked buggy, loud enough it shook the ground. Tattoo and Glove wore helmets and Glove a leather coat. Glove came up close. His plastic bag had cooked crumbled meat. Water in a plastic bowl that smelled like gasoline. She barked at Glove so hard a hot and rippling blackness came over her in a gush. It was death. Her legs crumpled and she fell down, silent. In blackness there was boot scuff and somewhere the trill call of bird. Deep in her belly something itched and then it moved. It fluttered. Her eyes fluttered. She woke. She let Glove lift her head to the water. After that he took off his glove so she could lick the bumps where once were fingers. Then she found her feet and cleaned the bag of its meat. Baez went in the back of the buggy with the big-shoe boy. The babies in her, or what would become babies, were going to live.

Now the sound of the buggy comes close. Its rumble grows deep in her jaw, spreads through her teeth, from raw root to spiked tips. Her children scratch at the plywood. Then they rush it. The barrier between them buckles and shifts. They yowl, they whine. They are hungry. They are too long caged. They are too much coyote.

In the furthest corner of the pen Baez makes herself small. She rolls onto her side. The smell of her own dying is thick. Dying wants out from inside her. She licks to get at it like she had licked sticky blood from her children, right here in this corner. Birth had stained the hard hot ground she shrinks into now.

That was two years ago.

Her babies had no eyes. She was their eyes, their warmth, their food. From the other side of the fencing, Glove and Tattoo had watched her nurse. When they entered, they came soft and quiet. There was more meat in her bowl now and the water fuller. The bunched-up blanket Glove pushed at her became a nest when she lifted each baby by the scruff and set it inside.

Her babies suckled until her teats touched earth. As they grew strong, she weakened. The hunger she and her coyote-mate gave those babies did not end, and neither did their yowling, twisting, thrashing. It was the desert trying to wrestle its way out of their sturdy muscled bodies. Still tries. With bagged meat and leather sleeves Glove and Tattoo tamed her children just enough to take them bounty hunting. She watched each one go and come as it was tested for the night's run, and then, when Glove and Tattoo's meat was not enough, her children turned on her. The plywood wall went up between them.

It is still early, and as yet too dark for their return, but the engine buzz is Glove and Tattoo's. Steady, unforgiven, in a wash of headlight the desert buggy winds its way up the hill. Glove unties tonight's lone bounty from the back of the vehicle. The bounty is something not boy or teen, but sweeter, nuttier, somehow. Instead of a peaked cap, a sort of twisted scarf covers both head and face. Round, glassy eyes peek out, taking in the shapes and shadows of this place — animal pen, trailer, a bright, blanketing moon. Together Glove and Tattoo lead the bounty to the lean-to. Tattoo readies the rope. The clattery alarm bells sound as the bounty is tied up. Across the plywood the animals who were her babies clamour and swell, yearning for quick release. Fear bruises the air. Baez licks her belly faster.

HONEY

She steps from desert to roadway and she turns left, pulling herself towards the milky glow in the western sky that she knows to be Buzzard City. She has to bend down and touch the hot tar to believe in it. She uses both hands, right then left. There are few cars. Each one that passes casts a meteoric light, then a rush whips against her body. She keeps to the gravel shoulder. Up ahead, radiant neon glows and then blazes into shape: a gold star on top of a pickle-shaped cactus which pulsates in the dark, steady as a pumping artery. But the sign is still so far down the road, half a mile at least. She keeps on and on towards it, dragging her horrible feet until it is right before her. She gazes up: Motel Roma.

Two-storied white stucco buildings with road-facing balconies form the courtyard. Pea-stone gravel scuffs against her shoes. The motel café swells with tin music and the voices of men who've got nowhere else to drive their trucks, nothing to drink, and nothing much to say so they yell instead. Above each room there is a light bulb. The general yellowy murk brightens the way to a corner beside the elevator where the office is tucked. A kidney-shaped swimming pool lingers behind a stretch of chain-link fence that sags — maybe from being so often climbed. The pool's flat, grey water is full of stones; on the smashed-up patio, the crumpled wings of plastic umbrellas slump or have fully toppled.

A homemade notice is stuck over the office door.

NO DAR LES DE COMER A LOS NIÑOS. Do not feed the boys.

The markered lettering is as stark and hard as the eyes that greet her from behind the counter.

A woman who must be Roma slouches at the counter, a lacy web of shawl slung over otherwise naked shoulders. Her thick black hair is short, curled tight, and the rings she's wiggled onto her fingers have turned the surrounding skin algae-green. The air conditioner behind her roars and when its cool air meets Honey's skin it is painful. The swell of her brain retracts. Degree by degree, her temperature falls.

"Please give me water."

Roma stands. The air conditioner's exhaust blows the shawl from her shoulders—plump, marbled with fat. Roma's mascaraed gaze falls down Honey's body, landing at the two tennis sneakers on the linoleum floor.

"Cash," Roma's lips are tight, a horizontal zipper. "*Plata.*"

"Water."

Roma shakes her head, clutching at the shawl. Her fingers plump her curls.

"Visa?" Honey says. "You take Visa?"

Roma nods. "With ID."

Honey licks her lips. The coating of the driver's license she pulls from her wallet has melted, the photo rubbed down by the boy's dirty fingers.

"Okay," Roma says, squinting at the card. "Give me Visa." Roma's accent is European. Hungarian? Is she in fact some kind of gypsy?

With Roma's fingernail file, Honey pries her credit card from her university faculty card. Roma snatches the Visa. She then surrenders a bottle of water and points to a chair; Honey sits and inhales the water in great gulps. The plastic rim hurts her mouth and her stomach shrinks up.

"You lost, Señora?" Roma asks if she wants to phone someone. "Call home?" Roma's hand makes-believe a telephone: thumb to jangly earring, ringed pinky to puckered mouth.

She shakes her head.

She looks out the window. But for the pickups lined up in front of the throbbing café, the parking lot is empty. By the pool, something shifts; a difference of light playing out in the layered shadow.

"Buzzard. How far?" She says this in Spanish.

Roma squints. "Thirty miles driving." Does she have a car? No.

Roma fills in the ledger according to the information on the credit card and driver's license. There is soap in the room and a towel. "Anything else?"

"Tylenol. Cigarettes. Cold beer. Large flip-flops." She doesn't care how much it costs or who brings it to her room. "And a sandwich."

Roma nods. The bar is open until two a.m. Checkout is at ten. There's a café in the bar for breakfast. "My *marido* cooks a good home-style mess."

"Breakfast," she repeats, the thickness in her tongue diminishing now.

"204." Roma squints. "You should call someone, Señora. There's a pay phone in the hall."

She says she will call in the morning. She wants to be alone for now. She turns, faces Roma. "Why can't I feed the boys?"

Roma shrugs, retrieving her slippery shawl. "You'll see. Farmers'll be here in the morning. This place'll be crawling with them —"

"With —"

"*Pollitos*," says Roma. "They come through the desert not far up the road." She lifts her hands. "For some reason this is where they get picked up. We should be so lucky."

Her room is at the far end of the corridor, overlooking the parking lot and the café. She leans against the balcony. She cannot remember where she put the key. Somewhere in the dark beyond, just across the highway, is the desert. It is all inside her now, just like Marianne had said she read in some book. "There is one inside each of us, Honey." Yes, it was in her all along.

In the room's grey fluorescence two beds are pushed into the centre. There is a midget fridge in the corner, a dial-up microwave on top. Bleach cannot conceal the room's history of beer and sweaty bodies, sulfur and cigarette—and the air conditioner unit rattling under the window does not quite melt the heat or diffuse a tinge of canned seafood. She gets a flash of the overheated Ventura and then quickly blocks it out.

Bent over the bathroom sink, she drinks hard. She frees herself of the running shoes, Marianne's denim, filthy underclothes, the festering rag that is her tank top.

She is thankful for the rusty safety bar in the shower stall. She holds tight. When the water touches her skin, she cries out. She doesn't wash, just stands there.

Her right arm is stiff but the pain is down to a four. She rinses her underwear and tank top in the sink, drapes them on the chair in front of the air conditioner. She shivers in a damp towel, and when there is a knock at the door she jumps.

"Beer, Señora," says a voice.

Someone has packed her a tube of Tylenol, a twenty-pack of Pilots, four cans of warm Bud, and a man-size pair of flip-flops. The sandwich, wrapped in plastic, is salami and mustard on cornbread. It is the most delicious food she has ever tasted. With her arm instinctively cradled against her chest, she drinks the beer quickly, swooning from the alcohol. The numb of the Tylenol kicks in. The bedspread, pocked with cigarette burns, is gritty with crumbs and sand. She curls up on it, waking once to shut off the light.

ON THE OTHER SIDE of the door the world is bright white, and the sunshine swallows her up like the night would do to a shadow. She cringes.

Last night's trucks are gone from the motel lot. In their stead are work vehicles, rusted out and dirty, filled with tools and ropes, guarded by mongrel dogs: shepherd, pinscher, bull, all with some degree of coyote mixed in. The slender nose gives it away. These dogs pace their truck beds — ribbons of tongue waggle and drip — overseeing shovels and tarps while the drivers drink coffee in the bar that is now, wiped down of beer, a café.

A flutter and a flap resound in the parking lot below. A man, tool belt clanking, chases a flash of fleeing boy. The boy is dressed in a grey T-shirt, jeans, and a backwards blue ball cap, all of it dirty; his skin is ruddy brown and badly scratched. The man hollers something at him, something angry, something Spanish.

Where the motel grounds meet the highway, the man comes to a sharp halt. But the boy keeps going, dashing across the asphalt, diving into the ditch on the other side. She remembers how Chávez had pulled out Keith's business card and rubbed his fingers. Now Chávez, like Baez, is probably dead. After a time, the man turns, spits, and walks back towards the café. He nods up at her where she stands frozen, clinging to the balcony rail. She waits for the boy to show himself. If she prays a bit maybe he will come back. But he is gone.

The café's only free table is in the window. Cigarette smoke cuts through the grease. Above the bar another sign warns not to feed the boys. Taped beside that, the handwritten menu says breakfast is all day and costs $3.99.

The man from the parking lot brings coffee in a paper cup.

"Breakfast, Señora? Bacon and eggs?" He reaches for his pen. The patch on his breast pocket says his name is Carlos.

"Yes, white toast. And a whiskey and Coke, double."

Carlos doesn't flinch. "Right away."

That boy Carlos was chasing could not have been Chávez. There is just no way. Ocho and Juan and Chávez had dropped her off on a rocky hill at the bottom of which was the highway. She'd stood by the dune buggy, unable to move. Juan was leaning up against the gun mount, polishing the vehicle's search lamps with his sleeve.

"No go, Chávez." She remembers trying to say in Spanish: "Please don't leave me alone now."

Ocho revved the engine at her. The boy, when she spoke, watched her lips and shook his head. "What are you saying, *vieja*?"

She had nothing but ache inside her, ache and the certainty that this boy had inherited some part of Marianne and so how could she let him go like this? Die like this? "You do understand me, *niño*. You do."

Ocho put some music on, the stuff Buzzard ghetto kids play as they race the main drag when people with jobs are asleep. Then Juan shouted at her and Chávez, laughing. Something about a kiss goodbye. Chávez looked at her and pointed with his bound hands where she was to go. Once she thought his eyes were like hard round pennies, but that moment they were all heartbreak to her, pools of it. And then in a spray of dirt and sand, Ocho turned the buggy around and drove away. She watched as they retreated. Chávez's head was bouncing. He did not turn around. She was afraid for Chávez, afraid for Baez. More, though, she was afraid of the sadness and regret she knew was going to come and drown her. She can't think about that now. Not without Keith there to help.

The men at the counter are in boots and jeans. Their skins are burned; whether black or brown or white, all is red. Grey hairs infiltrate their heads and half-beards. They whiten their coffee with cream capsules and sip it slow, fingers rarely touching the cigarettes poked in their mouths.

She feels their eyes on her. She hears their hushed talk.

"Some kind of walker."

"Crosser."

"Lost hiker."

"Desert had a good chew on her."

"Roma says she came stumbling in last night, drank a dozen Bud all alone in her room."

"Brain damaged, I bet. Some of the pickers I got have it. Kind of crazy and stupid from all that sun."

Early news blares on the TV behind the bar. *Hotter than normal temperatures; water rationing in effect; house fires raze half of eastern Buzzard; rash of drug-store invasions; family poodle coyote-nicked, and in front of the kids too.*

The men say how the coyotes are coming in more and

more now, easier to live in the city than out there in the desert.

"Then there's the illegals. How do they survive that son-of-a-bitch crossing?"

They shake their heads.

"Well, many're used to it, that terrain, like Africans are. Or like the Indians before taps and toilets were given to them."

"Yup. They get so it's wired in their blood."

She watches across the road. No matter how hard she stares, the boy in the blue ball cap Carlos chased does not resurface.

"*Huevos*, Señora." Her breakfast is a pair of fried eggs on toast, refried beans and sausage rounds glistening alongside.

"That boy," she says, looking up at Carlos. "The one you chased?"

"Who?" Carlos sets down her drink and wipes his hands on his shirt.

She points to the road. "He had a blue cap."

"There's many, Señora. Can't tell which is which."

She forces herself to use her right hand to lift the icy drink—the whiskey is barely detectable through the sugar—and her jaw works slowly on the toast. Salty butter soaks into the cracks of her tongue. Behind her the men keep talking.

Day is brightening in the parking lot. Traffic picks up on the highway. A few cars pull in, a truck. A white Control van completes a slow U-turn in the lot, then heads south. And that is when the boys come out. They fall in from the shadows, creep from under the patio furniture, crawl out from the bushes lining the front of the office or up from the ditches along either side of the road. Milling by the gravel shoulder, they sip sodas scooped from the machine by the pool, kicking cans, sharing bread. A few have treasures to trade: a china plate, a Bible, a magazine, an oversized T-shirt that had been Marianne's. These boys are battered and ragged, they clutch plastic bags and knapsacks, water bottles both empty and full. And their ball caps are of every make and colour: stamped and patched and decorated with magic marker, worn frontwards, backwards, some on the side; one boy, with face burned to charcoal, has a hat with no beak at all. Yellow caps, green, denim, net, mesh-backed, canvas, a lone white one, but there is no blue.

One boy turns a crushed beer can into a soccer ball; two-litre water bottles serve as goal posts. They keep the game to the road's narrow shoulder, away from the passing cars and the motel's driveway. Between frying eggs and pouring coffee, Carlos dashes out. With the hammer in his tool belt, he drives back those among them who stray too close to the café.

She signals for another drink. Behind her the TV shows images of the border wall, against which the Río Loco trickles, orange with filth. The newscaster wants to know what those watching at home think about this latest attempt to curb undocumented migration. "Will this finally plug the hole?"

A blue pickup pulls in, almost colliding with a lanky kid in rubber boots and a purple cap.

The boy jumps back, stumbling over his flopping rubbers. His playmates hoot and laugh, kick him the beer can. He fires it at the opposing goal, sending it wide, into the road.

The truck parks in front of the café. With a shaking head, the driver ducks out, slamming the door. He wears a yellow cap and denims; a scraggle of grey-and-yellow ponytail drips down his back. He leaves his window down a crack for the dog inside then strides into the café.

"Hey!" the men at the counter yell, over the news and the fryer grill and clinking cutlery.

"You got any treasures today, Marty?" a crab-faced man asks, loud.

Marty leans against the counter. He casts a look around.

Outside a small boy in an Gulf ball cap scores a goal. His friends shout. High-fives all around.

Honey feels her smile disappear as a shadow falls over her. Marty takes the chair opposite, signals for a coffee. To go with his tobacco scent, his face is cracked, especially around the eyes, watery-pink. Sunglasses perch atop his cap and his T-shirt, under the open button-down, says something about an aquarium.

"I thought you were dead," he says.

"Me?"

"You."

The coffee arrives. Marty wraps his fingers, long and dirty, around his cup. A boy is taking a penalty kick. He slips and, falling, takes a swatch of skin off his knees.

"One of your *coyotes* drop you here, Marianne?" Marty points to the soccer game, leans in close. His breath smells of his cargo. "Coyotes and chickens, isn't that their game?"

"Is that what it is? A game?"

"But with the little boys, it's different. You think: they're kids, so you can trust them. You think they can't hurt you." Marty nods towards the parking lot. "Look at them playing."

The sun is blinking white and the sky is bluebell. Way

beyond the highway and along the horizon, mountains rise. The peaks and gaps through which Ocho drove her rise up sharp.

"They're all the same," Marty says.

"No," she says. "There are good ones and bad ones, like any other kind of people."

"Sometimes I think they're smarter than us." Marty gestures with his thumb. The boys are comparing ball caps, sharing water from jugs.

"Maybe so. And maybe if I took one of them home to raise up, he'd be just fine."

Marty lifts his chin and runs his fingers along a prickled throat. His eyes narrow. "Maybe. Maybe yes, but it'd have to be right from a baby."

Her head buzzes. "Where'll they go?"

"Don't you know that, Marianne?"

She says she wants to hear his version.

"They're waiting on a ride. Farmers come for them, or contacts in the city."

She tells Marty their parents have gone north and become lost. "Whole villages with no parents. Imagine? And now no boys either. Just girls and grannies."

Marty shakes his head, fingering the slink of hair that has crept over his shoulder. "Don't know about that." He sits back, satisfied, runs a finger up and down the edge of his cup, catching a drip. "Well—you need a ride to Buzzard?"

She looks out the window. "No."

He leans in, closer now. Bitter coffee on his breath, smoke in his hair, in that yellow hat. "You know I could've turned you in, lady, helping the other side like that."

She slurps the end of the whiskey.

Across the table Marty stares back.

"I'm a good person," she says. "My daughter loves me so."

IN THE PARKING LOT the boys are puffing hard and laughing harder. They call each other *coyote* and *pollo*, depending on the team. She comes in close. Someone whistles and they stop, stand back, and stare, a rainbow of T-shirts and hats and shoes, jeans. Forty boys, maybe fifty.

"Hey, it's El Esqueleto," one says.

"What's she doing here?"

A boy in a big canvas cap with Coors on the front juts out his lip. "What you want here, Esqueleto? We're sticking to our side of the line."

She shows them open palms, her arms extended. "Chávez. See him?"

They shake their heads, shuffle their feet. "No, Esqueleto," Coors says. "We don't know that kid."

One boy kicks the can to another and slowly the game resumes. They run around her, laughing and crying out.

"Hey, spindly saguaro," they say, knocking her legs. "Fuck off, *vieja*. You're getting in the way."

"Hola! *Vieja*." Small fingers tug her jeans.

The boy in a pinstriped engineer hat stops at her knee. His wide brown eyes are rimmed in old-man red. His front teeth are too big and his right eyelid droops. He says he knows Chávez. Chavito, he calls him. With the eyes.

"He here?" She looks around. "*Niño*, tell me. I give him money," she says. "I take him to a good school. He be so lucky."

"Chávez?" the boy says, his eyes clouding. "In a school?" No, he says. Not him. "But why not me?" he says. "I want to be lucky too."

Another boy runs over. "Hey! Yeah! Give me money too! Either that or fuck off so we can play." Then another boy joins the first one, and another after that, and soon she's in the middle of a tight ring of boys, their upturned faces laughing at her in quick, lilting Spanish.

She breaks through their circle, knocking one boy to the ground. Marty's been watching. The farmers are coming out of the café now, carrying take-out cups. At their calls and whistles, the boys abandon their game, gather their belongings, rush towards the pickups. They hoot and holler, clamouring to get in the back, the drivers honking their horns. A rainbow of hats and shirts sit crammed into the truck beds, clutching sacks and bags and each other. The trucks form a line, waiting to pull out onto the highway—some going north, others south.

Leaning over the rail, she strains to find a blue ball cap. But they—boys and caps—blend in together, all different and also all the same.

"Chávez! Chávez!" she shouts, waving her arms, crazy. Then she shouts all their names, the only one she can be sure of: "Niño!" But if they hear her, none of them show it. She does not know their language after all.

And then, from the opposite side of the road, a figure pops up and comes running. In a backwards blue ball cap he dashes across the asphalt. The boys who see him cheer him on, call for him to hurry. A pickup, just turning north from the motel, slams on its brakes long enough so the boy can toss his knapsack in the back and jump inside. He lands in a pile of bodies which wrestle him up, cheering and laughing. She is sure it is him. She is also sure that he is dead somewhere, shot in the back as he ran away from the boy he loved.

She will see him in everything now.

As the pickup pulls off down the road, she catches the orange glow of eyes — and he catches her eyes, too.

CHÁVEZ

In the *vieja*'s photograph the doctor had silver hair, silver glasses, a long, thin face.

"And she has glasses too," he says. "Big black ones. And short hair, light-coloured. Bleachy. But I bet you'll just know."

Ishmael bets it too. But really the *vieja* could be any one of the tall, skinny white ladies going in and out of the sliding glass doors or sitting smoking at the bottom of the Moses statue.

The problem is there are about ten different entrances to the place. Chávez and Ishmael take turns waiting at the main entrance while the other one walks back and forth between the others. Along with the sliding doors, there are ramps for wheelchairs. People in pyjamas stand by the door smoking, as do ladies who must be nurses except they don't wear skirts and hats like he remembers from picture books. Instead they wear pyjamas too — papery ones in pink or blue, plus wide-toed rubber shoes.

As soon as morning breaks, cars and people and ambulances start pulling in and out of the roundabout. He feels jittery, like his very insides, heart and lungs, are sweating. Ishmael says they both just need to sleep. Ishmael talks about Hal — that's the street sweeper — and how maybe they can find him again.

"Hal can get us work, I bet."

But why will they need to work once he gets his money?

"It's a whole five thousand," he reminds Ishmael, training his eyes on the sliding doors across the road.

Because of the hospital guards they have to keep shifting their spots. They go from one bench to another, from this side of the road to the front of the Trust building right across the street, where there's a whole different set of guards who get to know them pretty fast.

"It's sort of like a war everywhere," Ishmael says of the straight-faced men, sunburned, black, some women too, with chunky belts and shoulder badges. "Like where I come from. Except they'd be our age 'cause all the men are gone."

They can see the highest peak of the Entrada Mountains from their favourite spot on the low wall in front of the Trust building. The mountain looms, wide and gloomy blue. When Ishmael learned Chávez had climbed through that range to get here, he had whistled.

"They watch over everything, don't they?" Chávez said. "Many eyes in that rock. Secrets too."

Ishmael is buying hot dogs from the cart up the block. The hot-dog man is half-black but with Chinese eyes and a thick goatee. They bet he was a picker once. Before he pays for the hot dog — they are going to share a jumbo — Ishmael talks to the man for a while. He shows the man the doctor's business card. When he comes back, his half of the hot dog already eaten, Ishmael tells him that Hugo the hot dog man said after work he'd go inside and ask for the doctor.

When the sky is dimming, Hugo's wife pulls up in a van that would be white were the doors and hood not all different colours. While Hugo takes the card and goes across to the hospital, Chávez and Ishmael attach the cart to the van's trailer hitch. They know how to from farm work. They tell this to Hugo's wife, Veronica, who speaks Spanish. She is staring at Chávez so much he wants to tell her to take a fucking picture. When she asks, he says he has no mom or dad or job. She has a tight ponytail that makes her eyes look closer together than they are. She is chubby, maybe even fat, like plenty of people here—Abuelita would shake her head at that. Veronica fills a clear bag with all the cooked hot dogs Hugo didn't sell. The bag steams up.

"Take it, my love," she says. "You want ketchup too?"

Hugo wades back through the traffic like he's crossing a fast-running stream. He holds up his thumb, way up. "Doc's on the twentieth floor. Like the card says."

Chávez tells Hugo and Veronica they really do have a place to stay—their friend Hal's house has a swimming pool and a TV in every room—and finally they drive away, cart weaving behind. Then he and Ishmael sit on the Trust wall, watching. When it's dark and the bag of hot dogs already empty, a really tall man comes out of the sliding doors. His hair is silver and, like the *vieja*, he is thin. His glasses—so big they cover half his face—are different than in the photograph.

Ishmael sees him first. Chávez says, yup, it's him.

They cross the road, the cars fewer now, and follow him—half-running because the man's crazy long legs carry him so fast—to a parking lot on the next block. The car he unlocks is sparkly blue and very clean. He disappears inside, folding in one leg then another. The headlights flick bright. He drives to the booth, shows something to the man inside. The mechanical arm goes up. From the doctor's spot, number 165, they watch the shiny blue car drive away.

The brand of car is Ventura. He must be a specialist or a

big cheese, Hal says, when they tell him of the regular hours Doctor Keith keeps. He comes every morning at seven. Weekends he's there at ten, hardly ever leaving before dark. His shoes have hard soles that clap when he walks and he has many ties—the green ones are his favourite. Along with a briefcase, he might carry a backpack with a tennis racket sticking out. He and a doctor with a brown beard, who also has such a bag, will drive away at lunch and come back two hours later. On those days the doctor will stay until ten or eleven at night, the pink hospital a blazing tower against the blue-black sky. Moses out front keeps steady and strong, even if his dress has splats of pigeon poo on the front and there are cigarette butts between his chipped toes.

Hugo won't approach the doctor for them. "Security'd be on me, boys, no way."

Instead, he tells them to write the doctor a note for his wife and stick it under the windshield wiper of his car. Or why can't they attach themselves to the car, sort of like an undercover cop on TV? But, whatever it is, they have to do something.

"The rich bitch should pay up," he says.

Ishmael won't let Chávez do the attaching-himself-to-the-car thing. This is not TV but real life and he could get killed doing something so dumb. One day the *vieja* is going to come to work with her husband. Maybe she'll drop him off like these other ladies do—offering lips or cheeks for husbands to nip before they slide out of their sleek cars that always have leather seats and hood ornaments of stars, leaping jungle cats, some that look like cobras.

"You have to be patient," says Ishmael. "But not be *a* patient."

Ishmael laughs so hard and then Chávez laughs, once he understands.

They live on the rice and beans Veronica brings for them in old margarine tubs. Veronica wants them to come home with her and Hugo. "Who is this friend? This Hal?" She wants to meet him. They say, tomorrow, tomorrow, and keep sleeping in the bushes—the best ones are under the Trust building windows—and washing themselves in fountains, of which there is no shortage in downtown Buzzard City. Chávez fishes out the coins at the bottom, and when he buys burgers or milk with the harvest Ishmael pretends he doesn't know where the money is from. Sometimes they do see Hal. He takes them for rides in his sweeper car if he's not in too much of a hurry, usually stopping for takeout at the Pepsi restaurant where he knows the lady in the pink rubbers behind the counter, who turns out not to be Chávez's mom like he sort of prayed she was.

But he and Ishmael are always in the parking lot at seven in the morning when the doctor's blue Ventura pulls in. If the silver Buick is parked next to it in 167 like usual they'll lie underneath, waiting for the cool air to billow out as the doctor opens his door. The air smells like *her*, sort of bleachy, a bit like leather. The doctor never sees them. His eyes are a million miles away. And he doesn't walk; rather he sort of runs on those legs.

But the attendant has called the hospital guards on them a few times. They're too quick to get caught, though, especially when the guards have such big belts and asses, and why the chunky shoes? They should be in Nikes.

When they're not waiting in the lot, Chávez and Ishmael stick near Hugo's stand. They have a good view of the front doors from there. Hugo watches too. He says the best thing would be if the doctor came and bought a hot dog.

"But I doubt he'd stoop to that, man."

He says the guy probably goes in for lobster. Sometimes Hugo won't go to the bathroom for the whole day. He doesn't think he should just pee in the bushes like Chávez and Ishmael do. The mini-park around the corner is nice and private if you just don't look at all the bums.

"We'll watch the cart, Hugo." But Hugo says no. He's disciplined.

It is boiling hot summer when the Ventura doesn't pull into 165 at seven a.m. Maybe Doctor Keith is just late. Or he's on vacation.

Hugo says, "It's summer, right, and these doctors'll take their wives to Italy for the whole goddamn month." But he also says, seriously, they should think about what would happen if his wife never shows up. Maybe they're divorced now. "And, anyway, five thousand isn't that much."

Ishmael frowns. "I bet it's enough Chávez can get us a hot dog cart." He brags that Chávez knows how to hawk stew and bread from back in his village. He could learn hot dogs real quick.

Hugo shakes his head. Before anything, they'll both need work papers. "Otherwise you're as good as garbage here," he says. "*Maybe* five grand will cover that for you both."

Chávez is going back to wait in the lot. Ishmael will stay with Hugo and watch the doors in case the doctor comes in a cab. The attendant in the booth is the one who's always reading, so it is easier than usual to sneak past. The lot is about half-full. Going low, he makes his way between the cars. Every other one, he tries a door—just in case—but they're locked. The silver Buick is in 167. It always is. That Buick doctor works more than Doctor Keith. Ishmael thinks maybe the car belongs to a patient who can't ever leave the hospital. Maybe the owner even died?

Footsteps come — sharp and fast like a lady in those high heels. Chávez rolls under the Buick. The ground is stained with oil. The footsteps stop and then an engine turns over. Wheels crunch. Then comes the creak of the mechanical arm. It all happens again as another car pulls out of the lot. Must be night nurses leaving. But then a car pulls in, and with a squeal turns right alongside him in 165.

The engine cuts out. The door clicks open and the familiar billow of cool air washes over his face, but the smell of bleach is stronger. He waits for the clap-clap of the doctor's shoes to hit the pavement. But instead there is a soft pat-pat. He rolls over on his side. There are pink Nike swooshes on the backs of the shoes. Big shoes, but a lady's. The feet dance around, up and down, as she does something in the car. Her ankles are bare. When Chávez sees the *vieja*'s tattoo, he is seized with fear. He can't hear anything but that — the cold thud of being scared. Then she shifts. The left ankle is tattooed now too: a black sun the size of a silver dollar. The rays are expert, sharp, and the ink so deep and shiny it is reflective.

His eyes get wet. He could just curl up under this car. He's so tired suddenly. His heart weighs a million pounds. And after all his two years of waiting — more than two years — he's forgotten what he's come here to say.

Slowly, still concealed by the Buick, he eases his body closer to her feet. Then he reaches out. He watches his hand as it closes in on her ankle. He wishes for Ishmael. If

Ishmael could see him, he'd tell Chávez to be cool and calm. Because if she screams—then what? Then it's all over. Ishmael would also remind him that all that anger in his heart is enough to make him sick. It does make him sick. To get rid of it, he wants to hear her scream. But he wants his money more. He pulls back his hand, tucks it in his armpit where it will behave. The ankle tenses and pulls as the *vieja* fusses around in the car.

Chávez rolls out from the back of the Buick, ducking the tail pipe. He crouches, peering around the rear bumper. The *vieja* towers above her car. Her blond hair is long enough it brushes her jawbone. She wears some kind of long, flowery shirt over her short pants. Her bare shoulders are wide and very strong. Man shoulders. They were not like that before. There are no glasses on her face, but a pair of sunglasses are perched on her head. She is fiddling with her purse, the very same one. Then she opens a briefcase up on the hood, shuffles the papers inside.

The breath he takes is deep and whistles through his nose. He steps away from the Buick.

"Hey *vieja*." He half shouts. "Hey lady."

She turns. Her blond eyebrows pull together above her nose and her mouth puckers into a red, lipsticked O. Her face melts. Summer's tan bleaches. The silence is long.

"*Niño?*" she swallows.

"Chávez," he says.

She clears her throat, a paper drops from her hand. "Chávez, yes, of course." When she bends to pick up the paper her sunglasses slip from her head, catching on the tip of her nose.

"How —"

He steps towards her. She steps back, dropping more papers. A wet film covers her skin now. Her red mouth opens and shuts like a fish's. He suddenly feels sad for her. And happy that he is young and not a woman. He moves around her, gathering the papers — typed pages with red pen scribbled all over. Her hand, when she reaches out, is really shaking. Finally she gets the papers in the case and snaps it shut. She rummages in her purse, digging out a pill bottle. She throws back a few, then drinks from a bottle of Evian.

"My God." Her eyes are full of tears. Then they start dripping, making rain on her face. "My God, Chávez."

"You want a tissue, lady?" He points at a squashed-up box on her dash.

"Yes, yes," she says. "Your English —"

Chávez crawls inside the car, bleach and leather, just like her, and passes her the whole box. "Yes, I speak English now."

She wipes her face and blows her nose.

"Everything okay, ma'am?"

Chávez spins around, readies to run.

Though it's a million degrees out, the attendant wears a zipped-up jacket with the parking lot name on it. He never drops his hard eyes from Chávez.

"Oh, yes," the *vieja* says quickly. She grabs Chávez by the shoulder and gives the attendant a sniffly smile. "This is a friend."

"Well, you let me know," he says, shooting another look at Chávez, up and down.

She tries to keep her hand on his shoulder but Chávez steps away. Then she asks how he found her. With a flash of the business card he says, "I got my ways." Then they just stare, cars circling around them looking for spots.

"So where's the money?" he finally asks her.

Her face whitens. Her red eyes squint. "Huh?"

"Money, lady."

"Don't call me lady," she says. "My name is Honey, okay?"

"Okay. Money, Honey. Where is it? You owe me big time."

BUZZARD CITY LOOKS WAY different from a car. It is quiet, first of all, and also cool, but Chávez feels a bit sick breathing that fake air.

They drive right by the hospital, which is weird, especially to see Ishmael and Hugo. Is that how Chávez looks, too, to the people in the million cars that pass him each day? Just a blur of hat and T-shirt, maybe a slice of smile?

The *vieja* had to call someone from the attendant's booth to say she wasn't going in to work. Then she called Doctor Keith's secretary. The car wasn't going to be in the spot till later. But everything is okay, she said. "Not to worry, Brenda."

"Do you need anything? Some shoes? Are you hungry? What about a doctor?" She flicks her eyes over at his brown jeans and rag-bag PU LIC   MY shirt that smells of hot dog smoke and the crystals they sprinkle on the Trust building grass. There's so many questions and she's either driving too fast or so slow people honk. When she sails through a red light she starts crying again.

"Jesus fucking Christ," she moans. Can he find the pills in her purse?

Chávez rummages around in all her junk. He gives her two little white pills, then some water. She drives with one hand the whole time, though both work now. Two polished dots scar her right forearm. She keeps looking over at him.

"I always wanted you to have this money, you understand, but how would I ever find you?"

"Please look at the road, Honey," he tells her. That makes her cry more.

Her bank is on the other side of downtown. She explains that it is a special kind of bank, sort of private, and big withdrawals must be done in person.

"Just sit here," she says. "I'll be right back."

She stumbles out of the car then comes right back because she forgot her purse.

The bank is in a quiet green area with lots of palm trees and hibiscus and no high buildings. Some other range of mountains, crumbly orange ones, rises beyond an endless field of brown houses-upon-houses. Chávez sits low in his seat, hat down, because people keep walking by. Inside the bank the *vieja* is standing in a line, tapping her toe and turning to look at him every other second. Finally she goes up to a girl behind the counter and opens her purse. Her back and big shoulders are to him.

The glove box is full of maps and candy bars that say Protein-this or Energy-that. He shoves one in his pocket, then reaches around and unzips the gym bag he saw behind his seat. The smell of her explodes from within, that weird bleach. There's a wet bathing suit, small green goggles, a wet towel, bottles of shampoo. He takes the goggles and puts them in his pocket. He and Ishmael will laugh over those when he gets back.

Ishmael.

Chávez puts back the goggles and the Protein bar and slides down in the beautiful soft seat. There's a security guard outside the bank now. A brown man with curly hair and a sandwich. Chávez slides right to the floor and crouches there, sweating, for the sun is beating hard and it's not even ten.

The *vieja* takes forever. Finally the door clicks open. She takes a thick brown envelope from her purse.

"Thank you," she says as he takes it. "Thank you, Chávez."

"You're welcome." The envelope is heavy. Way thicker than he thought. He stuffs it down the front of his pants.

"What I really mean is that I'm sorry." She says this without looking at him.

"Me too."

They stare out the front window, going nowhere. The car fills with the smell of his shirt. There's so much ketchup and milk dripped down you can hardly see the crosshairs. So what? He can buy a new shirt. Any shirt. And a tape with rap music, something to play it. Cars pull slowly through the parking lot, competing for the spots closest to the bank. Any cars with the back windows rolled down have dogs inside. There's a lot of them.

"Let's get a burger," Chávez finally says.

"Like a hamburger? For breakfast?" The *vieja* frowns like a *vieja* should.

"Yup. But it has to be one of those drive-throughs. I haven't tried that yet."

THE PARKING ATTENDANT IN the booth at the hospital is the woman one now. The paper McDonald's bag is stuffed with food for him and Ishmael. The drive-through was no big deal. The *vieja* pulled up too far from the loud-speaker where you order so she had to really yell. Then she forgot to drive ahead and almost cried again when the truck behind honked and honked. She wouldn't let Chávez pay, just like he wouldn't let her stop in at a shopping mall and buy him new clothes. And he didn't want to go home with her, either, or see her friend Dinorah. But he took a piece of paper with her phone number and address and promised to call if he was ever in trouble.

"Keith has lawyer friends," she says. A man in those nurse pyjamas walks by the Ventura. Chávez has seen this guy. He drives a beige two-door with rattlesnake decals on the windows and always needs a shave.

Now she starts talking about how she went back to see Johnny-for-Jesus and they even put a proper marker on her mom's grave. She keeps looking straight ahead, seatbelt still clicked.

"Baez dug deep enough, good girl, we just left it." She is quiet. "I still can't believe she's dead. I miss her every day."

Then she wants to know about him, and how he got out of the Oro and what he's been doing for two years and does he really not want to come home with her? She goes on and on, and he wishes for a second he didn't understand her English because now that he does it's like she's a real person and not the old-lady *pollo* who followed him in her ripped up denims and smashed glasses. Now he feels mixed up inside. The rules that were there before are gone.

"I really got to meet someone, Honey, okay?"

She pops another pill and washes it down with her McDonald's milk. "But when will I see you —" She says he's the only one who understands what she's been through. And does he still dream of it too?

"Yes, Honey," Chávez says. "I dream of the desert over

and over." Then he opens his door. She grabs his hand and squeezes, a bit too hard. She is so sad he is afraid of her. She doesn't want to let him go. "Please," he tells her. "My friend's waiting. He'll be worried." He shuts the door. "Thanks. Okay?"

She yells out, really loud, "Call me. Call me, Chávez, anytime, please," but he keeps walking, right past the booth and up the street away from the hospital in case she's watching and is going to follow.

The parking lot is out of view, then so is the hospital. He cuts back into the mini-park where he takes a secret pee in some purple bushes. Then he transfers the envelope from his pants to the McDonald's bag. On a bench he drinks his fountain Coke and thinks and thinks until he remembers he's got a whole bunch of money and hasn't even looked at it.

There's only one bum, an old guy, lying on a bench next to a rusty drinking fountain. He rips into the envelope. It's all fifties, two stacks each held with elastics. He counts two hundred bills total and that seems like too much so he tries again. Two hundred fifties? That makes ten thousand dollars. He smiles and laughs. But then he gets mad that the *vieja* can just walk into a bank and come out with all this money and another person can't. The money is nothing to her. And the hamburgers are cold.

He takes two fifties from the envelope. They go in with the McDonald's food, tucked among the fries. The rest of the money goes back down his pants. Then Chávez leaves the McDonald's bag next to the bum, right by that grizzled salt-and-pepper head with a hat over its face.

That's fine, he thinks, cutting back to the hospital. He and Ishmael will start fresh. First they'll get some lunch.

Then they'll talk future. He can hardly wait to show Ishmael the money. He already has the words picked out for when he comes up to the hot dog cart, where his best friend in the whole world is going to be waiting: "We're in this together."

BAEZ

The moon hits the height of the grey wall, turning it blue. The wall was not even as high as the hill when Baez first came here. And the river still had some water. The sunburned men working below did not look up at her pen and did not nod at Glove and Tattoo coming and going, nor did they seem to see the tied-up brown boys or the Cactus Men who came to claim them. And then one day, a day after her babies were born, the tents of the working men came down and the trucks got packed and they left.

Tattoo returns the male and the bitch to their side of the pen. He feeds them, gives them water. Her gate creaks open. Tattoo whistles at her, but she does not move. Then Glove is there above her too. He is smoking and he is drinking from a brown bottle. Glove and Tattoo talk. Glove crouches beside her and rubs her head. She licks his bare hand when he offers it. The textures of the scars ignite her tongue. It is Tattoo who takes out a gun. It is black and fits in his hand— Speckled Man had one like this too. The nub is hard against her head. She closes her eyes.

But then there is a voice behind them. The bounty is calling out. The calls are high, scooping up into the sky. Glove and Tattoo stride out of the pen, locking the gate. They yell at the bounty, who is standing now, jumping. The bells on the rope shake and split. And then, angry, Tattoo tears the scarf from the head of the bounty. The hair that spills out is long and thick and, despite the coating of dirt and oil and dust, very black. This bounty is female. She is so small, so very young. Her skin is brown, her eyes are big and boiling over with being alive. Her chin is narrow, turning her face into an upside-down triangle.

Niña, they say, laughing. *Niña, niña, niña.* A girl. A girl. A little girl. Glove and Tattoo shake their heads at the brown girl, at each other, smiling.

Baez stands then. She rushes the fencing of her pen. And she barks for the girl, for the *niña*, barks louder than her own children, barks until she feels their bodies charge the plywood that divides them. The wood breaks open, her children come shooting through. They circle her, growling. As teeth begin to tear into her, the wings of the bald birds sweep open. The birds squawk, frenzied, but then there is a great fiery crack. At the sound of the gun, the birds retreat and her children pull back.

Tattoo steps up, and, one eye shut, aims the gun at Baez. There is no hesitation. He releases the shot. A gust of white, a starry twinkle, slowly explodes. She can't see Old Blue but she can smell that flesh, that fibre, that smoke. That smell of Old Blue will always live. And also for that slow, unwinding loop of time, Baez can hear the brown-girl-bounty. She is clattering the alarm bells. The words she calls are high; they echo. She finds the brown girl's eyes. These eyes become her own and with them she can see herself dying, the heap of her body, the growing oval of blood soaking the ground. The pain is already gone. Then, even though her eyes are wide open, the world somehow goes black, blacker, blacker still.

ACKNOWLEDGEMENTS

Janie Yoon, my friend, my editor: this book exists thanks to all your care and encouragement over the years. Thank you for sticking with me and *El Niño*.

Thank you to the Ontario Arts Council, the Canada Council for the Arts, the Banff Centre for the Arts, and Barb Stone Bakstad for the generous financial support while writing this book. At the Banff Centre, Dick Hebdige, Lynn Coady, and Carolyn Forché contributed invaluable editorial insight, for which I am grateful. Joanna Reid: for all your friendship, advice, and contributions to the editing of this book, I am so thankful and indebted.

Thank you also: Siobhan Una Neville, Simon Rogers, Brendan McLeod, Calvin Dale Smith, Lila Graham and Andrew Lupton, Maurice Carroll, Kim Harrison, Sixmilebridge, Jen Mousseau and Nisi, Felipe Belalcazar, Ed Dunsworth, Brenda Chalas, Murray and Shirley Layman at Ranchos Bonitos

RV Co-op in Yuma, AZ, Sarah MacLachlan, Laura Meyer, Alysia Shewchuk, Melanie Little and everyone at House of Anansi, my mom, my brother Michael, my dad and Sara, public libraries everywhere, all the beautiful music, all my beautiful friends. That there is "a desert inside of each of us" is from Carlos Fuentes.

A portion of the sales from this book will be donated in perpetuity to Frontier College's Labourer-Teacher programs, which support migrant agricultural workers in Canada through literacy training.

NADIA BOZAK is the author of *Orphan Love* and *El Niño*, the first two novels in her Border Trilogy. She is currently working on the third novel in the trilogy, *english.motion*, which is a timely retelling of Joseph Conrad's *Heart of Darkness*. She is also the author of *The Cinematic Footprint: Lights, Camera, Natural Resources*, a work of film theory.